Paperback: 978-1-7362987-1-8

First paperback edition July 2021.

Edited by Alyson Montione
Proofread by ScribeCat (ScribeCat.ca)
Cover art by Jake Bartok

Schara Reeves Press

ScharaReevesPress.com

ACKNOWLEDGEMENTS

Editor:

Alyson Montione

Proofreader:

ScribeCat (ScribeCat.ca)

Rebecca Schmid

Cover Artist:

Jake Bartok

General Support:

Jesus Christ

Family

Friends

Schoharie Library Writing Club

Beta readers:

Jubilee Schmid

Zebulun Schmid

Emma Panzera

Becky Rowling

PRONUNCIATIONS

Aekon (AY•kon)
Alkemar (AL•keh•mahr)
Ateli (ah•TEL•ee)

Baey (BAY)
Baeno (BAY•no)
Bethynese (BETH•eh•neez)

Ckaknimaen (KAK•neh•mayn)
Crysen (KRY•sen)

Emarian (eh•MAYR•ee•in)
Esmer (EZ•mer)
Estasia (es•TAY•zha)

Gaevno (GAHV•no)

Hytat (HY•tat)

Jaythos (JAY•thohs)

Kaedna (KAYD•nuh)
Kaedovarna (KAY•doh•VAR•nuh)
Kovian (KOH•vee•un)

Kovo (KOH•voh)

Lytho (LY•thoh)

Maeko (MAY•koh)

Namaya (nuh•MAY•uh)

Patelayna (pah•tuh•LAY•nuh)

Rugo (ROO•go)

Sefen (SEH•fehn)
Skayla (SKAY•luh)
Syvil (SIV•uhl)

Tiskli (TY•slee)

Vek' n'Vol (VEK noo•VOHL)

This book is dedicated to Becca. Without her it never would have existed. Thanks for being my fellow writing nerd.

TO TAKE A WORLD:

THE GHOSTMAKER

A DAUGHTER'S RANSOM: BOOK II

BY NIAMH SCHMID

THE GHOSTMAKER

A world fallen to chaos, a place lost to time,
Once a beautiful country, full and better than mine,
Jealousy and hatred blinded me to fame,
So I stole the countries' people, and turned them to my name.

Fire, ice, and death I brought,
Complete and merciless destruction I sought,
To take a world, and make it mine,
Mine for time eternal.

A friend to stand against me, an ant for me to trample,
I tried and failed to catch him, and make him my example,
Eluded me he managed, for a time he led the fight,
To win the people from me, to banish me to flight.

Fire, ice, and deception I brought,
Complete and merciless domination I sought,
To take a world, and make it mine,
Mine for time eternal.

All but one I stole away, all but one I caused to fade,
A rebel to stand against my world, to try and tear all I had made,
But none can stand my fire, none can stand her mind,
For stronger one was never seen, to undo all her kind.

THE GHOSTMAKER

Fire, ice, and chaos we brought,
Complete and merciless control we sought,
To take a world, and make it ours,
Ours for time eternal.

The last shall fall, I swear,
The last shall fall, I'll leave not one,
To take a world, you must set the snare,
I'll take this world.

It's done.

PROLOGUE:

Sven:

A melodramatic beginning, to be sure. But after all, our world is quite prone to dramatics. It wasn't like Baeno had whined up a storm to The Creator until he gave them the guardians they so wanted. It wasn't like they jumped off the proverbial cliff when the Drogans first arrived.

It wasn't like they were all too eager to take different sides when my sister betrayed us all.

…But I'm getting ahead of myself.

You see, I was going to die. At least that or something worse. Such was the problem with walking into a trap. That and the fact the bait was so intriguing that no matter how certain you were you'd be caught, you had to go anyway. Which was why I was awaiting my doom out here in the middle of the night. A little cliché but true nonetheless.

The fate of this dying world was resting on my shoulders now, and with one sister missing and another my quarry, I had no idea how I was ever going to handle it. Moira had been the 'wise one,' the 'patient one,' but more practically the one that could bring time back if anything dared go awry. Both Moira and Skayla had always been the ones in the public eye, ready to make these life-and-death decisions. But now I was alone.

Moira vanished one year ago—and then, not even a week later, the war had gone downhill. Now all that was left was the Isle of Rugo and the countries of Gaevno, and Kaedovarna, where the capitol city of Kaedna resided and where Duke Emarian acted as the last line of defense should everything else fall. But, honestly, everything else on the world of Baeno was taken. Rugo had a very strategic landscape to fight the mysterious Drogans, and the only reason Kaedna and Gaevno hadn't been defeated was because Skayla couldn't navigate her spies quite that deeply yet— what with the maze of a mountain range that held Kaedna hidden safely away from prying eyes.

But there was still hope. Well, I would keep telling myself that, anyway—would keep repeating the promise of The Creator: I was about to make a dangerous gamble tonight, and if I didn't make it out alive, the child I was about to save would be our only chance. All I could think of, however, was how, if this worked, they would most likely destroy Skayla. The bond of siblings was a funny thing. Or perhaps it was just the relics that bound us that made me feel like I was losing a part of myself with her betrayal.

"Get a grip, Sven," I whispered to myself, trying for the hundredth time not to think of everything that had gone wrong. No time for that, now.

There was a whirlwind sound as some invisible force stirred the night air, and my heart choked. The sound of Drogan wings. Those wretched beasts that had shown up and started this whole mess.

I wasn't ready for this. Not ready to face Skayla again, not ready to fight her. But when did I get to choose when things happened?

The sound of the Drogan grew louder and louder. It was like a windstorm was on top of me. The wind billowed into my eyes and mouth until I could neither see anything but the bowing trees, nor breathe in anything but the suffocating dust from the road as it swirled around in added chaos.

Then that familiar monolithic beast landed, long, black-feathered wings resting neatly by its side, showing off the silver tips in the moonlight. It was like a Dragon in stature, but with a narrower muzzle, leaving it more like some half-breed of a Griffon and a Dragon. All its body was covered in feathers, and its long neck craned high and regal as it laid like a cat on the ground, allowing its master to slide off its back.

And oh, I knew her just as well as I knew the Drogan. She was tall, fitted in dark brown leather armor. Over that, she wore a long, robe-like coat that ran down to her ankles, the neat ripples trailing behind her and blending in the folds of night. But the neatness ended there. Her blond hair held itself in a half bun while the rest hung carelessly caressing her shoulders. It was a large contrast to the once poised and disciplined sister I had known and loved for so long. And that wasn't even mentioning the insanity that pierced the darkness with those glaring violet eyes.

Skayla. My Skayla. Then I felt a little part of me die inside as I saw, hanging around her neck, a golden chain with a pendant. It was too far away to see any details, and yet I knew exactly what it was: Moira's watch. I could just barely catch the glint of moonlight bouncing off the crystal lens that protected the little clock. My worst fears seemed to be closer to reality than nightmare.

Then she turned back to the Drogan, reaching up and dragging another figure off the beast. It was a little girl. The child's wings rippled in terror, changing from crimson to black and back again as she tried to breathe through the fear I saw so clearly.

The last Esmer. The last of the people I had known so well—that Skayla had murdered.

"Come out, come out, wherever you arrrrre…" Skayla continued to drag the girl across the clearing as she looked around, seemingly deaf to her captive's yelps.

My teeth grit and I stood up, one hand gripping the sword that Moira had given me, while the other hand gripped the illusion I had created of a blade. "Let her go, Skayla."

The laugh that penetrated the air was chilling, followed by her crazed purring voice. "Sven. How nice of you to finally pop by to see me."

The words seemed to echo everywhere, and, as she spoke, I noticed men slowly coming out of the forest and into the clearing. I was surrounded. "I've simply been dying to see you again."

My hands were lead, clumsy and locked in place. I couldn't bear to raise my sword against her. My hand tightened on my blade—the hand that held the ring and source of my power—and I strengthened my resolve to fight against her Curse of Mind. She wouldn't take me with her.

"Shut up. We aren't twelve, Skayla. Give me the girl, *NOW!*" As I yelled, the ground erupted between Skayla and the little child, separating them and pushing the girl across and towards me. Skayla looked surprised, undoubtedly shocked at just how real the illusion appeared.

No one else in the clearing moved—no one even flinched. I saw the violet in the eyes of the soldiers even as I saw the wicked glare in the Drogan's, and I knew they would not move unless their mistress bid them.

"It's going to be alright, darlin', don't worry," I whispered to the girl that now hid behind me.

"That was pretty convincing for the Master of Illusions, Sven," Skayla's tone wavered to something akin to forced patience. "But I'm not here for games. I want you back, come on."

Hear but don't speak, know but don't read. Reality. Stay rooted in reality, not Skayla's words.

The numbness her words caused wavered, and I felt strength return. "No," I said firmly, desperate and yet trying so hard to hide it, "This ends tonight." And with that, I made night fall like it never had before, a darkness so thick even a moonless night would have shone brighter than this nothingness. The girl cried out at the same moment Skayla's screeching laughter rent the air.

My fake blade vanished to nothing as I grabbed the child by the arm, running through the fray of blinded soldiers and confusion. The Drogan's roar blended with the cries in the night. I had to get the girl out of here. We could both get away—Skayla, along with the rest of Baeno, underestimated my abilities...but I had not come here just to save the girl. No. The real bait? Skayla.

I heard the sound of the Drogan taking off and ran faster, with the little Esmer stumbling courageously behind. Finally, I stopped, knowing I only had a few moments before Skayla would be upon us again. The light of the moon returned and we stood in the twilight, the Esmer girl trembling as I knelt before her.

"Shh, shh, darlin', you'll be alright. I've got you—you remember me, right?" I gave a small smile. "Remember me, Baey? Sven? I'm a friend."

There was an unsteady nod.

"Good girl." I looked up at the sky quickly, before returning my attention to her.

"I'm scared." Baey's trembling whisper matched the terror in her eyes.

I nodded my head and sighed. "Yeah. Me too, darlin'," I said with all honesty. "But I need you to listen very carefully."

There was the not-too-distant pounding of wings against the night wind, and I tried not to show a physical jump as my heart plummeted to the pit of my stomach. Skayla was almost on us again. We were currently in a spot with treetops too thick for the Drogan to land, but that would only keep us safe for so long.

"Do you know how to find north?" I asked. Esmers knew navigation practically at birth.

She nodded.

"Good. And you know what the Crest of Valdon looks like?"

Another nod.

I was sweating now; time was running out. "Excellent. Go east until you find a cliff. There will be a section with a waterfall. Follow the cliff north from there, and eventually you'll find a place with dark orange moss over a splotch of black rock. Walk into the rock. Don't be afraid. It's a secret cave. It's the only place where they won't find you. Stay there until my friends come find you. Understood?" It took a lot more effort to keep my voice calm than I would have liked to admit.

Again, she nodded, but her brow was furrowed. "What about you?"

I was caught aback for a brief second. Baey was only about eight years old, and I hadn't been expecting such a question. I didn't let her see the dread that was threatening to close my throat. Instead, I just winked at her and put a hand on her shoulder. "I'm an old hat at this, darlin'. Don't worry. I'll be fine." *You liar. You are about to be the biggest idiot this century; and it will cost you your life if your gamble is wrong.* But I had so easily gotten the better of Skayla back there that a new brazenness rose in my chest. If I got Skayla face to face with me—

alone—I could stop her. I could change her mind. Get her to tell me what...what she had done to Mum and Da. What she had done to Moira.

The Drogan must have found where we were. But while there wasn't the sound of wings anymore, there was instead the sound of soldiers crashing through the trees. They were practically upon us now, and I took one last deep breath.

"Now, I need you to do one last thing for me. Keep this safe. Don't ever tell anybody you have it, and don't ever lose it." I took off my ring and handed it to her, pressing it deeply into her palm. If things didn't go as planned, Skayla could not get my ring. "I'll return for it before you can even bat an eye." It was a dangerous ploy. I wouldn't be nearly as powerful without it. But If things went south...it would be even worse for Skayla to have it. The relics were powerful objects.

Little Baey blinked. "But what if someone sees it?" she asked in a scared little voice.

I winked. "Don't worry, darlin', no one'll ever see it except you and me."

The noise of soldiers in the forest grew to a frenzy. In fact, it almost sounded as if the Drogan had landed—we were out of time.

I made a little shooing motion with my hands. "Now, no more questions. Just run. Don't fly until you are a good way away. Go!" I pushed her off, and she ran swiftly into the night, wings darkening once more, disguising her from the hunter's eyes.

I hoped the temporary illusion I had placed over her would hold. Those never looked pretty, but, in the night, it would be just enough to keep her out of sight until she was far away. Besides, Skayla was after *me*.

I turned my attention to the Drogan that barreled into view not from above but through the undergrowth. Soldiers crowded in from behind, and soon I was surrounded. Skayla once more dismounted from the beast, entire demeanor loose and seemingly without worry. As if this all were a game. As if she hadn't caused a war.

"That wasn't very polite now, was it?" Skayla laughed. "Now, where is the little friend? Has she tried to run away?" she scolded with a tut-tutting sound. "Well, we'll just have to find her. Come on now, tell me where she went."

I pressed my lips together, looking her firmly in the eyes. She could spin those tricks with others but not with me. It had been so easy with my ring that, surely, I could manage it even without.

Oh, how I hoped I wasn't wrong.

"Come on, Skayla. Stop avoiding me. What is going on?" I made it sound like she had indeed simply stopped talking to me and hadn't just gone completely psychotic and tried to...recreate the world.

"Oh, you're fun, Sven." She laughed a little, still acting as if she was just a child playing with her little brother.

Hear but don't speak, know but don't read. Reality. Stay rooted in reality, not Skayla's words.

With a sigh, Skayla came up closer, smiling sweetly as she played with the little clock brooch that hung around her neck. For the first time, I was able to get a closer look at it. Close enough to see the crack in the lens.

My throat felt thick as my eyes refused to wrench their gaze from the relic and the ugly scar it now sported.

"Come on, Sven, you've missed me. I see it in your eyes. Don't you want to stay with me? It could be as it used to. You and me, saving the world. That's all I'm doing."

I started to feel the sensation of my mind numbing, as if I was a thousand miles away. Then I realized what was happening. I was better than this—I was better than this! "Skayla. Stop skirting the issue. What have you done to Moira? Where is she?" *Hear but don't speak, know but don't read. Reality. Stay rooted in reality—*

Skayla pouted. "She didn't want to help. She was always the old and boring one." A wicked smile crept on her lips like the cold embrace of death. "I'm the oldest now."

No!

I shook my head. She could be lying. Stay focused. "Skayla. Come home."

"The world is my home! Can't you see? I'm making it so much better now! No one will fight each other, no one will ever rebel. Why did you and Moira always worry that Ovok was a bad influence? Why, he, Kovo, and I are going to change the world! It will be so beautiful, Sven! Come, help me."

The dark beast—Ovok—-made a sort of grumbling chuckle behind his mistress.

How disappointed Moira would be, if she knew even I had nearly given myself to Skayla's MindHold. *Reality. Stay in reality. Not her words. Hear but don't speak, know but don't read.* I repeated my anchor over and over to myself until her words slowly lost power over me, and I felt warmth in my mind again.

I was going to have to kill her. I was going to have to fight my sister and I was going to kill her.

"Sven, stop fighting. Just relax and let go. Don't you miss me? I can see it in your eyes."

"Stop!" I whispered, looking at her in dismay. It wasn't working. "What are you doing, Skayla? What are you doing? Come back to me. Come back or I have to kill you." My voice cracked, and my grip tightened on my sword. I was going to have to destroy her. As long as I kept her mind games at bay, I knew she was no match for me. This was how it would end. The Watchers would be their own undoing. All would remember us as the three who doomed the world, not saved it. What a letdown.

Skayla cocked her head and let out another one of her eerie giggles. "I already told you, silly. I'm saving the world. And I need you. Moira was an idiot. She thought she could outdo me just because she was supposedly the wisest one. Well...you see where that got her!" Skayla sighed and then made a point of dangling the watch in front of me. "But let's get to the point, shall we? I was hoping you could give me a present."

The numbness began to creep into my head again; I desperately tried to fight it off. Suddenly it dropped away, and I saw Skayla's eyes resting very pointedly at my right hand.

"Sven." This time her voice was cold as iron. "Where is it?"

"Gone. And now you'll never have it." I tried to harden my resolve, but every movement felt slower with the effect of her words, and even just lifting my swords seemed to take all my strength away. "You've tried your tricks, and I figured it was about time I tried some of my own," I said with a smile as I tried to keep up the illusion that I wasn't struggling to resist her.

Skayla let out an agitated laugh. "Gone? Gone! How dare you rob me, Sven! You dare take my right from me? I gave you the chance to help me, to bring peace. Instead, you choose death. Oh, you will regret your choice, mark my words!"

Well, if that wasn't the most melodramatic, perfectly tailored little speech in the history of theater. "A bit forced, don't you think, Skayla?" I gathered the strength for a twirl of the real blade in my one hand and fought against her influence. It was so much stronger than I remembered. So much more potent.

Hear but don't speak, know but don't read. Stand fast, stand strong. Stand fast, stand strong.

CHAPTER I: The Ghost

Baey:

I laid in my bed as I listened to the creaking of the heating pipes, fingering the small silver ring I always had on me. I'd kept it safe for eight years now, silently obsessing over the little thing. I never forgot the earnestness in The Watcher's voice as he had pressed it into my hand.

Sitting up, I closed my eyes, trying once again to picture that night, just as I had done so many times before. As always, the memory was fuzzy, with only Sven Mara's bright golden eyes and strong voice ringing through as he tried to soothe me—just like an older brother. He would have been twenty-nine this year, according to Namaya.

It was rather odd, really, how someone I had hardly known would leave such an impression upon me, and as I reconstructed Sven Mara in my mind, I got an ache in my chest. From all I had heard of the stories, he had been so full of life. So brave and strong. Why? Why did he have to die?

My grip tightened on the ring and I took a deep breath. Ugh. I was getting all worked up again. Typical of a sixteen-year-old. As much as I would wish otherwise, he was dead because of me and I had to make his sacrifice worth it. Somehow.

My thoughts turned to the events of the last few months. We'd been fighting a losing war here at Valdon, the last defense that stood between here and Kaedna. But I didn't mind being at Valdon. The mansion held some of the last Gifters on Baeno, and until now we'd still had a fairly strong force to combat Skayla's advancing army. Then Emarian had sent the urgent message that Skayla had somehow made it around us. Now she was trying to find the secret mountain pass that protected Kaedna and the last heads of the resistance against her and the Drogans.

But the need to cut off Skayla before she found the mountain pass had left our forces drained here at Valdon, and now only very few of us— the strongest of us—remained behind. Sefen the FireWielder, Namaya the Healer, Maeko Kuto, Jaythos KeenEye, and Tanner the Memory Keeper. And then, well, me. Though I really didn't count. True, Maeko and Jaythos weren't Gifters either, but they were just as capable of holding their ground in a fight. Me? I was feeling more useless with every passing day.

Stretching, I opened my eyes and looked out the window. Morning had not quite broken through the night's gloom, but with my keen eyes I could still easily make out each tree in the surrounding forest. I rose reluctantly, slipping out from under my heavy blanket and into the thick cold of the stone mansion. *Brr.* As the frigid air met my skin, I wrapped my wings about me, making a little sanctuary from the bite of the autumn air. We had to be sparing of the heating. With so many of us gone, there were not enough people to chop the wood necessary to keep the water and heating pipes running—and Skayla had long since limited Kaedna's ability to mine and transport coal. Indeed, it had been rare for me to wake to the heating pipes in the past few weeks. Sefen must have made an exception due to the cold of last night.

Still fingering the ring hanging from a chain around my neck, I slowly made my way to the window, the old glass fogged at the edge with mist. Nothing stirred in the morning grey, not a breeze, not an animal. It was as if the whole world was holding its breath, waiting for what would happen next. Each day I came to the window and wondered the same thing everyone else was.

How much longer would we have our free will? How much longer until Skayla and her MindHold took over the last of us?

"As long as Valdon stands, so will Baeno. We are the wall between the light and dark. We stand when none can see. In Maras' memory ever present, standing strong will be." I said the words Sefen had repeated to me for the eight years I'd been here, as if saying it aloud could drive away the shadows of fear. But then I added, "I'll find a way." Somehow. Somehow, I would be of use. I *knew* this ring I wore around my neck was important, and that if I could only find out how, it might help me keep Baeno from this disaster that was now almost complete. At times, I thought of telling Sefen or Namaya of my hidden burden, but whether because of Sven's words of warning, or my fear they would only take it from me, I stayed silent. With that off the table, it left me to only wish, and wish, and beg Sefen to let me help the Warriors of Valdon. But all he would do is tell me I'm too important, too young, or too innocent. It was just a nice way of saying I was useless.

"How am I supposed to save Baeno if I'm too...important...to try?" I grumbled to myself. I was done with everyone's excuses. They just didn't make sense. Sven Mara had saved me for a reason, but I kept feeling like I was wasting the gift of life he'd given. As it was, there was hardly anything left of Baeno to live *for* already. But hadn't The Creator left a promise? Sefen had said after Skayla's fall that The Creator had said an Esmer would rise up to replace her. And, well...I was the last Esmer left in Baeno. But what if I was the *wrong* Esmer? What if the right one had died? What if Sven had wasted his life on me?

All this, however, was nothing new, and I allowed the bone-weary thoughts to run their cyclical pattern in my mind as I watched the sun begin to peek its head over the ever-reaching treetops, its pale fingers of light creeping towards Valdon. The stone building stood as sentinel, as if waiting for the return of its long-dead masters. What if this place were to fall too? I tucked the ring away under my shirt where it would be safely hidden away. No. Valdon would never fall. Not while I was here to protect it. I could have laughed at myself in contempt with the very thought. Yes, I was definitely up for the job if it came to protecting it...*not*. I'd be squashed like the feathery nuisance I was.

I gave one last look outside only to catch my breath at the sight that greeted me. I pressed myself against the window.

There, just coming out of the forest, was a figure, moving effortlessly among the morning mists as it approached Valdon. It was tall, enveloped in a thick, dark coat that seemed to shroud everything. His appearance was like some ghost from another world, moving so silently towards Valdon that for a sickening moment I was too enthralled to move. He was like something from a dream, and I thought that perhaps he was. At first my heart had risen, thinking it was one of our friends returned home at last. But the walk, the stature, the eyes, none of it was familiar to me. One word filled my mind, and I stood there frozen.

Stranger.

Then, just like that, my senses returned, and I snapped out of the trance. What was *wrong* with me?! I ran, my bare feet slapping noisily against the stone floor as I burst out the door and sprinted down the hall, clumsily maneuvering my hurried steps around the giant wings that constantly found themselves tangled up and in the way.

Soon, I was at Sefen and Namaya's door, pounding hard and shouting their names.

But there was no answer. Desperately I knocked with more ferociousness—or panic. Yeah. Panic was probably a better word. Sefen was a light sleeper, how could this not wake him?! I quickened my banging on the metal door, panicking when the door handle remained dormant. *Come on, open the door!*

"Baey! What's the matter?"

I all but leaped into the air, hovering for a second until I realized who it was that had been behind me. Landing back on the floor, I gasped for air, startled half to death. There, standing in the dim light, was the familiar bearded face. "Sefen! You scared me!" Was all I could manage to say for a second.

His eyes were alight with concern, and he gave me a quick look over. "I scared *you*? Your shouts have probably woken up the whole house. What's wrong? You look like you've seen a ghost." Indeed, already I heard doors opening down the hall and the sounds of the others waking. Namaya was already right behind Sefen. But Sefen's words had brought me back to why I was frantic.

Ghost. Stranger. I regained my thought process, and controlled my adrenaline so Sefen could understand me. "There's a stranger. I saw him outside. Looks like trouble," I gasped. Last time we'd had a stranger…it hadn't been good.

Sefen's face turned from worry to warrior, and he quickly disappeared into his room. I stood there in the hall, lost in the air of dream and confusion as Namaya and several of the others that were now in the hall all stared at me.

Sefen reappeared from his room, "Maeko, Namaya, come with me! We'll meet this stranger down at the door. Jaythos, eyes on the roof. Tanner, go with Baey to the balcony!" He shouted at the half-awoken crowd in the hallway.

I needed no further push, finding myself beside Tanner as we rushed to the balcony that overlooked the door to keep a watch on the stranger, who was now almost at the doorsteps of my home. Neither of us said a word, the silence between us screaming *danger* more loudly than any worried whispering could have done.

Feyn:

This wasn't the brightest idea I had ever come up with. Waltzing up to Valdon, the final stronghold to the gifted warriors on Baeno—former sanctuary of the two Maras—with a forged letter and a secret mission. Valdon's warriors were all that was left to protect what remained of Baeno, and with the number of spies running around, they weren't the most likely people to put trust in a stranger that had just walked up to their *hidden* mansion. So, as I said, not the brightest idea I'd ever come up with, but then again, it definitely wasn't the worst. Not that I could remember what my worst *was...*

I adjusted the near empty bag of my supplies that hung over my shoulder, and gripped the forged letter in my free hand, trying to go over what I would say once again. Once they saw the unbroken seal of

Emarian, most of their suspicion would hopefully go away. Not many had seen it, and it was something even one of Skayla's spies couldn't fake. And trust me, I should know. I'd made sure to bury the stolen seal several days' journey back so that it wouldn't be found on me if searched—if that happened, the game would be up and I wouldn't be able to find help. I needed to know who I could trust, but I had to do it quickly...before Skayla found me.

Valdon loomed practically on top of me now, and I pulled the collar of my coat a little further over my face, glad to be rid of the horrid mask I had been forced to wear for so long. *That*, I had destroyed. Burying was not enough on its own.

With a shiver, I returned my attention to the building before me. Like some haunted mansion, it represented the age of The Crafters before the war: A mix of metal and brick, four-stories high with a third-story balcony. Windows lined much of the house, and I knew well the glass made from the Aldrack sand, which made the windows appear to simply be crystal mirrors. It was a beautiful building, modernized in its finest, while still sporting the traditional tower on the right corner. But I wasn't here to sightsee, nor to reminisce.

A movement caught my attention, and I looked up at the balcony. The outlines of two figures knelt down on it, with one lending a shadow that loomed behind them and blended with the shadows of the terrace. It was as if it was wearing a cloak that completely enveloped it. Aha. Wings. So, the rumors were true, then.

The clicking of gears and the creaking of old hinges signaled an opening door and brought me back to what I was doing now. I stopped as three figures emerged from Valdon, letting them come to me. I'd been around long enough to at least know better than to seem eager or in a hurry. The more you hurry, the quicker you die.

"You have five seconds, stranger." A tall man with a thick beard and grey frock coat led the group.

So much for not hurrying.

I raised an eyebrow, very unimpressed. "Or your little winged friend on the terrace will tear me to pieces, ah?" I asked idly, watching his reaction closely.

The man bristled and the grip on his sword tightened. "No. But I'll make you wish that *was* what happened." There was a fierceness in his eyes, but it did nothing to faze me. I was more intrigued by the way he had both replied with such an ardent "no" as well as a threat. Protective of the child on the terrace and yet doubting of her abilities? Interesting.

I undid the wrap around my face and pulled back my hood, walking forward slowly and handing the letter to the bearded man. I looked different enough that I didn't worry about being recognized. With the mask gone, there was little chance of that. "My name is Feyn Cavo, and Duke Emarian has sent me on a sensitive and urgent mission. This letter will explain the rest."

He didn't say a word as he took the letter from me. The seal caught his eye, and a flicker of doubt ran across his face. He looked from me to the sealed parchment, and after opening it and reading the contents, he handed it to the lady next to him, murmuring something that I didn't catch. Well, this was going nowhere fast. I was trying to be let in and playing a game of catch wasn't exactly how I pictured it happening. But that's what happened when people thought they could somehow stop fakes and spies from getting into their home. Funny how they already had one among them. But who? That was what I was here to find out. I couldn't trust them with any other information or reasoning for lying until I rooted out the spy.

While they were arguing over my letter, I slipped my hands lazily into the side pockets of my outer coat, my left hand slowly going to feel the trinket in my pocket. I was trying *not* to be paranoid, but after stealing something like this? That wasn't exactly the easiest thing to do in the world.

"Are you going to stand here arguing all day or are we going to get somewhere?" I finally asked drolly.

The lady looked at me coldly, "Why? You in a rush?"

Yes, actually. I was, a little. But I wouldn't say that. I was already hurrying, and the more you hurry...wait. I'd said that already....

Instead, I gave a half grin. "No. But it is cold out here, and I feel we would be all better off out of the weather. And, assuming you can read, we should all be able to go inside soon."

"Don't bet your life on it," the lady said, giving me another cold stare before looking at the man with another one of her clearly characteristic skeptical looks. I noted the ring on her left hand, and the way its match sat on the hand of the man I had given the letter to. But married didn't mean one or both couldn't be a traitor.

After a long pause, she reopened the letter, carefully reading the inscription. I'd written it myself, of course, and was able to call to mind the words.

Sefen Kalaesia,

It is with a hurried hand I write this. Skayla somehow found Kaedna Pass and is currently besieging Kaedna. Your troops arrived this morning, and their support is allowing me to send out a trusted messenger to give this to you. His name is Feyn Cavo, and he is to alleviate some of the burden you and your depleted forces may encounter. But he is also on a more dangerous mission; there is no way Skayla found the pass unless there is a spy somewhere. It could be someone close to you or Valdon. Offer Feyn any aid necessary to quickly root out the traitor. I will return those you have sent as soon as we have resolved the siege, but there is no further help you can give us that you have not already sent.

Emarian Draeshno

The ease with which I remembered the letter left me perplexed as to whether to be pleased my memory was appearing to hold a little better, or worry that I could remember that so clearly and yet so little about who *I* was. But I didn't have time to get lost in this, as the conversation moved on quickly.

It was the woman who replied, "So, *I* see. Emarian empties our forces to deal with the invaders in the Mountains. We hear nothing from him for weeks, and then he sees fit to just send some stranger to live in *our* home, snoop about *unsupervised*, and tell us what *we're* doing wrong. How does Emarian expect us to hold off a completely overwhelming force without any help? Oh, I'm sorry…" She looked at me scornfully. "I forgot. He gave us someone. *One* person." The expression hardened further, and I saw bitterness rooted there. "We had to abandon two posts already, and we lost men and women because of Emarian. Good people." She whipped her black hair violently from her face, staring me down like a raven as she passed the scroll back to the man. "Sefen? You're not going to stand for this, are you?" she asked the man. I quickly noted the immediate vehemence with which she had rejected the letter. Hm.

Sefen gave me an equally skeptical glance, seemingly trying to search into my soul. I gave the most bored expression I could find, sighing and saying, "I can only tell you what the letter already has explained; Skayla and Lord Kovo must have a spy here, or nearby enough to follow someone going in or out of the pass. Now, are you going to let me inspect and get the work done before there is no Valdon for your army to come back to, or are you going to send me back to Emarian? Because, at this point, if I'm not going to be allowed to do anything, I'd rather go back and die fighting than idly waiting for your foolishness to catch up with you." I took a gamble and hoped that it wouldn't get me thrown out or worse. After all, that was quite a bit of lying. The problem was, I couldn't quite remember what the truth was. Stupid memory…I only hoped I could at least remember my lie. What was I getting myself into?

"Just because Emarian is the last noble in this forsaken land, doesn't mean he tells us what to do, *spy*." Once more, the raven lady was the one to challenge.

Well, wasn't she jumping to conclusions? "And just because all of you at Valdon are possibly the last ones with any sort of Gifts on Baeno, that gives you the right to tell *me* what to do?" I shot back. This was useless, and I was feeling fit to burst with anxiety already. "But can we please stop fighting like wild dogs? Whether you lot like it or not, there's a problem. Skayla's spies have somehow gotten a whiff of where this place is, and I have been sent to make sure I find whatever is going on. I don't mean to disrespect any of you, but you could use any help you can get until you get reinforcements. You're looking a little understaffed, really." I had honestly expected more people at Valdon. No wonder Skayla was getting ready to strike. I only hoped I figured out who to trust before she got here.

I watched with a sigh as Sefen played with the scroll a while before calling to the man behind him. "Maeko?"

Well, weren't we just being democratic?

The man—Maeko—had been standing motionless this entire time and, really, I could easily have mistaken him for a statue. However, at Sefen's question, the sturdy man seemed to spring to life, thickly calloused hand rubbing his bald head, "I don't know, Sefen. But he looks too skinny to cause much problems." His thick accent instantly gave away where he was from: Rugo. I couldn't believe anyone from that once sunny isle was still free from Skayla, but people did have a way of getting out from under her. Once more, I looked up at the balcony, where the girl was.

"It's settled, then. Maeko will watch over you to make sure you don't try anything. If there *is* somehow a spy, I want them found quickly before any further damage can be done. But our trust is not so easily won through a letter, no matter who sends it."

I made a small, careless bow. "Thank you." I couldn't help but think of how oblivious they all apparently were, for the damage had already been done. They were hanging by a thread, and they didn't even know it. Kaedna was taken, and I knew Valdon would be next.

Then, without a word, everyone began to file inside. The lady first then Sefen. Maeko stayed behind, obviously waiting for me to go through the door first. Not wanting to keep him, I myself moved up to the house and into the door, and once I passed the threshold, I felt Maeko's presence close behind. I suppose I should be honored to have a bodyguard...but...not really. Though, if nothing else, this would allow me to start with clearing him. I would need to be as quick about this as possible, and who knew, maybe a Rugonian was the spy; after all, as I said before, that country had long since been taken. So how had he gotten away?

I didn't quite make it inside before Sefen stopped me with his arm. He moved in close to my face, whispering harshly into my ear: "Light between the darkness, hope in the night."

And here I thought they were going to make it too easy. I whispered back dully, hesitating a moment as I tried to remember those long-forgotten words, "Stand fast, stand strong, and see the daylight." It was reactionary. In fact, I didn't know how I remembered the words. That was new. Usually, I was lucky if I remembered my own *name*. Speaking of...

Sefen let go of me and grudgingly allowed me inside the intricate building. I took a deep breath of the cool air inside, memories mixing with the reality of how much Valdon had changed—and not exactly for the better, in my opinion.

It was surprisingly clean and had been kept up, but the placing of everything was all wrong. Either it had been changed, or my mind really was going. A giant grandfather clock now stood as grim sentry to the left, ticks echoing ominously and only adding to its looming presence. The stairs in the center of the room no longer had the polished white marble. At least, I had thought it had been marble, but maybe it always had been that dark obsidian. The banners that had once hung down from either side of the second story railing were no longer there, making the house feel cold and forgotten. I did, however, remember the ornate twisted metals for the banister and railings of the second floor, and the metal trim that ran along the brick walls. But my eyes settled on the coat of arms that hung on the wall above the second story hall; the thrice weaved cord, springing into a living tree; the sign of The Three Watchers. The glaring reminder of their failure. Funny how their sign still hung here, when two were dead and the third the cause. I didn't have time to really wonder why I remembered all of this, for again words broke my tenuous stream of thought.

"Maeko will show you to where you'll be staying. I trust you will not leave it unaccompanied," Sefen said. At least they weren't trusting me as easily as I had feared. Honestly, that would just be pathetic, even if it would have made my job much easier.

Then another voice entered the hub of the vestibule. "Sefen? Who is it?" We all looked up at the stairs, and there, almost floating down, was a girl. Her wings hung around her like a thick cloak, hiding the rest of her from view.

The last Esmer in all of Baeno.

THE GHOSTMAKER

CHAPTER II: Stranger Danger

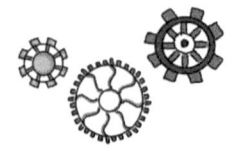

Baey:

"A messenger from Emarian," Sefen replied with that calm voice, which meant he wasn't very pleased with this at all and didn't believe this ghost to be a messenger. At least, not for Emarian. The calmer Sefen was, the worse the scenario.

I cocked my head and stopped at the bottom of the stairs, looking at the man that stood in front of me. The ghost from outside. But standing in the room now, he looked real enough.

He must have been traveling in the elements for some time. At least, that's how it appeared from the bag slung over his shoulder and the way he dressed. He wore not one but two coats: a sorely weather-beaten leather one, and a frock coat beneath that for insulation from the chilly air, the hilt of a sword peeking out from under its worn shelter. Old trousers were visible beneath the long outer coat, and he wore leather boots firmly strapped to his feet. Callused hands were very poorly hidden beneath torn-up, fingerless gloves, showing he was no stranger to the sword. His gaunt face showed he was used to going without food.

But what really caught my attention were those almost vacant eyes. His irises were a clear crystal, as if drained of all color besides the occasional green-blue flecks left behind. Those eyes cast me under a chilling spell, like I was staring right into the eyes of death. They seemed strangely empty, like a part of him was very far away from here—or nowhere at all. And while they certainly were not the violet eyes that signaled Skayla's MindHold, they were unsettling nonetheless.

And then...beyond that...there was something else. As if he had seen something truly horrible, and it was replaying over and over in his head. It flashed in his features, but almost as if he himself didn't realize it was being played. All I knew was the more I looked into his gaze, the more I wished to look away. A shiver ran down my back, prompting me to wrap my wings a little more around me and wishing to disappear from those empty windows to the soul.

I completely understood why Sefen didn't trust him.

Then Jaythos appeared by the bottom of the stairs, his crossbow fitted snugly to his arm as he studied the stranger with his usual aggressive skepticism. He didn't say a word, only watched. There was a lot of *that* going around.

Maeko moved up to the stairs and smiled gently at me, breaking his stern countenance for a brief moment. Then he turned to the stranger and said, "Let's get going, Skinny," and he was back to his old self.

I moved aside and allowed the two to make their way upstairs and vanish into the halls above.

"Baey. You are to stay away from him," Namaya said, as soon as they were out of sight. Her tone was stern, and she looked at me with that seasoned warrior expression of hers. She meant it, of course, and I honestly didn't want to see that man ever again. Yet, somehow her ordering me to stay away from him only made me wish to disobey. I really was getting tired of being treated with kid gloves.

But what did I say? "Alright." My answer was meek. Or rather, *weak.* Just like me. There was just no way out of it.

Sefen came over and put a hand on my shoulder. "We'll handle it. But best to be careful, just in case."

I hid behind a smile and nodded, not showing the unbearable humiliation I felt. I wasn't a toddler. I didn't need to be reassured and coddled. I wanted to help. I was *supposed* to help—supposed to be the one who saved Baeno, but instead I was watching it die. It and the warriors who protected it. Valdon was all the family I knew, and yet I had watched countless fade from its halls, falling to Skayla's merciless hand.

"Sefen. We need to find out sooner than later. The longer he stays, the worse it will be," Namaya pointed out, taking in a deep breath and looking upstairs with another doubting glance.

"So, why don't I just put a bolt in him now and we'll have it over with." Jaythos joined in the conversation. He always thought that was the solution to every problem.

"No!" I blurted out. Wait. Why was I defending him? He unnerved me, too. There was something odd about him, and the smell of death clung to his skin like it would to a grave. But still. I had this deep-rooted feeling that I couldn't explain…. Besides, if he really was a messenger from Emarian, whatever message he had brought had to have been important, right?

"Baey, what's the matter?" Sefen gave me the same concerned look he had given me this morning.

"I…I don't know, sorry." *Say it. Stop stuffing and letting them keep you out. You have to show them you're ready to do this.* Then the secret fear that kept to itself began to creep from the shadows again. *But what if I'm not? What if I can't handle it?*

"You look tired, darling." Namaya's hard voice softened back to a motherly tone, and her dark eyebrows drew together.

'*I'm scared.*'

'*Me too, darlin'.*'

I shook my head, trying to get the voices of that memory out of my head. Now wasn't the time. I was still scared, and he was dead, and his sacrifice was going to waste. It was rotting away, being plunged into despair just like the rest of Baeno.

"Why don't you go rest for a while. It's been a long morning," Namaya added.

"Coddling is not going to do anything but waste time," Jaythos muttered under his breath.

It was hard to tell if he was complaining about the coddling or the one being coddled, but either way I felt guilty for the waste. Without a word, I turned and started up the stairs, biting my lip to stop from speaking my mind. It was surprising that I had any lip left, at this point.

"Well? Who is he?" A voice greeted me at the top of the stairs, and I jumped. "Tanner...stop sneaking up on me like that." There he was, grey vest and trousers helping him meld in the shadow of the railing. He was always trying to startle me...I only forgave him because he was the only one that would talk to me without acting like I was five. But perhaps that was just because he was actually only a couple years older than me. So why didn't the rest treat *him* like they treated me? *Because Tanner can take care of himself. Because he actually has a Gift that's useful, that's why. He's not useless like you.*

Stuffing the thought aside, I joined him in the shadows, leaning against the wall and trying to ignore the distant chatter from downstairs

"Why don't you tell me? You're the one that can find memories, after all. I'm sure you got a hold of something. That's why you're hiding up here, isn't it?" Crossing my arms, I gave a mock unimpressed expression.

Tanner's face suddenly turned embarrassed, and he fiddled with his hands. "No...I didn't, actually. It was weird," he said softly. He took great pride in his Gift, and it was a little funny to see it fail him. I would have laughed at it, actually, except that even I was a little disturbed at the fact it hadn't worked.

"What do you mean?"

"I mean it didn't work," he answered, now sounding impatient. "I brushed up against him 'accidentally,' and all I got was a blank slate. Like he didn't *have* any memories."

My breath caught. "Do you think he's one of Skayla's? In a MindHold?" That would *not* be good.

"No, no." Tanner waved his hand in dismissal, now acting the expert...which, in this field, I had to admit that he *was*. "Even the people in a MindHold have memories, even if the memories are Skayla's and not theirs. But you know that already, I told you."

Now it was my turn to look embarrassed. "I know...it's just...his eyes make me nervous. And while they aren't the violet eyes, they look...unnatural."

Shaking his head, Tanner got up from where he had been sitting against the rail and stroked his chin like a right old sage, "His eyes are a little unsettling, yes, but they are technically *normal* eyes, Baey. Could be a weird thing he was born with. I've seen people's eyes when they're in *her* grip, and trust me, they don't look like that."

Ugh. He had to rub it in. And I just had to be bothered by it. Why did Tanner get to go out and help Sefen, while I withered away here in this stone-cold cage?

"*So,* do you know who he is or no?" Tanner reiterated his question.

I sighed and shook my head, trying to let his comment go. "Not any more than you saw from the terrace. All I know is he's supposed to be some messenger from Emarian, and the letter he gave us said something about a spy...but no one seems to believe it."

"As long as he's not The GhostMaker, I think I'll be fine."

As soon as Tanner said that name, a small shiver ran down my spine, and my fist clenched into a tight ball. The GhostMaker. The one who had killed the Queen of Rugo eight years ago. The one who had been responsible for destabilizing the country of Gaevno. The body count of Skayla's assassin only grew from there: the Ostinars, Delos Var...rumor had it he had even been the one to deal the killing blow to Sven Mara when he hadn't given Skayla what she'd wanted. And I couldn't help but wonder if he would have killed *me* if Sven hadn't saved me.

I shuddered. "If he is, I think I might kill him myself."

In truth, if he *had* been The GhostMaker, they would have known already; or, well, they would already be dead. No one lived long enough to get a close look at him, and the only description they had of him was that ghastly thing hiding his face. Made of metal but fashioned like some horrid masquerade mask, it was said to gleam in the sunlight just enough to signal your death.

"A little grumpy, are we?" Tanner commented curiously, looking a little taken aback by the sudden dark comment, and fortunately helping me to return from my devolving imagination.

I realized then that I had been holding my breath. "Sorry. I'm probably just tired," I said, letting out the breath in one big huff. In all honesty, my comment had even surprised me, and already I wished to take it back.

"Mhm, and I'm humble and not at all nosy. Spill it, Feathers. You've been off since we started talking." Tanner's smirk returned.

I hemmed and hawed, trying to decide whether to just walk away or spill my aggravations on Tanner. "I just...I mean, I'm just...tired of being stuck in here. Tired of doing nothing."

"Yup. Haven't heard this song before." Tanner rolled his eyes, leaning back precariously against the railing.

"Well, you asked!" I half shouted. He wasn't helping.

I realized I must have shouted a little louder than I had thought, as Tanner looked actually concerned. That and the noise from downstairs temporarily quieted. Ugh.

"Sorry," I whispered after another moment. I straightened and prepared to go down the hall and back to my room. It was where I belonged anyway.

"Look, Baey. I'm sorry. I know you're annoyed and all. But really, it's better that you're here. It's not all fun and games out there. Really."

"I have to go. Namaya and I, theoretically, still have our lesson. At least, as long as this morning hasn't cancelled it," I said curtly. Who was he to judge? How did he know whether I was cut out for it or not? But really, I was most angry at him hitting the mark. He was right, and I knew it. It *wasn't* all fun out there. It was awful and dark, and full of pain and loss. And I was afraid I couldn't handle it. But I *had* to try. I was *supposed* to stop it. So why wouldn't anyone let me?

"Careful, Baey, you'll—" Namaya's warning came too late. The stitch on the orange popped, and I felt a little juice squirt as my needle drove hard into the orange.

Ugh.

"Well, that's why we do this with fruit and not..." The way she couldn't even finish the sentence "with people" was somehow aggravating. Like she thought if she didn't say it, I wouldn't know. But maybe it was because she thought I couldn't handle it.

Maybe she was right.

All the same, I looked back to my "patient," whom I had soundly skewered, and extracted the needle from the thick skin. The area Namaya had sliced open glared at me, taunting my inabilities.

"Try and control the needle more, Baey. Don't be so afraid of it and it won't bite," Namaya coaxed as she looked over my shoulder.

With a deep breath, I tried again, wondering if I would ever really be able to help seal up an actual wound. Knowing me, I'd be stuck giving fruit surgical procedures for the rest of my life. Slowly, the needle pierced the skin again, but this time more gently so as to not puncture the fruit beneath. The hooked needle was better angled this time. I tried hard not to bite my cheek in concentration as I carefully pulled both sides of the string perpendicularly, knotting it, and cutting the extra floss. Now I just had to do it...ten more times?

"Good, Baey! Now, try again. Get more comfortable with it." Namaya's encouragement fell flat as it had been lately. Ever since I hadn't been allowed to even be in the room when Bazzo's leg was wounded in a fight, I'd been unable to believe Namaya's praise. Was I *really* doing well? Why wasn't I able to help then?

There was a nearly imperceptible snapping sound as I realized, too late, I'd pulled the next stitch too tight, popping the stitch and ripping the skin of the orange.

"Ugh," I grumbled as I threw the mutilated fruit down on the table. *This* was precisely why I wasn't allowed to help.

Namaya raised an eyebrow. "Let's stop for now. You've worked hard, and it has been a rather…exciting day so far. I don't blame your lack of concentration."

This only worsened my mood, but I nodded nonetheless. She was right; I was too distracted for this anyway. Too distracted to even perform surgery on an orange—an *orange!* And yet, it stung to know it was this easy for people to give me breaks when I wanted. Why did I have to be such a burden? Why was I so…little?

Feyn:

So, at least I was allowed to be alone in my room. Well, my *borrowed* room. I heard Maeko adjusting his position outside the door and sighed. Never completely alone, apparently.

Tossing my bag down on the end of the bed, I took off my outer coat, throwing it on top before sitting down next to it. The bed was clearly very unused and hard—not exactly the most hospitable room I could have been given. Somehow, I got the feeling they didn't care for me.

But that was fine, as I really wasn't sure *I* cared much for me right now either. Whoever *I* was. Memories of events and faces ran through my head faster than I seemed able to catch them, leaving me feeling constantly lost and exposed. However, as long as I didn't forget why I was here, that's all I needed to care about. Reaching over to my jacket, I dug into the pocket, just wanting to make sure it was still there.

Oh, great. My throat went tight as my hand failed to find what I was looking for.

"No, no, no." I muttered in a panic, rummaging through until I was certain it wasn't in there. No! Where was it?

That's when I realized I was searching in the wrong pocket. Holding my breath, I searched through the other one, and before long my fingers fell upon the cold metal oval. I felt a sensation beyond relief as I took the little watch by its chain and pulled it out. I stared at it blankly, trying to convince myself it was still there. I was very possibly losing my mind. Even more.

But if I lost this thing, I wasn't sure what I would do. My head was on the chopping block as it was, and if—or rather, *when*—Skayla found me, she would not be merciful. I could guarantee that right now she was not very happy with me. But I suppose that's what you get for deserting and stealing your master's prize possession. Whoops.

Getting up from the bed, I perused my room to see if it held anything of use. A chair, a candle on a small side table, a sink with a metal spigot, and a very pathetic-looking window. At least they had the sense to put me in a room that I couldn't really take a back way out of, it would seem. Instinct drove me to check for exits, however, and I went up to the little circular window, inspecting every inch. Well, if I really tried...I could probably get out this way. Peering out of it, I rolled my eyes.

"Yes, and fall to my death," I murmured. But I wouldn't give up on the window yet. For now, however, I felt content with just staring out of it and into the nearby woods.

I had scoped out the surrounding forest a great deal before actually "showing up" on Valdon's doorstep. If anything went wrong, I would need to know the area as well as possible—and trust me, I was worried something would go wrong—and this was even worse than I'd thought. Emarian was an idiot to have emptied the place of practically everyone.

On top of that, I still couldn't figure out how I was supposed to earn their trust before it was too late. They had already tossed me in a practical prison cell, and they seemed to have a very eager volunteer to stick me with a crossbow bolt. If they found out my other name, I would be finding a new place to stay...six feet underground.

But back to the most pressing matter. Looking down at my hand, I studied the intricate designs on the gold watch as I had done many times before. The pendant was made of gold strands woven together, nestling a little clock in the center with an ugly crack snaking across the glass lens. I traced the crack with a hard finger, feeling the way it called to me through the silence. It was mourning, broken and alone. I kept retracing the fracture across the lens, a memory tugging just out of reach....

With a great effort, I turned my attention to where to keep it. The worst possible choice would be here in this room. I would bet my life that my room would be searched *at least* three times a day—*at least*. Though they were not nearly as intimidating as Skayla's wrath, I was afraid of failing. Failing would mean the end for everyone.

So where to put it? Not many options remained. Of course, there was *one*. The one I had gotten away with thus far. But with the secret powers said to be hidden in Valdon, I wasn't sure how long it would last. I wasn't exactly as good as I once was at making things disappear. Well, maybe I shouldn't put it that way. I was still plenty good at making *people* disappear.

An involuntary shudder ran through my body, and I suddenly felt cold. Overtired and underfed, I could use some regenerating. Maybe that was why I was feeling so...chilled. But I had been a little uncertain of what falling asleep might bring. One more sleepless night. One more day without rest, just so I could get used to my new surroundings and be less paranoid about waking up without any idea of where I was...or who I was. Granted, I had enough issues with the latter already.

But was that *worse* than remembering? If it wasn't for the watch...not really.

The watch. Right. Well, so far, my little trick had held out, so, for now, I would keep at it. But I still needed a better way to keep it safe.

A muffled conversation from the other side of the door drew my attention, and I walked closer so I could hear.

It sounded like the word 'food' was thrown out there, and I was once more conscious of the gnawing in my stomach. I had fought through the feeling the last day and a half, but now I wasn't sure how much longer I could hold off.

There was a knock on the door, and I hurriedly put the watch in my pocket. "Still here," I shouted out.

A moment later, the door opened to show my bald bodyguard (though technically jailer would have been a more fitting description) holding a bowl in one hand and a glass cup in the other—and looking none too pleased, I might add.

"So, I'm not to be starved, ah?" I gave a half smirk as I took the food. The smell was torturous, and it was all I could do to not just suck up the stew right there. It was my own fault for not packing more supplies. Not that I would have had time to.

"You could use some food, Skinny. Would make bigger target for Jaythos." Ever so slightly, the man's lips curved upwards—as if trying to show his amusement and still be emotionless at the same time— somehow, he pulled it off.

"Well, I shall try to oblige them, then, and perhaps, in the meantime, they could give me the ability to actually do my job? No? Oh well, guess it'll have to wait then, ah?" I sighed and placed the plate and cup on the small little table by the bed, looking past the bodyguard and to the door. It was slightly ajar, and I could just catch the edge of a wingtip in the hall. Well, I could guess who he'd been talking to. "Tell the sparrow her gifts are much appreciated."

Maeko's stern expression returned with a fierceness, and he gave me a look that probably should have killed me. But I was hungry and did not yet wish to die.

"Everyone seems a bit overprotective of her, ah?" I pointed out.

"You should hold your tongue, Skinny. We do not trust you, and I was serious about the target." He didn't even flinch as he said the words. Yes, yes, he was *quite* serious.

I winked. "Oh, I didn't doubt you, my friend."

Maeko turned to leave, muttering, "Then you would be wise to be more careful about what you say, or I may kill you before Jaythos." And with that, he was gone.

As soon as the door closed, I went over to the food, grabbing the spoon and diving into the stew. But I stopped myself. I knew better. Eating after having such an empty stomach would not exactly be the healthiest thing to do...but I was used to it and so paced carefully. Of course, thinking on one's own brought a lot of challenges with it that perhaps I had overlooked....

"What am I ever going to do with you?" I murmured to myself. Sitting on the bed, I stirred the stew, forcing myself to have self-control. Finally, I took a very slow spoonful of the broth and sipped it. The taste was way too rich—as I had expected—but my body still groaned for more. I continued to eat carefully, mostly taking the broth, and leaving the harder vegetables and meat in the bowl. As much as I wanted them, my stomach would not appreciate it.

After finishing about half the bowl, I walked over to the small oval window and opened it, throwing the rest of the stew out. It almost killed me to do it, but I couldn't have them thinking I wasn't eating. They'd probably draw the irrational conclusion that I was somehow poisoning their food or something, and wouldn't that just be marvelous? Besides, it would stop any temptation to overfill myself.

I kept the window open after that, however, feeling less confined with it that way. I laid back on my bed and stared at it, breathing in deeply as a breeze found its way through the opened window. It touched my face, again reminding me that I was finally rid of that horrid mask. Free to feel the breeze and the sun. The sun that now shone through the window and into my room, glimmering and yet ever shifting and elusive, just like my memory. I was oddly mesmerized.

Whether I dozed off somehow or simply lost track of time, I wasn't sure, but I suddenly realized the sky outside was growing dim. Apparently, nearly a whole day had passed.

Outside, it was beginning to get dark, so there wasn't much one could see out of the window. I could still hear the birds, and the breeze, and know there was something outside of these walls. And there the feeling came again: The feeling that everything was closing in, with no way out, no way to escape. How could I possibly get away with what I had done? There was just no way out.

But what had I done? I jolted straight up, mind suddenly drawing a blank. What *was* it? What was so important? And…and where was I?

"Think! Come on, idiot." I ran both hands through my hair frantically and tried from the beginning. My name. My age…. "Don't panic. Don't force it. Just remember…" I mumbled. I closed my eyes and forced myself to ignore the icy grip that seemed to envelop my mind and take everything away again. Then slowly, ever so slowly, memories came trickling back. I slipped my hands into my pocket, wrapping them around the little watch and breathing a sigh of relief as I felt the cold, textured metal. The ice was gone, and my memory was functioning once more. Well, more or less.

I needed to be careful. Having a slip up like that while in this mansion could be a deadly mistake, especially if I wasn't alone when it happened. Granted, no one had ever gotten out of a MindHold before, so they wouldn't know what to look for. But if I started showing public displays of my mind skipping, I doubt it would take too long for them to put some warped pieces together themselves. And I had a feeling they would think I was somehow still *in* one—definitely a problem I could do without.

Suddenly, an idea came to me.

CHAPTER III: The Follower in the Shadows

<u>Baey</u>:

I lingered outside the door, hanging around and talking to Maeko. Well, trying to. He wasn't being very helpful at the moment. It had taken all of my skills to be allowed to take dinner to the two of them, but it hadn't helped me any.

"So, who is he, Maeko? What did the letter say?" I prodded, taking a sip of the hot tea I had brought up for myself. A little spilled from my chin and fell into my once-white, layered skirt. Ugh. Another stain. There wasn't much spare fabric or clothing since Skayla had destroyed the factories she hadn't taken over and repurposed, which meant wearing the skirt regardless of the embarrassing mark.

Maeko looked slightly amused, slurping up his stew with the utmost lack of care he could possibly find. "You are not subtle, Baey." He dodged my question, resting on technicalities.

My wings sagged, and I sat down against the opposing wall. "I know," I said with a sigh. "But I just want to try to understand some of what you all are doing. Why don't you trust him? Is it just the way he looks? Or is it actually what the letter said? Do you think he forged it?" More questions than I had intended poured out, and I wished with all I had that I could have stuffed them right back in. Ugh. I'd gone and blown it again.

Maeko gave me a slight smile, shaking his head and saying, "Little Baey, this is not for you. Do not worry."

But it was! It was supposed to be. How could I show them? How could I prove that I was ready? "I'm just curious, Maeko. It wouldn't do any harm in at least making me aware of what I should watch for, right?" I prodded, trying the technical route and ignoring the fact that he had called me 'little' Baey.

He raised his eyebrow but didn't look as amused as he had before. "Something is not right about him," he said simply.

"But what exactly did the letter say?" I pressed.

"It was from Emarian. He said Cavo had come to find spy. I do not believe this. How could there be? Valdon could not have spy, we are its— Protectors?" He stumbled over the word slightly.

I nodded. "Yes, that's right." I had taught the burly man Varnese since he had come here. His vocabulary had been extremely limited, but after six years, it was fairly hard to tell sometimes that he was still stumbling over words. I thought over what he had said for a moment then asked, "So, there's a spy in Valdon?"

Maeko sighed. "I hope not, Little Baey. He could have bad information. Or he may not be trusted. I do not know."

A sinking feeling settled deep in my gut, and I didn't ask anything more for a long while. Maeko ate his stew and I sat against the wall, trying to find safety in the folds of my wings…but none could be found. I felt as if the very foundation of Valdon was crumbling beneath me. What if this man was a spy? Or worse. What if Skayla had sent him to…to…

"What are you going to do with him?"

Maeko set his empty bowl on the floor and huffed. "I will take him out to search area tomorrow and judge him for myself."

That didn't sound *too* dangerous, right? "Could I come? That way if anything happened, I could fly for help. He wouldn't even have to know I was there. I could keep my distance." I knew he would say no. I knew I would be told to stay...but I was beginning to hit the edge. Though it frightened me half to death, I thought I might even be willing to risk Sefen's wrath to try and prove myself.

With a gentle laugh and smile, Maeko shook his head. "No, Little Baey."

But I might just. I really was thinking about it, and it scared me. How could I even think about doing something so selfish?

But was it? If I was supposed to save Baeno, I had to show I was capable—before there was nothing left of Baeno to save.

That night I lay curled in bed, wrestling half the night on what to do. I could stay far enough away that Maeko wouldn't see or hear me, yet my senses would let me keep track of where they were. But what if I got caught? I'd never be allowed outside of Valdon for the rest of my miserable life. I didn't want Maeko to get himself hurt, though, and as much as I hated it, I had a feeling that this stranger could very well bring down Valdon. I didn't want to see that happen.

I took out the ring once more, the thing that only I could see. Sometimes, I wished I could show Sefen or Namaya...or anybody, if only to help figure out what it meant. Suddenly, a strange emotion came over me. It was a strong longing, a longing to return to something that was just out of reach—but the feeling felt foreign. Staring at the ring, I let go, and upon doing so the sensation died down to just a faint thought in the back of my head. What did it mean?

I got up from my bed, this time with no hesitation or care for the cold. This was different. I had never felt this before, and I just had to find out what this was. So, with my hand now gripping the ring, I walked slowly to the door, trying to find where these weird urges were coming from. Did it come from the stranger? I shuddered. It couldn't be. This feeling was nothing like the one he gave me. His presence was of darkness and death, and a power that was grasping for something. No. This was different. It was lonely, searching. Like I was lost and would find my way just around the next corner...

"Baey? What are you doing up?"

I jumped up to blend into the shadows of the ceiling, fearing for one ridiculous, dreadful moment it was the stranger.

"Baey, come down. It's just me—and I can still see you, you know..."

It was Namaya, standing before me with hands on her hips and an amused smile. Exhaling, I fluttered back to the ground and stretched my wings in and out in embarrassment. "Sorry. I couldn't sleep...so, I went for a walk." I felt awful not telling the whole truth, but even if I had wanted to explain about the ring, I couldn't. She wouldn't be able to see it. Besides, some gut feeling down in me warned me against it. It always did.

"You really shouldn't be wandering, and so close to where that...man is staying." Namaya glanced nervously down the hall, and I followed her gaze.

Oh. I hadn't realized how close I was getting to his door. But...where was Maeko?

"Sorry. I didn't realize it." I whispered softly, ignoring the small urge that was still there in the back of my mind. "But…what are you doing up, Namaya? And where's Maeko?" I asked hesitantly.

Namaya put an arm around my wings and began expertly steering me away from the forbidden hall and back towards my room. "I relieved Maeko so he could get some sleep. I couldn't sleep anyway, so I decided Maeko could use the rest."

"Oh," was all I said. "What's his name again?" I asked suddenly.

Namaya stopped and stared at me oddly. "Maeko's…?"

My eyes went wide and I shook my head; perhaps I would have been amused, if not for the millions of things warring in my head. "No. No, no, no. The stranger's name. Sorry, didn't really specify, did I?"

Namaya just shook her head and started walking again. We walked for a little while, actually, until I realized she wasn't going to answer my question. I had thought maybe she was just remembering it or something, but I could tell now that she was clearly avoiding the subject. I didn't say a word or bring it back up, instead just giving her a quick look up and down, trying to see what I could catch by her appearance.

She looked on edge. My first impulse was that she, Sefen, and Jaythos had gotten into another disagreement. But her left hand was on her sheathed sword, while her right was still very protectively against my wings and back, steering me as if I might fly away if she didn't. Every little noise seemed to jolt her a bit—from the occasional sound of the pipes running at the base of the wall to even the simple echoing of our steps.

"There. Now, why don't you go back and get some rest, Baey? It's been a long day, and the last thing you need is to be up this late at night. Why, it's probably only a few hours before dawn already."

Was it? I resolved to look out my window as soon as I was back in my room. That couldn't be right. When I had been in my room earlier, it had only been an hour before midnight.

"Are you alright, Maya?" I asked softly. Of course, she was alright! She just must be on edge from everything today.

"What? Of course, why would you ask such a silly question, Baey? Go to sleep. You look all tense and strained. Goodnight, dear." She stroked my feathers in a quick, affectionate goodbye—just like she always did—and left quickly back down the hall.

After I watched her go, I went into my room quickly and over to my window. Just as I had thought. By the looks of the sky, it must be just about midnight now. That was odd. It was almost as if Namaya had been wishing away the night? She was usually so good at paying attention to things.

Nothing out of the ordinary, Baey. What's wrong with you? There is a dangerous stranger in the house, of course she'd be nervous. But I knew in my heart this wasn't right. Nothing shook Namaya. She was always collected and calm, ready for anything. Sure, she and Sefen had been arguing, and sure she had been pressing for us to abandon Valdon and move somewhere more secure, but really, I doubted she would blink an eye if Skayla herself was standing before her.

So, what was wrong with her? Why would something like this shake her so badly, while everyone else seemed to stay…well, normal and *fairly* calm, anyway?

My mind was resolved. I *would* follow Maeko and the man tomorrow—see if I could figure out what was going on. Maybe I could even get Tanner to help me.

61

Unfortunately for my guilt complex, I did not change my mind in the morning. Sefen and Jaythos had taken off early in the morning to evacuate one of the last towns that stood between here and Kaedna, as an impending attack that Tanner had discovered now left them exposed. I'd been to the town once or twice, but not in years—it being deemed 'too dangerous' as always. I missed even that small freedom, and the thought of the quaint town with its clock tower and cobblestone walks being deserted was a bitter image in my mind.

That being said, Sefen and Jaythos being gone meant the only ones to stop me following Maeko and Feyn were Namaya and Tanner. Tanner had agreed to keep his mouth shut—with the promise that I would keep him updated. The silly boy felt as left out as I was, though at least Sefen would let *him* help sometimes. Namaya had left right after to gather some herbs for remedies, in case Sefen and Jaythos ran into unexpected trouble. I thought this a little odd, since Sefen and Jaythos were only going to evacuate the town, not fight in a battle. But then again, Namaya had always been the pessimist. Or, perhaps, the realist.

The pale sun shot forth from between the clouds as I wove slowly between the tops of trees. Then I hesitated. Come to think about it, they had left Valdon rather vulnerable. Wasn't it unwise for Namaya to take off when we really should have at least one person here? Tanner didn't count. He could fight, but he wasn't a warrior. Sefen only really brought him along to get memories from the soldiers—locations, troop movements, things like that. That's how Sefen and Jaythos knew about that planned attack. They'd run into a patrol the day before Feyn had arrived, and with the intel Tanner had gotten from one of the men, we'd learned there was a raid planned on the next eclipse of the two moons. But the point was that Tanner wasn't a soldier. Should I go back?

Great. Doubting yourself again, Baey? It's too late now. Besides, surely Namaya will be back soon. She never takes too long gathering, and, knowing her, she'd hate being away long.

I slowed my flight, hanging even closer to the trees. Aha. There they were. For a moment, I had thought perhaps I'd lost them.

But what if something happened while I was gone? I started feeling gut-wrenchingly guilty. What if Tanner got overcome by Skayla's soldiers, and when I returned he was lying dead on the floor? Or worse. A MindHold. *Well then. How would you help at all?* The truth was a deafening blow, but it wasn't the first time it had slithered into my mind. It was true. I wouldn't have been any help anyway, and that was why I had come out here. To try. But what would be the use now? If no one was home, then who would I be going to call for help if something went wrong?

Oh, stop it, Baey! You've overthought this and now you have no idea why you're out here!

"Did you hear that?"

Ugh. I'd gotten too close and too caught up in myself. I let the wind catch my wings, shooting me up higher and away from the two I had been following. The voice had been that of the stranger and even at this height I could hear the response.

"Why, Skinny, nervous?"

"No. Why? Are you?" The stranger's voice sounded sorely unused, even as he shot the question back effortlessly.

Maeko just scoffed, "I am never nervous."

As quietly as possible, I settled back down to rest on the top of a tree that still held its summer color, noting how the pair surveyed each other. I realized suddenly that even as Maeko was trying to size up Feyn to see if he was trustworthy, Feyn was doing the very same to Maeko. It made me almost indignant—how could anyone think Maeko could betray Emarian or us? After all he'd suffered from Skayla?

"So why are we out here, again?" Was it me, or did Feyn look in my general direction? I resisted the urge to shrink or move in any form, but the paranoia was hard to ignore. I only hoped my wings were blending into the trees' color like they *should* be doing, not reflecting my current nervousness and sticking out like a sore thumb. Feyn looked away, and I tried not to breathe too hard in a sigh of relief.

"Skinny would want to be familiar with the woods, should a spy be watching us, yes?" Maeko waved his hand idly as he continued picking his way through the underbrush with his usual quietness.

Feyn sighed. "I need to be observing everyone *in Valdon*—I still think I should have gone with the other two to the town…." I had apparently missed some private argument. Again. Tanner usually kept me informed over things that were hidden from me, but I guess, in this case, he'd not given me the 'in.'

"Why? None of us would betray. We are all family—Skayla and Lord Kovo have taken much from us." Maeko's tone had an edge to it, and I knew why.

"Oh?" Feyn stopped moving and crossed his arms. "Explain; why not you?"

The silence made even my lack of sound appear to stick out; I barely caught the gasp that now stuck in my throat.

Maeko's usual cavalier expression twisted into something wedged between grief and anger as he turned to stare at Feyn. "I would never."

Feyn appeared so unaffected I could have flinched. "But why should I believe you?"

"Because if I ever see Skayla or her GhostMaker, I will make them pay for killing my Serafina."

Serafina. Queen Serafina. No one talked about her—especially around Maeko—but Tanner had told me the young queen had been like a daughter to Maeko. Tanner had seen the memory of what had happened, too. But he'd never told me anything beyond what everyone else knew; she'd been assassinated by The GhostMaker, and Rugo fell after her.

"What are we doing again?" Feyn's question jarred the silence out of existence, and the obvious attempt to change the subject was understandable.

Maeko just scoffed and turned around, fists still clenched. I prepared to take to the air again and follow them further when Feyn again spoke.

"Who—" He stopped whatever he was about to say, hands moving back and forth in a very panicky movement. What was wrong with *him?* It had almost seemed as if he'd been about to ask Maeko who Serafina was. I thought again of what Tanner had said about not seeing any memories in Feyn's head.

Then the stranger took off one of his gloves and…and…well, itched at one of his palms. Then I saw it. Little writing on the left hand. Writing he was looking at and obviously trying to make it look like he wasn't.

I locked my eyes on it, trying to see what it said. It was something like 'Watch Valdon Spy.' What was it for? I couldn't decide if that was good or not, but I would make sure to tell Sefen. But…how to explain this one?

Feyn:

I always had to forget things at the worst possible moment, didn't I? My burly bodyguard was suspicious of me already, and that moment had not been the time. But when had I gotten to choose when my mind worked? *Apparently never.* But what had triggered it this time? Something had triggered it…I was sure of—oh, but the more I tried to remember the more lost I felt, and suddenly I couldn't even remember my own stupid name.

Fortunately, I'd had the forethought last night to put a few memory joggers on my hand. It didn't take me long to at least remember some basics, but I had a surprisingly hard time remembering important things…oops.

Closing my eyes, I took a deep breath and tried to collect myself.

"*Kvanta? Co dayto ka.*"

"Patience, I'm listening." Well then, I had to be getting on Maeko's nerves if he was insulting me in his language. So, what had I said? I stomped my foot in a fit of exasperation. *You even remembered **his** name! You can remember everybody else's names. Everything else is* *important, but what's your name again? What were you saying? Can you at least manage that, you dummy?!*

Maeko was right. I was an idiot. My hands found their way into my pockets and to the watch. I relaxed as my left hand curled around it once again, and I calmed down slightly. Now to get back to business.

I wasn't lying to them. There was a spy. But who? I heard something from above and scanned the skies. Skayla hadn't found me already, had she? Nothing to make your day seem better than to have something go worse. But no, while the sound I heard was indeed those of wings, they were way too quiet to be a Drogan. It was the little winged girl, hiding up near the top of one of the tall, thick trees. Her wings had changed shade to blend in, but I had been able to catch her. Was she spying out of curiosity? With the way everyone treated her, I wouldn't be surprised, and I knew she wasn't the spy only because she was one of the people Skayla was so ardently looking for.

I thought about saying something about our little tagalong to Maeko but decided against it for now.

Now, what had we been talking about? I took a deep breath and *at last* reoriented, mentally crossing Maeko off my list of those who could be the spy and instead turning around the question: "So, your turn. Why don't you trust me, and how can I change your mind?" I only hoped I would be able to keep it together enough to get somewhere where I could write down that Maeko was innocent. No one who was as close to Queen Serafina as he obviously had been could take part in Skayla's plans, and the pain in Maeko's eyes had been too real.

Maeko's answer cut through that thought with a deadpan, "You stink."

...What...? I...I what? "Excuse me?" I swung around, not sure whether to hit him or laugh. What did *that* have to do with anything? Leave it to a Rugonian to get to the point.

"You stink. Stink of death."

I fought to keep my amused smile. I couldn't let him see how much that hit me. I hadn't actually thought of that possibility. No matter how much I wished it, I couldn't wash the blood from my hands. Shadows of whose blood exactly drenched me danced just out of reach, leaving me with a sense of dread without understanding why. One minute I would feel as if I finally remembered everything, only for the next to sweep it all away and leave nothing but gloom behind.

But if I didn't break the cycle, I would lose my entire self again. And so, I carried on, "I hadn't thought one could smell of death...well, not unless said person *was* dead. Are you insinuating something?" It probably wasn't the best answer I could come up with, but I had to say something before Maeko caught onto my trip-up in this charade.

My burly friend just huffed and looked at me with a scowl, arms crossed.

"So, then, how am I supposed to fix that?" I asked as we walked on, getting deeper and deeper into the forest. I lowered my voice as we went, knowing that Skayla's Drogans were beginning to get close to Valdon. I had a feeling Skayla had known its whereabouts for a while, now, and she was just waiting for the perfect moment. Which meant I had possibly just walked into a trap by seeking refuge at the ageless mansion. Just what I needed.

"I am not sure," came Maeko's noncommittal reply, just as quiet as my question.

Clouds blocked the sunlight, and all around us there was gloom and grey. I didn't like the feel of this part of the woods, and I could see that even Maeko looked uneasy.

"Something's not right," I muttered.

Maeko huffed and seemed to try to look unconcerned. "Besides you?"

"Shh!" I said sharply, closing my eyes and straining every nerve. A twig snapped, and I snapped my head in the direction it had come from, just in time to see a shadow running off into the woods.

"Quick, someone's out here—" and this person was *not* the winged girl. I took off without another word, chasing down the shadow as I jumped over logs, weaved through the trees, and tried my best not to trip over the general underbrush. Lack of sleep made me unforgivably clumsy.

Suddenly, Maeko ran past me, his strong limbs carrying him with ease and leaving me behind, breathless and angered with my own exhaustion. I was used to pushing myself, however, and with Maeko strongly leading up the chase I veered off to the left, hoping I would be able to cut off whoever it was.

But in another two minutes, I closed in only to find myself almost running right into Maeko, who was as equally empty-handed as I.

I knelt down to catch my breath, aggravated beyond belief at having let whoever it was slip out of our grasp.

"Who was it?" Maeko asked.

"What?" I wheezed. "You didn't have someone following us in case I jumped you?" My breathless laugh was bitter.

Maeko only answered with a simple, "No."

"Well, whoever it was must have stumbled upon us by accident with the way they took off. I think. Which means...where were they going?" And who were they? Suddenly a thought occurred to me. "Who was left back at Valdon again?" Stupid brain.

Maeko's frown gave the appearance that he was about to be very unhelpful, but fortunately he answered, "Baey, Namaya, and Tanner. Why?"

"Well, it wasn't Baey—the winged girl, right?" That sounded right. But how did I know her name? I must have heard one of those at Valdon say it in passing or something.

"Why? And why would it be someone from Valdon? It could have been an intruder watching."

I shook my head but didn't bother giving an answer. So, Maeko was safe, Baey was safe, Sefen and Jaythos were off in the village so they couldn't be the spy...so that left…

"We should head back." I announced quickly.

Maeko did not argue, and, for a while, we headed back in silence.

Then I decided to test my luck.

"*So, tell me,*" I changed to Rugonian, mostly in case the person we'd chased doubled back to overhear us. They might not know we didn't see who it was, and I preferred them to be on edge—it would make them easier to spot in Valdon. "*Why should not I be suspicious of any of others?*"

Maeko's shoulders shot up in immediate tension, and he stopped and stared at me.

"Yes, I speak Rugonian. Figured I would see if my accent was any good." I said just as carelessly, giving him a meaningful glance and hoping he would catch it.

"It stinks," he replied.

"Really? Is that the only Varnese word you know?"

He just shrugged. *"At least my Varnese is better than your Rugonian."*

"If you want them no suspicious to me, tell me why should them I trust?" Wow, my Rugonian really *was* rusty.

Maeko sighed. *"Fine. Sefen and Namaya have nothing left. Their family is gone and they have no other home. They've fought here at Valdon for almost as long as Sven Mara has been dead. It's more likely Sven would come back from the dead than they would betray anyone."*

"And Tanner?" I asked.

Maeko seemed less certain now. *"He's just a child."*

"*So were Maras when they became The Watchers*," I said, glad to finally be getting some cooperation. The stranger in the woods must have scared him, whether he would admit it or not. Now he *knew* I was right; there was a spy. Someone had been in the woods for *something*, the question was why. Were they on their way to contact Skayla? I wondered suddenly if they were reporting on my appearance here.... How long would it take for Skayla to get here? She'd been at Kaedna searching through the spoils of the ruins when I'd left her. But would she go to the Kovian Fortress to regroup with Kovo before heading here, or was she angry enough to just come straight for me?

I touched the watch in my pocket and doubt seeped through. Yeah, she might be angry enough, for sure.

"Were you even listening to me?" Maeko asked, jolting me back and making me realize we were back in the clearing in front of Valdon…and I had missed every word Maeko had just said about—oh, what had we been talking about?

A noise from Valdon distracted us, and we saw the door open and Baey come running out of the house, constantly tripping over her long wings as they dragged along the ground. She was obviously upset, her wings shimmering into different shades of bronze and black as she made her way towards us. But what made my heart plummet was the blood all over her white shirt. "Maeko! You're back! There was an ambush! Jaythos and Sefen are inside, but Jaythos is hurt."

Maeko's casual stride broke right there, and he ran up to the girl, briefly muttering something to her before rushing inside.

So, there we stood, she and I, face to face for the first time since I'd arrived. She stared at me awkwardly, seeming to wonder whether to run inside after Maeko or say something to me. Then she decided, opening and closing her mouth several times before actually speaking.

"What are you doing here?" she asked, pulling her wings close around her as if that would hide her. She looked at me and then back at the house, seemingly unsure of what to do and not sounding terribly intimidating.

"Helping," I answered softly. I cocked my head slightly to one side, brows furrowed as I studied her. "But I think you have slightly more pressing problems at the moment." And with that, I walked past her and through the door. Perhaps I could help them, and maybe, just maybe, earn their trust. But let's not get ahead of ourselves.

CHAPTER IV: Disaster Helps…Sometimes

Baey:

Stupid, selfish, thoughtless girl! What had I been thinking! I never should have left Valdon, never should have followed. I wasn't there when Sefen and Jaythos had gotten back—and had needed me. Tanner had covered for my whereabouts but, with his complete ignorance of medicine, had been unable to help. Namaya had somehow still not returned and I'd been shooed from the room as soon as we'd gotten Jaythos settled in a bed.

And here I was now, following the stranger inside, torn between making sure he didn't try anything funny while no one was watching, and running back to try and offer help again. He apparently decided for me, following the sound of commotion and all but running up the stairs.

"Where are you going?" I asked as I desperately tried to keep up, stumbling as I always did over my wings. Ugh, these things were so much more useful when flying.

"To help." He dodged down the left hall and soon found Jaythos's room, occupied with Sefen, Maeko, Tanner, and Jaythos, the latter sitting up stubbornly on his bed with his arm wrapped in a blood-soaked cloth. He looked even paler than when I had left him.

Everyone looked at us for a moment, but Sefen quickly went back to trying to convince Jaythos to stay put. It wasn't working.

"I'm fine, Sefen! It's just a scratch, which is more than can be said for those spineless idiots." He started to get up, almost toppling over in the process. Stupid warriors always thought they were invincible.

I heard a wry chuckle from Feyn and felt sick, thinking he was laughing at the wound and the awful mess that was unfolding before him. But then in a flash he was by Jaythos, helping Maeko and Sefen push him down.

"Well then, isn't this just wonderful? You've gone and almost gotten yourself killed, but you took a couple of them with you, ah? I hope that comforts all your friends when they have to bury you for idiocy." We just looked on in shock as Feyn stood in front of Jaythos, taking some of the spare cloth and ripping it violently into two pieces. "I'm so glad you think you're alright, because maybe that's what we'll write on your grave. What do you think, ah? 'He died, but he was alright.' Does that sound fitting? Death by idiocy? That's just what Skayla needs—idiots like you getting yourselves killed because you ignore scrapes like these."

I couldn't process this. I don't think any of us could. The fact that Jaythos wasn't strangling him already meant that either he was in shock, or the words were somehow actually hitting him—which would be a first.

"Who's the healer here?" Feyn asked as he started inspecting the wound on Jaythos's arm.

"Namaya...where *is* she?" Sefen looked right at me, and I shrugged helplessly.

"She said she had gone out to gather herbs in case." What if something had happened to her?

"Well, does anyone *else* know where she at least keeps her supplies? This needs a disinfectant if you still have that sort of thing out here—and stitching before we bandage it up properly. The quicker we get that done, the better."

Without thinking, I gave a quick "I'll be back—I know where it is." Before anyone had a chance to tell me otherwise, I was running—and tripping—down the hall towards Namaya's supply room, grabbing everything I could think of that would be of use and running back into the room. "Here—this should be everything. This is Namaya's own salve—it works miracles and there's just a little bit left from her last batch." I handed the vial to Feyn as I set out the rest of the supplies on a little side table.

"Great. I need a second set of hands to help with the stitching. I take it you usually act as Namaya's second?" Feyn didn't even turn around as he asked. He didn't wait for an answer before continuing, "Get the needle threaded and ready and come over here."

"I don't think—" Sefen was cut off by Feyn.

"Not the time for arguing, please."

I heard Jaythos let out an audible hiss and guessed the salve had been applied. Needle threaded, I quickly headed over to Feyn's side. "All set." I handed him the stitching implement.

"My hands are all slick from handling the salve, can you do it?"

"What? No, she's just a child, Feyn, this is—"

"—Can you do it or not?" Feyn asked louder, voice almost vehement.

I don't know what possessed me to nod, but as I looked down at my unsteady hands I began to wonder if perhaps it wasn't just my whole body shaking.

It's just like the orange; it's just like the orange. Right, the orange I'd maimed forever. *Just* like that. Feyn helped hold the edges of the skin in place as I began to work. One stitch. Two…three…the more I did, the more natural it became and the less I worried. True, I wasn't breathing, true Jaythos's occasional grunt reminded me this was no longer a fruit…but my hands steadied, my shoulders relaxed and allowed for smoother movements, and, twenty-five stitches later, Jaythos's wound was closed.

A strange thrill ran up my back, and I stepped back as I inspected my work. "Not a bad-looking orange, if I do say so myself."

"I'm…sorry?" Jaythos blinked, stare blank.

Come to think of it, most everyone was staring at me…. Right. They'd all probably thought I would faint. But before I could think further, Feyn again stepped in, this time addressing Jaythos and not me.

"Now, do you think you can behave like an actual soldier and get rest, or do I need to let you borrow *my* guard?" Feyn's question to Jaythos sounded more like a hidden threat.

I had a feeling it was a jab at Sefen for posting Maeko to watch his every move, and I wasn't sure whether to laugh or be as indignant as the others seemed to be. Indignant…and embarrassed. They'd all locked him up and he had helped us. That had to count for something. Maybe he wasn't a spy; maybe I was just fretting for nothing. Maybe. But he still gave me the chills.

Jaythos said nothing in return, only glared at Feyn. But that was as close as any of us would get to a 'yes,' so we filed out of the room. Sefen stayed behind a moment longer to talk to Jaythos.

Feyn immediately took off in the direction of his room—no doubt to get changed and cleaned up—and I watched him go. I wasn't sure if I was just seeing things, but it almost looked as if his hands were shaking.

Once he was out of sight, I breathed a sigh of relief. Maeko looked at me with his thick brows knit tight over his eyes. "You alright, Little Baey?"

"Huh? Yes, I'm...much better than Jaythos, at least." I realized my satisfaction at actually doing a half-decent job was not really a fitting mood for the situation, and the reminder of everything that had gone wrong today dampened the victory. I thought again of the way Feyn had seemed to so purposefully look at me in the woods and worried what he might do if he had seen me. Would he tell Sefen? A knot formed in the pit of my stomach, and suddenly I just wanted to run after Feyn and get the whole thing over with. At this point, I might as well tell Sefen myself...but I couldn't. Not right after he'd just finished dealing with Jaythos, and whatever had happened at that town. But perhaps, more selfishly, not after I'd just finally been allowed to do something *helpful*.

"Are you going to go back to keep an eye on Feyn?" I found myself asking Maeko, wondering how the events of the day would affect the stranger. I also wondered about the chase in the woods. So, Feyn was right? Was there a spy?

Maeko sighed and nodded. "I...should." He started walking off but went slowly, as if I were hanging onto his ankles.

"Little Baey?"

I forced a small smile. "Hm?"

He shifted and gave me another look. "Have you been here all day?"

The suddenness of the question did nothing to calm my fears. Ugh. To lie or just get out with it? I couldn't lie...but what if I told the truth? Would it stop me from ever being allowed into what was going on? "Mhm." I managed to force the sound out, pursing my lips and trying not to look undeniably guilty. Ugh, lying was pretty awful.

"Why don't you get cleaned up? You look like a murderer," he said, seamlessly changing the subject in a way that made my head swim. Did he know? Had he seen through the thin lie?

I forced my paranoid questions down and answered with a simple, "Alright," before making my way to my room.

It wasn't until I was in my room and in front of my mirror that I noticed the blood. Ugh. No wonder Maeko had kept looking at me like that. I looked like I had just been murdered or something. My long, stained skirt was now completely beyond hope, and the sleeves on my white blouse were not much better. Only my pinstriped collared vest had somehow missed the dark stains of Jaythos's wounds. I was going to have to suck it up and get rid of this shirt *and* the skirt. At least we would have some cleaning rags for Namaya.

I sighed and stared at myself, covering the blood with my wings and wishing it to go away. My wings were still that irritating dark bronze, but I didn't need to see them to know how I felt, obviously. That's probably how Maeko knew I was lying. Wings were useful, yes, but mine had the habit of showing what I was feeling…which was less useful.

I rolled my eyes at myself then as I noticed a twig in my messily bunned hair. Oh. Whoops. If my bad lying hadn't clued Maeko in, the twigs and leaves in my hair probably had. Who was I kidding? I couldn't do this.

Now beginning to feel very itchy, I decided I should probably get washed up. There was a sink in my room, and I turned on the faucet, the pipes creaking and groaning as the water sputtered into the porcelain bowl. It took a while, first the wings, which had gotten a little blood while helping pin Jaythos down—before Maeko had gotten back—then my face and hands. I had to change and find a creative way to get the stain out of my once-white clothes, even though I knew it was a hopeless cause.

About an hour later I gave up, throwing the awful things on the ground and making up my mind just to rip them up and use them as a rag or something. It wasn't worth it, and I didn't feel like wearing something that had my friend's blood on it. Still, I felt guilty for tossing the shirt when fabric was so precious.

I sat down on my bed, wrapping my wings as closely as I could to my body. This day had gone terribly wrong. I had the most bitter taste in my mouth, along with a disturbing, yet unknown, fear sticking in the back of my mind.

Why had Feyn and Maeko been speaking Rugonian? I wished more than ever that Maeko had taught me more, as I hadn't really been able to understand anything they had said. Granted, if I had known Rugonian I might have stuck around instead of heading back to Valdon, and that would have meant getting caught red-handed by Sefen. Or worse, not being there at all and unable to help.

Help. It always came back to that. Instinctively, my hand went to the ring, and I pulled it out, fingering the small, intricate carvings in the flawless silver. In the middle was that smooth green stone, and I rubbed it soothingly, trying to clear my thoughts.

What did the ring do? Too many years I had asked that, but for some reason, at this moment, I felt I might actually be able to find out. The strange urge of longing returned, and I felt pressed to go out of the room. However, my fear of who I might run into outweighed it, and I stayed, getting up and pacing instead. Something drew me to my window and I soon found myself overlooking the darkening sky. It wasn't that late yet, but the stern look of the clouds had hidden the sun away, and even now I could see the rain beginning to fall.

I thought of the town and the vague memories I had of walking through it in the evenings when I was very young. The shadows of the tall clock tower had once felt so comforting and yet now it seemed shadows only held a sense of foreboding.

Then I thought of how Sefen and Jaythos had been ambushed and wondered how in Baeno Skayla's men could have known they'd come. *Spy.* The word rang in my head, and my shoulders slumped as I stared into the evening. It seemed everything was being met with failure these days. Stepping back from the window, I stomped my foot. I had to do better! I had to find a way. I thought back to that night, *the* night. The darkness, the fear I felt, then him. The confusion I had felt when he had pressed the thing into my hands. Over and over, I played it in my mind, and I closed my eyes, trying to pick something out—anything out—to help me feel like I was there. My mind settled on the sword Sven had used to protect me. It had been so beautiful, with the same silver that the ring appeared to be made of.

It had such beautiful markings on it, working gracefully into that odd shape. Curved so elegantly. I sighed, opening my eyes once more. Suddenly, I gasped with fright, jumping back as I tried to get the thing out of my hand—but it disappeared first.

It…it…the sword! It had been in my hand!

Feyn:

80

I stared at my shaking hands which were smeared with black ink. And blood. Blood everywhere. Had I killed someone? What had I done this time? What had I been made to do? Vainly, I tried to slow my panicked breaths, closing my eyes again and focusing on something—anything that would help me remember what had happened. My breaths steadied, and my hands stopped shaking. Valdon. The watch. The spy in the woods and Jaythos.

Relief trickled slowly through my body like an antidote to a poison, reviving life into my numb limbs. No one was dead.

"You really need to stop doing this to yourself." I sighed as everything came back. At least the memories came back a little easier this time, though part of me selfishly wished some of them wouldn't come back at all. I rewrote the little words in fresh writing on my hand, adding a few: Maeko, Sefen, Jaythos. Those who I had cleared. All that remained were Namaya and Tanner...and Namaya was the only one not there in the mansion. Hm. Odd for a healer to be absent when needed most. But then, what had Baey said when Sefen had asked? Namaya had been gathering herbs in case? Why would she have thought they would need some?

The soft pattering of rain broke the silence and I went over to my pathetic little window, watching as the rain hit against the glass. I cleaned the window until it seemed the clearest crystal in all of Baeno. That reminded me. I was now covered in blood and could use some cleaning up. But before I tried to get washed up, I made sure to take the watch from my coat pocket and place it on the table, where I could keep an eye on it.

There was a washing bowl on the table, and I turned the faucet on and set to cleaning off the rest of me, careful to keep the writing on my hand intact. After, I changed into the one spare set of clothes I had and then tried to clean my old shirt with the water, eventually leaving the shirt to soak in the sink.

There was a knock on my door then, and I frantically grabbed the watch and shoved it into my trousers' pocket. Even though no one could see it, I still panicked that the trick would give out.

"What may I help you with, Maeko?" I called out, already knowing who it was.

The door opened and in entered the silent Rugonian, looking as severe as ever. "Sefen wants you," he said, stepping aside from the door in an obvious gesture for me to leave. This would be interesting.

Having no wish to provoke my stern-faced friend, I grabbed my coat and went out the door, closely followed by Maeko. Down the hall we went, past Jaythos's room and to the last door on the left. Maeko ushered me in.

I found myself in a much nicer room than I was staying in. A bookshelf lined one wall, lit from the light of a small overhead chandelier. A large, oak desk sat in the middle of the room, and atop of it sat an hourglass, pearl-inlay fountain pen, and, most unique of all, a typewriter. They all seemed relics of a past we'd never see again—creatures of fairy tales. I tore my eyes away from them and to the man sitting behind the desk.

"Feyn Cavo," Sefen said in greeting, getting up from the chair. He made his way around the desk and up to me.

"That was my name, last time I checked," I replied with the raise of an eyebrow. Except it wasn't my name. The problem was, which name was my real one? It seemed on the tip of my tongue—

Sefen did not appear amused. He was probably still upset over my insistence on Baey helping. "I think I must thank you," he said with a small sigh. He leaned against the front of his desk and narrowly avoiding the fragile hourglass with the precision of someone who more often sat *on* his desk rather than behind it.

"You think?" I raised an eyebrow. "Though I suppose you aren't wrong. Baey deserves the most gratitude."

"Maeko told me what you saw in the woods," he finally replied, completely ignoring my statement. But I was too distracted by sudden obliviousness. What was I doing again?

Stupid brain. This ebb and flow of my mental tide was really giving me a headache.

Did he mean the girl? No. That wouldn't be it. There had been something else. It was…oh, what was it? I had to contain my frustration, trying to keep my hands from fidgeting as I vainly tried to force back the lost memory. How come I could remember exactly what kind of trees were in the forest, but not what was so pressing?

"Well?"

"Hm?" I gave the vaguest noise possible, trying to give me time to think. Woods…the girl… "What exactly did Maeko tell you?" I asked. Maybe this would get him to tell me. Then the memory would come back. Hopefully.

Sefen sighed, seeming very fed up with my games. "The figure in the woods. He told me you both tried to chase them down but lost sight of them."

Yes! The floodgates were opened and the memory returned—and with it my seriousness. The spy. "Yes. I think they were either watching Valdon or on their way to deliver Skayla a message. And if it's the latter, then I'm sorry but my suspicions are correct: Someone here is a spy." Skayla hadn't been kidding. She really was close to getting all of Baeno, wasn't she? Spies were everywhere.

"Did you get a good look at them?" Sefen pressed.

"No. But after talking to Maeko, I have ruled out him, you, and Jaythos. That leaves the boy and Namaya."

I heard Maeko let out a groan of seeming frustration.

Sefen's eyes widened, "What? No. That's impossible. Tanner is more than trustworthy, and Namaya would *never* betray us. It's out of the question. The spy isn't here, don't be ridiculous."

"Why? Why not Tanner, and why not Namaya?"

"My *wife* has lost enough to Skayla and Kovo. She would never even think of selling us out—and I would be careful before letting her name cross your lips in such a way again."

I was undeterred, whether from exhaustion, conviction, or desperation. I refused to tell anyone about the watch until I'd shut up the spy, but what if I couldn't find them before they got word to Skayla that I was here? That had to have been where they'd been going—and where was Namaya? "But I didn't see Namaya here today. Is she back yet?"

Sefen's glare was deadlier than my blade, which was more impressive than he even knew. "She. Is not. A spy. In fact, if she doesn't come back tonight, I would be more concerned that the spy found *her*, and if she died trying to stop them, so help me I will *gladly* inform Emarian of *just* how much help you were."

This was going to be difficult. The more I thought about it, the more likely it was that Namaya *was* the spy—the boy had been here when we'd returned, and while it was plausible that he'd doubled back....

"Yes. Please inform him how I helped save your friend Jaythos. That would be appreciated. Now, can I leave, or are you going to continue to throw away my attempts to help? Skayla has been so far ahead that you can't plan anymore. You're so busy *defending* that you can't attack. Valdon is too close to the Kovian Fortress. A week away is your doom. Your other strongholds have stood abandoned, the factories have been destroyed, and half of the towns you are protecting are now abandoned or burned. You should leave here and find a different way of attacking. *Of course*, there's a spy—how do you think word got to Skayla and Kovo's men that you were evacuating that town? Who else could have possibly known?"

The hourglass on the desk fell over, and the resounding clang it made was worse than the silence. At least the thing hadn't broken. "You really push your luck, don't you?" Sefen's entire body was rigid, and yet I saw he was really thinking about it for the first time.

"It comes with being a youngest son," I said with a sarcastic smile. "Think on it. Just not too long. In the meantime, I will continue to observe the two *I* deem suspicious." Not waiting for a reply, I turned and let myself out, brushing past Maeko and walking back in the direction of my room. The best thing I could do for him now was allow him to think on what I'd said.

I noted Maeko did not follow me out, and for the first time I was alone.

I tried to keep my mind on the last two obstacles in my way: the boy and Namaya.

I recalled yesterday, when the kid had 'run into me.' What if he was really trying to do a little 'grab-n-go'? He could have been trying to get in my pockets to find the watch. What if there was more than one traitor? What if they were *both* spies? I felt the paranoia sinking deep, and I began flexing my fingers to try and get this suffocating feeling out somehow.

Just in time I reached my room, slipping inside before I could allow myself a breakdown in the exposed hall. Safe and alone, I paced violently back and forth, hands working frantically as I tried to do anything to calm myself. I was tired, and it was seriously wearing on me. But I couldn't sleep. If I woke up without any memory of who I was or what was going on…. I didn't want to even think about it. I couldn't go back, and the fear of such a possibility pierced worse than any physical knife could.

I sat down on my one solitary chair to think, realizing pacing was only going to make me more tense. But then I got the opposite problem. As soon as I sat, I realized how exhausted I was, and my eyelids began to feel as if they were weighed down by a mountain. I fought it but couldn't bring myself to stand up.

Everything in the room distorted, spinning one way or the other as if reality itself bent. No! I couldn't fall asleep now! I needed to think. I had to figure this out.

But everything felt heavy, and I would finally pay the price for ignoring my screaming body. Slowly—ever so slowly, my head drooped, and I felt myself drifting off into the world of long forgotten sleep, leaving me with nothing but a tortured conscience and a tangle of yarn with loose threads, waiting to unravel Baeno.

CHAPTER V: Keeping My Own Secrets

Baey:

I sat on my bed, staring blankly at my hands. I had been dreaming—that was it. It had been an eventful day, right? Maybe I was in shock. Maybe I was hallucinating.

But deep down, I knew better. It had been real—it had felt real. So, what had happened?

I took a deep breath. Maybe if I tried it again. If it did it again, I could be sure. A suspicion formed in the back of my mind—the stories I had grown up with about The Watchers and their Gifts. Sven Mara, the martyr of Baeno, who died for someone who was only *probably* the one The Living Stone had talked of.

But Sven…he was called the Master of Illusions. That had been his Gift. I grasped the ring tightly, taking it off the chain and staring at it. Could it be? I closed my eyes, but I couldn't think of anything. What should I try and picture? The sword again? With all the excitement, that memory was now distorted and fuzzy. No, it had to be something fresh—something recent.

Focusing as hard as I could, I tried to picture the lantern that hung in my room. I held my hand out, trying to pretend I was holding it. I thought of the clear glass, held in place by bronze wiring that curled up and twisted like the roots of a tree.

Well, here goes nothing.

I opened my eyes, and there, clear as day, was the lantern, dangling from my hand. The funny thing was, it was in the wrong place. For some reason, the handle was halfway *through* my hand, and it looked like my hand had been impaled by the lantern. I laughed a little. So, I wasn't exactly good at this so far...

I moved my hand away, and it blew through the illusion as easily as if it wasn't there. Because...it *wasn't* there. Then the lantern started to shimmer, looking foggy and all out of shape. Before I knew it, the thing was gone altogether, disappearing into thin air.

Huh. This seemed to take quite a bit of focus.

Oh, how I wanted to run and show the others. This could be really useful if I could get the hang of it! But then the words of Sven came back to me.

"*Now I need you to do one last thing for me. Keep this safe. Don't ever tell anybody about it and don't ever lose it.*"

Would I be betraying him if I showed even Tanner? He could keep a secret. I looked back down at the ring. Sven had said that no one would be able to see it, and he had been right. No one had. It was as if it was invisible. But now, I realized it was because Sven Mara had probably put an illusion around it—which meant, theoretically, I could take it off, right?

I could actually show someone and not have to carry this secret alone anymore. Still. I would be betraying Sven; I knew that. What if something awful happened, all because of me? I would be responsible. No, I couldn't tell anyone, not yet, anyway. Not until I got good at using it—or at least figured out if I could be. And yet, part of me now didn't *want* to tell the others. After all, this was *my* secret. My charge. My responsibility, and, as scary as it had been, I knew it was the one thing that made me useful. Maybe.

I flopped back on my bed, my wings sending a small cloud of feathers up. As I settled down, the feathers that had been flung up slowly floated down, some on the bed, some on the floor. Ugh. I'd have to clean that later.

I laid there for a while, just thinking. So many things had happened today. I had been such a rebel, spying on Feyn and Maeko. But really, I had been an idiot for going out in the first place.

Then, there was Feyn. He'd been the first person to ever really ask for my assistance, let alone do it without blinking. He hadn't even seemed to consider I wasn't up for the task, and...and even more, he'd been right. I'd actually done a decent job with Jaythos. Feyn, a stranger I'd known barely more than a day, had put more faith in me than those I'd known for a near lifetime. But why did I still have this awful feeling about him?

Someone knocked on the door. Getting up from my bed, I tried to smooth my ruffled feathers a bit before going over and opening the door.

"Oh. Tanner. Come in." Relieved, I stepped aside. Tanner came in and I closed the door behind me. "Sorry about the mess today. I shouldn't have gone."

Tanner shrugged. "It's fine. I'm just glad Jaythos is alright. Namaya just got back. She said if he stays down and doesn't try anything, he should be fine—she said using her salve was a good call, too. And your stitches didn't look half bad." His grin faded and he paused, running his thin fingers through his hair before lowering his voice, "Did you find anything out?" He was clearly referring to my little escapade earlier in the day.

91

"I...I don't know. There was someone in the woods, but I couldn't see who it was. They chased after so fast I couldn't keep up, and by the time I found Maeko and Feyn again, whoever they'd been chasing was gone. I headed back after that." If only I was a better flier, I could have perhaps caught whoever it was. Then I *really* could have shown my worth. That I was ready.

Tanner looked *actually* stressed. "That's not good. Between that and the disaster with Sefen and Jaythos—"

"—What happened?" I blurted, interrupting him. Oops. "Sorry...I just. All I know is there was an ambush?"

Tanner sobered. "It was a trap. Sefen and Jaythos should be glad they got out with their lives."

I shuddered, feeling numb all over. "And the town?"

"They'd long since been taken by Skayla," he said quietly, confirming what I'd already known deep down. Tanner looked upset, and I understood. He'd been the one to find out about the potential raid. When he, Jaythos, and Namaya had hit one of Skayla's patrols, he had taken the memory off of a soldier. I wondered if he doubted his information—if perhaps he'd missed that it was a trap. Was I the only one who second-guessed such things?

I wanted to say something—wanted to tell him it wasn't his fault—but every time words formed in my head, they seemed superficial or unsympathetic. I finally settled with a simple, "I'm sorry."

A big grin plastered itself on Tanner's face, and he shrugged. "I'm fine, Feathers."

Oh, Tanner. He was always convinced that if he just pretended, the world wouldn't get to him. But I said nothing, completely at a loss for what to say, and not wanting to make it worse.

Instead, my mind wandered once more to the ring, and more than anything I wanted to tell him about it—everything. He would understand more than the others, and I knew he'd keep the secret.

"Um...Tanner?" I tried to sound casual about it, but I failed epically.

Tanner perked up, instantly looking interested. I was terrible at hiding emotions, so I was sure "secret" was written all over my face.

Doubt crept in my mind, and I buckled. "Never mind."

He looked slightly disappointed but said nothing about it. "So, Feyn Cavo was quite the rebel. And, I daresay, he wasn't the only one." Tanner acted as if nothing had even been said in the first place.

I smiled a little, but as much as I wanted a chance to bask in my brief moment of usefulness, I couldn't help but turn my attention to the mention of our guest. "What do you think of Feyn?"

Tanner stretched and put on a bored expression, moseying over to a chair by my bed and sitting down, letting out a great big yawn. Uh oh. He was worried. "I don't know. He's so...I don't know...hollow? I don't know if that's really the word. But I still can't understand how I didn't get a memory from him. Not even one. I told Sefen that—he didn't like the sound of it either. But again, Feyn isn't in a MindHold. I don't know, Baey." He sounded so uncertain. Then he added suddenly, "But...at the same time, what I've seen of him, I kind of like him. I mean, he actually let you do something, for once."

93

"Yeah." I couldn't help but smile as I sat down on the floor and let all my limbs take a break. My wings were still so tired after all the flying I had done today.

"What do *you* think of him?"

I sighed. "I…don't know. He unsettles me. Like what I would expect if I ever…ever met Skayla. He just…I don't know if it'll make sense, but he…sort of has the smell and feel of death on him." I shuddered.

Tanner nodded. "No. It makes perfect sense. Maeko keeps saying the same thing, actually."

"Yeah, I know." I recalled his words to Feyn and couldn't help but smile. "His exact words to Feyn were 'you stink.'" I laughed then, and Tanner joined in with me.

"Good old Maeko," he said after we settled down.

"But anyway, he doesn't seem bad. He seems almost lost…. Oh yeah. There was something weird that happened in the forest today. I can't believe I forgot." I recalled the moment where I thought I'd been discovered.

Tanner cocked his head, shifting his position so he almost looked like a cat ready to pounce. Always on the move. "What?" His eyes shined with anticipation.

"How do I explain it…. He just stopped while they were in the forest— I thought he'd seen or heard me. But then he acted like he'd forgotten what they were doing. Then he looked down at his hand, and I saw some writing on it."

Tanner shifted once again; attention caught. "Writing? What did it say?"

I closed my eyes, recalling the memory as vividly as possible. "Watch Valdon spy," I recited, opening my eyes once more to catch his reaction.

"Hm," was all he said. There was a long silence after that, a silence I dared not break. When *Tanner* was quiet, it usually meant he was actually taking time to think—which was rare.

Then, as quickly as the silence had come, it went, and Tanner said, "Well. I actually came to let you know I finished cooking, so dinner is just about ready." He laughed sheepishly. "Almost forgot that. So, when you're ready, you can come down." He got up from his perch and got ready to leave.

I bolted up, a little miffed at the fact that he had so quickly dropped the subject. But I would give him time, and I figured we would talk about it later. "I might as well come down with you then. Not much to do in here by myself."

Right before we went out the door, Tanner turned to me, looking rather serious. "You know, Baey. Maybe you should tell Sefen that you followed Maeko and Feyn. Or at least tell him about the writing on the hand. I don't think Maeko saw it."

He was right...I knew he was. "Maybe I will," I replied simply, following him as he resumed walking. We made our way down the quiet hall, hearing the dim noise from downstairs as everyone else sat down to eat.

Then I felt that strange urge again. That urge from the ring. I wanted to follow it, and my stride slowed until I was standing still as a marble statue. My wings twitched and itched to fly me to where I was being called, but when Tanner gave me a bewildered expression, I tried to shove the feeling down and kept walking.

Downstairs was cozier than my dark room, the bronze lanterns all automatically lit at sundown by Sefen. The dining room was especially bright. The long table was laden with candles, and the larger chandelier above it illuminated the meat and soup set in the center. Most everyone had already taken their seats, and as always, Sefen sat at the head.

"Tanner, Baey, there you are. I was just about ready to go up and fetch you myself. Sit down and eat! Baey, Namaya apparently found some game on her way back, so we have nice fresh food." He smiled gently at me as I took my place on his right. I caught the tension in his eyes, though, and the way he'd slipped in the "apparently" as if he was a little annoyed at the fact. To my surprise, I found so was I. But why? Namaya hadn't exactly been idle all day—*apparently*, she had been hunting to help with our food supplies. Apparently, she'd just left us at a bad time unintentionally. Ugh. No. I was just misunderstanding the situation; that was all. I was sure Namaya had a perfectly good reason. She had to—after the mess she'd left us to clean up.

As if on cue, Namaya entered the room—the only one missing besides Jaythos. "There. Now Jaythos has no excuse to get up. No good one, anyway," she stated with satisfaction, plopping down in her seat at Sefen's left side. She and Sefen stole a glance before she caught me watching.

"Well, hello, Baey, I don't think I've seen you all day. Are you alright? I'm sure you had a bit of a shock with Jaythos." Her voice was gentle as always when dealing with me. "But you did a good job. Hopefully you won't have to do such a thing again. I'm sorry I wasn't there."

Not do it again? I swallowed the lump in my throat. I hated how everyone was so worried that whenever something disastrous happened,

I would be put into a huge tizzy. Plenty of things had happened, and I was still here. But really, I hated it because so many times they were right, and that just proved why I shouldn't be out helping them. After all, I'd been practically frozen until Feyn had snapped me out of it.

"I'm fine, Maya. Starved half to death, though. And you even saved me the embarrassment of having to resign from eating." I forced a laugh, looking at what had clearly been a Kear—a pygmy deer. Everyone chuckled, knowing full well the first and last time we had ever had any sort of fowl. What should I have done? Wasn't I technically part bird? So, what exactly would happen if I had *eaten* a bird? As you can imagine, to an eleven-year-old child, the thought had been simply terrifying. Everyone still had that dinner imprinted in their brain, and it always got a good chuckle. It was always the easiest way for me to divert the conversation away from my uselessness.

There was silence for a little while, and then one by one we stood, every face at the table looking solemn. Sefen raised his glass, and with grave ceremony said, "To the Maras."

"To the Maras," we all echoed, toasting the two fallen heroes. I always found it odd how technically Skayla was a Mara, but everyone acted like she hadn't ever been related to Moira or Sven. I suppose killing your two siblings was on the level of being disowned.

"Wonderfully done, Tanner." I forced myself to contribute to dinner conversation.

He rolled his eyes at me, always proud of the fact that he could cook better than anyone else, and always trying to hide *just* how proud he was. Honestly, his skill was just as important as Namaya's. A cook and a healer were always greatly needed.

I finished before anyone else but still sat at the table, mind wandering as I kept finding myself staring at the empty seats all around us: the seats where those who had left for Kaedna usually sat. At the table, no one was allowed to talk of it, and it brought back a sense of normalcy. But lately…lately, it just felt fake.

"Good as always, Tanner." Sefen wolfed down a huge piece of meat, speaking as he always did, between bites. Warriors had no sense of manners.

Turning a light shade of pink, Tanner rolled his eyes, trying and failing to look 'cool.' "This is one of Tali's recipes."

Tali—the woman who had found Tanner and raised him. I had never met her, but Tanner said she was quite the character. Or had been.

"Well, I owe my life to that woman," Namaya said with conviction. "If we had let Sefen cook, Skayla would be the least of our worries."

Everyone at the table chuckled. Sefen gave an unimpressed look and resisted the temptation—but not for long. Again, the show of good spirits felt just that—a show. I couldn't help but catch the constant looks that passed between Sefen and Namaya. Usually, I loved the distraction, the lack of gloom-and-doom conversations, but not tonight, and, before long, I became more and more distracted. The surrounding conversations turned into background noise as my thoughts rested on the weight around my neck. It was exciting and terrifying at the same time, with the thought of being useful constantly being weighed against the consequences of what would happen if I did tell someone. But I couldn't…especially not with a stranger like Feyn here. Speaking of Feyn...

"Is Feyn not coming to dinner then?" I asked, too late realizing I'd interrupted Tanner in the middle of his story.

Everyone sort of stared awkwardly at me or their food, and I realized that all of us had sort of...well, forgotten about Feyn. "Shouldn't it be better that we have him here, where we can see him? What if he went somewhere? Or...or what if—"

"—Baey, calm down." Sefen made as if to get up. "It's alright. I don't think Feyn is going to do anything." He only sounded sort of certain, which made me get up.

"Well, he has to be hungry. We haven't been very hospitable so far. What if he tells Emarian?" I tried to laugh, but it sounded awkward and misplaced. Everyone at the table seemed just as uncomfortable and nervous as I was. Tanner was giving me looks like I was supposed to just sit down and not say a word, and Namaya had that same odd expression that she always held when Feyn was involved.

"Little Baey is right. Skinny is probably hungry," Maeko chipped in.

I bit my lip nervously. "I'll bring him something—if you don't mind Sefen." If I went and brought him food, maybe I could get some more information on him too.

Sefen did not look pleased with this at all, but Namaya spoke up first. "No, Baey. He's dangerous," she said flatly.

I felt turmoil swirl in my chest until I was almost queasy. The more I thought of it, the more I just had to go see him, and it was as if something was pulling me to seek him out—something other than me. "He helped Jaythos," I pointed out.

"What is the matter with you, Baey? Aren't you listening? He can't be trusted." Namaya had gotten up and was leaning over the table, looking dead serious.

I looked desperately over at Sefen, who was clearly perturbed at Namaya's behavior. He cleared his voice—in that 'if you would please stop bickering like five-year-olds' way—and said with a tone on the verge of losing patience, "Namaya, I believe you are mistaken. I believe Feyn Cavo is who he says he is—and I thought we had all agreed long ago to leave such serious matters for later and not talk of them here."

"But Sefen, it's bad enough you let us stand here to be slaughtered like animals when Skayla finally locates Valdon; you would put a child in harm's way?"

The room got deathly quiet.

"With Sven Mara's protection upon Valdon, it is our best place of hiding. Or would you have me give up and run into Skayla's arms, Namaya? Or give up Baey to Lord Kovo myself?!"

"You *are* running into their arms, Sefen. If we had taken the Kovian Fortress, that would've been something. But no. You said it was too risky. How can you just sit and wait? What kind of plan is being the cheese in a broken trap?"

Sefen's face was going crimson, and I sank low in my seat. What had I started?

"Oh, I see," Sefen spat back, jaw clenched. "You would like to lead Valdon. You know so much better, all of you. I am too much a fool. Well, where were you today when I needed you? When Jaythos needed you? You left his fate to a *child*, Namaya! I thought you'd been killed!"

"We could *all* be killed! There is no hope!" Namaya shouted back. "You were always the one pulling at strings that weren't there. You—"

"—Right. Because leading a full-out attack on a fortress we can't find would've been a *much* wiser option."

Namaya clenched her fists and rested them hard against the table. "Fine then. We could send Baey and Tanner to Kaedna once it's secure and retake the pass." She sounded less angry and more serious. "One man can hold off a thousand there, and we'd be better placed strategically."

"And let them gain even more ground? If we fall back, then there is no going back, no gaining ground. They will wait us out until we are too tired and too spent. They have Drogans. We don't know how to kill them. We don't know their weaknesses. No one has lived long enough to really find a way to kill the beasts, only to wound and rout. Now this is enough foolishness, Namaya. Maeko, can you please bring food to Feyn?" Sefen returned to the issue that had started this all.

"But—"

Sefen shot her a glance even I knew better than to argue with, and though it wasn't directed at me, I slouched even lower with that knot of anxiety in my stomach. My wings drooped drearily around me like a dog would hang its ears while sulking, but I said nothing. I knew better.

"Maeko?" Sefen reiterated.

Maeko nodded mutely and got up from his seat, giving me an attempt at a reassuring glance before he left.

Namaya said nothing, only left with her fists still clenched.

Sefen sat down again but did not touch his food. Finally, I couldn't stand it any longer. The words they had said; the things they had talked of doing. They wanted to send me away? Send Tanner away? I didn't have to see his face to know that he was just as confused. He was probably indignant, too. But I was just disappointed and angry at myself. This proved what I felt. I was useless, and they held back because of me. Namaya wanted to banish me from all the people I had ever known, just to let them die like Sven Mara had. Was I always getting people killed?

"May I be excused, Sefen?" I asked softly.

Sefen only made a small hand motion.

I got up and turned around as hot tears of anger slowly streamed down my cheeks. Ugh. As if it hadn't already rained enough. I did my best not to run out of the room, walking with a straight back and arched wings, glad my back was turned so they couldn't see my tears. I felt like screaming or taking off into the night sky and not caring where I went. But I wouldn't. The tug from the ring returned, and I thought of my secret. As I made my way slowly up the stairs, I was suddenly glad I could tell no one about the ring. As I thought about it, I realized if I told them, they really *would* take it from me. No. This was *my* secret. *My* puzzle to figure out—and maybe I could show them I was ready.

Feyn:

"*Come on, Skinny, wake up.*" I felt someone shaking me and jolted awake, sitting up straight in my chair. I blinked once or twice, trying to clear my blurry vision as panic set in. There in front of me was a very burly man, bald as a desert, with a stern face to make you curl up inside.

But I wasn't panicking because of what he looked like. I was panicking because I had no idea who he was…. I blinked again and opened my mouth once or twice, trying to figure out whether it would be wise to ask this man questions. Was he a friend? Had I known him? Why didn't I remember anything? I felt the panic increase, but something told me this wasn't the first time this had happened.

And why in Baeno was he calling me 'Skinny'?

The man huffed impatiently and gave me a little shake as if not convinced I was awake—and at this point, neither was I.

I raised my hands in protest and got up hurriedly from the chair, having enough problems being dizzy without this stranger shaking me to death.

"I'm awake! I'm awake!" I replied in protest, if nothing else then to stop him from killing me. The words felt funny in my mouth, and though I understood them, the words he and I were speaking didn't seem natural. *"What do you want?"* I asked, hoping this would help me remember. Maybe this was some prison I was in? But why would I be in a prison? And why would it be so nice? I looked quickly around the room: clean, nice bed, and a little window made of clear glass. No, this couldn't be a prison. In fact, it was better than the place Skayla had kept me.

Skayla…had I escaped? Or…was this another mission?

That was when I realized my stomach had woken up with me, and it was trying to convince me I was starving. It wasn't enough that my head hurt with all the shaking, my stomach had to feel fit to eat me alive, too?

"I brought you dinner, Skinny," he said as if reading my thoughts, pointing to a bowl and cup on a nearby table.

I felt as if my heart would melt right there, and all I wanted to do was gulp the food down, but some inner instinct warned me against it. And before I ate or did anything, I needed to figure this out. Who was I? I wanted to beat my brains out until I could remember, but I was afraid of exposing what was going on to this man in the room, in case he really was an enemy.

I started to run my hand through my hair but, as I did, something caught my attention. There were words written on my hand. I stared at them for a moment, trying to decrypt them. They weren't like the words the man and I had been speaking, and, at first, they just looked like scribbles of nonsense.

"*Skinny?*" The man sounded confused.

I ignored him, focusing on the words and trying to get them to make sense. Finally, it all clicked.

Watch, Valdon, Spy, Sefen, Jaythos, Maeko.

It all flooded back, and the weight of the memories almost made me fall over.

"*Are you alright?*" Maeko—he was Maeko—grabbed my shoulder, and suddenly I realized I *had* sort of fallen over. My vision cleared, and I found myself gripping the back of the chair, Maeko holding my shoulder to keep me upright.

"I'm fine," I said in Varnese, "Just lost my balance for a moment." I slowly straightened back and let go of the chair. "See? I'm fine." I brushed by him and over to my table, snatching the mug and swigging a good gulp or two down to try and prove it.

"Skinny make fat lies," Maeko said, switching to Varnese as well.

"No, I'm just optimistic. And you're being a bit nosy—don't you think?" I took another gulp of the drink and raised an eyebrow at him. "Just got dizzy for a moment. I'm fine, now," I said truthfully. Now that I remembered everything and the initial toll of it had rushed through, I was starting to regain my senses, and everything seemed to fit back into the puzzle. Sort of. I sighed and ran my hand through my hair again. Why did sleeping bring such dire consequences? I had to find some way to bring back my memories without causing suspicion—at least until I could find out who I could trust. That was the real problem, wasn't it? Who could I trust?

"You look bad." Maeko said flatly, still speaking in Varnese.

"I'm not exactly sure what to say to that one," I replied absently as I took the bowl of stew and began examining it as if it was some foreign object.

"Was there anything else you needed?" I turned and waited, giving the silent, yet very strong hint to *leave*. I didn't need any more nosy questions as to why I looked bad, why I had woken up in a fit, why I was acting so weird, and other useless things. That was for me to worry about, and not have strangers poking around trying to weigh it as evidence for or against me. I felt as if the whole room was closing in on me, and the sudden need for some air left me trying not to explode.

I shook my head and blinked, alarmed at myself. I had to keep it together a little more. These side effects were really making for some out-of-control emotions. I really was in no condition to be keeping secrets. In fact, I was in no condition to be trusted with this thing in my pocket!

"You look bad. Shouldn't be alone, I think. Why don't you come downstairs?"

I sighed. He was right. I should go downstairs. Being with the others could help me find out which ones I could trust and which ones I couldn't. Perhaps I could even weed out the traitor.

But first…

"I'll come down after I've eaten," I answered.

Maeko seemed slightly satisfied with that answer, at least, and left the room, allowing me to eat a good half of the stew.

Then, feeling much more refreshed, I left my room and made my way towards the stairs. Slowing my pace, I tried to first evaluate my options. Again, I came to the same conclusion; it was either the boy or Namaya.

I sincerely hoped the boy wasn't the spy. I needed him, and everything would just get so much more complicated if he was really working for Skayla—but I did need to expect the worst. Other than him, all that was left was Namaya. She'd left with an excuse that seemed slimmer than my chances of all this working out, and she'd been the only one missing when Maeko and I had returned. She wasn't doing herself any favors, and her relationship with Sefen appeared to be almost the entire reasoning for her being innocent.

I made my way down the stairs then, as prepared as I really could be for this.

THE GHOSTMAKER

CHAPTER VI: When All Else Fails

Feyn:

The living room was a well-lit, cozy, little room, with pinstriped wallpaper hidden behind several bookshelves. In one corner sat a reading desk with a quaint magnifying lens to aid reading and, in another spot, stood a collapsed metal and gear ladder that could be unfolded for grabbing books. My eyes flitted to an obviously vacant spot where perhaps an upright piano had once sat. But why had I guessed a piano? The whole room seemed like something out of a dream, but again, any specific memory evaded me.

"Feyn, nice of you to join us. Please, sit." Sefen closed the book he'd been pretending to read and sat up straighter in the chair he was occupying by the bookshelf. He motioned to the collection of cushioned lounge chairs and the solitary couch that together formed a sort of crescent shape in the center of the room, the latter of which was taken by the blond-haired boy. I nodded in thanks and slowly made my way to the seating options, evaluating Sefen and the others as well as the room I was in.

I noted how all activity had stopped in the room now that I was here and found it dually interesting that everyone was present except for Jaythos…and Baey. The two I had voiced doubt about to Sefen were both in the room, and Maeko, who had been the only witness to my conversation with Sefen. Was this a set-up? If so, then for whom?

My attention was drawn to the full-length windows at the other side of the room, where the shadow of Namaya stirred from where she'd been staring out into the dark. She turned, eyes settling on me. I noticed the wariness, and perhaps...the slightest bit of fear.

A voice intruded upon the tension: "I don't think we've officially met. I'm Tanner." The boy got up and extended his hand. Suspicion flared, but the last thing I needed to do was seem hostile and refuse. Wasn't this swell?

So, with a grimace-like smile, I took his hand, shaking it. A very unpleasant sensation ran through me, and it felt as if someone was searching my very soul. I all but yanked my hand from his, my grimace growing dark to mirror my displeasure.

The boy cocked his head and gave me an innocent grin. "Are you alright?"

"Just fine," I replied, trying to seem collected. Innocent. Sure. Panic rose as I wondered what he was looking for—the watch? I only hoped my mind was fractured enough to protect any information. I looked to Sefen as I sat down, catching the look that passed between him and Tanner. This had been planned. Sefen wanted verification on who I was. That didn't exactly make me sigh in relief. But by the lack of horror on the boy's face...nothing *really* compromising had been found. I hoped.

"*Now* will you listen to me, Sefen?" Namaya continued to back up a conversation that had apparently already been going on. "Jaythos is out of commission now, and if Feyn is right and there is a spy, we should leave or prepare for the worst."

She was suggesting fleeing? It rang of someone already giving up.

Tanner spoke up then. "Leaving shouldn't *be* an option, if you ask me. It wasn't for Sven Mara. Why, he went and faced Skayla head on! *One* person. Watcher or no Watcher, that was insanity, but he did it."

"Sven Mara was a fool," Namaya spat back.

"On that, we can agree, at least." I wasn't sure who was more surprised over what I'd said: me or everyone else in the room.

The room got deathly quiet, and I heard Maeko move from his position. "*I would be careful what you say, Skinny. You're standing in the former sanctuary of Moira and Sven Mara. This is all that's left of their legacy.*"

I knew that, and I didn't care. They were fools, the lot of them. Skayla had completely decimated the world she was supposed to protect; Moira had been stupid and tried to fix the problem by herself; and Sven...oh, Sven. He'd not only fallen for the same thing, he'd gone and—

"You have a tongue that's quick to judge, Feyn. Especially The Watchers," Sefen joined in.

"One of which is Skayla, right?" I cocked my head. "Wasn't she one?"

Namaya snorted. "You boys go ahead and keep arguing over the dead. I'm going to go check on Jaythos." She collected herself then and started out of the room as if giving up on the whole thing.

I fought the urge to get up and follow her, not exactly relishing the idea of her being where I couldn't see her. Something seemed to be upsetting her. Was it guilt over not being there when Jaythos had needed her? Or something else? I noted the way she and Sefen were avoiding eye contact.

Tanner got up as well. "And I should go check on Baey."

And tell her exactly what you saw in my stupid head. I wished I knew what it was, and if I should be worried, but I would not fall into that trap. Asking would show I was concerned.

The two left, leaving just Maeko, Sefen, and I. Sefen put his book away and walked over to the seat Tanner had been in, sitting down across from me and putting on a very thoughtful expression.

"Feyn," he started, "Maeko said you speak Rugonian. Where did you learn?"

"There was a greater wealth of knowledge before the Great War, Sefen. One could learn almost anything," I replied vaguely.

"Except a civil tongue, it seems," Sefen said with a twinkle in his eyes. Slowly, he seemed to be warming up to me. Sort of. "But come, who was your teacher?"

"A man named Aekon Toa, who lived on the island of Rugo for quite a while. I lost contact with him when the war started."

"Aekon Toa?" Maeko's interest was piqued at this.

Right, I should have known better than to bring it up to Maeko.

Sefen's curiosity remained. "One of the Rugonian Queen's guards? Wasn't he the noble who helped The Crafters in the outlining of the first steam engine line? However did you become friends with someone so high in status?"

I shrugged. "It was a different world back then. I was a diplomat for Patelayna, and my family had helped bring The Crafters' innovations there as well. Aekon Toa liked my country's vision, as you could imagine." Why did this feel like less of a lie than I was intending?

This seemed to better satisfy Sefen, and he moved on. "So then, what are you by trade now?"

I gave him an incredulous look. "What do you mean?"

"What are you good at? The sword, scouting, accusing my wife of treason?" A wry smile tugged at his lips, but I saw the doubt forming in the rest of his features. The fact he'd voiced my accusation was show enough.

"A little of everything, if you put it that way," I said resignedly.

Sefen raised an eyebrow. "And what is that supposed to mean?"

"It means I can do what I need to in order to survive." I got up from the chair and made my way to the misty window. It was still pouring outside, and one could hardly see a thing past the rain. It seemed as clouded outside as it was in here. I only wished I could think straight long enough to find out if I was doing this all wrong. "And right now, that's finding out who the spy is."

The eerie silence that settled on the room told me that my answer had been unwelcome. I needed to keep my behavior in check, because if I couldn't get him to think otherwise, he would never believe me. What was wrong with me? Why was I acting so...unlike me? Slandering the Maras? Testing Sefen? My mind was a tortured mess that left me struggling to think straight and apparently leaving my attitude to suffer for it as I fought to keep my guise.

I decided it best to remain quiet, looking out and trying to see the surrounding forest. I wondered with caught breath if Skayla's Drogans were out there, waiting for a signal, and once more I felt the icy grip of paranoia slip its hand around my chest. Now was not the time. Now was the time to keep a level head and not be stupid. I doubted I had many more days to get the Guardians on my side. I only hoped whatever message the spy was likely trying to get to Skayla would take time.

"What do you intend to do?" I spoke suddenly.

"What do you mean, Skinny?" Maeko asked before Sefen could say anything.

I resisted the urge to sigh. "For all you know, Skayla could be on her way here right now. Valdon's been compromised, and Skayla could easily crush it." I turned from the window and back to Sefen and Maeko.

"I talked to Namaya earlier. I only told her you suspected Tanner," Sefen replied.

It took a moment for me to hide my utter dismay. Had Baeno fallen so far as to have these bunch of idiots protecting it?! "What were you thinking?"

"I was thinking we'll see how she reacts to this and know for sure whether it's her or Tanner. I didn't tell Tanner anything, but he did insist on taking another go at your memories—" another twinkle in Sefen's eyes—"so, we'll see what he finds. Besides, if it's particularly damning to you, he's probably the one you're looking for...right?"

I tried to relax, but some instinct told me there was something in my head I didn't want Tanner to see...but I couldn't remember what. It wasn't the watch...it was where I'd come from; who I was. But...but who was I? What had I done that was so horrible? I began to feel confused and realized I needed to get alone. "If you both will excuse me, I should return to my prison—I mean, room. I don't think this is going anywhere, as usual. Hopefully you'll have a *better* plan tomorrow and we won't all suffer for it." I turned to leave, waiting for Maeko to follow. But he didn't, he kept his place near the shadows, where he had watched the entire proceedings with hardly a word. So, without anyone following me, I made my way out of the room and into the darker hall.

Lanterns were lit, though they hadn't been before. Sefen's work, no doubt. His talent as a fire wielder apparently had more practical uses besides that of making war.

Wait. How did I know that? Who was Sefen? Where was I...?

My room. Just make it to my room—how did I know the way? I found myself practically collapsing through a door I only hoped was where I stayed, shutting it fast behind me and leaning against its closed frame. My breaths were heavy and unsteady; my head swam. What was I doing here? Where *was* here?

That's when I noticed the mess. Everything in my room was torn apart, the drawers, the bed—everything. Had someone searched my room or had I? What was I looking for, if so?

I ran my hand through my hair, panicked at how drowned in emptiness I felt, unable to grab hold of anything in the darkness of my mind. Who was I? Who was I? Why was I here? And who had been looking in my room?

Then...then I remembered one word: Watch. The watch. Quickly, I shoved my hand in my pocket until I felt the cold metal against my sweating palms. Taking it out, I stared at it in the dim lantern-light of my room, the crack whispering to me. I remembered; I'd stolen this from Skayla when I'd left.

That's when I remembered why I didn't want Tanner looking around in my head. *I* was The GhostMaker. Skayla's GhostMaker. Her agent of death. The horrible title echoed and lingered in the darkness. The one shred of my identity that always carried itself with me. The reality I couldn't escape.

Baey:

I sat on my bed, distracting myself by experimenting with the ring again. At first, I just did little things, making a lantern appear in the room or making a duplicate of my mirror. Then I slowly got more complicated ideas, but each of those didn't quite look right. When I made myself, it flopped in a big way. Let's just say that if people looked like mushroom heads…I would have been quite accurate.

Right now, I was trying to make my mirror look bigger than it was. I only sort of figured it out, though. I could make it bigger, but the real size could still be seen. Suddenly, there was a knock on the door, and I hurriedly slipped the ring back on its chain and around my neck. "Who is it?" I asked, already knowing the answer.

Instead of replying, Tanner just came in, and by the bouncing energy in his step, I could tell he'd been up to no good.

I stared at him, making it known under no uncertain terms that I was annoyed. "Fine, just come in like you own the place."

As he closed the door, however, it was clear he didn't care a whit. He was so excited that I was afraid he would fly right through the roof—and trust me, I would know.

"What is *wrong* with you, Tanner?" What had he done? I was dying to know.

He put on his finest grin, walking about my room and constantly tripping over his own feet as he paced. Tanner was not normally a klutz, either, and at this point I would rather have had each one of my feathers plucked than this suspense.

"I got one! I can't believe it," he chattered, making exaggerated motions with his hands. "I got one!"

I slammed my fist down on my bed and huffed, "Tanner Pardaya Armon, what in the world has gotten into you? If you don't tell me, I'll throw you out the window! First, you burst in here without announcing yourself, then you start spouting off nonsense and expect me to understand it?" I couldn't stand the feeling of ignorance anymore. Tonight just wasn't the night to dangle my lack of knowledge in my face.

Tanner stopped and his excitement instantly faded, replaced by concern. "What's the matter, Baey?"

My wings drooped, and I was sure they showed the dismay I felt. "I—just..." If I went into a long, emotional, unneeded monologue, he wouldn't tell me what he had 'gotten.' "I just really want to know what you're talking about. The suspense is killing me." I forced a smile and when he still said nothing, I made a little hand gesture to prod him.

"Well," he started, the excited sparks reigniting in his eyes. "You know how I tried before to get a hold of Feyn Cavo's memories?"

My eyes grew wide, already guessing what he had done. I gave a nod to show that I understood, desperate for him to continue.

"So, I realized I hadn't formally introduced myself. When Maeko said he was coming down for a while, Sefen, Namaya, and I got an idea. When Feyn came in to sit down, I introduced myself and extended my hand. When he shook it, I tried again." He paused, clearly for theatrical effect only. "And this time, I got something." He grinned triumphantly and plopped himself in my chair. "It was awfully disjointed and a lot of wacky out of context things. But he had memories. That was the most important thing."

So, he was waiting for me to press him. I gave in. "Come on, doofus, don't make me beg."

He squirmed in his seat like a caged bird, just itching to be let go. "I saw a bunch of weird images, mostly. Once they would start to mean something, it would fly out and I couldn't find it again, but I got some. He kept repeating those words that were etched on his hands, the ones you told me. Except there were some of our names, too. 'Watch Valdon spy' and then 'Sefen, Jaythos, and Maeko.' Then I saw this weird silver ring, with a small green jewel and odd designs etched all over it—"

I tried to interrupt then, but his mouth had been released, and I couldn't get him to see the desperation I now felt. It was as if my very life's breath was stolen away.

"And then I saw a woman and a watch but couldn't get a look at either memory before they disappeared. After that I saw a grand mansion that meshed metal and brick. The place seemed to make Feyn bitter and I got a memory for the wish to withdraw. It had some sort of sour memory attached to it, but when I tried to find that leading memory, it got dashed away like the others." He paused to take a quick breath there but still not long enough for me to blurt out anything about the ring. "And Baey..." He sounded thoughtful when he jumped back in, a little slower, this time.

My mind still swirled from the mention of the ring, and I felt like I had a bunch of burrs for words. All I was able to do was utter an unintelligible, "Hm?"

"I think I found out what's wrong with him." The excitement returned. "I think he's having memory problems. Like, full out amnesia. It would explain why I didn't get any memories from him when I bumped into him, and why all the memories he has now are vague and easy to lose. I think the harder he tries to remember, the more he forgets." And with that, he finished. He stopped squirming, stopped looking cooped up and uncontainable. He had finished his news and now he wanted my opinion on it all.

And that's when my words were finally released from their prison. "Amnesia? How can that be? How would he remember what he's here for? I mean...it does make sense, it does... but...how?" The realization of it all struck me, and I recalled the time in the woods, when he had asked Maeko what they were doing. "The words on his hand!" I blurted out. "That must have meant to watch Valdon and look for the spy! Maybe that's how he remembers. But...why the names?" *And how does he know about the ring?* "We have to tell Sefen. This isn't good. We can't have someone who can't even remember their name running around here—what if Skayla somehow did it to him?" Why would Duke Emarian send such a messenger? Or had something happened to Feyn on the way? Or....

Tanner nodded, "Yeah. We need to know why."

"Why don't you go tell him now?" I asked. This was serious.

Tanner sighed and rolled his eyes. "Because he's still down with Feyn, and I can't go and make Feyn suspect something. So, we're stuck until they're done."

I let out a huff, completely overwhelmed with information. What did it all mean? I was most worried about the memory of the ring. What if Feyn knew I had it? What if he really *was* sent by Skayla to get it? Panic surrounded me. My ears pounded, my wings twitched nervously, and I felt as if all my senses were being magnified by a thousand. What if Feyn was outside the door right now? What if he was just waiting to make his move?

Ugh. I had too much of a wild imagination. I shook my head and moved on to the next question. I should get as much information as I could. "So, the ring. Do you know what that may have been? Is it something of his, maybe?"

Tanner looked confused. "I don't know. It was a fleeting memory. But the way it appeared in his head, it was something he had either seen a long time ago or was looking for," Tanner replied, once more the expert.

That wasn't good. What if he was looking for it? A shiver ran through me.

"But it wasn't a really pressing memory. It was almost buried, actually. I wouldn't worry about it. None of those memories seemed really important, except maybe that watch. Of course, it's hard to tell when all of his memories seem distant. But I think Sefen will be really just worried about the fact that Feyn is having memory problems, and that he didn't tell us."

"Definitely," I affirmed. But maybe this would clear everything up. Maybe it would finally all be explained, and we could find out for sure if we could trust Feyn or not. I was leaning towards mistrust, and yet I kept getting this weird turmoil. It was that feeling I got whenever I held onto the ring, but even when I wasn't it was starting to gnaw at me. Was it warning me against Feyn? But it wasn't like it was a feeling of a person, but of something it had been missing. But a ring couldn't miss something...except an owner. But besides the fact Sven Mara was...well...a long time resting...it wasn't that sort of feeling. No. This wasn't the sort of feeling of an object to its master. Never thought I would assign emotions to an object....

"You seem pretty worried about this, Baey. Don't worry. We have the information now. You know Sefen. He'll get the truth out of Feyn now." Tanner put on a big grin, but the confusion hidden beneath was obvious. I was probably acting really weird.

We both jumped when someone knocked on the door.

"Baey? Tanner?" Even when I heard Sefen's voice, I didn't relax.

"Oh...Sefen. Come in." I stumbled, trying to calm my thumping heart. By the look on Tanner's face, he was struggling with the same thing.

In a moment, Sefen had slid through the door, and when he stood before me I felt a little more protected. Now, more than ever, I wanted to tell him about going into the woods today.

"Tanner. I thought I'd find you here." He looked from Tanner to me, then added, "Is everything alright, you two?"

THE GHOSTMAKER

CHAPTER VII: Plans Gone Wrong

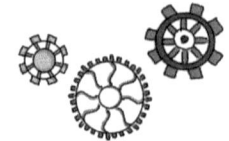

Feyn:

I hated hating sleep. All I wanted to do was rest, and yet sleep meant waking up and wondering who you were. Sleep meant time wasted remembering what you were doing. Sleep meant waking up in a panic. Sleep meant...what was I talking about again?

It had actually taken me longer to remember when I had woken up this morning, if that was possible. Of course, I could remember exactly what I had for dinner. Whoever made their food could cook—but that wasn't the point! Cake and lovely dishes of meat didn't define the future of the world! At least, if I remembered my history correctly...oh dear.

I walked over to the small window, watching as the rain poured down mercilessly onto the earth. Lightning flashed, and a moment later its whip cracked in the distance as it wrestled with managing the rain. It seemed to be having an even worse time than I was. Controlling rain had a fitting resemblance to trying to herd all my lost thoughts into one place.

My hand found itself in its usual place, touching the small gold watch. A slight urge arose, but I ignored it as I always had. Stupid thing was supposed to be broken, and I was already trying to ignore the thing it was looking for.

There was a knock on the door, and I heard Tanner from the other side. "Breakfast," was all he said before leaving, no doubt moving on to the next door to announce that food was ready.

It was probably a good sign that I was invited to join them, but after the stunt they'd pulled last night, I wasn't so sure I liked the look of it.

But no matter. I would go anyway and prepare for the worst. Or try, at least.

I pulled on my coat as I walked out my door, feeling chilled. Perhaps breakfast would at least give a clue to who had searched my room last night. Again, I found myself realizing that it could feasibly have been Tanner or Namaya. Both had excuses, and both could have left in a hurry when they'd heard me coming up the stairs.

"Good morning." A small voice came from behind me, and I jumped around to find the winged girl facing me, her big blue eyes staring back at me in guarded mistrust. Her wings shimmered from silver to dark grey, and they quickly wrapped themselves around her in a protective barrier.

I made a quick, polite smile, saying, "Good morning." Then I turned and started down the stairs again. That stupid watch started pestering me again, and I did my best to ignore it as she walked behind me down the stairs.

Then a thought came to me. "Baey...." If Tanner had *actually* gone to Baey's room, it was less likely he'd have had time to do as extensive a search as had clearly been done in my room. "Was Tanner with you last night after dinner?"

Her cheeks reddened and she looked guarded. "Yes...why?"

"Was he there long?"

Now she looked indignant. "I don't know. We tend to spend the evenings doing *something*; it can get so boring here. I don't really keep track of time." And with that, she brushed past me and hurried forward in an evident move to avoid further conversation.

It was looking more and more like the spy was Namaya. I would talk to Sefen again today—and *really* try to make him see. If not...if not, then I would have to play my hand. Right? Oh, wonderful. I knew I'd had a plan in case I'd found the spy and they wouldn't believe me...but what was it?

My train of thought was completely derailed by the piquant smell of some exotic variety of food wafting up to us as we reached the main hall, and I found myself wondering who in the world had cooked breakfast— because apparently that's all this empty brain could hold onto.

Baey seemed to read my mind. As she led the way to the dining room, she said, "Tanner cooks. Don't question it; just eat it. He's definitely something."

I just shook my head and followed her, and soon we both came into a smallish room, lit with candles and adorned with a beautiful looking breakfast. Tanner must have had way too much time on his hands; I couldn't quite understand what I was seeing. Granted, I had not eaten diversely in recent years, but I doubted anyone would have understood what this food was. There was something that resembled bread, but with a pinkish tint and an almost sour aroma. Beside it was a large silver bowl filled with a sweet-smelling liquid.

I tore my eyes from the food, realizing that we were apparently one of the last two to arrive at the table. Even Jaythos was sitting at the far-right end, arm in a neatly made sling. I did a quick examination of the dressed wound and concluded that Namaya was definitely gifted with medicine. And being a traitor. And being late to breakfast.

Sefen got up from where he sat and gave a polite nod. "Nice to see you could make it. I doubt if you've ever tasted anything like what Tanner cooks up."

I gave the food another skeptical glance but said nothing. Looking around the room, the others were acting slightly off, and I was about ready to accuse them of poisoning the food—even though I knew that was ridiculous. They all seemed to be staring at me, as if they suddenly knew for certain I had some secret and were now trying to find it out. The fact that Baey had actually *talked* to me meant something was the matter. Where had I slipped? Certainly, if they knew my identity, they wouldn't have bothered hiding the fact.

Soon, everyone who *was* here took a seat—the girl to my left—and one by one they raised their glasses. Not quite sure what was happening, I did the same.

"To the Maras," Sefen said, and there was a mumble of agreement. I forced myself to join in, sipping my drink and somehow managing to swallow it. I doubted I took that comment the way Sefen meant it.

The food was dished out, and everyone began eating heartily, conversation being thrown back and forth. I had not seen so many spoons before me for as long as I could remember—not that it meant much—and wondered who had the time to set the table properly anymore. That boy must get bored.

"How's your arm?" I tossed the question to Jaythos, trying to take part and grasp a little of their routine.

"It's doing fine. Namaya worked her usual magic with it," Jaythos replied, his voice mirroring the glare he gave me. "I guess I must thank you for helping, though. I have no idea how one *remembers* all of those remedies—especially so quickly."

Alright. That wording was definitely not by accident....

"Where is Namaya, anyway?" The girl piped up from next to me, eyes locked on Sefen.

Yes...where *was* she?

Sefen cleared his throat, taking a swig of his drink before he spoke. "She had to leave last night. She'll be back by this evening, hopefully."

This evening. That wasn't enough time. In fact, that wasn't any time at all. Though in reality, all this time had been borrowed. My suspicions felt confirmed with the way she was constantly disappearing, and I glared at Sefen for his stupidity. I'd told him it was Tanner or Namaya, and he'd just up and let one of them leave. *On their own*, of all things.

"Eat up, Skinny. Before I call you stick," Maeko spoke up.

I looked from him to my bowl and repeated the movement several times. "I thought I was doing pretty well," I replied. Honestly, it was getting a little sweet, and I didn't think I could stand much more of it. Besides, if I'd had an appetite, it was gone now. I *had* to talk to Sefen.

"You don't like it, do you?" Tanner stood up and leaned across the table, trying to see how much I had left. "I knew it! You all have just been being nice." He made a face at my half-eaten food and plunked back down in his chair, looking very dull.

Lovely. So nice to know the last hopes of Baeno were being fed by an immature child.

"If that makes you feel happy, go right ahead. But it's not a crime if someone's full only halfway through their food," I replied dryly. I was waiting for something to shatter. This was too ordinary, too shallow. If Namaya *was* the spy, her absence a second time couldn't be good.

Conversation around me continued, but I was lost, retreating into the deep recesses of what the memory brought up. There was a roaring in my ears, paired with the tingling sensation that kept running through me, and I couldn't decide if it was that stupid watch again, or if it was me dreading what would happen by tonight. I knew why Namaya had left. She needed to find out what Skayla's next move was. I knew Skayla couldn't be far from Valdon now, and it appeared this would turn out badly. Oh, I hoped Sefen believed me.

"Feyn?"

Feyn? Who was Feyn? That wasn't my name last I had checked. I felt someone prod me, and my vision cleared. And why the cheery attitude? It didn't sound like anyone from the Kovian Fortress.... Then I looked down at my half-finished breakfast, and it clicked. Aha. I looked up again and saw everyone looking very intently at me. The girl—Baey—prodded my arm again, and I blinked, still feeling confused and out of place.

"Yes?"

"Skinny, alright?"

I cleared my throat, which due to the lump in it made me cough, which made me have to take a gulp of my drink, which then almost made me choke. This could be going a little more smoothly. "Yes. Sorry. Just something in my throat," I mumbled, pretending that's what he had been asking, even though he had asked it *before* I had coughed.

"Feyn. What's the matter?" Sefen's more guarded voice pierced the increasing awkwardness, and I turned to face him.

"I need to talk to you." I looked around the table then back at Sefen. "Alone."

Sefen's whole body seemed to tense for a moment, then he collected himself and got up. "Tanner, Baey, why don't you two clear the table? Jaythos, go up and get some rest. I'll talk to Feyn and Maeko."

And Maeko? What part of 'alone' did he not get? Though I suppose it wouldn't make much difference. Maeko knew the full scope of what was going on anyway.

I forced myself to nod and rise from my chair, trying to ignore the dizzy spell. My brain was fogged, and I was having a hard time focusing. Constantly the questions of "Why exactly are there three spoons?" "What was I doing?" and "Why am I being called *Feyn?*" bombarded me, and sometimes I couldn't find the exact answers. I just needed to hang on for a little longer. Just a little longer, and we could get out of here.

I followed the two men—Sefen and Maeko, those were their names— out of the dining room and across the main hall once again. I'd been here before...or was I imagining things?

"Stop it," I whispered to myself, trying to pound some sense into my useless brain.

"What did you say?" Sefen stopped and turned around.

I made a nervous smile and shook my head. "Hm? Nothing."

He looked none too convinced but turned and continued into the room we had been in before.

By the time we entered, I felt more in control, the fog spell seemingly having passed.

Maeko closed the door behind us, and with it I realized this was now my last chance. But just as words came, Sefen spoke first.

"Feyn, Maeko and I have noticed you haven't been acting right since you've gotten here," Sefen began.

Wait. What? "What do you mean?"

"I mean that you are not exactly in condition to be searching for a spy," he finished.

I became incredulous. "I don't quite understand how that could be…" I replied, now lost. Was he implying I was sick?

Maeko made a grunting noise and stepped in. "You don't look good, Skinny."

"I'm fine," I said, sounding a little more defensive than I had meant. This wasn't important at the moment; couldn't they get it?

"Really. Memory's fine, then?"

Great. So, they had figured it out. "What? That's fine." I scowled even as I inwardly panicked. *Don't lose track of your thoughts, don't lose track of your thoughts, don't—*

Maeko grunted. "Then what did we do yesterday, Skinny?"

Useless, weirdly retained memories were about to come in handy. "We came across someone in the woods. It was in the area of the forest with the Ketha trees. Found it odd, as Kethas usually grow higher in the mountains."

Unfortunately, this did not satisfy either of them. My deeper suspicion came to the surface. The boy. He had shaken my hand last night. Somehow, he must have gathered I was having problems.

"Aha." Sefen seemed to think very hard. Uh oh. "How many days have you been here?"

"Three."

"What is my name?"

"Sefen."

"Where are we?"

I opened my mouth, but nothing came out. I couldn't just stand here like a confused duck!

"A house," I said sarcastically, trying to hide my paranoia. But this house was significant…why?

"Having trouble remembering the name? That's funny." Sefen smiled coyly now.

Time was up. It was now or never. At least I remembered what I was here *for*. "Sefen. We don't have time. I need to try and explain, but it might be too late. My memory is the least of your problems. I think Namaya's the spy. She's the only one consistently away at the perfect timing, and all she's done is combat my claims. Skayla is on her way now from Kaedna and Namaya has probably been relaying with a Drogan or message bird, and she's leading Skayla. She's already—"

The door was thrown open and Namaya came storming in, followed closely by the rest of the household, all looking confused. "Sefen! Thank The Creator you're all safe!"

I felt as if I had just been stabbed with a knife. No. No, no, no. What was she playing at? Did she know? Had Skayla told her who I was?

"Sefen. Please, let me finish," I broke in, fruitlessly trying to retain my calm demeanor, but even I could hear the hurry in my voice. I was about to go down in flames.

"No!" She pointed her long, thin finger at me, giving me the same look she had the day I had arrived. "Don't say another word or I'll kill you myself, GhostMaker."

Baey:

My heart jumped in my throat, and every muscle in my body tensed as I heard Namaya. Jaythos, Tanner, and I had all still been in the kitchen when we had heard her burst into Valdon. We'd all followed her in here to see what was the matter, and now, as she uttered those horrid words, I almost wished I hadn't.

The GhostMaker. Feyn Cavo. A sudden dizzy spell overcame me, and it took all my strength not to fall over. It all made so much sense now. The feeling of dread he'd always given me when I was near him, the vacant look in his eyes, it all pointed an accusing finger at him, and I believed it. Worse, I wanted to kill him myself—to avenge all of the innocent lives he'd taken.

"N-Namaya, what do you mea—are you sure?" Sefen's words were disjointed, and he stood utterly still, pale as the moon.

"Yes. As sure as I am that I'm alive. I tracked down that no good spy that Maeko and *he* had seen the other day. So, you see, I was right. There was someone watching us—not Tanner. Tanner is *innocent.*" I was completely confused by the vehement statement. Wait, what? They'd thought Tanner was a traitor?

"Tanner is innocent," she repeated, "And *you're* the spy. No doubt you thought you could gain our trust and pick us off one by one, eh, GhostMaker?" Her voice dripped with a contempt that was completely justified. Everyone here knew that he'd killed Sven Mara and very possibly Moira Mara as well. Maeko had a personal hatred that was even stronger, as the Queen of Rugo had been murdered by his hands.

131

Looking at Maeko now, I knew that if someone didn't hold him back, there would be another murder taking place pretty soon.

"But it backfired. That worthless piece of scum was supposed to be spying with you."

"Where's the spy now?" Tanner jumped in. I turned and looked at him questioningly, only to find him as pale and dumbfounded as I was.

"Dead. I had loosened his bonds to get him to talk more, and he jumped me. Before I realized what I'd done—he was dead. But he made sure to sell you out first, just like you'd done for him. He even told me…" She trailed off, walking up close to the…the…GhostMaker…and putting her hand out to take the sheathed sword that hung at his right side. "Exactly how to prove it to you all."

He jumped back, almost quicker than I could process the movement and put his hand on the hilt. "Get back, *traitor.*"

"Traitor? What in the world do you mean?" Namaya looked taken aback and confused. Then her face hardened, "Last time I checked *I* wasn't Skayla's personal assassin!"

The GhostMaker looked dismayed, turning from Sefen to Namaya. "Sefen. You need to understand, she's the traitor. She's sold you out to Skayla, and—"

"—What?" Sefen's face went from pale to beet red. "How dare you? Don't you try to turn around and accuse my family, Feyn—or should I say *GhostMaker?*" He took out his own sword, making it clear he would have no qualms in using it. "Namaya, what was it that the spy told you?"

"Well, if you remember, The GhostMaker took Sven Mara's sword when he killed him," she said, seeming to try and hold back emotion. "Haven't you noticed how he keeps his sword on him at all times? Always beneath his coat and out of sight? If we were to take out the sword, we would still see the inscription Moira had put on it when she had it made for him."

I stared deadpan at Feyn, watching as his expression turned from dismay to near anguish. So, it was true. I could see by the look on his face. Here, standing right in front of me, was the murderer of hundreds. Including Sven.

"No, you don't understand. Just let me explain—"

"—You lost the right to explain when you came here and lied!" Sefen shouted at him, putting the sword up in an offensive position. "You had me there. Made me doubt my own *wife*—no. No more lies. You shut up before I kill you myself."

It all took place in a second. In an action that was clearly instinct, The GhostMaker drew his sword and angled it against Sefen's.

The sword hit the light of a nearby lantern, and the small lettering near the hilt reflected the light perfectly—and with it, sealed his doom.

As quickly as he had brandished the sword, The GhostMaker dropped it, stepping back and putting his hands up. "Sefen. I know you won't listen, but you—"

And that's when Maeko came upon him.

Hand to The GhostMaker's neck, Maeko lifted him up and pushed him up against the wall, speaking violently in Rugonian.

"Yes, and I am...very...sorry...about...that..." Feyn choked, sounding as sorry as one could when your life was being choked out of you.

I just stood there numbly and watched. It was as if the whole world had started to close in around me, and I could do nothing about it. I couldn't move, I couldn't breathe, I could only watch.

Sefen, Namaya, and a one-handed Jaythos were finally able to pull Maeko off of Feyn, and The GhostMaker slumped against the wall, breathlessly holding his choked throat.

Sefen stooped down and picked up the sword that The GhostMaker had dropped, handling it like a delicate flower as he examined the lettering we had all seen. He turned to Feyn; his free fist clenched tightly. "Namaya. You and Jaythos take this murderer down to a cell. We will decide what to do with him in a moment."

"Sefen...you don't...want...to do this," The GhostMaker dared speak, still trying to regain his voice.

"Be quiet," Namaya spat, grabbing him by the arm with her free hand, while holding her sword in the other. "I told you, Sefen. We should have left."

Jaythos came up and grabbed Feyn's other arm, and, together, he and Namaya practically dragged him away. I shivered as they passed me, and my blood ran cold as for one anguished second The GhostMaker's eyes locked on mine. His vacant gaze seemed to plead with me, and he opened his mouth to speak. I was relieved when Namaya and Jaythos shoved him forward, stopping him from saying anything.

They left the room, and I ran over to Sefen, who was staring blankly at the legendary blade. Tanner was close behind me, and put a comforting hand on my shoulder.

"I say kill him." Maeko's tone was frightening.

Sefen said nothing, only staring at the sword.

"Well, if you don't kill him, I will."

Still not tearing his eyes from the sword, Sefen spoke. "No, Maeko. You will go search the woods."

There was a grunt of dark disapproval, but Maeko obeyed, barging out the door.

It felt like a nightmare. The GhostMaker, in my home. I just couldn't wrap my mind around it. It was a wonder we were still all alive. I thought of Jaythos, and wondered...could The GhostMaker have been the one to leak the information on the evacuation to Skayla?

"Sefen..." I whispered, not really sure what I'd wanted to say but wanting to say *something*.

"I'll be back," Sefen said shortly, acting as if he hadn't heard me. He turned to Tanner and handed him the sword, stomping out of the room and slamming the door.

"...May I see it...?" My question was barely audible, and my hands itched to have the sword in my hand.

Tanner said nothing, apparently still in shock, but handed me the blade.

The tips of my fingers tingled as the cold metal brushed against them, and when I gripped the handle I felt a thrilling sensation, followed by a chill. This had been used to kill hundreds of people. Once, it had been used to protect thousands. Carefully, I ran my finger along the curved edge. The handle was sorely beaten and not in the polished state it had been when I last saw it, and it was in sore disrepair. As much as it was obvious it had been used, it was also clear it had not been taken good care of. My heart fell to my feet and my wings followed as I touched the hilt, and the inscription upon the base of the blade. The writing was in

135

short-script, allowing for much longer phrases than usually could fit in such a small space.

"May you never be quick to use this. Your sister, Moira." I wondered with a sickening feeling how many people this had murdered in cold blood, and the inscription felt like merciless irony.

My hand wrapped around the once-ornate hilt then, and I grit my teeth. "Oh, what it would be to have him killed by the blade he stole." I wasn't quite sure why I had said it, but deep down, the thought had been lurking for years, and now, with the murderer of my rescuer so close, I wanted nothing more than to avenge.

"Baey," Tanner called my name in a breathless wonderment, sounding none too concerned. "Don't think like that. You couldn't kill someone…and…and besides, we need him alive. This really is good, you'll see. Think of all the information he's going to give us. We could find out Skayla's moves, and what his plans had been. Once we get more information from Namaya, we can find out what exactly is going on." As he continued, his confidence seemed to return and the excitement in his voice built in momentum. I felt bad for not really listening.

I knew I wasn't the kind of person who could kill someone—even someone who deserved it. But never before had I wished to be. And then there was the awful feeling that the whole reason he'd been here was to get the ring. That must have been it, and that meant Skayla knew about it, and knew where it was. Guilt crushed me, and I felt that I really might have to tell Sefen…but not until he calmed down a little.

"I'm going to go see if Sefen needs anything, or Namaya, or anybody at this rate. Are you alright?"

I managed a nod.

"Alright…if you're sure…" Tanner looked me up and down skeptically then extended the sword, hilt first, back to me. All the while, he looked nervously from the window to me. "Promise you won't go crazy and try to go kill him?"

I gripped the hilt tight, giving a more vigorous nod. "Deal."

"Good. Then stay away from the windows and keep safe until one of us comes back. Who knows what could be coming." A visible shiver ran down his spine, and he gave a very weak smile before disappearing out of the room.

I looked down once more at the sword, remembering when I had made it materialize in front of me. How different it looked now: hilt grimy, scuffed, and slightly dented, once something that had helped protect Baeno. What if we were failing Baeno just as much as it had?

Feyn:

"I'll kill you; you hear me?" I whispered to Namaya, pouring every inch of the anger and frustration I felt as they cuffed my hands into the cold iron shackles that hung from the wall. I strained against them, willing myself to break them and just get at the no-good vulture. "You've signed the death warrant of everyone!" I shouted now, not caring if I sounded deluded or even pounded the final nail into my coffin. She would see—unfortunately, they would all see very soon. I had to get out of this! Had to somehow get free and stop the complete disaster that was about to unfold, but I was helpless, and it was exactly what Skayla wanted.

The bars closed, and Namaya locked the door. "Jaythos, let Sefen know that the spy is locked up," she spat through clenched teeth.

Jaythos gave me a very characteristic glare. "You should feel lucky, worm. If I had my crossbow, you'd be dead. But maybe that would have been merciful." He smiled wryly before exiting. Well, it would have been merciful compared to what was going to happen now.

As soon as the door shut, I made as much of a yank against the chains as I could, nearly throwing both of my shoulders completely out. "Namaya, whatever ridiculous thing Skayla has promised you, it won't happen. You're betraying your friends—your *husband*—to death or worse—"

"—Oh, please, don't talk to me like I'm in a MindHold. You don't know me or understand. And really. Accusing *me* of not thinking clearly?"

"Well then, enlighten me, because you are about to become just as bloodstained as I am, *vulture*." I cut deep, trying somehow to knock her out of whatever glory craze or bloodlust she was caught in. She was talking nonsense, and if I didn't know better, I would have said she was even crazier than I was.

"I am trying to stop the bloodshed, *GhostMaker*, not spread it like you. Don't lecture me about having a red ledger, we know yours would fill a book."

If she called me that one more time, I would wring her neck. The weight of the title was enough to crush me. "You are the one who cut communication for Skayla and gave her the way through the mountains to Kaedna, weren't you?"

"Shut up."

"You got them all killed! Are you *listening?*" I shouted. "Everyone who went to Kaedna is *dead*. Trust me, I killed them myself—I saw it!"

"You're lying. You'll say anything to let me get you out of here. Skayla promised—she'll talk reason into them. You know *nothing*," she hissed, "*nothing*, you hear me! So be quiet or be silenced." Her right hand flicked a knife from her pocket, and she held it by the tip of the blade. "Now. You stole something of Skayla's, and she wants it back."

"Really? Then I guess she'll just have to wait until she gets here," I said flatly. "When she walks over the cold corpses of your family."

She winced but hid it quickly. "The only corpse here will be yours, GhostMaker."

CHAPTER VIII: A World Gone to Ashes

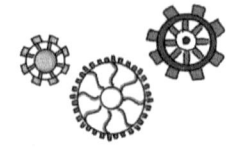

<u>Feyn:</u>

I thought I might explode if I didn't move soon. Everything seemed to close in around me as I just stood there, not even having enough chain length to pace about the musty-smelling room.

"Come on, idiot, think." There had to be something. Time was almost up, and all I'd done was fall into exactly what I'd hoped to avoid.

For all I knew, the next person to come down those stairs could be Skayla. I couldn't let her have me again. I wouldn't let her use me. The memories of my time with her wailed like the sound of mourning, and I could barely swallow the panic that begged to scream with them. I couldn't go back. The very thought of it made the bile rise in my throat and my vision cloud.

I could have jumped right out of my skin as the door opened and someone came slowly down the stairs.

"You have five seconds to explain yourself before I hand you over to Maeko." I could not explain the feeling of relief that spread through me as I heard the taut voice of Sefen, and soon I found the man standing in front of the bars to my cell.

"Is there a point?" I asked helplessly. "You didn't believe me when I was Feyn; what's changed since you found out I was The GhostMaker?"

"Three seconds left. Start talking."

"You're not going to believe a word—" I would have thrown up my arms in desperation if I could—"but I escaped Skayla's MindHold right after I found out she had a spy in Valdon—"

"—Escaped a MindHold? Try to make your story a little more believable, at least." Sefen's contempt was clear, and I sighed with exasperation.

"There *is* a first time for everything, ah?" The hopeless situation fought tirelessly against my will to drill the truth into Sefen, and right now I wasn't sure which would win out. I had an impossible story. No one had escaped a MindHold before, no one had gotten away from Skayla, and on top of all that, I was The GhostMaker. "But if you want me to finish before Skayla gets here, I suggest you keep your interrupting to a minimum."

Sefen didn't look too happy but said nothing.

"I came here to warn you of the spy and using a stolen emblem of Emarian I forged the letter and came here to try and find out who it was— now let me finish!" I said as his face grew red and he started to open his mouth. "Think about the town you and Jaythos went to. How did you think *I* knew how to get to Valdon?"

"Valdon cannot be found. Someone who knows of it must willingly show you," Sefen argued.

That's right, interrupt, show my point for me. "Exactly," was all I said, partially lying. No one had shown me. Sven's little illusion upon Valdon was quite clever, but I had a way around it, you could say.

"No...no one here would *ever*...."

I sighed and shook my head. "Sefen! Don't be a fool! How often does Namaya disappear? Wasn't she on the raid where you found out about that town? And the patrols that were getting close to Kaedna, who do you think told Skayla the entrance to the mazed mountains? Think!"

The last word echoed hauntingly around the room, disappearing into silence.

When it was broken, it was by a barely audible whisper. "Oh, Namaya...."

Oh, how that name disgusted me. "Yes, Namaya," I responded in a barely civil tone, even as I fought to remember *my* final name. The one that wasn't that title of death. Oh, what was my name? It was important, I knew it, but I just couldn't seem to grasp it long enough for my stupid memories to really take hold.

Sefen covered his face with his hands and started pacing with a vengeance. "No...no, no, no..."

I watched him, very confused. He believed me? How? I waited, waited for the other hammer to fall, for the glass to break and the trap to spring.

"I don't...I don't understand. Why did she do it?" His voice was soft, the kind of soft that came before the explosion, and I could see the pure anger building in his eyes. The solitary lantern in the room flared up as he ranted. "How! If Jaythos hadn't told me himself..."

Hope flickered within me. Aha. Jaythos's skepticism must have led him to wait at the top of the stairs after Namaya had dismissed him.

"What did you steal from Skayla?" he asked me.

"Moira's watch."

The color drained from Sefen's face, and he came up once more to the bars. "What?"

"We don't have much time. You need to get everyone out of here before Skayla gets here, Sefen." I started feeling panic welling in me again, and I had to fight to keep calm in the midst of this idiocy. "Namaya went last night to seal the action, I imagine. Skayla will be here any moment, and she will want this watch, and all of you."

"Once Maeko returns."

"You need to let me out, Sefen. I'll show you where the watch is, and if I'm lying you can kill me, but if you don't let me out, you're all dead. You need to at least have the children leave."

"I'll send them to Kaedna—"

"—No. You can't. Kaedna's been taken for weeks, thanks to Namaya's treachery," I interrupted again. "Sefen, there's no time to explain everything, and honestly, I don't even remember it all. Now let me out, or you might as well go up and hand yourself over to Skayla now, because there's no time to argue."

Sefen just stared at me, shock rippling over his features. The flames from the nearby lanterns blazed to match the ire in his eyes. "Wh-what? What about the—"

"—All dead." I had no time to soften the blow. "Skayla killed them all." Another memory flitted just out of reach. Memories of how they had died. Of what I had been made to do. "We can't grieve now, Sefen. Please, Skayla will be here any minute. You here at Valdon are all that's left."

"Tell me where the watch is first." Sefen choked out the demand.

"I'll do better than that," I said, the chains scraping as I slipped my hand into my pocket and slowly took the watch out by the chain, stopping my little trick so he could see it. Once out of the pocket, I let the thing dangle in front of me, swinging spastically back and forth. My mind hadn't felt this clear in a long time, and I realized it was time to explain as much as I could as the last puzzle piece *finally* clicked into place. At last, I remembered who I was. Who I *really* was. "Now let me out, ah? I'm not about to let just anyone handle all that's left of my sister."

Baey:

My palms were sweating, my heart was threatening to pound right out of my chest, and my eyes were darting so quickly from one movement to another that I now had the most throbbing headache. Once again, I came back to the window, hoping that Maeko would reappear from the woods alive and unharmed. He'd been gone for too long, and I was beginning to worry he wouldn't come back.

Finally, I couldn't stand it anymore and all but ran to the door, throwing it open and going into the main hall. It would appear that Tanner had pretty much been doing what I had been. In fact, his forehead was so dripping wet that it was reflecting the light of the lanterns. His own short sword was clutched in his white-knuckled hand like it was a lifeline, and he jumped as I burst into the room.

"Where are the others?" I asked without skipping a beat.

"Jaythos went and took Sefen aside just a little while ago. I don't know where they went. But Namaya was getting the rest of her weapons." He turned and gave a nod in the direction of the iron door that led into what I always had called the cellar—it had really never been used. Just then the door opened, and Sefen came out, followed by…by…

Tanner's sword went out in a defensive stance, and he looked frantically from Sefen to The GhostMaker. "Sefen? What's going on?"

"Where's Namaya?" Sefen countered without even bothering to answer, looking from Tanner to me. What *was* going on?

"She's in the armory getting some defenses up," Tanner replied slowly, apparently just as utterly confused as I was.

Sefen's face went white, and he looked Tanner dead in the eye, almost talking faster than I could process. "Get a few things together for a flight. Easy food that will keep—Baey, guard the door and let me know as soon as Maeko returns. Namaya's—" He choked. "Namaya *is* the spy." And with that, he ran down the hall with The GhostMaker close behind, leaving Tanner and I more in the dark than we had been before.

I was speechless. Had I really heard him? That couldn't be right. It just...couldn't. Turning to Tanner, I opened my mouth to ask him, but he spoke first. "No time to think, Baey. Just do what he says." He sounded scared and looked it, too. As he ran to the kitchen, I saw his hand shaking and his weapon threatening to fall out of his hand. My hands were little better as they trembled at my side.

But he was right. There was no time to think. I went up to the door and peeked through the secret hole, allowing me to see outside the door. What if they came from behind? There just weren't enough of us anymore to see all the avenues for attack.

I saw movement at the edge of the trees, and almost choked in fright. But then I caught sight of the familiar build, the bald head, and my shoulders relaxed a little. It was Maeko.

"Maeko's coming out of the woods!" I shouted at the top of my lungs. "Where is he?"

I leapt into the air and pointed the sword down to the ground where I had just been, scared to death. Seeing who it was, I wasn't sure if I should be relieved, or enraged. "Tanner! Don't scare me like that!" I floated to the ground and took a breath.

Tanner shifted from one foot to the other impatiently. "Where is he, Baey? I need to make sure he's not in a MindHold. If Skayla herself is coming, she could have caught him—and their eyes don't always change immediately."

I peeked through the hole. "He's running up, he's literally—"

Before I could finish there was a rapid series of knocks on the door. Tanner unbolted it and pushed me out of the way, preventing me from seeing what he was really doing.

"Give me your hand, Maeko."

A moment later the door was completely opened, and Maeko rushed in. "Where Sefen?" he asked, completely out of breath. He must have been running for a while—which meant terrible news.

"In the armory with The GhostMaker—I don't know what's going on," I answered, trying to search his eyes and see if maybe he would know, if he would understand.

He put his large hands on my shoulder and moved me out of the way, trying to force himself into a sprint.

"He says Namaya's a spy," I called out to him before he disappeared, hopelessly lost in the storm of events.

"I'll be back," Tanner said in a rush, disappearing again into the kitchen.

I didn't know what to do. I just stood there, Sven Mara's sword in hand, wings flicking every which way in nervousness, and my whole world collapsing at my feet.

There was a flurry of noise from the hall where the armory was, and suddenly I saw Sefen and Maeko practically wrestling Namaya.

"What's happening?" I shouted in a panic, running towards them and tripping constantly over my wings. I stopped before them, just in time to see them tie her with sturdy Varnese rope. I wanted it to stop. I wanted them to explain to me what was going on—why The GhostMaker was not the one tied up—but my feet were stuck, frozen to the stone floor like ice.

The GhostMaker came out, and just as Namaya opened her mouth to speak, Sefen shouted, "No! No more lies, Namaya. Jaythos heard you! Don't deny it! Now be quiet or be silenced!" I'd never heard him so close to tears.

My fingers felt numb, and Sven's sword threatened to fall to the ground from my loosened grip. What was happening to my home—my family?

"Watch her. I'll get Jaythos," Sefen addressed Maeko shortly, then turned to me. "Go see if Tanner is packed and tell him to come here. Quick, Baey!"

I was startled back into reality, and as swiftly as possible ran to the kitchen. Sefen had never shouted at me like that. But I shook myself and pushed any emotion on the matter aside. Ugh! No! This was no time to cry, silly!

"Tanner! Are you done?" I stopped at the kitchen and saw him putting some bread in a travel pack. "I think so."

"Good. Sefen needs you, now." I managed to choke the words out and was glad not to say another word. He threw two packs at me and was somehow able to burden himself with three. That's when I realized; medicine. We would need medicine.

"I'll be back. I just have to run upstairs, quick."

"Baey, what—"

I was gone before he could even finish asking, taking the back set of stairs from the kitchen. I tore down the second-story hall and to Namaya's supply closet, stuffing as much as I could in the packs Tanner had given me—he'd given me the ones with fewer things in them, of course. Then I took a medicine bag from under one of the shelves and stuffed it full of anything I could think of that we might need. That done, I ran back down to the hall, this time taking the main stairs so that I would end up where everyone else was.

"Baey! There you are!" Sefen called from the bottom of the stairs, where everyone stood in the foyer with weapons ready—even Jaythos, who was no longer wearing his sling. Maeko was watching the peep hole in the door, every once in a while looking back at the others. Namaya was now tied to the base of the stairs' railing, and the other three were standing around talking in hurried voices.

"We're leaving, *now*," Sefen said with a forced calmness.

Namaya strained against her bonds, and I found it hard to even look her in the eyes as she spoke. "No! Sefen, it's too late. You don't understand. She promised if you laid down your weapons, you won't be put in a MindHold. I tried to tell you, but you would never listen! Your stupid false hope was going to get us all killed, Sefen, just like Darin and

Varina! We've *lost*, and I wasn't about to watch you kill the only family I had left! We've *lost*, don't you see? Skayla's Drogan himself is coming."

I couldn't even process this. Namaya...she really was the spy. Her words sealed it, and now with the reality of it all staring me right in the face, all I could do was look at Sefen, wishing he would deny this all. Like he would somehow tell me it wasn't really what was going on.

But all I saw in his eyes was the same hurt that raged in my stomach, and his voice mirrored it as he spat back at his wife, "How could you, Namaya? You doomed our friends to death when they left for the Kaedna Pass. How could you do this to *me?* You *knew*. You were the one who gave Skayla directions. You aren't doing anything but joining the ones that *killed* our family, not stopping it from happening again."

"No! Sefen, it's not like that. Can't you see?"

I watched Sefen's shoulder slump. "No, Namaya. No. You've lost who you are..." He sounded on the verge of tears, whispering something I only just caught: "You aren't the woman I married." With that, he turned back to us, sorrow etched deeply in his face and eyes. Sorrow from the soul, and I felt it too. So broken. "Baey, Tanner, Jaythos, and Maeko. Leave through the tunnel."

The shock from the conversation wore off as I could take it no longer. "What?! No! Sefen, please, don't make me leave! I'll do anything! Don't make me leave our home, please!" More tears began to find their way, threatening a flood. No, no, no, no—NO!

"Baey, there's no time. If everyone is caught, it's over. No questions, now." Sefen's voice was now incredibly soft and gentle. He came up and knelt by me, whispering in my ear. "I know what you have, Baey. I need you to keep it safe, just like Sven told you."

I was lost, drowning in the turmoiled sea of this disaster. What. Was. Going. On. "H-how?" I tried to form words, but it wasn't working. How could he possibly know? I looked from him to the others, and my eyes settled on The GhostMaker. His memory. He *had* known…but he was our enemy, right? What was going on?!

Sefen pulled back from me, forcing a smile. "No questions, Baey. Just go and be safe, please."

"And…" The GhostMaker said, coming up to us and taking off his overcoat.

I backed up. "Don't come near me." My grip tightened around Sven's old blade with a new vigor.

The GhostMaker took a step back, a brief glimpse of hurt flashing in his eyes before it was masked behind understanding. I didn't care. He was a murderer, and no matter what anyone said, I wouldn't let him take me in as well.

"She'll need this, Sefen." He handed his coat to Sefen and then turned back to me. "It's cold out there, and you'll need it if you want to stay warm and alive…darlin'. I am sorry." His expression softened with the word, and he looked sad as he said the nickname. Darlin'. Wait. What?

I couldn't speak. It was as if every bone in my body had turned into a stone, and no matter how much I wanted to move, I couldn't. My tongue was cold as glass in winter, and my eyes were probably bulging bigger than a bug's. "How…"

"They are here." Jaythos's announcement was almost lost in my shock.

"They need to leave *now*, Sefen," The GhostMaker said, voice practically bursting with anxiety. "Otherwise, even with a distraction, the Drogan will find them."

Sefen didn't need any further push and turned to Maeko. "Maeko, you know where to take them."

The man nodded, taking up three of the food packs as if they were nothing and heading off towards the back of the house. "Come!" he commanded.

I was about to follow when Sefen pressed the coat into my hands. "Take it, Baey, and be careful." He looked up at Tanner. "Both of you."

Not daring to argue, I wrapped my hand around it. As I did so, there was a sudden, uncontainable urge to take it—the urge from the ring, and I grabbed the coat and put the thing over my shoulder.

My whole body was numb as we raced down the hall, passed rooms I knew and had played in, read in, learned in. We were about to leave it, and I knew deep in my gut that I would never return. Anguish stirred, and I felt as if I would melt away from the mere thought. I couldn't leave! But my feet rebelled, moving one after the other closer to the back of the mansion.

Maeko turned right then into the room of maps. Sefen had always liked this room. Its walls were empty except for the large shelves of scrolls; he had said there was nothing in there to distract him.

As I came in, the familiar scent of old paper wafted into my nostrils, but I found no comfort. But why were we in here? This wasn't the back door.

Before I could say anything, Maeko went up to the bookshelf by the far wall and took hold of it, pulling one end out. Behind it was a small hollow just big enough for Maeko to crawl into, leading immediately down into a hole.

"Come," he said, motioning us to get down into the hole. "Jaythos. Bring lantern." He motioned to the lantern that hung on a peg by the door, dimly lighting the room.

Tanner was first, not even blinking before he disappeared into the dark. Then it was Jaythos, who dropped down his crossbow to Tanner before he jumped down, the light from the lantern hardly visible after he had gone.

A panic overcame me. "No...no..." I choked, backing up. Ugh. I couldn't go down there. It was the opposite of the sky, and what if something collapsed? What if something...something...

"Little Baey. We need to go." Maeko extended his hand and gestured encouragingly. "No time."

"Ugh" was the most intelligent noise I could make, taking a deep gulp and heading over to the hollow. Closing my eyes, I knelt down and forced myself into the hole, my wings cramping uncomfortably into the tight space. I made a little squeak as my hand dropped down where the hole was, and I almost fell in face first after it. Ugh. Opening my eyes, I looked down, and saw Tanner and Jaythos in a much larger tunnel at the bottom of the hole.

"Come on, Baey, you can do it."

I gasped for air. "I don't think my wings will fit!" I said in a panic.

Suddenly, something pushed me from the back, and I plummeted down the hole and right onto Tanner.

He sort of caught me, sort of gave me something soft to land on, and I felt bad for screaming right in his ear. "Sorry," I murmured as I got up and brushed myself off, face flushed in embarrassment.

"Out of the way, you two," Jaythos said gruffly, moving us to the side so that Maeko could hop down. He brought with him a rope that went back up above us.

Tanner took the words right out of my mouth, "What's that?"

Maeko gave several long, smooth tugs to the rope, and we all heard a light thump. "Closes shelf," he replied simply. He looked at Jaythos and motioned to the lantern. "You do not know where to go. I will lead."

Jaythos handed him the lantern and took back his weapon from Tanner, shouldering his crossbow. "I'll take the rear," he said, waiting for Tanner and me to follow Maeko first.

We all filed in and began down, first Maeko, then me, Tanner, and Jaythos. "Where did this tunnel come from, Maeko?" Jaythos asked.

"Sefen said Maras made them. Only he knew of them," Maeko replied. "For emergencies."

A lump formed in my throat, and I whispered, "What is going to happen to Sefen?" And The GhostMaker, I added in my head. My mind went back to the way he had talked to me before we'd gone. So different from what "Feyn Cavo" had been like, and had it just been my imagination, or had he sounded exactly like…like—

"Do not worry, Little Baey."

But I did worry. I worried that I was leaving the last home I would ever know, worried that we wouldn't make it, and worried that Sefen was going to die.

CHAPTER IX: Skayla

<u>Feyn</u>:

"You should have gone with them," I muttered.

Sefen grunted. "Right. Your story is so obscure that I'm still not sure I believe it."

I knew that was only partly an excuse, and I didn't completely blame him.

"Sefen, please—" Namaya's interruption was an unwelcome one, and my jaw clenched.

"Be quiet," Sefen croaked, voice somewhere between harsh and pleading.

I added nothing to the conversation, instead leaving them to go down into the armory. The room was in bad shape after Namaya had been in it and only half the weapons were still functional.

She had gotten to three of the unstrung bows and broken them in half. The arrows had been snapped, and some of the swords had apparently been jammed into the iron door and bent. But at least we had gotten ahold of her before she destroyed everything. I was able to find the last two undamaged swords, but that was all that remained; everyone else had taken what they would need.

As I ran out back into the main hall, there was a huge thumping sound from the roof, and I sighed. "She's here," I whispered as Sefen finished gagging Namaya.

"Now?" Sefen asked, as more thumps came upon the roof.

155

"Not yet."

A loud crash exploded from upstairs, and a cold shiver raised the hairs on my neck. "Hide," I whispered, slinging the crossbow over my shoulder and brandishing one sword in each hand. We both took to the shadows, Sefen under the stairs and myself right across from him, hiding in the gloom next to an old wardrobe. We had drawn all the curtains closed and Sefen had dimmed the lanterns to the point where there was hardly a flame. Everything was so dark I could hardly make out Sefen's form.

The noise from upstairs jarred my nerves, and my heart stopped when the sound of footsteps on the stairs echoed around the room. I didn't have to think twice; I knew who it was.

"*Sveeeen.* Come on out. It's not nice to run off and hide like a coward. And after I'd been so nice and let you stay with me. That's *not* very nice. Don't make me regret not reuniting you with Moira."

There were few things I was afraid of in this world; my death was not one of them. What Skayla had made and would make me do in a MindHold, however, was definitely something I was petrified of. The way she called for me was more painful than the worst physical agony someone could think up. It made me want to curl up and hide in the midst of the nightmare; memories danced in my mind and scenarios of what would happen if she got me back under her hold were all too tangible. I held my breath, closing my eyes for a moment before looking over at Sefen. I shook my head. Not. Yet.

I could see Skayla's form now, right at the bottom of the stairs. "What have we here?" she cooed, stopping by Namaya. "You fool. Where are they?" Her voice was a little harder as she addressed the quiet woman, who stared pale and voiceless as she sat before the half-crazed Skayla.

I gave a short nod to Sefen and then, without warning, all of the lanterns burst into roaring flames. They lit every room of the house like a bonfire and caught the tapestries along the walls on fire.

Skayla didn't even blink, but Namaya wrenched against her bonds. The door was thrown open, and Skayla's soldiers rushed in among the panic. I instantly saw the violet, faraway-looking eyes of the ones in a MindHold, but they were few and far between. The majority of them were Bethynese soldiers, already pulling up masks that would filter through the smoke. They'd expected to burn this place to the ground anyway.

"Now!" I shouted, and both Sefen and I sprung from our positions and into the flames, catching the men off guard and taking out a few almost immediately. Skayla screeched.

There was a roar from the roof, and another crash. In moments, a coal black Drogan with ice-white tipping his feathers came crashing down the stairs, barely fitting into the room and completely obliterating the staircase—freeing Namaya in the process.

Ovok.

Its black-feathered tail swung about the room, hitting its own soldiers as well as Sefen.

But I felt an unnatural ease amid the chaos, ducking the Drogan's thrashings and weaving through the mass of soldiers. You could see the fear in their eyes as I clashed with them—they knew who I was. Or rather, what I had become.

The GhostMaker. The one you saw before you died. Only now they weren't hiding safely behind Skayla's skirt, for I had gotten out from her grasp. An arrow whizzed by my head and I spotted a soldier with a recurve; his expression was one of panic upon realizing our eyes had locked. I could use a bow. I leapt through the mass chaos, the Drogan's claws, the soldiers' swords. I ducked the archer's last-ditch effort to pick me off, and, before he could so much as flinch, I was upon him, one of my swords plunging through him.

I left it there and sheathed my other blade, taking up the recurve and throwing the quiver over my shoulder as I dodged to the side, narrowly missing the blade of another soldier as he tried to avenge his friend. I kneed the man in the chest and ran, disappearing back into the flames of the mansion.

I made my way up to the massive Drogan, nocking an arrow and loosing it in the same motion, hitting its mark right under the animal's jaw.

There was an ear-piercing screech from the thing, and its tail came flying for me, but I ran between its legs just in time.

"Insect!" it garbled out in a scraping, screaming growl.

Running out from under the Drogan, I took out another arrow, dipping it in flame and loosing it at the beast's neck. This one it saw coming and batted at it with its claws, hunching as if to pounce as it glared at me contemptuously.

I felt someone behind me, and just as I was about to turn, I heard Sefen's voice.

"What a way to go out," he breathed as we both leapt out of the way of the beast's lunge.

I just grunted, watching as Ovok's failed leap only turned him to another focus: the building supports. "With any luck, he'll collapse the building before the fire does." With any luck, we *would* be killed and Skayla wouldn't get us. But I knew we wouldn't be so lucky.

I swept my leg under a soldier as he came running at me, searching the chaos until my eyes fell on Skayla, who was by the bare doorway leading to outside, grinning like a crazed cat.

"Remember what I told you," I muttered, hoping that we would both be able to escape being trapped in a MindHold. I didn't have my ring, which meant our chances were slim. But Skayla didn't have the watch anymore, either, meaning my abilities might just match hers at least a *little* more evenly. Still, I had never tried to keep someone *else* out of a MindHold. Would my anchor even work without my ring? Last time hadn't worked out so well.

The flames grew, and I started towards Skayla and the door, using the recurve when possible and the sword when needed.

Instead of trying to run away, Skayla stepped sideways to block the door, giggling. "Oh, you're funny." She shook her head.

I blinked through the smoke as my sword clashed against Skayla's, and I ditched the recurve as I knew I would need my hand free. She would be no match for my skills, and she knew it. But that's why she'd brought help—just like last time.

"Sven, come back to me," she cajoled as she barely jumped in time to avoid my attempt to trip her. The jump left her off balance, however, but as I went to drive the sword into her temporarily vulnerable chest, I was distracted by a lunge at me from behind, which I had to roll to the side in order to dodge. Thought turned to instinct as I found myself surrounded by four soldiers—all in a MindHold, explaining their quick response to Skayla's distress—and I danced with their blades as one by one I eliminated them. But it was hard to fight through the flames and the toxic smoke, and I found myself struggling to breathe through it all.

All the while, Skayla laughed in the background, glee spilling over like some spoiled child.

"You have become a monster!" I shouted as the last man fell. Time stood still. I was seething, and now, barely out of reach of striking distance, I faced her. Years ago, I would have been loath to end her life. But now, all I felt was hatred and betrayal. I was beyond words. Everything else around me blurred, and all I cared about was her and what she'd done.

"Oh, Sven, silly, *you're* the monster." I lunged at her as she said the words, but I was too late. An arrow came from somewhere to my left and struck me in the side. As pain seared up and down the left side of my body, I managed to break the shaft of the protruding arrow and stumble to my feet, trying to locate Skayla. My vision blurred and all sound faded, but I forced myself to remain standing, pushing myself on through the ash and lunged my blade in Skayla's direction. But another man jumped suddenly in front of me, bringing down his sword over mine. The sheer force of it plus my own weakened state allowed the sword to fly from my grasp, and I was shoved to my knees against my will as two more men helped bring me down.

The crackling of the uncontrollable fire seemed to intensify even as the screeches of the Drogan rang in the air, and as I struggled against my captors, I caught a glimpse of Sefen also being subdued.

"Take them outside before we are all cooked for dinner!" Skayla shouted over the roaring flames.

The Drogan was last out, all but crumbling the already decimated mansion as it burst through the front wall. At least the tunnel would now be completely covered. No one would know where the others had gone.

Once outside, we were both searched and bound with rope, forced to our knees before Skayla. I fought through the pain of the arrow in my side, but it was a battle to keep my concentration. I *couldn't* lose focus now. Our minds depended on it.

"Now, Sven, time to be reasonable," Skayla said as she stood in front of us, sighing as if this all was just some great, unavoidable tragedy.

My gaze searched the crowd of soldiers, and I saw the confused eyes of Namaya boring into me as she mouthed my name. *Sven.* If I didn't know any better, I would have thought by the shade of her face that she had died and come back a ghost. So, Skayla hadn't told her.

"Sven Mara! Look at me!" Skayla's long fingers grabbed my face, painfully forcing me to look her in her startlingly violet eyes.

No. I couldn't do this again. I struggled to breathe through the arrow lodged in my side, but still I managed the reply. "Whatever can I do for you, my darling sister? Murder? Torment? I am ever at your bidding." My voice dripped with the bitterness from nearly a decade of her voice in my head but still I remained calm, waiting for Skayla to try a MindHold and hoping that I would be able to resist it even through my wound. For both my sake and Sefen's.

"Careful what you wish for." She looked from me to Sefen, expression that of a gleeful toddler. "Tell me now, or I will set you upon your friend. You always were my best interrogator."

"*No,*" I spat, even as a shudder ran down my entire body.

She only clucked like a mother hen. "Oh, be reasonable. Come back, I miss you. Don't you miss me?" Her voice was as pleasant as the sound of running water, and I expected to feel the urge any moment.

"No," I repeated, completely unaffected. In fact, I didn't need to use my anchor...or any effort at all. It just...didn't affect me. How odd. Not that I was complaining.

"Oh, don't be so difficult, Sven." Even though she held herself with the utmost confidence, I could tell Skayla, too, was startled, and she let go of my face, stepping back and stroking her chin. "Hm...well, I suppose we will just have to try your friend then." She laughed a little, turning to Sefen.

"Maybe you will help me, hm?" Her voice turned once more to that of a playful child, smiling disarmingly and constantly laughing to herself. "You look so brave. You can help me bring peace, stop any more bloodshed. I'm just trying to save the world, you see."

I jerked my head to face Sefen, staring at him hard and saying, "Remember what I told you."

"Shut up, Sven!" Skayla screeched, smacking me across the face.

"Namaya told me all about you, Sefen. She says you would do anything for your family. Help me, help me so that I can bring in your friends peacefully. I don't want to hurt anyone any more than you do. Be smarter than Emarian." She smiled as she said it, that last phrase was meant for me. Every moment I was remembering more...and it wasn't pleasant. The death, the years of being under her. The friends she'd made me murder. I wrenched myself out of that devolving train of thought, concentrating instead in diluting the potency of Skayla's words. Like my

Gift, hers was based on an illusion and twisting of reality. Only hers was the illusion of words.

"Hear but don't speak, know but don't read. Stand fast, stand strong," I heard Sefen mutter, and Skayla's face went red. But she kept calm, sighing like a disappointed mother and turning to me.

"Oh, Sven," she said, shaking her head, "What have you done, you idiot?" She turned around and looked up at the black Drogan as if to share a moment of exasperation with it then back down at me. "You think your little trick is enough, Sven? Hm? Your power is *nothing* to mine, nothing! Illusions, ha, you were the weakest then and you're the weakest now." She turned to Sefen, shouting, "*Tell me what I want to know!*"

"To see is to remember, to do is not to die—-"

"SHUT UP!" Skayla's yell was piercing, but as quickly as she had lost it, she was back to her pretended, maniac calm, turning to Ovok and saying sweetly. "You're right. They chose the hard way, the fools." She made a tutting sound.

The Drogan nodded, eyes boring into us with the depth of an abyss. "Search The GhostMaker, first," it said in a gravelly, jarring rumble.

Skayla came over to me once more, searching in my pockets and trying fruitlessly to find the watch.

"It wasn't yours, Sven. You shouldn't have been jealous and taken it." She straightened back up.

I grit my teeth, spitting out, "It wasn't yours either."

"It was more mine than yours!" Her demeanor changed into the red-faced brat she had become. Then the brat disappeared, and she giggled. "But I will have it. Don't worry. I'll fix the mistake you've made."

Then she turned to her soldiers. "Make sure they're secure, and let's get moving! Put them on some of the horses you kept in the woods. I need them alive and in one piece, and the long ride is going to be rough on my poor little brother," she ordered, making a pouty face at me before turning around. The black Drogan laid down and allowed her to climb up, and, in a second, they were in the air, hovering above us in the sky as we were dragged towards the woods.

Baey:

It was beyond suffocating to be underground in such a closed space. The smell of earth reminded me of death, and every time I saw a mouse or rat, I squeaked more than it did. It didn't help my sense of claustrophobia that the tunnels seemed endless, turning into more of a maze as we walked through numerous side corridors and came across more than five forks in the path. Once or twice, we actually walked through...well...a wall. One of Sven Mara's tricks, but at least Maeko knew we were going. I just had to keep telling myself that.

In the meantime, I tried to distract myself, rubbing the ring hanging against my neck. Sven. That brought me back to how Feyn—The GhostMaker—had spoken to me, and an awful feeling surfaced. Suddenly his presence, as haunting as it was, rang familiar, as if from a dream. The voice had changed and grown both quieter and raspier, the face thin and almost twice as old as he should have seemed, and the eyes were not the brazen gold I remembered them being...but could it really be him?

164

"You alright?" Tanner's whisper came from right behind me.

I flexed my wings in and out repeatedly in an attempt to soothe myself, focusing on that and not the walls closing around me.

"I'm fine," I muttered. Absolutely fine. My home was about to be overrun with Skayla and her soldiers, Sefen and The GhostMaker were waiting to be slaughtered, and we were running away—*I* was running away.

Again.

I felt like we had been down here forever. I was starting to think that maybe Maeko had taken a wrong turn, and we would be stuck for good. *Oh no, please, no.*

Then, just when I thought that I would scream if I didn't get out of this death tunnel, a fresh, evening breeze blew through my feathers. It was intoxicating and a tingling sensation ran up my wings into my back. More than ever, I yearned to fly.

The breeze got stronger and stronger until, suddenly, we were above ground, now being engulfed by the wind. I was surprised to see the sun fading behind faraway mountains. I had thought it was just my mind playing tricks on me, but it now seemed that we had indeed been under the tunnels almost a whole day. I closed my eyes and took a long, deep breath, drinking everything in like a thirsty hound. Then, as quickly as the pleasant feeling had come, it vanished, replaced once more by the severity of our situation.

"Now, Sefen said you know where cave is to hide in, by the Nethani Cliffs?"

I tilted my head to one side and looked at Jaythos, mystified, "What...?"

"Baey Tihali Mornaro, focus!" Jaythos startled me with the vehemence in his tone.

I turned to him, shaking my head. "I don't know what you're talking about, Jaythos. Maeko, what cave?"

"The one Sven Mara showed you, Baey! Where Emarian's men found you!" Jaythos snapped.

"But...how—"

Jaythos interrupted me. "Later. Now, where is it?"

My breath was gone, and I felt as if someone was sitting on my chest, crushing my ribs to powder. Could it really be? Had my wish come true, only to be burnt and turned into a nightmare because of me? Had *The GhostMaker* really been—was he—

"Baey." Maeko's voice was low but deathly stern. It snapped me out of it—sort of—and I looked to the evening sky, orienting myself as to which direction was north.

"Follow me." I choked out the words, taking flight just above the ground and flying swiftly through the forest.

The others ran close behind, shadows in the quickly fading light of day. Soon, the two moons reared their faces, rising just above the cliffs that were still far in the distance.

I paused and landed, catching my breath. It had been a couple hours, and still we were nowhere close. "I...I don't think...we'll make them...until tomorrow..." I wheezed.

Jaythos leaned over, coughing raggedly and trying to regain his breath. "That's no good…we…we'll be caught before the sun…rises. It would have been better…to stay and fight," he stammered, looking over at Maeko.

Maeko just stood there, breathing heavily, yet still looking like he could run a couple more miles without batting an eye. "We will make it. All good to keep going?"

Tanner—who had just plopped down on the ground—let out a groan. "I think I might rather just die," he muttered.

"Don't wish that, Tanner. It could come true." Jaythos went over and patted Tanner's back cheerily.

"Lovely," Tanner managed to say, grunting pathetically as he made himself get up.

And with that, we continued. I had it easy, in comparison, my wings allowing me to glide without too much strain. Well, I thought so, at least, until it became *painfully* aware how much my wings were lacking in exercise. On top of that, I had to carry the stupid coat Sefen had made me take. Though somehow, I got the sense that something truly precious was hidden within it.

By dawn, we were all spent, and the four of us collapsed under a very tall Tafne tree.

"We must go on soon," Maeko grunted, refusing to sit down when we stopped.

Now that we had a moment to catch our breath, sit, and listen, I realized I could hear the far away screeches of Drogans. We were being hunted. Self-consciously, I looked up, scanning the sky and expecting to see one of the great Dragon birds. It made it hard to rest.

No one spoke while we sat, all hoping that by being quiet, nothing would come, but it made for even higher tension. My wings itched to move again, and I felt that this was worse than being in the tunnels. How would we ever make it to the cliffs?

Suddenly, there was a screech that was closer than usual, and everyone looked up in a panic.

"Scatter!" Jaythos whispered hoarsely as he jumped up, taking his crossbow from the strap on his back and loading it. He pressed himself to the tree, just as all of us did the same under different ones.

My breath caught in my chest, and my heart pounded so loudly that I was afraid the thumping could be heard even from the sky. I cocooned my wings around me, turning them the color of the surrounding forest and hoping they would shield me from the sharp eyes of our hunters. A shadow passed over, and another screech wrenched the air.

The beating of wings slowly faded, however, and soon it was just another sound melding with the other hunters. After about ten minutes, it faded all together. Not daring to breathe a sigh of relief, I slowly peeked through my wings, seeing if it was safe. Jaythos had just peeled himself from the tree, and I saw the others begin to come back.

Ever so carefully, I opened my cocoon, getting up and moving towards the others. The coat was pressed closely to me, and my wings still almost enveloped me completely, but nothing gave comfort. I just wanted it all to stop. I wanted to wake up.

"We must keep going," Maeko said. I didn't know if my wings would work. I was almost paralyzed with fear, and I felt I might just cry if I opened my mouth, but something inside me kept going. Some inner strength I didn't have made me move my wings—made me fly—made me do what I could not.

For a while, every ten minutes or so, we would have to duck as a Drogan passed, and each time I thought we were done for. But gradually, the closer we got to the Nethani Cliffs, the fewer instances we had. It was common knowledge that the Nethani Cliffs were a dead end, and no man being pursued would head for them. The Drogans were probably thinking that we were heading for the River Tusand, where we had kept a boat in case of emergencies. Namaya would know of that. My heart sunk at the thought of her.

We arrived at the cliffs by evening, everyone so out of breath that if a Drogan had seen us, there wouldn't be much of a fight.

"Where...where's the cave, Baey?" Jaythos gasped out the question.

I looked up and down the cliffs, trying to remember. I recalled the orange moss and the black rock next to it, but that wouldn't help us much in the dark. I looked up at the two slits of moon, shining pitifully down upon us.

"Quickly, Baey. We're exposed," Jaythos added impatiently.

I clenched my jaw and muttered, "I know, I know...I'm trying to remember." The stone, the moss...the stone, the moss...there had been something else...something that I had seen when I'd gotten there—the water! The waterfall. I turned to the right; my sharp eyes still able to see fairly well in the dark. Straining as hard as I could, I looked down the seemingly endless cliffside, desperately trying to catch a glimpse or hear the sound of the water. Nothing. Despair began to set in, but I turned and looked left.

"This way!" I forced an excited whisper and gathered up the coat in my arms, running—and tripping—in the direction of what I'd seen: a small glitter reflecting the light of the moons. The others limped after me, not much running left in them. But we were almost there. Almost safe.

By the time we reached the roaring waterfall, we were all about to collapse, but new life surged within my bones. "Almost there!" Northeast. He'd said northeast, right? We went on, and, soon, I saw it; the rock, still covered with the moss, as if nothing had changed.

"We're here," I said with satisfaction.

Tanner's eyes bugged out. "What?!" he rasped. "It's a…a…wall!"

I shook my head. "You doofus, it's like the walls in the tunnel. Follow…follow me…" I half walked, half stumbled, into the black stone.

The sound of running water greeted me, and I was transported back eight years, when I had stumbled in here as a scared child. Time liked repeating itself, it seemed. I was still a child, I was still scared, but by now I should have known better.

I looked about the large room of the cave, a few stalactites and stalagmites littering the room here and there. There was a pool of water in the center with steam rising out of it, and a trickling fountain of cool water coming out of the wall on the left. I closed my eyes and breathed in the smell of must, letting it take me back in time.

The others came in behind me, but for a while I did nothing, only stood there lost in recollection. Then the spell broke, and I was back.

"At least it is a little warmer than outside," Tanner commented, all but falling down onto the hard ground and pulling his coat around him.

I looked over to the back wall, where a meager mound of supplies was still stacked. Jaythos followed my eyes then dragged his exhausted body over to it, rummaging through and pulling out a couple of musty cloaks. "Well…if we could get them dry…" he said darkly, staring at them skeptically. Then his eyes went back to the pile, and he dropped the blankets. "Now this is better," he mumbled.

I ignored him and went over to the steaming pool, sitting down in front of it and using it like a fire, just as I had done so long ago.

"Maeko." I called his name, and soon I felt his presence behind me. "How did you know all this? Who told you?" I managed the whisper.

Maeko took a deep breath then said, "Not now, Little Baey. Rest." His voice was as burdened as I felt. So much had happened—so much had gone wrong—that it was hard to even know where to start processing. But I couldn't get past The GhostMaker. I needed to know.

I turned around, looking up at him defiantly. "No! Please, don't torture me. I need to know. I just need to know." Just the look on his face proved that I was right. Proved that I had failed to see what was right in front of me.

Maeko sat down next to me, heaving a deep, deep sigh, "How would you say it?" His tone was bitter. "Our heroes are not always who we think."

The more he tiptoed around things, the more it made me hurt. What had we done? I hugged the coat in my hands, bringing my knees up as close as I could and surrounding myself with my wings.

"The GhostMaker—Feyn—he has also one more name, I think you know," Maeko said quietly.

"Sven…" I whispered. When he said nothing, I repeated the name. "Sven. He was Sven Mara, wasn't he?" I looked at him, anguish piercing my soul. "How could we have missed it, Maeko? How did we let this happen? We were blind to Namaya…we didn't see Sven…. Is everything so hopeless that we can't see who's our friend and who's our enemy?"

"Names don't make friends. People change. We will see who friends are when the smoke is done," was all he said.

I couldn't stand it. "But our friends are still out there! Or were—and we left them. Sefen and Sven could be dead...*again!* We've gotten them killed because we were blind, and now what are we going to do?"

Maeko patted my back gently, getting up and turning around. "Rest. We are going to rest. And Sven Mara died long time ago. GhostMaker is all is left, I think." And with that he walked away without another word.

Numbly, I picked up the coat, shaking it out so I could use it as a blanket. No. How could he say that? Was he right? If Sven was The GhostMaker, then all of those terrible acts, the assassination of the Queen of Rugo, the many other deaths in battles and murders…. Had Sven simply turned with Skayla and now finally regretted it? Or had he been in a MindHold? But…none could escape a MindHold, so how? And surely someone would have realized The GhostMaker had been under a MindHold, if that were the case. A shudder ran through me as I realized no one saw The GhostMaker and lived.

Until now.

Then I remembered Tanner's discovery of his memory, and wondered if that had something to do with it. Perhaps he *had* been in a MindHold?

But as much as these thoughts swirled in my brain, I couldn't keep them, and exhaustion began winning out. Sluggishly, I adjusted the coat on my lap. The weight felt funny, and suddenly a thought occurred to me. Excited, I attacked the coat's pockets, looking to see if there was anything in them. That nagging feeling the ring around my neck had been giving me turned into an anticipation and I was compelled to keep searching.

Then I felt it. The rough texture of paper, and then the cold touch of metal. Without a moment's hesitation I grabbed hold of both, wrenching them from the pocket and holding them before me.

"Maeko! Jaythos, Tanner! Come here, quick!" I shouted, my hands practically shaking.

There in my hand was a note, and a small, intricately made gold watch, with a crack running down the lens.

THE GHOSTMAKER

CHAPTER X: Estasia

Estasia:

I hated not knowing where Skayla and her pet Drogan had gone. The Kovian Fortress was an unpredictable enough place without that madwoman and her pet running in and out. As if I didn't have enough trouble being everyone's lacky. The downside of being a slave...but, remember, Skayla was 'making a better world.' We should all be *so happy* with how things were turning out. Yes...my options were being brainwashed or scrubbing dungeon floors. What a life. I much preferred being a pickpocket. Oh, the good old days of freedom and being carefree, when all you had to worry about was eating.

Tanya brushed past me, whispering, "Back," as she did so. I took the rag I had been dusting with and threw it over my shoulder, running my grimy fingers over my long, snarled hair. Already? Or had I just lost track of time? Either one wasn't good; I knew better than to let my mind wander. That was a dangerous thing to do here.

The gaslight lanterns flickered as I walked down the hall, and the steam pipes and coils lining both sides of the brick hallway groaned and creaked more than the prisoners held below. I tried to think through what to do once more. I had a getaway plan already, but how would I get them *out* of the cell? Locks were easy enough to pick, but not the ones in this fortress's dungeon—and if I wasn't careful, this could go terribly wrong. Besides, all of this was banking on the fact that there *would* be a prisoner. Skayla usually got into her prey's head within minutes, and very few lasted beyond that. But this was The GhostMaker we were talking about. He'd gotten out of her grasp already, surely, he could hold out?

A whistle screeched out, signaling that indeed, Skayla had returned. The piercing sound was one I had long grown used to, but nonetheless jumped at whenever it broke through the thick, smoggy air of the fortress.

I kept walking, dodging a few violet-eyed soldiers as I made my way down the stairs and to the lower levels of the dungeons, getting into position for when they arrived. Another soldier brushed past me, not even looking as he made his way up the stairs. No matter how many years I had been down here, those vacant eyes hadn't gotten any less creepy, and the sight of them reminded me of what could happen to me if I wasn't careful.

If you aren't careful, you might be wishing that is what would happen to you.

I made my way further down the rank-smelling hall, ignoring the stench that greeted me. Some of it was the leaking sludge and dirty water from the pipes, ill-kept compared to those on the upper levels. No one wanted to be near the dungeons, even if that meant leaky pipes and bad heating. Not that it mattered to me; slaves didn't get heat. Why, I'd even broken a pipe valve or two just to get the satisfaction of walking by a few freezing soldiers who couldn't stand the winter's cold.

There were some groans or shouts from the cells but most of them were vacant. The only ones held here were those who had willingly disobeyed Skayla, receiving the due punishment. I settled the queasy feeling in my stomach as I remembered my time in one of those cells.

I walked down the familiar set of stairs to an even lower level; this one smelled even worse than the first.

And here was my job. I had put it off most of the afternoon, hoping I could wait until Skayla returned. This was almost completely empty, with usually only one or two unfortunate souls trapped down here. It had been empty for a week. But I knew that wouldn't last. Soon there would be a new prisoner. But I would get him out. I would help him, just like he'd helped me. As long as I wasn't too late anyway.

I saw the half-awake, greasy-looking jailor sitting lazily on his stool at the end of the hall, his keys clanging with every sluggish movement. With my usual guise of meekness, I shuffled over to him, eyes darting in pretended nervousness from him to the floor.

"You're late," he snarled, his rotten-smelling breath wafted unpleasantly in my face.

Yes, yes, I was. And I needed to be, if I was going to find out what cell they were in.

"Sorry," I muttered, mimicking a perfectly frightened little mouse. "H-how many do you have today?" I asked in a hoarse whisper.

The man sat back, chubby fingers rubbing his stubbled chin. "None today on this level. Just me, rat. The upper level has the same as yesterday."

I felt inwardly sick. "I'll be back with the food, then," I said, turning around and heading back towards the upper stairwell. But what if Skayla interrogated the prisoners already? What if they arrived in a MindHold?

Just as I was about to go up the stairs, there was a huge commotion right at the top of them, and I flattened myself against the wall, knowing full well that new prisoners were coming down. Relief spread through me, but I quickly fought to push the feeling down. Around here, anyone could be listening in on your thoughts. And by anyone, I meant Skayla, of course.

Two men came down the stairs backwards, seemingly quite occupied with containing a very unwilling prisoner.

My breath caught as I saw him, and even though I knew he had been coming, I had inwardly been hoping he would get away—and that I wouldn't have to pay back the debt I owed him—for his sake and mine.

"Hold him, you idiot!" one of the men yelled at the soldiers behind The GhostMaker, opening his mouth just in time for the captive to yank free and smack the soldier square in the jaw with his elbow. That was a good sign, in some sense. Unwilling meant his mind was free.

"You'll regret that one, GhostMaker," the man growled, finally getting a firm hold of him and helping the other three men drag him down the stairs.

The group passed me, and, as they did, The GhostMaker's eyes locked on me, just for a brief second. He looked so different without that garish mask Skayla had always made him wear. The cruel mesh of metal and gears was like some nightmarish masquerade prop, with only one violet eye ever visible from behind it. Yet even without it, I still found his appearance haunting. I had never seen his eyes without Skayla's influence, but the almost completely clear irises were equally unearthly and frightening in their own right. Only flecks of bluish green kept them from being utterly blank.

I took all of this in with mere seconds to observe before he was pushed on as he resumed fighting back. I was surprised at the feeble attempts he was giving—until I saw the way his side had been haphazardly bandaged, blood leaching through the fabric. That wasn't good. It looked like it had been hastily patched up for the trip back to the fortress, but it was obvious a good effort had not been made.

And then my day got worse. They had passed, and with the help of the grubby jailor, were shoving him into a cell, when another group came down the hall, fighting with a much livelier prisoner.

My heart plummeted. How was I going to get two of them out?

Before I could even think about *not* thinking about it, the gaslight lanterns on the second level burst into uncontrollable flame, threatening to blind everyone on the level.

"Oh, no you don't!" The soldier who had been getting The GhostMaker into a cell ran past me and up the stairs, shoving his way through to the disorganized mass of men trying to control this second captive. He took out his sword and gave the man a good tap on the head.

The fires died down, and everything was quiet.

"Now, get him into a cell!" the soldier yelled, huffing and heading in the direction of the upper levels.

I stared at the unconscious man as they dragged him through and evaluated him for wounds. Besides a good bump on the head, he looked well enough…for now, anyway. If he was any good at resisting Skayla's mind, he wouldn't be in good shape for long.

"What are you standing there for? Get going, girl!" The jailor yelled, threatening me with his heavy bunch of keys. It might not have seemed particularly dangerous, but I had felt and seen what that ring of metal keys could do, and I didn't feel like getting a permanent bruise on my skull. Again. I couldn't help but laugh inwardly at how little self-control he had compared to the Bethynese soldiers. The Bethynese, if nothing else, at least kept to themselves and had a little more refinement than the other mercenaries that joined Skayla willingly. Even if Bethynese soldiers were walking killing machines.

My mind raced as I reached the top level of the dungeons, constantly going through the process of guarding my thoughts and worrying that Skayla would find them. I wasn't in a MindHold, at least, but I had no idea if she could listen in, and I didn't intend to find out.

Just as I was thinking of that, I saw *her* coming down the hall, blond hair in a slightly messy bun. Instantly, I knelt down, eyes riveted on the rough stone floor as she grew closer. I could practically hear her smirking and knew she enjoyed every minute of subjugation she could force on someone. A shiver ran through me as she brushed by, but I dared not move until she and her tall companion, Lord Kovo, were down the stairs and on the next level.

Getting up, I tried not to hurry to the kitchen, not wanting to have another run-in with Skayla. Every time I saw her was an opportunity for her to find out what I was planning, and if that happened, not only would I be done for, but everyone that was helping me—and years of work would be lost.

Sven:

I tried to calm my breathing as I stood, shackled to the wall with my arms out to the sides. Both Sefen and I still had our minds but doubt pricked deeply. Or perhaps it was my throbbing side.... The five-day journey hadn't helped my injuries. Neither had it helped when my hands were put inside these hard-iron cases. Not only could I not sit down, my hands were completely useless—meaning I couldn't even inspect the wound. True, my captors had done a rough job of patching me up, but, somehow, I got the feeling my well-being wasn't really one of their primary concerns.

I heard a clattering noise from outside, and soon the thick iron door of my cell opened to reveal Skayla and her ever-present and lengthy shadow, Kovo. I despised the snake of a man and would have given anything to be able to wring his neck. I knew he had been responsible for getting the country of Bethyn on Skayla's side, and anyone who could convince a country to turn on its world was worth less than a worm in my opinion.

"Welcome to my humble home, *murderer*," I greeted Skayla obstinately, my eye contact with her never wavering.

"I do believe this is *my* property, GhostMaker." She grinned and shook her head, shoes echoing in hollow fashion as she walked around me. "And should I begin to list off those *you've* killed? Perhaps you've forgotten."

I gritted my teeth and said nothing, keeping my mind focused on anything except the information she was looking for. I knew, even now, she was looking for a way in. She wasn't going for a MindHold—no, she was simply intent on searching every corner of my already scattered mind. I'd had years of practice, but it didn't stop the panicked apprehension.

"Cat got your tongue?" Skayla came around to face me once more, the violet blaze of her eyes almost more unnatural in appearance than the eyes of those she controlled. Her smile grew. "Oh, see? You're already being good again."

Too many memories of being held silent in her presence surfaced, and I spat back, "I will *never* be your pet again. You'll have to do the dirty work yourself now."

She shook her head. "You're so adorable."

I could feel my face grow hot in my anger, and I fought to keep my mind focused. This is what she wanted, she wanted to see me lose my cool, wanted me to trip up and get upset—but I only had so much self-control, and it wasn't really enough to hold onto. She had done too much and being able to at last speak to her face-to-face after being muzzled by her for eight years was too tantalizing.

"I am *not* your toy," I said flatly, hoping the words would dig at her. I wanted her to feel the betrayal, to really understand. She had used me to kill hundreds! It made me sick just thinking about it. "But how do you sleep at night, ah? Is it a bit of trouble? Knowing what you have done? To Moira—our parents? You've got just as much blood on your hands as I do."

The back of Skayla's hand came crashing down across my face, and I soon tasted blood in my mouth. It would appear that I had gotten her upset.

Looking up at her eyes, I could picture sparks flying out of the mad things, like shards from beneath a blacksmith's hammer.

"You hit like a child," I retorted as I spit out the blood, raising an eyebrow and trying to appear unimpressed. It wasn't exactly a good thing to say, as that got me another smack across the face. Skayla had always had good aim in a fist fight.

"You have no idea what I'm keeping from you—what I'm sparing you from. You're still having memory problems even after the MindHold, aren't you?" She smiled coldly. "That was my gift to you. My failsafe. I can make you relive *all* of them, you know. So. Where is it?" she asked, tossing the question out as if she really didn't care.

"Then why don't you," I forced my voice to remain even, hiding the chilling terror at the threat. Somehow, I had a feeling I *really* didn't want that.

Skayla giggled, "Oh, I might. But so soon after you've torn up your mind getting away from me, you might break all together. So, I need to give you some *time* before I try anything like that. So, tell me now and I'll make sure I don't come visit you in a few days and show you just how miserable your life can be. Where. Is. It."

I returned with a taut, "Safe."

"I'm the only way to ensure safety, silly," she rebuked.

"Tell that to the dead!" Years of repression forced the choked shout out in response.

Her lower lip stuck out, and she gave a pathetic little look. "Aw, Sven, that hurts. But maybe you just need time, time to see more clearly. So, I'll let you think about it. And if I can't get to you, maybe I can get to your friend in the other room after Kovo's worn him down a bit more." She chuckled, shook her head, and left, closing the door behind her.

And that left the other problem…. Her snake of a shadow had stayed behind, the Lord Kovo. "*Mara.*" He spoke my last name in a bored state of exhaustion, like he was playing a game that had long run its course. "What am I going to do with you?" His expression was neither pleasantly charming nor crazed as Skayla had been. He had a different, calculated sort of charm about him, the kind of charm that could make you like him even if you *knew* he was a monster—I found it repulsing. And yet to not be afraid of Kovo was a grave mistake; I had witnessed his ferocity over the years.

I looked at him hard. He'd find it wasn't that easy. "I don't think the information would really be useful to a *worm*," I growled. But as Skayla had already said—that wasn't why he was here. He was just here to wear us down, to get Sefen or me to break enough for her to get past my anchor and into our heads. Just like last time.

"Who are you fighting for, Sven?" His towering figure cast a shadow like death over me, but I stood resolved. His face hardened, and he leaned in closer. "Last I looked, you killed anyone worth saving." He drew each word out slowly. "And honestly, you are an oddity in this world we know. I have seen more than you can imagine, and your stupid chivalry is rare. You are a dying species, Sven. Someone would have come around and abused power eventually; at least when Skayla wins, she'll have the whole world in peace."

"Peace? You mean mindless and without a will." I glared at him as I prepared for the worst, knowing better than to anger the worm, but not having the fastness to stick to common sense. "So why don't you crawl away whining and tell Skayla that if she wants to know, she can come back and drive it out of me herself."

Kovo sighed, taking a knife out of his belt and toying with it as a cat would a mouse. "This is much bigger than you can possibly imagine, Sven Mara. But unfortunately, you are too blind to see it. Now let's get this over with and pretend I can actually make you tell me what we need. And then you'll pretend withholding the information will actually make a difference in the outcome, and we can both live in a wonderful little land of make-believe."

My jaw clenched tighter, if that was possible, and I came back with a growling, "Sounds wonderful."

Estasia:

I walked into the kitchen, giving a quick smile to Tanya, who was kneeling over a wooden bucket and painstakingly peeling potatoes. The faint smell of horse told me she had gone to see her brother last night. It wasn't something anyone else would catch, perhaps, but I'd been around enough horses. She nodded back in greeting, and then we completely ignored each other.

There was a hub of general chaos as the sinks buzzed with running water to clean dishes, the bells rang from atop the door—signaling various needs for the officers of the fortress—and the stoves growled with the loud sizzling of cooking food. Even above this, various slaves came running in and out, carrying rough iron trays laden with various bowls and cups, some empty, some full. I took my time, weaving between them and heading over to the cook, Aekon.

"*Finally, it has arrived,*" I said in a mix of Rugonian, some random bits of other languages, and some words of Aekon and my own devising. It lowered the possibility of being discovered.

The cook nodded without turning to me, scraping some unpleasant smelling mush from a pan. "*How many today, then?*" he asked, pretending he hadn't heard me, instead referring to the number of prisoners he needed to feed.

I recited the number I had been keeping in my head. *"The usual on the upper levels—so fifteen. And then three including Kithro on the lower levels."* To anyone else, it appeared we were speaking some language from the west that just resembled familiar dialects. One might understand a word, without getting the message. We spoke it whenever talking to each other, so it made it look like it was just our casual way of talking. Aekon's first language was not Varnese, so it was perfect.

"There's a problem. There's two, not just him. And he's wounded. But it's true. He has freed himself of her will." I came back to the problem at hand. That was how we talked; he pretended to ignore me, and I explained every bad thing that could happen. It was probably the former thief in me: I had always had the motto 'expect the worst, be pleasantly surprised.' Aekon didn't really care for it.

"Go to Ateli and tell her how much food you need. You must go— you're already running late. The last thing we need is for you to get taught a lesson again. He won't be able to help this time. All will work out." Aekon didn't stop his rhythm as he continued to stir the pot over the stove, finishing another pan of gross mush and then making an idle shooing motion with his hand.

"I'm a slow learner," I replied dryly before disappearing into the hub of the kitchen.

I'd need to make several trips to Ateli, seeing as I couldn't carry all the rations in one go. After getting the first load from Ateli, I took the large tray of stale food and gross water and made my way back down the hall, making extra sure to pay attention to the sounds of footsteps. Too many times had someone come rushing down the hall, only to run into my tray. According to them, it was always the slaves' fault, and we didn't get to argue. And seeing as these were the prisoners' rations, if they spilled, they would not be replaced.

I stepped to the side as one such case came sprinting down the hall, a Bethynese soldier. Those were the most hated among the mind-free slaves, despising incompetency and all too happy to punish those who showed it. So, I made extra sure to wait lest another one of his friends was lagging behind.

In the clear, I made it down the first set of stairs, having just enough time to rush down them and out of the way as the sound of Skayla's shoes echoed down the hall. Anyone could recognize that gait.

Wrestling with my laden tray, I bowed down as always, not looking up as she passed. I waited a moment, but I didn't hear the footsteps of Lord Kovo. After waiting a little longer, I finally gave up and looked around. Skayla had been alone. And then it hit me like a sword to the stomach: If Kovo wasn't here, he had to be down with the prisoners still. Not good.

I tried to ignore the unsettled feeling in my gut as I slipped the rations through the slots in the doors of the upper level of the dungeon. After that, I made off quickly to the kitchen once more and repeated the run two more times.

At last, I returned to the bottom level of the dungeon, laden with the food for the two new prisoners as well as Kithro. I liked how he got a lunch ration while the prisoners were lucky to even get two meals a day.

"Finally. I thought you would never get back down here, rat," Kithro said, grumpy and impatient as always. He eyed me as I picked out his food—the only fresh and not-mush of the bunch—and handed it to him.

187

His grubby curled around it like worms on a carcass, and I suppressed a shiver as I picked up the tray of food again. Now, I could go feed the prisoners.

Suddenly, there was a commotion from the cell next to us—where The GhostMaker was—and the door unlocked from the inside, bursting open to reveal a quite piqued Lord Kovo, his charcoal hair a bit more tousled than usual.

As soon as the door closed, his body relaxed, though his expression proved his annoyance with the captive. It was rare to see much of any reaction out of the cold and calculating Kovo, and I wasn't sure which I preferred.

He looked down from my tray to Kithro. "His rations are to be half what you give the others," he spat at us both. "You're late today." He looked me up and down, eyes narrowing.

Naturally, he paid attention to every minute detail. Everyone thought Skayla was the one to be feared, but I had watched how Lord Kovo and Skayla interacted, and I sometimes wondered….

"Yes, sir, I was delayed with washing the hallway floors," I said with a humble bow of my head.

"No excuses. After you are finished here you can return with supplies to tend to the prisoner. And do that every day, as long as he needs it." He gestured sharply to the cell he had just exited.

Usually, no one wanted that job. It was frightening down here. This level was gross and ill-kept, and it was a reminder of what punishments could be inflicted for insubordination; most people would do anything to get away from the stench. But not me. Today, this was actually a really good happenstance, and I was amazed at the turn in fortune. However,

I did not want Lord Kovo to know this, so I put on my usual guise and pretended to hide a grimace. "Yes...sir," I mumbled, making a small, clumsy bow.

He gave no reply, only a long stare before turning around and continuing down the hall.

And here I'd thought this day was turning out terrible. Finally, it would seem things were going my way.

It had taken me longer than I'd thought to return to the dungeons for my new task. I had made a quick stop by the medicine room to get supplies from Ketique. Ketique was not a particularly savory character and had decided to interrogate me on who I was using these for. I knew better, though, and after wasting way too much time, got him to give me the normal supplies allowed for prisoners. Had he found out it was The GhostMaker, he probably wouldn't have given me much at all. As it was, this was a meager supply.

So now, here I was, heading down once more to the place where all the worst stenches of the world were kept caged and the prisoners with them, hoping that The GhostMaker's wounds weren't too severe. But remembering the way he'd come in...I just needed him to be able to get out of here. I wasn't exactly built for carrying people out.

"I'm back," I announced dully to Kithro, who smiled with those beautiful rotten teeth of his.

"Maybe this'll teach you not to lollygag, rat," he said, chuckling to himself as he practically rolled off his stool and grabbed a kerosene lantern. "Yell when you're done and not before." He opened the iron door for me and stuffed the lantern into my hand.

Taking a deep breath, I entered the cell, shivering as the cold darkness greeted me, only partly fought off by the lantern light.

The iron door closed behind me, and I was trapped. But at least things were going according to plan.

"*Now* who is it?" I faced the man as he spoke, the lantern's light stopping just short of him. His hands were encased in metal casts that were chained to either side of the wall, meaning he couldn't do much more than stand there, arms outstretched.

"I'd say your worst nightmare, but not sure I'm quite up for that job," I replied shortly, taking a step closer so he could see me and I could get a better look at him. I noted the food that had been slid under the door was still there. Looks like I'd be feeding this prisoner, too. Why wasn't I surprised? Kithro wasn't exactly the prime example of a nursemaid.

The GhostMaker's pale eyes searched me warily. I did the same, mimicking his look as I calmly set down the small wooden bucket of water. Without breaking his gaze, I placed the rag I had wrapped around the handle on the ground next to it, took the bottle of numbing ointment I had…borrowed…from Ketique out of my pocket to also set on the ground, and then walked closer. He didn't trust me, and, not surprisingly, didn't recognize me.

"GhostMaker," I said, nodding. The name didn't seem to please him very much, but I didn't know what else to call him, and though Aekon had hinted at him being someone else of importance, he wouldn't tell me. All I knew was that this plan was for more than just repaying him for what he had done for me. It wasn't about just getting me out of here to further our plans; it was also very much about The GhostMaker being free of Skayla. I was curious but knew that Aekon had his reasons for not telling me. He must have been a great ally against Skayla, indeed.

I took a couple more steps towards him, now close enough to really inspect him. It wasn't that good of a report either. "My punishment for being lazy was to come clean you up a bit. So, relax," I said, knowing a 'come to help' wouldn't really get him to trust me.

His eyes narrowed. He watched me with the best example of skepticism, but said nothing. I nodded again and went back to where my supplies were, first finding the wall hook for the torch so that I could use both my hands.

"What's your name?" he asked, voice hoarse. He still sounded wary but a little gentler. I brought the small bucket closer and then brought the other things over before replying.

"My name is Estasia." I finally said, picking up the bucket. I quickly turned back to business. "The water isn't terrible. Do you want a drink before I help you? No bugs, I scooped them out myself."

And there came that injured-hawk look again. I sighed and rolled my eyes. I knew he was worried I was just some spy sent in here to wheedle information out of him, but I wasn't. I was here to try and get him out. "Believe it or not, I'm here to help." My whisper was barely audible. Hopefully he would see that I didn't just mean with his wounds.

His brow furrowed over his dull eyes, and I started to see how tired he was. Tired and now confused.

"Please just take the water," I asked more desperately. I knew they wouldn't give him much in the way of anything to drink—the cup with his rations was hardly enough—and he'd only be able to eat when I came. I couldn't have him dying before I could get him out.

He made the slightest nod, and I picked up the small bucket and pressed it to his lips, tipping it ever so slightly so he could drink. After setting it down I made a small, triumphant smile. "There, that wasn't too bad now, was it?"

Now, to get to work. I grabbed my rag and dipped it in the lukewarm water, taking the vial of numbing oil and popping out the cork. "This might hurt at first, but I got something that will hopefully numb the sorest spots at least a little," I said, keeping my voice as low as possible so that Kithro wouldn't hear. If he did, I probably wouldn't get a hold of this ointment again.

"How'd you get that, ah?" The GhostMaker asked softly.

I didn't dignify that with an answer, only going about my work. He winced a little as I applied the rag to his side wound, but I was gentle. As I worked, I started to talk in a whisper, hoping he would believe me. "I'm a friend."

He let out a small, wry chuckle but didn't respond or look down at me. He seemed a little short on trust, but here, in this place, I didn't blame him.

I said nothing more for the moment, wanting more than anything just to tell him everything now. But I knew better. As short on time as we were, if I tried to force him to trust me, it would only make it seem like I was trying to get something out of him. No. I had to show him, earn it a little.

I worked the rest of the time in silence, being as gentle as I could in cleaning him up. After I finished, I was able to get him to eat, and, at last, I gathered up my supplies and forced a small smile. "I'll be back tomorrow." Then I let the facade drop, looking as worried as I was trying not to feel. "Be careful," I whispered.

He looked at me curiously but said nothing.

"Kithro! I'm done!" I shouted, and, after a while, the lock groaned and the door opened to reveal the very unpleasant face of Kithro. Without another word, I left, hoping The GhostMaker and his friend could survive long enough for me to get them out.

CHAPTER XI: Friend-ish-ship

Sven:

My head throbbed and my legs and arms ached as I now stood alone in the dark. Kovo's efforts had received nothing more than silence, half out of stubbornness and half out of the fact that, honestly, I couldn't really remember *what* he wanted. At least my stupid memory lapses were useful, somehow. But now that only made me wonder if Skayla would make good on her threat. Indeed, my mind was perhaps too muddled and fragile...but that wouldn't last, would it? How long did I have?

"Sven." I heard the muffled whisper to my right, and I twisted myself around to the wall it had come from. My body groaned in protest, stiff from the interrogation and the wound Skayla had inflicted.

"That's my name," I muttered to the voice in the other cell, suddenly not feeling so sure. Right? 'Sven' suddenly didn't sound right to me. I thought it had been Feyn.... Great. "Snap out of it," I scolded myself. Though, perhaps the memory problem wouldn't be so bad; I couldn't give them information I couldn't remember, after all.

"Good. You're still alive," the voice replied.

Who was I talking to? I tried to concentrate, but everything was a blurry mess in my head. There had been a woman in here a little while ago, right? That's why I had fresh bandaging. But this voice was that of a man. Who was it? I was exhausted and completely out of concentration, and now I couldn't even think straight enough to remember what I was doing here.

"Come on...come on..." I coaxed my stubborn blank mind. *Remember, you idiot!* "And you are, too," I called back to the man. I needed to find a landmark, something that would bring me back to what was happening. But what was happening? The more and more I tried to remember, the more impossible it became for me to do just that, and I was swallowed up by the maze of my mind.

"I think," the voice came back once more, breaking the nail-biting silence.

That's what I was trying to do...think...I closed my eyes—in truth not really making a difference, because it was completely dark in here already—and tried to think back to the last memory I could remember. Moira and Skayla arguing over the Drogans. But why was I here? I didn't recall stepping in or doing anything stupid, so how had I ended up in...in a dungeon? True, Skayla had seemed to be more distant and irritable of late, but *this* was a bit of a leap.

My legs ached from standing, and I shifted my position. Instantly, a pain shot up my side from the arrow wound.

Then it all came back. *Really* came back. The fight, Skayla, Baey, the ring, and the watch. I opened my eyes and sighed. This was a bad day. How were we going to get out of this one? As much as I would have liked, I dared not speak any more with Sefen. The jailor would clearly be able to hear every word we said, and I had a feeling Skayla had put us in nearby cells hoping for just that.

Skayla. My chest tightened as her words echoed in my head.

"That was my gift to you. My failsafe. I can make you relive all of them, you know." I knew she'd make good on that threat. How long did I have?

I could only hope my mind would stay the mess it was. Suddenly, getting better didn't sound so appealing.

I jumped a little as the door creaked open, revealing a figure with a lantern. My jaw clenched as the person came closer, and I forced myself to stand tall. "Namaya," I spat out.

She closed the door behind her and placed the lantern on a nearby hook protruding from the wall. Her eyes searched me earnestly, looking confused and almost concerned. She kept opening her mouth to speak then promptly changing her mind and closing it once again.

"Just be out with it, then," I managed to get some fierceness into my hoarse voice.

Taking in a deep breath, she took out her sword, coming up just a little closer. Well, she seemed nervous. "Is it true?"

I didn't say a single word, only glared.

"Sven, you-you don't understand." her voice was quiet, and she stammered as she spoke, sounding almost Human for the first time.

So, she *had* figured out who I really was. I didn't care. "Obviously."

"Baeno's gone. There's nothing left to protect. Emarian's city was taken—you know that."

I laughed dryly. "Yes. Thank you for the reminder." I could still see the flames. Still see...ugh, how was I going to deal with this if Skayla brought it all back? I swallowed hard. She was right. It would definitely break me.

"But she would have found it eventually, Sven. You know that, you had to have known it. There was only a matter of time before everything came crashing down. I didn't want to be standing there when the ashes settled and have everyone I loved dead at my feet. Skayla promised that she wouldn't harm anyone if I cooperated. I'm saving lives, Sven, by cutting this short."

Her words hit hard, though whether she meant to imply that what she had just described was my fate, I was unsure. And yet, it was. Everyone was gone and yet I was still here, having caused it. But still, I was disgusted. "I'm sure that was very comforting to the friends you sent off to be ambushed at Emarian's city. To be killed." My voice was emotionless as that memory resurfaced.

"No. They were taken. Not killed."

"I was there. I remember it. Skayla doesn't like having other Gifted around. Too much risk. You must have been pretty blind to have thought otherwise."

"Stop. Just...stop." Her expression turned defensive, and she returned to the hard, catlike Namaya I had known while at Valdon, but I could tell she was shaken. Very. Shaken. "If you are going to keep accusing me, then maybe you don't want *my* help getting out of here."

This had 'trap' written all over it. "And lead you to Baey and the others? Right now, Baey is the best chance we have of getting rid of Skayla. I don't think so."

She laughed. "Baey can't save anyone," she retorted dryly. "She's just a child. And you threw your life away for a dream."

No wonder Baey had no confidence in herself. I stared at Namaya a long time, unable to muster anything but the wrenching sadness her words brought. "We were all children once. They see more than we ever could, and I believe the promise of The Creator. Even if you have forgotten." Moira, Skayla, and I had just been children, and yet we'd been given the most powerful Gifts in centuries. "But if you think that way, why are you here? Just soothing your guilty conscience or trying to get me to talk?" Her argument was digging her own selfish grave.

"Because I'm your only option, unless you want to die down here." She sounded on the edge of her rope, just about ready to fall to her death. She reached into her jacket pocket and took out some salve and bandaging. "And I don't want…Sefen to die here." These words were said differently.

I made a shallow sigh, battling with my disgust of her betrayal and the possibility of her being honest. "Talk to him, then." I inched away from her. "Don't bother."

"Fine." She straightened. "I'll come back soon, and maybe you'll change your mind." She said nothing more to me, only shouted, "Kithro, I'm through with him!"

The door promptly opened, and the jailor stepped aside to allow the woman out. I couldn't tell for sure, but it sounded as if she went into Sefen's cell. If she had, however, she had kept her voice down, just as she had in here.

My suspicions were confirmed when I heard the door open to Sefen's cell, and some more muffled conversation. Then someone walked down the hall towards the stairs, and there was silence. I wanted to ask Sefen what she had said, but as completely out of it as I was, I wasn't that much of a fool.

The young woman—Estasia—kept her promise, coming in the next day. I wasn't sure what to think of her. Would Kovo really send two spies

in here to try and get me to tell him where the watch was? But if only one was a spy, which one?

I watched Estasia intently as she set the kerosene lantern in the usual place, bringing the bucket and rag up to me just as she had done before.

"Why were you sent here again, Estasia?" I couldn't remember what she had said yesterday, and really, she should be happy I could remember her name.

She offered the bucket to me as she had the day before. "Drink?" she asked, ignoring me.

Hm. I couldn't decide what to do with her. Granted, I'd been in and out of the Kovian Fortress many times in the past eight years, but her face stuck out more than I would expect from just any slave I might have run into. "You look familiar," I said barely audibly, entirely ignoring her question. I needed to know first.

"I'm a friend." She matched my quiet tone.

Was I supposed to remember her? *Was* she a friend? My empty brain ached more than the rest of me, and I was having no luck forcing it to reveal the answer. Come on…come on….

"Now drink," she said, not asking this time. The wooden bucket was pressed to my lips, and I got a few life-giving gulps down. It was probably not the best tasting water, but to me it was like a mountain spring.

"Are you taking care of my friend, too?" I motioned my head in the direction of Sefen's cell. It was agonizing not being able to talk to him. Not to know how he fared. Not to know if Skayla had broken him. She had been in here again this morning to try and work her tricks, and I could now say with certainty that it seemed to hold no real power over me. She could dig around, but every time she went for a MindHold, I didn't even feel like I was being dragged in that direction. But what about Sefen? It was harder for me to help through the walls of a cell, but, surely, he would have been taken out of it if Skayla *had* gotten him under her spell.

And then still Skayla had left with the comment that my mind was on the mend. That I wouldn't be able to hide behind forgetfulness forever.

Estasia nodded. "I was told to this morning. I'll make sure to get him some water, too." Her answer jerked me out of my devolving thoughts and back to the issue at hand.

Why was she doing this? "Why..." I asked slowly.

"I'm a friend of Aekon Toa," she whispered.

The hairs on the back of my neck stood up, and I felt a wave of alertness wash over me. "You are?" I had worried that after my escape, Aekon would be linked to the disappearance of the watch. Did this mean he was still alive? Or was she avenging a fallen friend? Or trying to trap me? I was too tired...too tired to think. Why was I here, again?

The woman looked back at the door, expression wary. When she spoke again, she was even quieter, if that was possible. "Yes, I am. And...we're trying to get you out," she said, going about her work as she spoke. I held in a wince as she cleaned my wounds. "Sorry," she murmured, pausing before continuing her story. "You don't remember me, though, it seems. But there isn't time to explain." She looked around again and then said quickly in Rugonian, *"Aekon said he taught you Rugonian. That true?"*

I nodded ever so slightly.

"Does your friend speak it?" she asked, once more speaking Varnese.

"No. I don't think so," I answered.

This seemed to disappoint her a little, but she said nothing. Instead—having finished patching me up—she began gathering all her supplies. "Is there a way I can still get a message to your friend—that I want to help?" she asked.

I weighed my options through my fogged brain. If she really was with Aekon—if she really was a friend—then perhaps we could get out. "Tell him I said to stand fast, stand strong, and we'll see the daylight." Hopefully that would help Sefen to know we weren't alone. Maybe.

Estasia:

I had seen the look in his eyes and could hardly contain myself. The spark—just one, but one was enough. He had started ever so slightly to trust me. Now, if only I could get his friend to do the same. Inwardly, I repeated the phrase I had been given as I headed off down the hall to change the water in my bucket. *Stand fast, stand strong, and see the daylight. Stand fast, stand strong, and—*

"Where're you going, rat?" Kithro demanded from his perch.

I took a deep breath and turned around, making myself act as fragile as a wilting flower. "Um, uh…sir, g-going to change my-my water and rag," I replied meekly.

Kithro laughed boisterously and even from here I could see the spittle go flying. "Haha! No need for that, rat. Dirty water will do for the scum."

"B-but if I don't clean it out, it will get them infected…and they'll die, sir." I pretended to be frightened for my life.

Kithro's face turned red, and he started to get up from his chair. "You challenging me, rat?"

My head shook vigorously back and forth, "N-no—" I was very proud of my nervous stammer—"I ju-just didn't want to-to get in t-trouble for getting them killed be-before Lord Kovo got wh-what he needed, sir...." That should get Kithro's attention.

As if on cue, the man stopped, turning from indignant to thoughtful...not that he had any brains to think with. "Uh..." he said very intelligently, scratching the top of his balding head. "Well—uh—get on, then! What are you standing there for?" He made a couple violent gestures with his hands, and I nodded eagerly, picking my bucket back up and hurrying down the hall like a good little slave, hiding the smug look trying to plaster itself on my face. Toying with idiots was such a pleasant pastime.

As I made my way through the winding passageways and up to the courtyard, I carefully thought over what had happened—and what would happen.

The GhostMaker had trusted me more after hearing Aekon's name. Aekon was not at all eager to tell stories or explain himself, and it often aggravated me. He told me things on a need-to-know basis, but what I felt he didn't understand was that sometimes, completely obscure things might need to be known. He had an almost unhealthy dose of mistrust. But then...didn't we all?

I opened the door that led outside to the courtyard, letting the fresher air hit my face. My sweaty, frayed hair didn't budge much, even when the wind picked up, but the breeze did cool me off and freshen me a little. I adjusted my grip on the bucket's handle and walked with purpose across to the wall where the large metal faucet allowed for the filling of larger buckets. Funny how this place had running water and heat, and yet they still didn't care to let *us* bathe or stay warm.

The bucket brimmed near full, and I turned off the water, hoisting both myself and the bucket up and walking back inside. My next stop was to Ketique to get some fresh rags. He wouldn't be as likely to give me new ones, and the argument I had used on Kithro wouldn't do much to fool him. Ketique was smart, smart enough to notice a missing bottle of numbing ointment, which led to why I would be returning it today. I may have had an ulterior motive for going to get the water cleaned. Ketique would be taking inventory this evening, so if I didn't get it back in that cupboard, I was done for.

But it was all part of the plan.

I didn't have much wiggle room before Kithro would get suspicious that I was dawdling, but I had hopefully just enough to switch out bottles. I'd been up late last night, using the common Getsi plant and a couple of Aekon's kitchen herbs to mimic the appearance and smell of the numbing ointment. For the ointment I had taken was more than just that—the plants it was made from also worked as a sedative, which was something I could definitely use. I had enough of the bottle to use it to help The GhostMaker's companion and drug Kithro and quite a few of the other guards—that would be Aekon's part of the plan. Tanya was in charge of giving food out to the soldiers.

After setting down my bucket further up the hall, I ducked down into an unused stairway, heading partly down into the dark. This fortress was so large that I had found several places where no one else went; something I used to my advantage. Quickly dropping to my knees, I searched the wall carefully, avoiding the pipes which included the steaming hot water pipes. Those left a mark.... At last, my hands maneuvered around the maze of piping and found the familiar loose brick, wiggling it out. Behind was the hollow spot I kept my—borrowed—items. Some glass bottles, a small amount of food that would keep, and a knife. That one was probably the riskiest of them all, but I had always liked a good challenge.

I took the only glass bottle that had anything in it—my fake ointment— along with another empty one. Taking the real bottle of ointment out of my pocket, I emptied its contents into the empty glass, and replaced the liquid with my impersonation of the ointment. Ketique wouldn't catch on until he used it next—which wasn't very often. Hopefully, by then, we'd all be long gone.

That done, I quickly put everything back and replaced the brick, making my way back up into the better lit, inhabited level of the fortress. After waiting until no one would see me, I exited the small passage and walked up the hall to get my bucket. I then calmly scooped the bucket up and continued on my mission, the bottle full of fake ointment hidden deep in my pocket.

I picked up the pace a little, hoping I wasn't running too far behind schedule. I only hoped Ketique wouldn't give me any actual trouble. Ketique *always* gave me trouble. He had been the one to accuse me of stealing some bauble of Skayla's four years back. That had gotten me thrown in a dark cell and almost whipped. Even after being proven innocent—which in that rare instance, I actually was—Ketique had been tirelessly heaping accusation after accusation until, thankfully, no one really believed him anymore. I had definitely capitalized on that fact.

Everyone thought I was just a meek little broken mouse, subdued after the first incident. Even though Ketique was now quite accurate when accusing me, no one bothered to investigate.

Putting my bucket down by the entrance to the medical bay, I took an extra moment to make sure it was where no one would trip over it. That was the last thing I needed right now.

I took a deep breath and entered the chaos. There were still quite a few soldiers in from when The GhostMaker and his companion had been caught. It appeared they'd made quite a mark after all. I weaved through the scattered cots that lay here and there on the ground, heading toward the way too familiar greasy figure. At the moment, he was hunched over a table. His dirty red hair was pulled back in an oily ponytail, showing off the burns he had gotten by experimenting with different chemicals and ointments. One of them had been caused by me, when I had been young and more *outwardly* the rebel. Probably the reason he hated me so much. Probably also the reason I had been changed to kitchen detail and was no longer one of his assistants. Seeing as the scars meant he might never be allowed back in Bethyn, I was very proud of myself. Bethyn and their requirements were a bit outrageous, even if it did turn out the best soldiers.

"Ketique?" I called the man's name, assuming my usual mousy posture and tone—not that Ketique was taken in by it.

He turned around, adjusting the monocle-like magnifier over one eye that he used for surgical procedures. "Yes, rat?"

He'd been the one to start that little nickname, too.

"I need some new bandages," I replied gingerly, holding up the gross ones in my hands.

"What for?" he spat, spraying me with spittle. He definitely knew how to treat ladies, now, didn't he?

"I have to care for-for more prisoners,"

He snorted. "The rags I gave you should be plenty for The GhostMaker."

Of course, he'd found out. "But it's not just for him," I pressed, treading as always on dangerous ground.

"Not my problem, rat. Now go find a dark hole to crawl in before I find one for you." His smug look made me want to give him a nice little punch square in the jaw. Maybe then some of those nice white teeth he bragged about would go flying. Oh, to see the look on his face...but no. Sadly, that wouldn't exactly land me in a good spot, and I had better ways of getting at Ketique.

"The-then maybe you can help me with another pr-problem?"

"What?" He spewed the word out, purely hostile now.

"I-I heard the other day that some of the officers' good...um...dinner meat went missing. Do you kn-know anything about that?" Ketique was just as much a thief as I was. The only difference was that I was better than he was. Much. Better. Bethynese soldiers were very disciplined. And it was clear Ketique was *not* very good at being Bethynese.

His face grew just the tiniest bit red, and he narrowed his eyes. "Rat," he growled.

I cowered, even though he knew the threat I was giving. The cowering was more for the benefit of anyone else in the room. "I th-thought maybe you could help me sh-shed light on the problem. Aekon hates th-thieves in his kitchen."

I was pleased to see the crafty man livid at the remark, and it took him a moment to calm himself enough to speak. "No one would believe a rat." Only, he didn't sound too confident when he said it.

One of Ketique's assistants, Lytho, came up and interrupted us then. "Sir?" the ill-fortuned slave said hesitantly, already cringing in preparation.

Ketique turned on the unfortunate soul, spit flying as he berated the young boy. "*What?* Have you no manners! I should have you whipped for such rudeness, cow!"

Ketique had a fondness for naming people after animals....

The cowering Lytho sputtered apologies, bowing his head as he begged forgiveness. "So-sorry, sir. It-it's jus-just that the-the—"

"—I don't care!" Ketique cut him off, slapping him across the face. I wanted to grab Ketique and give him a lesson he wouldn't forget, but I had had years of practice stowing those feelings away. Besides, I observed that the slimy man had already been given quite a lesson: There was a new-forming bruise by his jaw. Ketique's slack mouth had finally gotten him into trouble with a Bethynese officer, it seemed. Physician or not, all Bethynese were supposed to show a high form of discipline and respect to those higher than them—something Ketique failed miserably at.

"Bu-but sir..." Lytho's face was now red on one side, and tears threatened to stain his cheeks. "Captain Chukoan—"

Magic words for Ketique. His anger vanished instantly, replaced by his usual irritated impatience. "Well, why didn't you say so! Rat, get your cloth and get out of here." He gave me one last evil glare before following a very subdued-looking Lytho.

Heart pounding, I went to the small closet where the bandages and supplies slaves were allowed to handle were. I grabbed a handful of the cleanest ones I could find and then gave a quick look around. Ketique was occupied with the captain, and voices were getting a little raised— as always. The only one that was paying attention was good little Lytho, who gave a quick nod. I only had seconds.

Diving my fingers into my snarled hair, I took out the two small slivers of bent metal from within the mess, moving noiselessly over to a locked cabinet in the corner. I gave another glance over my shoulder before angling to get a good look at the lock. The cabinet was, of course, meant to be break-in resistant, an intricate mesh of gears and cogs holding it shut like a steel trap. The lock itself was also a highly sophisticated one that required a strange looking key in order to open it. But I had long ago figured out how to coax the lock, and, within seconds, I heard the satisfying click.

With another look around, I gathered with relief that Ketique hadn't been in here for anything and swiftly replaced the bottle in its place. My heart pounded as the familiar pulse of adrenaline flowed through my veins.

With a quick breath of satisfaction, I grabbed my rags and retreated from my crime, heading back out of the bustling room. Years of experience controlled my nerves and with ease I walked right out of the room.

But I was short on time to get back down to the lower levels. So, now burdened with cloth and bucket, I walked as fast as I could down the halls, expertly dodging any who passed. It was still rather chaotic, with soldiers running back and forth as if preparing to leave. I had gotten used to it in the past two weeks—they had been looking for The GhostMaker—but now I was confused. The GhostMaker had been caught, so who were they looking for?

The thought stuck with me as I stood once more in front of Kithro, waiting impatiently for him to get his lazy self up from his stool.

"You took your sweet time," he grunted sourly as he finally stood up.

He had nothing to complain about, seeing as I was the one now waiting for *him*. But I shrunk back and appeared to look terrified. "I'm sorry, I'll try to be quicker."

He just snorted, giving me a lantern to add to my already-full hands, and opening the other cell door.

Somehow juggling my burdens, I trudged into the dark place and set down my bucket, the door as always closing noisily behind me. This man was probably a good fifteen or twenty years my senior, but the thick beard could be affecting my judgement. He eyed me curiously, chained in the same way The GhostMaker had been.

"I have a message for you. From your friend," I whispered.

The man's eyes bored into me, and I knew he was trying to search out and extract any hint of fallacy. Perhaps now would be a good time to relay the message. "He said to remind you to stand strong, stand fast, and you'll both see the daylight," I said, hoping it was what I thought it was. I was no fool—secret messages were very familiar to me, and this one was definitely the kind you'd find from some silly hero tale. Why were they all so uncreative?

The man eyed me closer, tilting his head to one side in deep thought. Meanwhile, I did exactly what I had done with The GhostMaker, hanging the lantern and dragging the bucket up to him. "I'm just going to dress your wounds," I said reassuringly as his whole body tensed.

He wasn't in the best shape either, but he would be able to walk. Good. I would need that. Hopefully, he'd still be able to in another day or so. Hopefully, he'd keep his mind his own, too.

"Now before that, do you want a drink of water?" I said, prepared for the same battle I'd dealt with The GhostMaker.

The man narrowed his eyes and looked guardedly at me but nodded. Either this man was really too quick to trust, or the message from The GhostMaker really hit the spot.

I gave him a drink and then went about my work, patching him up as quickly as I could so I could have a little time to talk to him before Kithro got suspicious. This man seemed more reasonable, and though it could come back to bite me, I needed information.

"What is Skayla looking for?" I whispered.

For a moment, I thought I really had made a deadly mistake, for the man's face twisted up in a protective anger. Then he looked at me and asked, "Didn't he tell you?"

I shook my head. "He's not terribly well off," I half lied. He wasn't well off, but he could still have told me. This man seemed led more by the heart than by the head. Probably half the reason he was here, too.

I got a skeptical glance and then a whisper, "Friends of ours."

That was definitely not the whole thing. I could see the irrepressible look on his face; this man was not quite the liar The GhostMaker was. But I wouldn't press. At least I knew they had friends that were free. We'd need them.

"Do you know where they are?" I saw the fire alight in him and added quickly, "Don't tell me! I just need to know so that—" I lowered my voice even further—"so that you can get us there when I get you out."

His defensive demeanor lessened, but he still didn't look very convinced. I needed to know. If they did have friends on the outside, it would be easier for us to hide once we were out. Unfortunately, all my sources were here on the inside, or in the few other cities Skayla had left standing—such as Hytat, which was not exactly a day's ride let alone walk from here. Hence why I needed to get out. We needed better relay between the cities where I had contacts.

The man did not answer aloud, only nodding slowly. But that was enough.

I wanted to stay and talk more, but I was out of time. I had taken long enough with everything else, and I didn't want to give Kithro any reason to get me in more trouble. "I have to go. But I'll be back," I whispered before gathering up my things and calling as I always did for Kithro to come get me.

The door opened and Kithro's ugly mug appeared, allowing me to drag myself and my bucket out of the room. I was a little surprised—and apprehensive—to see we weren't the only ones down here. There in the hall, looking incredibly impatient, was a tall, raven-haired lady, long spindly fingers drumming restlessly on the pommel of her sword. She seemed to be trying to hide bitter uncertainty behind a stiff demeanor. Hm. She shot me a questioning, icy glare, which I made myself not return, instead looking at Kithro.

"I'll be back with supper in a little while," I assured him, already seeing the irritated look in his eyes. He would survive another hour.

"It had better be," he replied.

"Kithro. I don't have all day. Are you going to let me in, or do I have to report this to Skayla?" the lady butted in.

This made Kithro very indignant, and as he went to open the door to The GhostMaker's cell, I could hear him muttering darkly under his breath.

I didn't want to leave—worried at what the lady was doing down here—but Kithro would kill me if I didn't get going, and I couldn't afford to trip up now.

So, swallowing dread, I headed back towards the kitchen, knowing a long day of scrubbing pots and floors awaited me to keep my dread company.

Sven:

"Will you let me help now?" Namaya asked as she toted the medical supplies in front of me. "You and Sefen are going to waste away down here, and whether you like it or not, I'm your only chance at getting out. I'm working on a plan, but for the meantime, I need you to stay *alive*. You're looking pretty bad."

"I...I'm confused," I whispered, tired and feverish. Hadn't she just been in here? "I thought you already had a plan..."

"What?" Namaya stared at me. "No, I—" Her eyes narrowed. "I haven't figured one out yet. Who else have you been talking to?"

Stupid brain. There had been someone else, right? At this point, I guess I could have made them up, but regardless, it hadn't been Namaya. What had the woman's name been again...Estasia? That was it. She was real. She was real, and I had just let it slip to Namaya. I was such an idiot. "I don't know anymore, I can't even remember why I'm here," I lied—but only this time. If she'd asked twenty minutes ago, it might have been the truth.

Namaya looked exasperated but disguised it with a scoff. "It doesn't matter. The only one that would be in any way insane enough to help you would be a slave, and they can do nothing."

And people wondered why Baeno was in this whole mess to begin with. This attitude. Things had been handed to them on a silver platter by me and my sisters to the point that no one bothered to solve their own problems—no one had hope after we weren't there to give it.

"Whatever you say." I blinked, realizing my head was drooping against my bidding.

"Hold still, I'm going to see what I can do about you. You look sick." Namaya's tone changed, and I heard her come closer. I was too tired to make any objections this time.

Whether I liked to admit it, the salve made a difference even if I was still fevered. Whatever that salve was had to have been influenced with Namaya's Gift, however, as no natural remedy could have made me feel this improved *this* quickly.

Still, I did not give a thank you. Was she baiting me? Was she trying to get me to lead her back to Baey and the others, only to turn them in to Skayla?

"That will hold you for now, at least. But I can't properly heal you until we get out of here."

I didn't say a word.

Namaya huffed, and I watched as her hands clenched and unclenched fiercely. "Fine, don't thank me. Don't believe me. You'll see— I'll make this right. I will come back soon, and I'll get you both out. Just— don't...go anywhere." She swung around and headed for the iron door. "Kithro, you slob, get up off that stool and open this door!"

The door was opened, and soon I was once more left alone in the darkness. It wasn't exactly a good thing. I tried to keep my mind from wandering, but that wasn't exactly something I was good at anymore.

Skayla. Think of Skayla. I didn't want to. More than anything I didn't want to see what she had become—and I didn't want to remember who she had been. What had happened? In the eight long years she'd been mercilessly in my head, I hadn't found out. The eight years I had been forced to grovel and do her every bidding—still I had not discovered it. The change had just been so drastic, so startling. Or had she hidden that, too?

Yet I remembered the day I could best trace it back to. It was the day the Drogans had appeared in Baeno. I remembered Ovok, claiming they'd been on some world called Eatris and hunted. And then, the protests against the beasts...and Skayla always against them. I'd been against them, too, at first. Until Skayla had started to change. She'd stopped talking to me, stopped confiding. First, she'd withdrawn, then....

"Stop it Sven, you're wandering," I whispered harshly to myself, exasperated. I needed to think of what was happening *now*. What if I became so focused on what had happened that I forgot all that was taking place now? A shudder ran through me, causing me to wince. I couldn't afford to get lost in my head. Not here. Honestly, I was surprised I'd remembered any of that.

I strained my eyes against the darkness, again inspecting my restraints. Even though I had already looked at it many times, I tried to find some flaw—anything. It was like the predicament the world was in. But my old strength from before this nightmare was long gone, and there was a reason Kovo and Skayla were keeping me this weak. Weak meant I couldn't use my Gift to escape—it kept me trapped here, under Skayla. Again. Always in her grasp.

CHAPTER XII: To Free a Prisoner...Or Two

Estasia:

I couldn't sleep. One more day. That's all I had between now and when I would try to get them out. If I waited too much longer, they might not be able to walk out, let alone *ride*—even as it was, it was doubtful if The GhostMaker would be able to. What in the world was I going to do? I only hoped he would at least be able to stay on a horse. If only I could get them out in the morning but no. No. The pipes' maintenance was scheduled for the day after tomorrow and that meant the engineers—glorified slaves, themselves—wouldn't be in position until then. The burst pipes would be a vital distraction to keep us from being spotted as we rode out of this nightmare.

Which led to my next problem. The horses of Skayla's soldiers were always shod with a special bar across that set apart their tracks from others, so that a stolen one could easily be tracked down. The only way to steal one was if they had just been brought in by locals or from somewhere other than Bethyn. That was the other reason I had to wait another day: The horses seized after the attack on Kaedna had been brought in late last night—a full day later than I'd hoped. Tanya's brother Jeth was a stable boy and in charge of getting three unmarked horses set aside for us, but now he wouldn't be able to secure both that and the confiscated tack in time to leave in the morning—and I couldn't do it in the evening; we needed to drug the soldiers during the morning meal.

I suppose it wasn't a horrible thing to have the whole day tomorrow to make sure all was in order, but I worried for the two men in the dungeons. Both had actually looked surprisingly better this evening, and the fresh bandaging on them had not come from me; perhaps Kovo had decided to give them some proper care in the hopes they would last longer.

I sighed as I lay on my cot, staring at the ceiling and listening to the rumble of the fortress around me.

We just had to make it through tomorrow. They could hang on for one more day.

Right?

I didn't get any rest that night, tossing and turning as thoughts raged like an ocean in the storm, trying to find a way to even out the odds against me. Now, against my will, I had one more day to figure it out. I had to force myself to calm down. What was wrong with me? I'd taken plenty of risks before, gotten away with my life plenty of times, and done last-minute changes before. The only difference was that now, I had lives other than my own hanging in the balance, and that was something that I didn't like gambling with.

I forced myself to eat the usual breakfast rations, even though I hadn't the stomach for them. I'd need all the strength I could get before what would happen.

Then, just like always, it was down to the dungeons, past the rows of solemn prison doors and down the stairs. The hurried steps of someone behind me startled me, and I moved to the side, quickly kneeling down as I recognized the heavy, irritated steps of Lord Kovo. My jaw clenched and a deep-rooted dismay rushed to the surface of my thoughts, and I wished that I could will the heartless piece of dirt to turn around.

Don't go down those stairs, please. Just be checking on one of the other prisoners on this level. Anything. Please. My heart stopped as he paused a moment in front of me, and I dared not look up.

"So, on time today, are we?"

Still not looking up, I nodded, not needing to fake anxiety this time. "Yes, sir."

Without another word he turned and stalked down the hall, vanishing down the stairs.

Taking a gulp of air, I forced myself up, walking down where he had just disappeared. I heard the eerie sound of a cell door closing shut, and I winced. If only I could have gotten them out yesterday. What if, even now, I was about to be too late? Stupid horses.

I walked up to Kithro, swallowing my sudden doubt and asked, "How many today?"

"Five on the second level, two on the first. These two get none. And then me," he replied, sitting back in his stool and leaning against the wall, biting his dirty nails like some toddler.

I nodded quickly and turned, leaving as fast as I calmly could, but my senses were now on high alert as my anxiety spiked. I walked up the various stairs, flinching at every sound that rang through the hallways. The click of the mechanical messaging system that shot scrolls through chutes to various rooms in the fortress, the clacking of a typewriter's keys as I passed one of the military conference rooms.... I was almost thankful for the constant noise of the kitchen as I arrived, even if the smell of a million pans of pottage cooking made me nauseous. I was not at my best—but that didn't matter. I had to be.

I went up to Aekon, forcing my heart to stop pounding. *"We should have found a way to get them out today,"* I said.

"You have a plan, you'll do fine," he said calmly, stirring a big iron pot with a stained wooden spoon.

"I'm worried about him. The lord went down into the dungeons this morning." I forced the panic out of my voice, making sure not to refer to Kovo by name so his name couldn't be recognized should someone be listening in.

Apparently, Aekon still managed to catch my worry, however. *"Esa, relax. You say yourself that panic is a merciless enemy. It'll work out. Don't lose hope. Give Ateli the ointment today so she can give it to Tanya. Do you have it with you?"*

I nodded. *"Yes."*

"Then give it to her—and Esa?"

I looked intently at him, waiting as he tasted whatever he was cooking.

"How many today?"

I sighed, rolling my eyes as some of my tension released. Good old Aekon, always pretending nothing was wrong. *"Seven, including Kithro."* I replied. He gave that shooing gesture as always, and with that I went over to Ateli, repeating the rations for her. The girl started loading a tray for me, taking things off a nearby counter.

"Here. Let me help," I offered, taking one of the dishes and going to put it on the tray. Then, just before it reached the tray, I fumbled, dropping the plate so it clattered noisily on the floor, the meager contents spilling on the floor.

I was instantly on my knees with Ateli, feigning dismay and trying to help her pick it up. "I am so sorry, Ateli. Here, let me help."

In one movement, I slipped my hand into my pocket where the little bottle of ointment had been stowed, and then in the next I brushed my hand against Ateli's, slipping the glass vial under her palm. She didn't even blink, instantly knowing what to do, even though she hadn't expected it until tomorrow morning.

"Wait, wait," I said, giving her a knowing look so she knew that she was still not to give the ointment to Tanya. Hopefully, we could wait until tomorrow—but just in case. "Why don't we get a broom or something?" I suggested to hide my earlier comment.

Ateli shook her head. "No, it's fine. I understand." She paused just for a second there and then continued, "You were just trying to help. Why don't you finish loading the tray, so Kithro doesn't kill you for being late with his food?"

"Thanks," I said, taking in a deep breath and doing as she suggested. I then hurried out of the kitchen, balancing the tray expertly through the flurry of slaves and cooks.

I made it out of the kitchen, but I had barely started making my way down the hall when someone grabbed my arm and pulled me into a quiet side passage. My heart raced, but instincts forced me to keep calm.

There in front of me was the tall lady from yesterday, looking just as irritated and impatient as before.

"Well?" she asked, drumming her fingers on her sword.

"What?" I asked incredulously, not bothering with a guise now. She didn't seem like the type that liked cowardly mice.

"Sven. He talked to you, didn't he?" she pressed.

"...Who is Sven?" The question was genuine.

The woman gave an undignified grunt. "You're not fooling anyone."

Actually, I was. Quite a lot of people. At least…I hoped.

"But you're confusing me," I countered. Well, just me, that was.

"You're the one, aren't you?"

The lady, as antagonistic as she was, was so sure that I knew exactly what she was talking about that I couldn't help but be the slightest bit perturbed. But I did have to tread carefully—I didn't know much of who this lady was, and for all I knew, she could be a dear friend of Skayla.

Then it clicked. Skayla…Skayla Mara. She'd had a brother—Sven. I fought the instinct to catch my breath as a sudden thought occurred. You had to be kidding me.... The GhostMaker was *Sven Mara?* I forced myself out of the startling revelation and back into the problem before me.

"I'm not anyone but myself, and if you'll excuse me, I need to get this food down to Kithro before he kills me." I went to leave, hoping that she wouldn't stop me. Even worse was the fear that she knew something and would tell Lord Kovo. I did not want that.

The lady stepped in my path, and my heart plummeted like a dead bird from the sky. Great. This was not going to end well. I held my breath as the lady reached into the pocket of her coat, pulling out a small vial. It was the vial I had just put into the cupboard the other day.

"Is this yours?" She looked suddenly quite pleased with herself, and I rebuked myself for having shown my open dismay. How had she gotten it? "I saw you go into the closet and found this. It's a good duplicate, but it doesn't *quite* smell right."

What was I going to do now? I tried to come up with options but to no avail. However, I was not going to continue to let her see how apprehensive and panicked I now was, and with every conscious effort I could muster, I kept a calm demeanor. "I don't know what you're talking about," I replied.

The lady rolled her eyes. "Stop lying, or I'll bring this right to Lord Kovo," she threatened me, and I wasn't sure whether to be hopeful or even more anxious. This meant two things; either she hadn't brought this to Lord Kovo yet, or she was just saying that to get me to confess.

"I don't have anything to confess." I stuck to my lie, closely watching her reaction. The panic had been, as always, replaced with adrenaline, and the small hole of an escape started to urge me on, clearing my mind. "Search me. I don't have the ointment."

The lady sighed. "Of course, you don't, you probably hid it in some corner of this forsaken place."

Hm. The way she said that was quite interesting. "Is a confession all you want? If so, you might as well bring it up to Lord Kovo now, because I'm not giving one." I stood firm and hoped my gut wasn't leading me to my death.

"No. I want the truth," she urged. She wasn't very good at this, was she? The more I watched her, the more I noticed the sweaty palms, the nervously darting eyes. Aha. I recognized those symptoms well.

"Why don't you give *me* the truth?" I turned the question on her, seeing now that she really wasn't in control. Only, she didn't know this yet.

She looked taken aback by my question and didn't answer for a moment. "What?" was the highly intelligent, very thought over answer she gave me. It only affirmed my suspicions. So now to capitalize on her 'disease.'

"Lying isn't going to make me want to tell you the truth," I pressed. Come on, come on. Every move from now had to be calculated. I needed to push her but not too far. This lady was practically being driven by what ailed her—guilt.

She looked incensed, taking several staggering breaths before managing to get herself under control enough to reply, "I can leave, and I *will* tell Lord Kovo that you stole the ointment, and he will see to it that you never do so again."

I was hanging on the edge of the cliff, hoping my instinct wasn't just leading me on. "But then you'll get Sven killed," I said.

The lady stopped dead there, staring at me with guilt-ridden, conflicted eyes. I saw the words working over and over in her mind as she tried to decide which voice to follow, and I only hoped she picked the right one. "So, you *are* the one," she finally said.

I still wasn't quite sure what she meant by that, but I was *not* going to tell her that. "I didn't say that."

"Tell me why you took the ointment." Her voice turned hard again, and I feared I'd lost her—but her eyes said otherwise.

Here came the biggest gamble of all. If I was right, I might gain an ally, but if I was wrong...I didn't want to go there. "Go ahead and run to Lord Kovo. It doesn't matter to you."

I watched her break, slowly seeing that she was not going to win this argument. I made myself not breathe out in relief, just in case.

She looked around quickly and then addressed me. "I want to help."

CHAPTER XIII: Sacrifices

Estasia:

It had been a long day. After giving out rations, I'd been scrubbing floors until evening, and after that I'd had to do evening rations—which I had just finished. My head ached with tension. So far, both Sefen and The GhostMaker—Sven Mara, if that *was* who he was—looked to be hanging on. I wondered if Namaya was the one tending to them.

My footsteps echoed hollowly across the hall as I made my way back to the slaves' quarters. Tonight was the last night, and I didn't know if it would come together tomorrow. Plans always seemed better until you had to execute them.

I entered into the ill-lit room, slaves scattered throughout, some preparing to sleep and others talking in hushed voices to each other. I immediately spotted Tanya and made my way over, knowing I was being watched closely. Skayla always had a spy in here somewhere—and you never could know for sure who to trust. But I usually had an eye for it.

Tanya saw me and met me halfway, managing a small smile in greeting, "Esa, I was beginning to wonder if you'd been locked down there, yourself." Her tone was that of relief.

I had been terribly late because of the...discussion...I'd had with Namaya. To say the least, Kithro had not been very pleased.

"How's Jeth?" I dared to ask. She only saw her young brother when he came in for his rations or if they somehow crossed paths during the day. Today it was vital that he get to her, so he could relay whether or not he had gotten the unmarked horses.

Tanya shrugged. "He didn't have much time. Only said he was doing alright and that the horses kept him busier than ever. Some had even almost gotten a man killed, they were so frisky. But he said all went well and that he's not been scratched in the least."

Good. Very good. At least that had gone well. "That's good. Horses can be dangerous." I continued the conversation so that any undesirable listeners wouldn't catch on to the fact that Tanya had been relaying a totally different message.

"Yes. I worry for him, Esa." Tanya was sincere as she spoke, eyes darkening. It took me a couple seconds to realize why she looked so anxious. Jeth could take care of himself, so I saw no reason for worry. Only in this last year or two had I started to form a bond with those that were helping me, and really, I still often found myself uncomfortable with the feelings of attachment people had with each other. Even now, I kept myself separate.

"He takes care of himself, don't worry." I tried to sound reassuring, tried to sound like I knew what I was talking about. But no, at twenty-six, I still had very little idea what it really meant to have a family, or friend, or anything. My very small experience with it hadn't really made me want to ever put real effort into having any of those.

I banished the bitter thoughts, needing a clear head for the plan tomorrow. I said goodnight to Tanya and made my way to my bunk, plopping down and trying to refocus. But my mind wandered, finding its way to Sven Mara, his friend, and then Namaya. What if I couldn't get him out of the cell? What would happen if I couldn't even do that much?

And Namaya. She had tried to wring it out of me what I was going to do, but I'd refused. I touched the glass vial she had given me. Right before she had finally let me go, she'd pressed it into my hand and told me to use it on Sven. She said it would help him. But I had limited knowledge of medicine, and not being able to find out what it was, I dared not use it on him. Perhaps Lytho would have a clue—but I couldn't get to him. The women were always kept in a separate room from the men, and I couldn't risk getting caught the night before I would escape. But if it really was something useful, it would have helped me feel a little less doubtful about this strange woman.

I had asked Sefen—Sven's friend—and he had said she'd betrayed them and turned them over to Skayla. That would be the reason for the guilt that was eating her up. But could I trust her now? Traitors were not only cowards, but ones with little idea of what side they were on. You never knew when they would switch. So what side was she on? I just hoped that if my plan did go awry and she was there, she would help. But again, hopefully I would not have to find out.

A guard came in and the few lanterns in the room were put out, and everyone was ordered into bed. When the guard left, I turned over on my mat, once more going over the plan.

Ateli had gotten the ointment and would put it in the soldiers' food tomorrow morning. Lytho had told me it would take until about noon for it to completely take effect, so I would just take my sweet time getting down to care for the two prisoners, making a stop at my secret corner to get the knife from the back—just in case. Kithro would also be getting a good dose of it, so hopefully he would be out cold by the time I got down there. I'd then get the keys, get the two out, and we would head for the stables.

Jeth had transferred the food from my secret store to the stables and with that we would have enough for a couple days. The problem was, would they be able to ride?

I had to believe everything would go well. We'd planned this, it had been good in theory. Ketique would hopefully be blamed for poisoning the food, as Ateli would make sure to put some in Jeth's food, and Aekon's, and herself, along with a couple other slaves. The only ones to blame would be Ketique and me. It was Ketique's medicine, Ketique's food wouldn't be drugged, and he was disagreeable enough that it wouldn't be hard to get the others in the fortress to point fingers at him. The only thing that wouldn't be able to be explained away was the planned bursting of the pipes. It would help stall any scouting parties, but would they just think I did it? Or would they know of the other slaves' participation?

Doubt still crept in the corners of my mind, but I fought it off. No. This was not the time for doubt. Curling up under my one very thin and insufficient blanket, I closed my eyes, not letting that word out of my thoughts.

No.

Never in my whole history of thievery and risks had I been this nervous. As I made my way down to ask Kithro for the usual count, I could feel my palms sweating. What was wrong with me? I relied on my steel nerves and wit. If I managed to lose those, I was dead for sure.

Usually, the adrenaline rush was a thrill but not today. Today, I had more hanging in the balance than myself, and I didn't like it.

"On time, rat? That's a surprise." Kithro's voice heralded me from across the hall, and I forced myself to remain calm. I felt as jumpy as a rabbit.

"Yes, sir," I mumbled. "How many today?"

"Two on the first level, none on the second. The two worms in these cells get food and water today." He jerked a grimy finger in the direction of Sefen and Sven's cells. "If they're alive, that is. Kovo wasn't too happy with that one." He pointed to Sven's cell, and my heart felt faint. No, no, no. He'd been looking so much better yesterday. He had to be alright. He would be, even if I had to make him! Kithro's foul grin made me want to hit him over the head with his own keys, but I only cowered, making him think his warning had worked on me.

"I'll return with your food," I said quietly, turning and making myself move as slowly as I always did. I couldn't mess up only hours before. The adrenaline pulsing through me urged me to run, to fly, to do anything but walk, but years of dealing with this had helped me rein it in and harness it. Still, today was not the most in-control I had ever been.

I entered the kitchen, the hustle and bustle overwhelming this morning. Everyone seemed to be making some sort of unnecessary noise, disturbing my already stirred-up thoughts. But I stuffed the feelings down, deliberating every step as a step closer to freedom. Not just for me, but for the two that were down *there*.

"*All is ready?*" I asked as I came up to Aekon.

The Rugonian nodded and stirred his pot. "*How many today?*" he asked casually.

I sighed, not really knowing whether his calm demeanor right now was helpful or stressful. *"Four, and then Kithro. The two at the bottom are to get food today. Not that that will matter much,"* I replied, calming my nerves a little as routine and Aekon's confidence began to sink in.

"Good. Are you ready, Esa?" He turned to me for a moment, his eyes searching me.

I nodded. Yes. Yes, I was. I knew part of Aekon still wondered if I really had changed, if I really was different from the thief who only cared about surviving. But I knew I was. *"Yes, Aekon. And I will be in touch as soon as possible"*—although who knew when that would be. *Hopefully, I will be in touch*, I thought doubtfully.

The usual shooing gesture was given, and I went off to Ateli. The girl looked dead calm, smiling at me like nothing in the world was the matter. I wished I felt that way.

"How many today, Estasia?" she asked, cocking her head.

"Four and then Kithro," I repeated, going over to help her with the food. It didn't take long for her to ration it out, having very few numbers this time. Helping her calmed my nerves a little and seeing her so collected reminded me of how unprofessional I was acting. I'd been doing things like this practically since I was born; *I* was the one who should be calm and untouchable. I usually was. So, with a deep breath, I forced myself to be. I reminded myself of the thousands of other times I'd gotten myself into huge risks like this, and how I had always come out with my skin intact.

Taking up the tray, I nodded farewell—and good luck—to Ateli and headed out of the kitchen. Too late to turn back now. I passed soldiers in the hall as they went to get their rations, hoping there was enough in the bottle for what was needed. We couldn't drug all of them, but it would hopefully bring enough chaos to the scene to help us go mostly unnoticed.

I walked with a determination down the hall to the last set of stairs, reminding myself that today would be the last day in this stink hole. I was getting out. But I also reminded myself of all those that were helping, who weren't able to leave. I wouldn't abandon them. Just as I had promised, I wouldn't abandon them.

"Hurry up, rat!" Kithro yelled at me as I made my way down the hall, looking with impatient longing at the food.

Little did he know that this food would give him quite the coma later. If all went as planned, and if Ateli had put the proper amount in.

I laid the tray down and picked up Kithro's food, and no sooner had I gotten it off than he snatched the plate from me, gobbling it down hungrily.

I moved on to the rest of my job, sliding the plates of food under the small iron slits. Soon, they wouldn't be here any longer, anyway.

I finished a little sooner than I'd hoped and realized I would have to stall for time if I was to get back down at noon. But with my reputation that shouldn't be hard.

I walked slowly back to the kitchen, watching the soldiers closely as they passed me in the corridors. I looked for signs of drowsiness, or anything that would show if the stuff was working. I knew it hadn't been long since they had eaten, that I needed to be patient and wait for the effects, but it sounded so much easier in theory.

Upon returning the tray to the kitchen, I noticed that Ateli and Aekon were actually looking a little drowsy. It made sense—slaves ate early in the morning when they arose.

After helping with some of the dishwashing, I plucked myself up and next headed off to Ketique's domain, suddenly apprehensive that Namaya had told him about the missing ointment. Even if she had, it hopefully wouldn't have complicated things—unless Namaya or Ketique had also told Skayla and Lord Kovo.

I masked my nervousness as I walked in, going over to Lytho to get supplies for the two prisoners. Ketique would notice me soon enough and shove the boy out of the way and going to Lytho instead might get Ketique in an even more argumentative mood.

"I need supplies," I said as I came up next to the short boy. He looked at me with eyes that showed how nervous he was. I was still not the one to trust people fully, and I wondered if he—or any of the others—would really have the strength to keep our group secret if one of them was found out. Lytho was just a boy and skittish at that. What would happen if they saw his nervousness after we escaped?

Not now, Esa. I rebuked myself.

Lytho averted his eyes then, taking a breath and seemingly trying to calm himself. He was just about to speak when I heard a roaring voice.

"Rat! What are you trying to pull, ah?" Ketique came storming up, his eagle nose poking itself in others' business whenever given the chance. Right now, he was just doing the predictable and unknowingly helping me out tremendously. I needed a good way to waste time right now.

"I'm ju-just getting the s-supplies for the prisoners." I countered.

Ketique snorted. "You know very well you are to come to me for that, rat." He seemed to puff up to twice his size, and I just sighed.

Lytho quickly ducked away, not wanting to get in the way of two arguing thieves. "O-o-oh I'm s-so sorry. I forgot," I said innocently.

This did not seem to please Ketique in the least, and he started huffing in and out like a fevered cow. "Forgot? Aren't we a clever little rat now?" His lips twitched into an unsuccessful smile, and he put his hands on his hips. "I will get your supplies this time, and you will not be bargaining for anything," he spat.

I watched him with satisfaction as he disappeared into the supplies closet, emerging minutes later with an empty bucket and two rags. "This is all you get. If you dare drag your worthless self in here again today, I'll wring your neck."

Little did he know that I wouldn't be back in this room ever. If everything went well, that was.

I nodded and gave another innocent look, retreating from the room with my bucket and meager supply of rags. As slowly as I possibly could, I made my way up to the courtyard. Once at the well outside, I took my sweet time lowering the bucket, watching in assumed exhaustion as the bucket hit the bottom, filled with water, and sat there.

That done, I started back to the fortress, wary and ready for the task ahead.

Then I began to notice it: As I entered back into the fortress halls, there were fewer soldiers, and some of the soldiers I passed seemed to be walking in mud, each movement slowed. It was working.

By the time I had made it to the floor above the upper dungeon, I saw a soldier or two passed out on the floor or slumped up against the wall. Hope surged within me, and for the first time, I felt the normal effects of adrenaline. Energy pulsed through every part of my body, and I felt ready to take on Skayla herself—not that I *wanted* it to come to that.

Hopeful, I reached the bottom dungeon, and to my joy saw Kithro leaning listlessly against the wall, snoring.

I dropped my bucket and ran up to him, quickly inspecting him before going for his keys.

Suddenly his hand moved, and he grabbed my arm. "What are you doing, rat?!" he asked fiercely, an evident, sluggish drawl showing the effects of the drug. I had been too quick. Taking the knife from its concealed place, I brought the hilt down on his head. Kithro was almost completely out cold as it was, and the smack completed it. I breathed out, relieved, then took the keys. My hands were steady as I found the key that unlocked Sefen's cell door, bursting in with a lantern.

The man was startled, apparently having been asleep, and now forced himself to stand up, his chains having been loosened enough so he could actually sleep on the floor. He looked defensively at me before realizing who it was.

"What are you doing?" he asked, a look of bewilderment on his face.

"Getting you out of here like I said I would. Can you walk?" I asked, coming up and finding the key that went to his chains.

He nodded and gave a hoarse, "Yes."

I put another key in the lock, and this time when I tried to turn it, I heard the satisfying click. Soon, I had the man completely free, and he used my shoulder to steady himself a moment. "Where's Sven?" he asked, concern etched in every line of his worn face.

"I haven't let him out yet."

He nodded and unsteadily followed me out the cell door. I instantly set upon Sven's lock, throwing the door open as quickly as I could. My heart plummeted. Sven Mara was no longer where he had been, for

Kithro had released Sven as well so that he was now lying in the corner of the cell. But unlike Sefen, he was not awake. Both Sefen and I ran up to him, and to my dismay he was still completely unconscious.

Sefen knelt down, shaking him. "Sven, Sven, you idiot, wake up!" he urged with his sorely scratched voice. I thought about using the potion Namaya had given me but still decided against it. What if it was really something to kill him?

I knelt on the other side, stopping Sefen. "Careful, you'll hurt him," I said quietly, "Let me try." He backed off a little and I bit my lip, trying to look as if I'd done this a million times. I only looked like I knew a lot about medicine.

Even in the dim light of my lantern, I could see Sven Mara's pale face, his chest rising shallowly up and down. "Take this," I muttered, handing the lantern to Sefen. I took my keys and started to search for the ones to unlock Sven's restraints. Finally, I found it, and the case clicked open.

"Sven," I whispered, taking his hand and squeezing it, hoping the sudden pressure might wake him. "Wake up. We need to get going. You can't just walk out on us now." I tried to will him awake, knowing every moment was precious. "Sven Mara. Stop being selfish." He wasn't, but I was desperately trying to find any angle that, if he could hear me, would give him the will to come back. "You don't have time to rest. We need you."

My heart jumped up to my throat and my stomach fluttered as I saw his eyelids twitch and then slowly open to reveal those hazy, haunted eyes. His skin looked clammy and fevered. Not good at all.

"There you are, idiot," I muttered in doubtful relief.

"Hm?" he said faintly, looking confused.

Sefen helped me prop Sven up, and I winced with every movement, hoping we weren't hurting him, but knowing it was impossible not to do so.

"Who…wh-where…" he murmured disjointedly, looking hazily from Sefen to me.

Sefen sighed. "Naturally, you had to forget now…Sven. It's me, Sefen Kalaesia. We're in the Kovian Fortress, and if you don't get yourself together, we're going to become permanent residents. I didn't think you were *that* fond of the place." There was a bad attempt at cheer there.

I watched as something in Sven's delirious mind clicked, and his eyes forced themselves open a little farther. Ever so slowly his arms moved, and his hands braced against the ground as if to get up.

"You can't walk," I said desperately, not catching myself in time to stop. Unfortunately, if he could somehow manage to stand with our support, it would help. "Let us help, at least," I added.

"No, no…" He looked at me for a moment, as if seeing me for the first time. "I'm—" he stopped and winced as he vainly tried to get up—"fine."

"No, you're not, and if you don't want to get us all killed, you'll let us help you up." This seemed to shock him into obedience, and together Sefen and I were somehow able to get him to his feet…sort of.

With painful slowness, we made our way out of the cell, leaving the lantern behind. I cast a quick look at the unconscious Kithro and had to remind myself he was asleep. Then, step by step, we started up the dungeon stairs. My senses felt magnified to ten times their original strength, straining to hear if any footsteps were near.

We managed to get up to the second level of the dungeon and still we ran into nobody—as expected. However, as we neared the next set

238

of stairs, a wild, muffled commotion started making its way down. The whole place was probably in an uproar, with half of the soldiers drowsed, drugged, or completely passed out. The pipes were scheduled to burst soon, meaning even more chaos would soon erupt.

To my horror, I heard the sound of hurried steps coming towards us, and we had no time to find any place to hide ourselves before the person came down the stairs and stood face to face with us. When I saw who it was, I wasn't sure whether to be relieved, or terrified.

"Namaya," Sefen said through gritted teeth.

She looked in dismay from the half-conscious Sven Mara to Sefen. "I hoped I would find you down here, still. I smelled that ointment in my food and had a feeling something was about to go down. What—what happened?" She took a step closer, and I started to feel for my knife. Which was hard when also supporting a man.

"You, Namaya." Sefen let out the tortured, growling reply.

She stared at him a moment, deep hurt in her eyes. "Let me help, I can help divert the soldiers," she said at last, the pressure of guilt beginning to disappear a little from her eyes as the prospect of making amends came closer into view.

Before Sefen could say anything, I broke in. "Fine." We didn't have time, and I could see that she did want to try to make things right. We needed all the help we could get.

Sven said something, but I couldn't hear, his voice was so soft.

"We need to get to the stables," I said.

"Follow me." Namaya's eyes were alight, almost to the point of madness, and she took off quickly. I wondered if she had forgotten that we had a very wounded Sven Mara to drag with us, but she reappeared as swiftly as she had vanished. "It's clear," she said breathlessly as she ran back down the stairs, coming up to us then and relieving a begrudging Sefen of Sven's weight.

She and I got him up the stairs and to the next flight that led to the top level; then she disappeared again.

It was nerve-wracking, and every noise made my heart jump.

Namaya came bounding down the stairs right before we made them, shaking her head violently. "Wait. Let me distract them," she said quickly before running up the stairs again, without much except trust for an explanation. This was definitely a trial by fire.

I heard her yelling but couldn't distinguish what she was saying. Hopefully it was *not* giving our position away. I put my hand where my knife was, just in case.

Naturally, Sven took that opportune time to go limp. Not good.

"Bad timing, *bad timing*," I said with a grunt as I had to let go of my knife and grab him. Sefen made a very similar noise to mine, having less success than me in holding him up.

Namaya came down then and instantly ran over to help. Between the three of us, we got him up the stairs and set him by a wall.

"Wake up," I said through gritted teeth, shaking him a little and trying to get him to open his eyes again. For a dreadful moment, I thought he wouldn't, but then the eyelids flickered, and his eyes were visible once again.

"Sorry…did I…miss something?" he whispered feverishly.

I tried to smile. "No. You're fine. Let me help you up." I took one side and Namaya took the other, and once again we started down the hall.

As we continued along, we began to see the carnage of Tanya and Ateli's well-done job. Soldiers lay slumped against the walls, groaning or completely passed out. They'd come through once again. Then I noticed other bodies...bodies of the dead. I gave a brief look to Namaya. I guess she really *was* helping us.

As we got closer to the courtyard, however, we started running into more and more soldiers who were awake and panicking. Then, soldiers started to notice us. Namaya let go of Sven and took out her sword, taking care of those in the way. I swallowed the bile in my throat. I was a thief and a risk taker, not a killer, and it wrenched my gut to see death. No matter how much I'd seen it.

We managed to make it to the door to the courtyard, and once more Sven fell.

"The Drogans will be outside. I'll get them out of the way," Namaya said.

"Don't you think we accounted for that?" I asked even as I noted the water dripping down from the ceiling. The pipes would keep the fortress nice and busy. "That being said, go ahead and double check that the coast is clear, by all means." She'd played look out well, so far.

Namaya threw a glare my way but didn't argue, leaving Sefen a short sword before disappearing behind the door.

I turned my attention back to Sven. "Come on, Mara, don't desert us now." I said softly, "We're almost there. Just hang on." I took his hand and squeezed it again, hoping it would work just like it had before.

It didn't and I resorted to shaking him. Namaya reappeared then looked down at us.

"All clear. Go get the horses you need and bring them here," she said.

I didn't know what to do. I didn't want to leave Sefen and Sven to Namaya. What if she was setting us up? Doubt crept back in, and I hesitated.

"There's no time!"

She was right. Whether she was a traitor or not, if I stayed a minute longer, we could all wind up dead. So, knife in hand, I nodded, getting up and slipping out the door.

A cold breeze greeted me, and I was thankful that the sun was hidden deep behind dark rain clouds. Good. Rain to hide our tracks, and the dark to shield our eyes. After being in the dungeon for so long, I had a feeling Sefen would not easily adjust to any sudden light.

Soldiers ran helter-skelter around the courtyard, shouting and trying to reach the nearest door inside, a few of which I knew for a fact were locked, thanks to some of the slaves. Anything to add to the chaos.

It only took me seconds to make it across to the stables, and I rushed inside, quickly searching the horses for the three Jeth had saved. They were already out and tied to the barn wall, saddled and ready to go. I noted the supply bags and whispered a thanks to Jeth even though he wasn't here. A thought occurred then, and before grabbing the horses, I found a rope lead and slung it over my shoulder. Then I somehow managed to grab the reins of all three horses and keep them in check. They all were very calm—Jeth had chosen well. I only hoped this wouldn't change when the chaos outside rushed upon them.

I led them out, instantly lost in the flurry of commotion as soldiers ran around like ants who had just had their hill stamped out—many carrying sandbags and other materials that were clearly meant to try and stop the rush of water the burst pipes inside had released. As quickly as I could,

I made my way to the door on the opposite side of the courtyard, where I saw Namaya waiting. When I reached her, she took the reins from me. "Sefen will need your help with Sven. I tried to help him but didn't have much on me," she said, jerking her head at the door.

I nodded and slipped back inside, finding Sven still on the ground but awake—barely. The worst of his wounds were better bandaged with what seemed to be Namaya's shirt-sleeve, but physically, he was only getting worse. With more difficulty than the other two times, Sefen and I got Sven up, but at this point he was giving us almost no help. Not good *at all.* I opened the door, and we emerged outside.

The first challenge was to get Sven on the horse, and somehow, we succeeded. He looked like death as he teetered from atop the horse, but he did stay on, gripping the pommel of the saddle tightly, half-conscious as he was. Then I took the rope I'd confiscated and used it to tie Sven to the saddle, hoping it was enough to keep him secure should his consciousness wane again. After that, I helped Sefen up. He was a mess as well, but at least would be able to steer the horse. Then I got on my own mount, pulling my horse back to where Sven was so that I could keep him and his horse in check.

I could almost taste freedom, and I couldn't believe we were so close. Would it really work? "We need to go around back to the side gate," I ordered our group as Namaya hopped up behind Sefen on his horse, and together we rode through the oblivious fray of the fortress. The chaos seemed to reach a new level, and I heard shouts about a flood inside. Perfect.

"You three wait out of sight while I check the gate," I said as I got ready to slip off my horse.

"No, let me." Namaya was quicker to dismount. "I'll be less suspicious should anyone see."

My jaw clenched, and I wanted to refuse. But at this point, honestly, if she'd wanted to turn us in, she would have done it by now. My biggest concern at this point was more that she was trying to tag along in order to see where Sven's friends were and report them to Skayla—and that was a problem we could sort out after we at least got a day's journey away from this awful place.

So, I nodded. "Alright."

I grabbed hold of Sven's reins and led his horse over to the shadow of the gatehouse, where we watched Namaya get the gates open.

That's when I saw her, her blond hair half up and half splayed in the wind, her face twisted up in disgust. "And what do you think you're doing?" Skayla's voice rang loud enough for me to hear. I swallowed hard.

Panic washed briefly over Namaya's face as she stumbled for a reply, "I-I saw someone slip through the gates. I was going to follow them."

"Oh?"

"Yes—I think they were trying to escape in the middle of the chaos."

"Do you, now? Then why does it sound so much like you're *lying?*" Skayla took a step closer and bile rose in my throat. Oh no.

"I-I wasn't."

"Please. You can come clean with me, Namaya. You're so torn up inside. I understand. What's weighing on you?"

Even though the words were not directed at me, I felt the allure of them. Skayla was using her Gift, and we were all about to be made. Slowly, I started contemplating what we could do now. My hand rested by my dagger.

"You." Namaya's answer rang clear. "You're what's weighing on my mind. You told me they would be safe—that no one would harm them. You told me you'd see to it personally. And instead, my husband is trapped in your horrid dungeons wasting away!"

"So, you're betraying me then? You're leaving?"

"Yes." I saw Namaya sway as if in a trance, but her grip tightened on her sword. "I'm going to leave and find my friends, and I'm going to get them far away from you. I can't save my husband, but I can save the others from you."

Huh. Namaya wasn't betraying us. Even in Skayla's influence, she showed a strength I'd seen missing in so many. None could resist Skayla's tug, but Namaya instead was twisting the truth...buying us time. And she wasn't giving us away. Not even that we'd escaped.

"You insolent worm," Skayla laughed. "You can't hide anyone from me. To think you believed I actually cared about any of you—you're all a threat. A threat to the peace I am bringing the world. *Peace!* I can't believe you would throw that away. Ovok was right that none of you could be trusted with the power of—"

Skayla was cut off as Namaya lunged for her, blade brandished even with the unsteady half trance she was in. Skayla did not even flinch, only stepped to the side and drew her own, shouting a violent, "Stop it!" That made Namaya stop dead in her tracks. It was so potent that I felt my heart might even stop its thunderous beating.

I heard Sefen breathe in and turned in my saddle to put a violent finger to my lips.

I looked back just in time to see Skayla run Namaya through.

Barely did I keep my own gasp stuck inside my throat as Namaya gasped, kneeling to the ground as her eyes went sightless.

"Fool," Skayla growled, "can't you see I'm helping the world? Why do you never see?" And with that, she walked away, back to where she'd come from. I heard her shouting over the din to inspect the inside, and knew we had to leave *now* if we wanted to get out with our skins.

I turned in the saddle to see a stricken Sefen, his eyes wide as a single tear escaped them. Even before I could tell him we had to go, he spurred his horse and raced ahead to where Namaya's body lay.

I dared not risk shouting at him, instead grabbing hold of Sven's reins and riding over to the gate. I dismounted and finished the job Namaya had begun with the gate, and then turned to where Sefen had dismounted to cradle—oh. Bits of conversations and reactions pieced themselves together now as glaringly obvious as their matching rings: Namaya was his wife.

"We have to go, now," I whispered through my teeth. "She could come back any moment and we'd all be dead." Perhaps I should have been more understanding. But our lives depended on it. At least the traitor had used her last moments to redeem herself.

Sefen made as if to try and pick up Namaya's body, and my heart lurched. *No!* We couldn't afford literal dead weight! Was he insane?

I turned in desperation to Sven, unsure whether I was making sure he was still alive or whether I was begging for verbal backup.

Sven swayed precariously in his saddle; face twisted in a grimace. "Sefen…I'm sorry," he whispered. "But we do…need to go…" His hands clenched the pommel until his knuckles were white.

Now, I thought.

Sefen let go of Namaya's limp form, but I noted how he took the ring from her finger. With a trembling breath, he forced himself back on his horse, staring at his wife's body one more time before following me out of the gate. I dismounted once outside and forced the gate closed, and before I knew it, we were riding away into the darkness, Sven barely able to stay mounted but for the sturdy rope that held him.

And so, I tasted my first moments of freedom, somehow given at the expense of a traitor I'd never known.

THE GHOSTMAKER

CHAPTER XIV: To Mistrust or Death!

Estasia:

We'd been traveling for over six, nerve-wracking days. The Drogans were on the hunt for us by the end of the first day, Skayla undoubtedly having checked the dungeons after confronting Namaya. Miraculously, it began to rain almost immediately after we'd left the fortress—and not just rain but pour. It continued well into the night and then the next day was foggy. After that, it rained on and off, bringing bad weather for tracking and excellent conditions for hiding. However, not really prime conditions for my two companions. But as much as I hated being soaking wet, rain also meant that the Drogans wouldn't be able to see a thing, giving us a little extra shelter from the eyes of our hunters.

I didn't know how Sven Mara kept awake, but something Namaya had done had given him some sort of strength. Sefen said that she had given them both some potion. But whatever it was had started wearing off about two days ago, and now they were both having trouble staying on their horses. Sven was getting steadily more critical. It had gotten to the point where I'd actually administered some of the special vial Namaya had given to me. Seeing as she had died getting us to safety, I took a bet that it wasn't poison. I dared not use much of it, however, as we had a long journey ahead and I still wasn't quite sure what it did. But at the very least, it was keeping him alive.

We zigzagged this way and that, trying to do anything that could confuse Skayla's soldiers as we had been doing the last couple days, though now at a much slower pace. Sefen had taken the lead, though barely staying mounted. I turned again in my saddle and stopped my horse so that Sven Mara would come up by me. He was just about to fall off, and I barely had enough time to catch him. Great, the rope had come loose somehow.

"Woah there, come on. You're heavy," I said, somehow pushing him upright. The horse moved nervously to the side, and I hoped that it wouldn't jerk away and cause Sven to fall off.

I heard Sefen get off his horse, and soon he was beside us, trying to steady Sven. But it wasn't working. The horses shied apart from each other, and Sefen had to let go of his own horse to catch Sven as he fell out of his saddle, the rope that had held him completely undone.

I slid quickly off my saddle, grabbing the reins of our horses before they had a chance to realize they were free. Sefen hardly had the strength to catch Sven, and was forced to lay the unconscious man as gently as he could on the muddy ground.

Rain poured down upon us, and I couldn't see a thing as I tied the horses to a nearby tree and then knelt by Sven's side. "Come on, Sven. Wake up. Wake up!" I repeated a little more forcefully, shaking him and even slapping him lightly on his very pale cheek. "You can't die now, idiot. Not after all the trouble I went through, please. Gah! Don't make this a stupid waste of time!" I tried to sound angry, but I was more desperate. Through the torrents of rain, I couldn't tell if he was breathing. Quickly, I fumbled with the vial of medicine and put a little more to his lips. "Come on."

Sefen tried to help me revive his friend, shaking him and calling his name as well. "Not again, Mara, please."

Suddenly, amid the noise of falling rain, I heard the sound of a twig breaking, and instantly I was up and turned towards the noise, knife out and ready. Two figures appeared in the mist of rain, and my heart almost stopped beating altogether. No, no, no....

"Sefen!" one of the figures called out, walking quickly towards us. He sounded not much older than myself.

I brandished my knife offensively, unfortunately knowing exactly how to wield it. "Take one step further and you're dead!" I shouted, hoping I was ready to use it.

I felt the presence of Sefen next to me, and he put a hand on my arm. "Wait," he whispered, then said, "Jaythos?"

The figures appeared a little more clearly, stopping just a yard or so before us. One was a tall, lanky man with a crossbow and a few knives around his belt. The second was a very sturdily built, fierce-looking man with a bald head and no weapons at all. He looked a bit like Aekon, and my first guess was Rugonian.

"It *is* you!" Sefen limped over and embraced the lanky fellow, which didn't seem to please his friend very much.

"Wow. What did they do to you in there, Sefen...?" the lanky one asked, patting Sefen's back uncomfortably and trying to wiggle away. "Hug Maeko, next time."

I watched the Rugonian's eyes wander, and a scowl marked his face as his gaze settled on the limp form of Sven. I took a protective step back to where he lay, still far from trusting these strangers.

"We were on our way to find you," the lanky one said as he pulled Sefen away from him. "You do look terrible. Told you I should have stayed."

Sefen suddenly sounded irritable. "Jaythos, we ordered you to leave if we didn't meet you within the day—but later. Sven Mara's hurt badly. I—" I knew what he was about to say. It was what I was thinking. He didn't know if Sven was dead.

Without taking my eyes off the wary Rugonian, I knelt down and tried to wake Sven up again. The Rugonian started to move forward as if to inspect, but I raised my knife once more. "I will use this," I said between gritted teeth.

"Estasia. These are friends."

"Not this one." I saw no worry in his eyes as he looked upon Sven, only distrust. "Don't come a step closer," I growled before turning my attention back to Sven.

Come on, please.

I tensed as the Rugonian completely ignored me, kneeling by my side and making as if to put his hand on Sven.

"Don't touch him!" I snapped.

"What is wrong with him?" he asked.

"He's *dying*," I spat back. "Now step back while I try and help him."

The lanky one—Jaythos, I gathered—came and tapped the Rugonian's shoulder, who quickly moved aside for him. "Let me see." He put two fingers to Sven's neck. This man appeared at least a little more genuinely concerned with Sven's well-being, but I sensed doubts in both of the newcomers. Doubts towards me, but more so doubts over Sven. If they'd really been Sven's friends, I had a feeling they would be at least as panicked as I was. Apparently, they had known The GhostMaker first.

"He is alive. But not good. I don't know if he'll make it. Still want to kill him, Maeko?" The last bit was sorely sarcastic and directed at the Rugonian.

"We need to get moving. Skayla's men are not far behind.... How far are we from the cliffs?" Sefen interrupted, rubbing his beard anxiously.

"About half a day," Maeko answered.

Jaythos nodded in agreement. "By horse, that's correct. Especially if you've been making a good pace."

Aha. So, they must have come on foot from the start then. "Well, we need to go now."

There was a fevered cough from next to me and a very faint, "Yes. Before…something…worse…happens." We all turned to find Sven, barely awake once more and trying vainly to get up.

"Woah, woah, woah." I put a hand on his shoulder. "Let me help," I said, knowing that he could hardly even keep his head up. I was surprised he had woken up at all.

"For one that complained about warriors getting themselves killed, you seem to be following the same path." Jaythos seemed to lack grace in his humor. "I knew I should have stayed behind with you two," he said yet again as he put Sven's arm around his shoulder. I helped him; Sven feeling as limp as ever.

"Go get the horses. I guess I'll have to ride with him to make sure he doesn't fall off and drown in the mud," Jaythos said. "Sefen won't be much help, and Maeko is about ready to kill him, as it is." He eyed me suspiciously.

And, clearly, he didn't trust me. That was fine. Sven was taller than I and, even sorely underfed, he would be impossible for me to keep on the horse if he decided to go completely slack. Besides, a person up there with Sven was better than the rope.

I went and untied the horses, bringing them over as I listened through the rain for the screeches of Drogans or shouts of soldiers.

"Who…are…you?" I heard Sven's weak voice cut through the drumming rain.

Jaythos sighed. "Annoyed, wet, and tired. Not that you care, you big lump," he said gruffly as he and Sefen strained to get him up and slowly over to the horse. Jaythos was probably doing more of the lifting, considering Sefen's injured leg.

They got to the horse, and I heard Jaythos give a groan. "Ugh. Sefen, I really don't know how in Baeno we can get him back on."

"Let me," the Rugonian—Maeko—suddenly broke in, pushing past me and up to the others.

I instantly sprung to life, drawing my knife. "You touch him, and I have no problem ending your life, Rugonian."

"Touch *him* and I'll kill you, stranger," Jaythos said, almost before I'd gotten the words out. "But don't worry; if Maeko kills him, I'll be sure to reprimand."

"Will you all stop! Sven is going to die while you sit around bickering. Maeko, if you can get him on the horse, then do it. But Estasia is right. Don't harm him. I know how you feel, but unlike Namaya, he didn't have any choice—and we need him alive." Sefen's voice rang clear through the curtain of tension, and even I didn't argue.

Maeko scooped up Sven from the men's arms, and somehow got him onto the horse with what seemed like ease. "There," he said shortly.

254

Perhaps it was my mind playing tricks on me, but I thought I heard Sven murmur a low "Sorry." However, through the rain, I couldn't even tell if he was conscious anymore. As it was, Jaythos had to leap up onto the horse as quickly as possible in order to make sure Sven didn't just slide back off.

Maeko and Sefen got on one horse, and I got on the other, and once again we rode off in the rain, this time with what I was told were friends. They didn't really seem fond of Sven though. It made me angry. Had they no idea what sort of man he really was? How much they owed him, even when he was The GhostMaker?

I lost track of how long we'd been traveling—a few hours at least—my nerves completely shredded as I tried to keep track of Sven, Sefen, and our two new additions. I loved the rain for the cover it gave from the Drogans but hated it because it was so loud we would have a hard time hearing if soldiers were ahead or close behind. We came close at one point, barely jerking off our path in time to have a group come by. They had been a group of Bethynese soldiers, and we were lucky the weather was as bad as it was, for not much got past the Bethynese.

Once the scouting group had gone past us, we continued on, everyone tense and silent. The greenish grey gloom turned darker, and I guessed the sun was preparing to give leave to the two moons. Then, without warning, we were greeted by a small open plain and a sky-high wall of cliffs. My heart leaped to my throat as I realized that we were almost to—well, wherever we were going. Sefen had said it was a safe place, though to all others running from Skayla, the Nethani Cliffs sounded like a death trap.

After coming to the cliff wall, we followed it north for another ten minutes, passed a roaring waterfall, and then stopped. I was confused. Sefen had said it was a cave, but we were stopped before nothing. Then, to my disbelief, I watched as Jaythos and Sefen rode straight into…well…into the wall. Well, this week couldn't get any worse, that was for sure.

Baey:

When Sefen and Sven failed to show up, Jaythos and Maeko had decided to leave and inspect what happened at Valdon. They'd found nothing but ruins…ruins and the bodies of soldiers. Convinced Sefen and Sven were alive, they'd been scouting the surrounding area and coming back to the cave whenever they could, replenishing our food supplies so that we could last the wait. Tanner and I had begged them to let us come and help but to no avail. Instead, we had now been cooped up here for what felt like a decade, pacing and coming up with all sorts of horrible scenarios that could have played out for Sefen and Sven. I didn't even know how long we'd been here anymore. Days? Weeks? It could have been years.

And every moment Jaythos and Maeko were gone only left *more* room to worry.

I paced back and forth in the eerie cave, my hand fumbling with the broken watch that now hung around my neck alongside Sven Mara's ring.

"What if they're caught, or dead, or worse? It's been so long—we should go find them."

Guilt overwhelmed me; I couldn't believe that after all this time, all this wishing against all the evidence...that *he* was alive. Sven had been right under my nose. Why hadn't he said anything sooner? Would we have believed him? But why did we now? The note had explained something vague, but all I knew was Namaya was a traitor, Feyn—The GhostMaker—was Sven Mara, and that just as I'd found him, he'd been lost again.

And Namaya...the closest thing to a mother I had...why? What was I to believe?

"Baey, stop it. You're making *me* panic." Tanner intruded upon my thoughts with the same nervous energy of my steps.

I stopped pacing and turned to him. "But what if that's what happened? What do we do?" It made so much sense now. Sven forgetting, the eyes, the way he acted. It had been the MindHold. Tanner and I had puzzled over both what Jaythos had told us and the message for days, and after Tanner searched the paper's memories, we had realized how it all made sense. But we were too late...always too late. I couldn't stand this anymore. I'd stayed idle and useless too long, and now it might be too late. Besides Tanner, everyone that I'd ever known or loved could be dead.

Even Kaedna was now gone. All our friends...I thought of Adrian who'd always used to give me piggyback rides when I had been small. Or Ednis who used to read to me at night. I wondered whether they were dead or in a MindHold and shuddered. Which would be more merciful? I didn't want to think about it.

Then, suddenly, the clattering sound of horses' hooves broke the air like thunder, and I whirled around, clutching Sven's sword tightly as my heart skipped a beat.

Words could not describe my relief as Sefen and Maeko entered the cavern, mounted on a dark bay horse and soaking wet.

"Sefen!" I cried, tucking the sword away and half running, half tripping, towards them. "You're alive, thank The Creator, you're alive!" But then my joy soured as I noticed Sefen's poor condition. Maeko got off the horse first, helping Sefen as he practically fell off of it. He looked badly beaten up and barely even managed a weak smile.

"Hello, Baey," he said quietly. My throat was dry, and just as I was noticing the apparent absence of several others, there was the sound of other horses entering the cavern. Jaythos came in on a silver dappled mare, keeping an unconscious Sven Mara barely in the saddle. Sven looked even worse than Sefen, clothes tattered and face as pale as moonlight. In fact…I couldn't tell if he was alive….

I ran over, hoping to help Jaythos as he dismounted and tried to get Sven off the horse.

"Wait! Let me help!" The voice of a stranger split the tense silence, and I turned to find yet another horse in the cavern, a lady just dismounting it. Her soaking, snarled, umber hair clung stubbornly to her neck, making her look like some wretched beggar. The rags she wore completed the look, just as wet and dirty as the rest of her.

She beat me to the horse, easing Sven out of the saddle, keeping him somewhat upright with Jaythos's help, her wary eyes seeming to watch everyone at once.

"There is a makeshift bed over in the corner," Jaythos said to the lady, and together they brought Sven over to where we had made a pile of somewhat usable blankets.

I felt lost as I followed them, torn between helping Maeko and Sefen, and following Jaythos and Sven. Worse, I felt invisible; here and yet useless...only able to observe as I desperately tried to get a grasp on what was happening. They weren't dead...but as I began evaluating Sven's wounds even from where I followed, I couldn't help but ask myself how long it would stay that way.

Ever so gently, they set Sven down and the lady was instantly kneeling beside him, running her thin hands over her hair and then reaching out to feel Sven's forehead. She turned around and looked up at Jaythos, looking distrustful as she spoke. "Do you have any bandages or medicine?"

"We have bandages and other supplies." Finally, my mind cleared, and I answered for Jaythos, shock subsiding as something clicked in my brain. This woman clearly had no idea what to do—proper dressing couldn't be done until their wounds were better cleaned and sewn up. Namaya wasn't here; I was the only one that could help. I was the only one that would know how to help Sven or Sefen. "I'll get them. Sefen, come and sit down over here, it will be easier to help both of you if you're nearby," I shouted over to where Jaythos and Sefen were, for the first time feeling useful. I swiftly glided over to the pile of supplies, rummaging through and finding our supply of bandages, stitching implements and thread, and a small bottle of cleaning ointment. I ran back over, kneeling by the lady.

"Are you familiar with medicine?" she asked hesitantly, eyes darting from me down to Sven.

I nodded. Namaya had shown me many things in the time I had been at Valdon, even if I hadn't really been allowed to get practical experience in helping with the wounded. But I no longer doubted being able to keep a clear head around it. I'd helped Jaythos; I could help them.

The lady shoved a small, finger-sized vial full of a sky-blue liquid into my hand. "Then here. I've been rationing it to him, but I don't know what it is. Will it help?"

I popped the cork, smelling it even though I already had a strong suspicion of what it was. I got a little excited as my suspicion was confirmed. "Yes. Yes, this will. But he needs all of it now." This might just buy us some time. Sven would probably already be dead if the lady hadn't been giving it to him, but a larger dose would be much more likely to help him now. I could see by Sven's clammy complexion that his wounds were becoming infected.

The lady gave me some space, and I opened Sven's mouth, pouring almost all of the liquid in. I wished it would work immediately, but I knew it would take time.

Just then Sefen came and clumsily sat against the wall, his breath ragged.

"Jaythos, go get some dry blankets. These two will die of cold if we don't get them a little dry—Sefen, drink this up." I handed him the vial, giving the best bossy look I could muster.

He obeyed and drank up the rest with a weary and almost mystified expression. Satisfied, I turned my attention back to Sven.

"The main problem is this," the lady pointed out, moving some of his tattered shirt away to reveal a bloodied, ill-bandaged area on his side.

I winced as I pulled the rags aside to inspect it. It had been a bad enough wound without the infection. But hopefully Namaya's ointment had helped. I wondered why she had given it to this lady—if indeed Namaya was a traitor. And then, where was Namaya? But my first job was helping Sven and Sefen, and I shoved any other questions from my mind for now. Lives depended on me.

Sven coughed weakly, vacant eyes opening in confusion. Good, the ointment's initial strong effect had brought him away from death's door, for now.

He blinked at me, looking as lost as a baby bird fallen from its nest. "What…" he whispered, bracing against the floor as he tried to sit up.

The lady next to me put a hand on him, pushing him down. "Oh, no, you don't."

I shot her a glance, not sure whether to be thankful or wary of her, and returned to inspecting Sven's wound.

"Is he going to be alright, Baey?" I heard Tanner's voice from close behind me but didn't turn. How would I answer? I was skilled, but so much of Namaya's skill had been from her Gift, and she could not teach me instinct. I could only hope that her potion and the abilities I had would be enough.

"The potion helped," I said, distracted with the momentous task before me. "Sefen, how are you holding up?" I didn't turn as I asked, focused more on Sven, for the moment.

"I'm fine," Sefen grunted.

I allowed a brief turn in the man's direction, doubt and worry mixing together in a terrible combination. Jaythos had apparently been giving Sefen some form of inspection, however, and nodded in confirmation. "Few bumps and bruises, but rest and some better care will fix that. How's Sven? I thought he was gone there a couple of times."

"Who are...you?" Sven once more tried to sit up, kept down by the lady.

I turned back to my patient and talked as I worked, "It's me, Baey. Remember?" I bit my lip, trying not to think; only act.

"That's...right..." He sounded incredibly confused and faint as he tried to get up for the third time.

"Would you stop that, Sven," the lady said through gritted teeth, pushing him gently down again. "You're worse than an old lady who's lost her spectacles."

It was a long process, with several wounds in need of irrigation and disinfecting. Then the salves I'd packed from Valdon were used, and I left Sven only when he was at a point where the lady could bandage him up. Then I went and repeated the whole thing over again with Sefen, conserving as much of the supplies as I could. This was all we had.

At last, I finished up. "Now, all of you who've been out in the rain ought to change. We should have enough for everyone, though I can't promise how well they'll fit..." I knew the lady that was with us was too tall for me and would likely end up wearing something meant more for Jaythos. I turned back to Sefen and Sven. "And then both of you need rest." I looked especially at Sven.

He said nothing in reply, only giving a weak nod.

I took in a deep breath. "Thank you," I said in a whisper.

Everyone changed or was helped, and I was glad to see Sven and Sefen's shivering finally subside.

"Tanner, can you go grab the coat over by the pool?" I turned my head and looked up at my worried friend.

Tanner's head bobbed, and he sprinted off like a hunted rabbit, returning with the coat bundled in his arms.

I took it and spread it over Sven. He still had a fever and was now completely unconscious. He would be alright...he would be fine. I couldn't let myself think otherwise.

I saw the woman standing nearby, watching our every move as if she worried we might try and kill Sven or something at any moment. I turned and addressed Tanner. "Could you just keep an eye on him—make sure he doesn't try to get up or-or anything?" I stumbled, feeling the adrenaline begin to fade from my system. I felt shaky, exhausted, and I didn't like it at all.

Tanner nodded and sat down next to Sven. The lady moved closer and took a spot by Sven's other side. I didn't trust her, and she didn't trust us. Hopefully, it wouldn't stay that way.

I turned my attention to Sefen, who was still conscious nearby. Jaythos and Maeko were with him. I heard Sefen murmur, "She...she was doing what she thought was best."

Namaya. They were talking about Namaya. I came over quietly, kneeling by Sefen without so much as asking permission as I inspected him for signs of a fever.

"Doing what she thought best?" Jaythos snapped. "Getting us all killed? Getting everyone *else* killed was what she thought best? She realizes she sent Bato, Kesh, and all of the others to their death in Kaedna?" He spat on the ground. "Did what she thought best. Yeah, right."

I winced but couldn't say I didn't feel the sting of the betrayal. Sefen's expression did not hold any malice though. Only grief. Grief and loneliness.

"She believed the lie. She didn't want us to end up like...." He trailed off. "Like all the other dead. But she did what was right, in the end." His voice was hoarse, and it wasn't from his wounds.

I felt out of place, and now done, I stood up, unsure whether I should leave.

"You can stay, Baey," Sefen whispered. "You have a right to know, too."

Know what?

"Namaya only wanted you safe, you understand that?" Sefen was looking me right in the eyes now.

I bit my lip. How was this all safe? How could she have believed a lie? "Try and remember her with fondness, Baey. For me."

Remember her? "What do you mean?"

Silence. I felt Maeko put a hand on my shoulder.

"She's dead, Baey. She died." Sefen's cheeks were wet. "She died getting us out."

I wasn't prepared for the emotions his statement brought with it. I had thought that with her lies and betrayal, I wouldn't even care what happened to Namaya. How wrong I was. I felt numb but didn't cry. I'd seen death before—and I had been grieving everyone who'd fallen at Kaedna for days now. But this was different. It was like the day I was told

Sven wouldn't be coming back. When I'd found out he'd gotten himself killed for me.

"And what of this woman?" Jaythos shattered the somber mood with the reality before us, and we all glanced over to where the stranger was with Sven. "Can we trust *her?* Because she definitely doesn't trust us."

Sefen sighed and set his head against the stone wall, closing his eyes. "As far as I know," he replied quietly. He sounded tired. Really tired. "She's pretty much the reason Sven and I are still alive. Not sure why she's helping us, though."

Jaythos gave a brief glance before he sighed with his typical impatience. "Time isn't something we have, Sefen. Too many times we were caught waiting. Too many times. We don't have time to wait and meet another stranger to see if she is or isn't a spy." He looked bitter, and his fists clenched

Getting up the courage, I broke into the conversation, my voice coming out as an embarrassing squeak. "Who is she?" I asked.

"Her name is Estasia. She was a slave in the Kovian Fortress. That is all I know," Sefen replied.

Maeko broke in, then. "And how do you know The GhostMaker is the Sven Mara? He does not look like Sven."

I couldn't help but agree in one aspect at least; Sven didn't look anything like he once had. His eyes, for one. For another, he looked as though much longer than eight years had passed since his disappearance. It was still hard to rectify the youthful, lively young man I'd been rescued by with the gaunt, weatherworn one that Sven now appeared as. Honestly, when I'd first met Sven as Feyn, I had guessed him to be closer to his forties at least. Not the mere twenty-nine that Sven was.

Sefen sat up straighter and stared him directly in the eye. "Maeko. I understand your skepticism; you have a right, I know. But he *is* Sven. What's left of him, at least."

"But we see nothing, and I ask how we know it was not simply a trick Skayla did to your mind?"

To my surprise, Jaythos was the one who came to Sven's defense. "Maeko, will you stop going after him? There isn't any time for stupid theories. You're telling me he doesn't ring familiar to you now? I'd never met Sven Mara before this, and *I* can tell..."

I didn't seem to be the only one startled by this remark.

"At least, I can see it *now*. No one else could have ever made it out of a MindHold except someone as powerful as a Mara, and what Tanner saw in his mind seems obvious signs of breaking from one. It's proof enough for me at least. There's no point in him tricking us—he's *dying*. If he indeed has found some way out of Skayla's prison of the mind, then why should you hold it against him? Did you hold it against me when I deserted the Bethynese army?" His voice held a fervor I had not experienced before, and his fist was clenched tightly.

Sefen broke in, trying to ease the building tension. "The point is, we need him on our side, and this is one person you don't want to doubt. Now will you both shut up—" Sefen broke off the last word in a small coughing fit.

I chided myself with getting so caught up in the heat of the argument that I had allowed Sefen to continue to talk and stay up when he needed rest just as much as Sven.

"No. *The point is* you need to sleep. They can talk to you later." I summoned my best commanding tone.

"As you wish," Maeko said softly, grinding his teeth and turning stiffly.

Jaythos followed suit, murmuring a, "Don't die on us, Sefen." Before he turned around, however, I caught that quick flash of some secret burden he let show through every once in the blue moons. Jaythos had arrived at Valdon shortly after I had arrived, and no one ever talked about his past—no one had ever questioned the Bethynese man for being at Valdon. But now, I wondered if I'd just gotten a piece of the puzzle.

However, now was not the time.

I sighed, turning my attention back to Sefen, "Now rest. I'll check back on you in a little while." Hopefully my voice sounded…semi-authoritative, anyway.

He nodded and lay back, eyes closing into what I hoped would be a peaceful slumber.

I returned to where the others were, intent on checking on Sven again. Him, I was *really* worried about. While Sefen seemed certain to recover…Sven, I didn't know. Unfortunately, Maeko had taken it upon himself to come over here and keep a vengeful eye on Sven—seeming to have gotten in an even worse argument with Jaythos after I'd shooed them off. To say it plainly, everyone around Sven was giving each other evil stares; I rolled my eyes and huffed. This wasn't good. We had enough trouble without killing each other.

"What's the matter?" I asked, already knowing the answer.

The lady—Estasia—said nothing, instead turning her burning stare on me.

Tanner answered what everyone already knew. "I am having a hard time trusting someone that shows up with Sven Mara half-dead," he muttered darkly.

The lady pursed her lips. "I showed up with him half-*alive*. Better that than all dead. If I'd wanted him dead, then I wouldn't have brought him at all, or Sefen, for that matter."

That...was a good point. But I needed to focus. I knelt down by Sven and quickly checked his pulse, feeling like I had a gaping hole in my heart. But soon I realized that it wasn't my feeling, but the feelings of the objects that hung around my neck. They were feeling his pain—somehow, I just knew that's what it was. I didn't understand it, but it wasn't exactly a lovely experience.

"Stranger tell of herself; we will tell of ourselves. We both are friends of Sefen." Maeko sounded very short on patience.

"And Sven," I added, giving a glance his way. I understood he was angry, but it wasn't an excuse.

The lady didn't seem to like this idea very much. "One of you has already betrayed him, and at *least* one of you wants him dead, so I'm not in a hurry to just give you information." She stared at Maeko.

"Then why did you bring him here?" Tanner piped up, cocking his head and looking bemused and frustrated.

Estasia didn't take her eyes off Sven. "Because there wasn't really anywhere else to go, and he was going to die. Sefen said they had friends—I just didn't realize he meant only *he* had friends."

We had to break through this wall. If we didn't at least find out *whether* we could trust each other, we could be in this stand-still forever—which really wasn't an option. Besides, we needed Maeko to realize Sven wasn't the enemy anymore, or else I was afraid of what he might do. I'd heard the stories of what happened after they'd murdered the Queen of Rugo.

So, I decided to try and get at least *some* productive dialogue going. "Did you know Sven Mara before? Sefen said you were a slave. Why aren't you in a MindHold?"

This seemed to amuse her, and she thought a while before replying. "Only as The GhostMaker. And Skayla likes to think she can strike enough fear into people without needing a MindHold. Lord Kovo never seems to like it, but it makes her feel in control." She paused. "But Sven Mara was the only one I'd ever seen who fought against her hold." This last comment seemed pointed at Maeko.

A shiver ran down my back and through my wings, but I tried to hide the unsettling feeling Skayla's name brought me. The memories it dug up. "Lord Kovo was there as well?" This was news. Last any of us had heard, he had gone to Rugo to quell a small rebellion that had been stirring. We had actually been hoping something would come of it but to no avail.

"He returned a few days after her pet Ovok. It was for the invasion of Kaedna—at least, that's what I think now." A shadow passed over her face. "If I'd known beforehand, perhaps I could have somehow gotten word. But there's only so much I know of what's been going on inside the fortress."

Another shiver.

"When was Kaedna taken?" Maeko finally broke the silence, voice hard as he addressed the lady.

"Two months and a week ago was when Skayla and Ovok left. They didn't bring any prisoners back with them. But after that battle is when Sven finally found a way to escape. And I do have a name—Estasia. You may even use it, if only to stop any name calling." Her eyes twinkled slyly. "But come, why don't you all tell me a little about you? This is supposed to be going two ways."

I gave her another look up and down. As much as I didn't want to, I would honor our side of the bargain, and hopefully Maeko and Tanner would do the same.

"I'm Baey. Sven saved me when I was eight, and we all used to live in Valdon. Do you know the name?" I asked. Someone had to say *something*, and honestly, at this point, I would be surprised if she didn't already know half of this.

She nodded but didn't relax as I'd hoped. "And you are?" she turned to the other two, raising a doubtful eyebrow.

"Tanner."

"I am not answering until you tell why you help." Maeko said stubbornly, his eyes like wildfires as he sized up Estasia. He was clearly not pleased that she seemed on Sven's side, and her objections to him being even in the same area as Sven made it worse—not that I disagreed at the moment. This was just a mess. Maeko was usually better than this! Why was I the one trying to negotiate? I now wished I had told Sefen to stay awake and help get these three under control. I wished I had seen that Feyn was really Sven. I wished I had never left him that night, and he had been forced to carry me off! Oh dear, this wouldn't do….

"Am I the most adult one here?" I asked as my frustration spilled over.

Estasia laughed a little then, shaking her head. "You're a plucky one, Birdy."

I wasn't sure whether that was a compliment or an insult. "We're on the same side," I said. Until proven otherwise, that was.

"What's your name? There's really not much harm it can do." Estasia said, again addressing Maeko. "I mean, Skayla already knows all your names anyway, I imagine."

"Maeko," he said begrudgingly. "Now why do you help?"

I was finally able to breathe a little. Maybe we were finally getting somewhere.

"How long have you known Sven Mara?" Estasia countered, and I was back to holding my breath. Ugh.

"Can we please stop acting like this is a battleground? Sefen and Sven are hurt, and we need to do something other than sit around and wait for Skayla to come and kill us all. She probably knows more about all of us than we know about each other, right now." Tanner sounded equally as frustrated as I was, seeming to have broken out of the cycle of mistrust at least enough to see arguing back and forth was pointless.

This put a small kink in the other two's death stare. Estasia was the first to budge. "Alright. We'll take turns. I'll say something first, just to show you I have nothing to hide."

CHAPTER XV: Memories

Estasia:

I didn't like showing my hand, especially to someone as outwardly petty as this Maeko. I also didn't like the way he stared at me, as if I was going to put a knife in the girl's back as soon as he wasn't looking. His glares at the helpless form of Sven were even worse. The problem was, I was afraid that the moment *I* wasn't looking, he'd put a knife in *Sven*. Unfortunately for the negotiations, I had a pretty good feeling my fear was slightly more founded than his. Too late had I stopped my instincts and forced myself to give these strangers a chance. Now we'd taken two steps back for every step forward, and I wasn't sure I could undo what I'd done. Still, I had to try, and as much as I absolutely despised telling anything about myself—telling anything that could give someone power over me—I had to try and fix this. Besides, I wouldn't tell anything too revealing.

"My name is Estasia. I've been a slave almost as long as Skayla's been in power," I started, watching each of their reactions. I liked the winged girl. She seemed smart and more observant than the rest. She already seemed wrapped up in what I was about to say, even before I said it. She would be the best shot at gaining their trust. "I knew Sven Mara first as The GhostMaker." I paused, watching as the Rugonian stiffened even more. The girl looked embarrassed, her wings curling around her like a blanket of comfort. Hm. "He'd helped me once. So, I decided I would pay him back if I ever got the chance. Your friend just happened to end up being part of that bargain." I cut the story short, leaving out details that I didn't want to share with anyone but Sven. I just hoped he would live to be told. I also didn't want to risk my whole underground network over gaining the trust of a few strangers. That is, if it survived *this* stunt. I only hoped Aekon and Ateli were not found out.

The winged girl bit her lip and looked down, while the young one, Tanner, nodded, extending his hand.

"Alright. Here's to trust," he said, waiting for me to shake it.

Now, I was desperate to show faith, but I wasn't *that* desperate. This boy was definitely clever, but I was good at catching 'clever.' Something in his eyes told me that, somehow, he had an ulterior motive for me shaking his hand, and I had a feeling that, somehow, I wouldn't really like it. So, I went as if to grab it, then suddenly withdrew, putting it up just in time to cover an only half-faked sneeze. "I guess we'll have to wait on that...sorry." I said with a small smile, wiping my snot-stained hand on my trousers.

"Er...I guess it's the thought that counts," Tanner replied, looking rather downcast. My suspicions were confirmed by the disappointed looks on the faces of both him and the others. Hm. I knew Valdon had been the home of the last of the Gifted, and I had a feeling that that played into what had just almost happened. I would have to be careful to try and avoid contact with the boy—until I knew more.

"I'll get you a blanket," the girl said, getting up slowly and heading off. That was actually a good idea. My sneeze had only been a partial ploy, and I really was beginning to shiver despite my change of clothes.

I looked down at Sven again, biting my lip as I tried to find some sign that he was getting better or worse. His chest rose and fell shallowly, and in intervals that were rather far apart, but at least he was breathing. He had a hideous black eye as well. The girl had done a much better job cleaning and dressing his wounds than I had, and though he was pale, he wasn't that death white he had been earlier.

"Here." The girl—Baey—came back, handing me a very ragged blanket. But anything was welcome at this point, and I wrapped it tightly around my shoulders.

"What was in that vial that I gave you?" I asked her, curiosity getting the better of me. I also wanted to know if, really, I should have given it to him earlier.

"It was something to counteract the infections. A…uh…friend of mine had created it—is that where you got it?" She looked away.

Ah. Namaya. She knew.

I wasn't quite sure what to do. I didn't really buy into any of that emotional nonsense. "I see," I said, stopping short of giving any condolence.

"Where did you get vial?" Maeko repeated Baey's question.

Oh, dear. Hopefully he would not press the question past this. "Namaya gave it to me—said it would help him."

The girl nodded, biting her lip as if to stop herself from saying something. She sat back down, and as she did, an all-too-familiar pendant fell dangling from a chain around her neck, having been tucked beneath her shirt.

"Where did you get that?" I stood up suddenly, eyes riveted on the small golden watch. I had seen that many times before, dangled in front of Sven by Skayla to torture him. I could only guess at why, but I knew it was beyond important.

The girl clutched the thing and it disappeared within her clenched fist. "Why?" she asked, defensive.

I narrowed my eyes and looked her up and down again. "Sven gave it to you, didn't he?"

So that was what Kovo and Skayla had been looking for; Sven Mara had stolen Skayla's precious trophy. Well, that explained why Kovo had been so enraged. Skayla had always seemed to make it a point to flaunt it in front of The Ghost—er, Sven, and Kovo had never appeared happy about it.

Maeko took a protective step towards the girl, his body language reeking of anger and warning towards me for standing between him and his revenge.

"Do you know what that is?" I asked, completely ignoring their hostile attitudes.

I heard footsteps echoing faintly in the cavern and turned around to see Jaythos coming towards us, looking very bored. "Maeko. Stand down." He didn't sound very committed to the command.

Maeko's stone face didn't even twitch, but I could see he was hesitating. I felt like I was being cooked in a stew and that, at any moment, it might boil over.

"You all are being very unsympathetic to Sefen and Sven," Jaythos continued in the same dry, careless voice. "If you're going to argue like children, do it where they can rest and not have to listen to you squawk." He stopped before us, caressing his crossbow like a pet bird.

There was a lot of distrust in those eyes. More than the rest of Sefen's company. It made sense with him being Bethynese, and yet that only left me wondering why he was even on their side at all.

"Baey, stay with Sven. Maeko, Tanner, Estasia, why don't you step over this way so we can bicker a little more respectfully?"

I didn't like being ordered—I'd had enough of that at the Kovian Fortress—but I did know that unlike Maeko, Jaythos didn't want to murder Sven where he lay, and he was ordering *Maeko* to leave as well, so I was alright with that. Baey seemed unsure as to whether or not she liked this arrangement but nodded. Tanner looked embarrassed, and Maeko just kept that stone face. This was definitely an interesting group of misfits. I only hoped they were worth all of this trouble.

Baey:

I clutched the watch in my hand as I sat by Sven, remembering what the note with it had said. '*Protect this with your life, Baey. I know I am always leaving you with such burdens, and I'm sorry.*' Already I was being careless, letting it slip into view like that in front of the stranger. Naturally, Estasia knew about it, too. I could only guess at what it was. Was it the source of Moira's power the way the ring seemed to be Sven's? It would make sense, but when I had tried to fiddle with the watch, it had done nothing—but could that be because of the crack in the lens? Even though the others knew I had this, I hadn't told them what I thought it was. They still didn't even know that I could use Sven's ring, and I didn't want to tell anyone about it until I could ask Sven about it, myself.

In fact, if it wasn't for the fact that Sven had said to protect it with my very life, I would have guessed it to be just an ordinary timepiece.

The night passed slowly, and I only drifted off here and there as I kept a close eye on Sven. He'd never woken up—not even when I'd checked his wounds again and applied more salve. Not even after hours had passed, when Sefen had woken up.

I bit my lip and checked Sven again. He was still unconscious, and I was pretty sure he'd caught some form of cold from exposure. I hoped he hadn't slipped into one of those death sleeps. His breathing was steadier, but one could never tell. I still remembered Kenten slipping into it, two years back.

Shuddering, I returned my attention to the here and now, putting a hand fretfully on Sven's neck to check his pulse for the millionth time. Stronger than earlier but still weak. I wanted him to just wake up. It was so nerve-wracking sitting here in the dark, with nowhere to go and no idea what would happen next. Suddenly feeling quite claustrophobic, I got up stiffly, heading over to Sefen, who had woken up once more about ten minutes ago and refused to go back to sleep.

"How are you feeling?" I asked in a whisper, kneeling down beside him. The potion had worked its magic and already he seemed revived, which is why he was no longer listening to me.

"I feel like I could fly," he reassured with good humor. "Though I leave that one to you, for the present."

I was too worried to be amused, and my brow furrowed as my thoughts strayed back to Sven, the watch, and how Estasia had seen it.

"What is it?" Sefen sat up straighter, wincing a little bit, but brushing away my hand when I tried to stop him.

"I...I'm just distracted—worried," I corrected myself, not really able to hide the overflow of anxiety. "We've lost, Sefen. Everything is gone now, isn't it? Kaedna was the last free city. Valdon was the last defense…Sven could *die*. What can we do? There's no one left to fight, and nowhere left to go." I had rambled a little more than I'd meant, and I bit my lip, covering myself with my wings until they almost completely encased me. I just wanted to hide, to wake up, and find out all this had been a dream. But it was time I grew up. Things weren't going to get better, and they definitely weren't going to go away.

Sefen pulled my wings out of my face, putting a comforting hand on my shoulder and smiling gently. "Not yet. I mean, we're still alive, at least. And so is Sven." But I saw that look in his eyes. He was as scared as I was, and it terrified me that a grown man like Sefen—a *warrior* like Sefen—had the same fear as me.

"But what now?" I struggled to say the words, sounding a little desperate. "What can we do now, Sefen?"

He sighed, all his false confidence withering away like a doomed spring flower. "I don't know."

This wasn't like in Valdon, when Namaya had warned him and he had insisted on other ways. I'd always known that even though they had fought, that if anyone could have found a way, Namaya and Sefen could have…only, Namaya had found one without us….

I bit my lip, forcing myself to breathe. All I'd ever known was gone. I was scared, and those I knew were disappearing. Was Sven next? Was I condemned to let him down twice? Only this time, I really *would* be responsible for him dying; I was here and able to save him, and yet couldn't.

"Baey. Get some rest. These things always seem worse when you're tired. Leave the worry to me." Sefen's soft smile returned as he spoke. "I'll wake you if Sven stirs or anything."

"But *you* need to rest," I urged desperately. I didn't want to sleep. It might be more pleasant than being awake, and to be stuck wishing for a dream was awful. I needed to stay awake—I needed to devote every last breath to trying to fix this.

Sefen shook his head. "I'm feeling much better," he endeavored to convince me, but he was still quite hurt. As much as he tried to hide it, I could see it plainer than if it had been painted on his weary face.

"And I'm better than you. So, get some rest and I'll be fine." I was surprised at myself for sounding so stern. "Please," I added meekly.

"Alright." With another worried expression, he sat back, pretending I couldn't see his half-opened eyes.

I crept back to Sven's bedside, checking on everything in my newly formed obsessive routine. Nothing had changed, and I wearily plopped myself down, my wings sagging around me like old rags in sore need of cleaning.

"I don't know what I'll do if you never wake up...." I stumbled over myself, barely keeping my voice from shaking. "You just have to," I finished with a gulp. Too many worst-case scenarios were forming in my head. Too many questions were spinning around, and too many nightmares were coming true.

I folded my wings around me once more and withdrew deep into their folds, the feathers almost darker than the cave itself as they showed my overwhelming fear. I just sat there, playing with a feather nervously and closing my eyes to the dark. No more. I couldn't take it. I knew I would regret my wishing and still I had wished. I found myself whispering to him, not really realizing that I was saying any of it out loud. "I never got to tell you thank you, or ask you why you didn't come with me. Why you had to die—but you didn't die, I suppose. Was the MindHold worse? Please tell me you didn't endure that for nothing? You told everyone that I was supposed to save the world, but there isn't a world to save anymore, Sven. So, you see, you just have to wake up. If you don't...." My voice broke off there, not wanting to imagine the possibility. A stray tear fell onto my now *terribly* stained skirt.

"Well...this is...awkward..." I heard a voice as it spoke amid a small coughing fit. My wings sprung into full alert mode, and I barely kept from leaping in the air. His eyes had just barely opened, and he looked up at me blankly.

"Sven! You're awake!" Really awake. The fever seemed to have broken and the potion had actually done its job. New life surged through my cold veins.

"Um...." he said with a wince, trying to pick himself up into a sitting position.

"Don't get up—you'll hurt yourself." I put a hand to his shoulder, trying to push him back down while still being gentle.

He stopped and just stared at me, and I realized that he probably had no idea what was going on. "It's me, Baey. Estasia and Sefen got you out. We're in the cave you sent me to, remember, Sven? You gave me this?" I released my grip on his shoulder to take out the watch that dangled around my neck, stopping its uncontrolled swinging motion so that he could get a good look at it. His eyes widened, and a mental spark seemed to light up as it clicked. His vacant eyes filled in with more blue-green color, and he looked less like his ghostly self and more like an actual Human being.

"Oh, good. You found it," he said softly, ignoring me and sitting up. My chest tightened as I saw the pain he tried to hide, but he refused any order to lay down. His eyes were riveted on the watch. "How long have I been—here?" he asked with a cough, gripping his side as it wracked through his body. Ugh. Yea, definitely a cold. That wouldn't help the cracked rib from the arrow wound.

"About a day," I replied, desperate to make him take it easy. "You really should lay back down," I added. "You're very sick." He could use a warm drink about now. But we'd not dared build a fire—we might be hidden, but fire could still send off smoke.

"No, no...I'm, fine, darlin'," he wheezed.

Mhm. No. But what could I do? I was useless, and felt ashamed that my own relief that he was awake was clouding my judgement on how to care for him.

"Where's...everyone else?"

"Resting. Like you need to be."

He just coughed. "I-I need to talk to Tanner. I need—" Another wheeze left his sentence unfinished.

"To rest." I gritted my teeth. "If you don't stop talking, Sven, you'll choke yourself to death. Just be quiet and heal, please?"

"No time," he said impatiently, tapping his fingers on the ground. There was clearly more on his mind, and I wanted him to say it—but not until he was more recovered.

"Sven, please. You're awake now, but only an hour ago I thought you were going to die...please, lay back and rest."

281

His eyes riveted on the watch and ring around the chain I wore, and I could hear the drumming of their yearning. It was kind of scary, honestly. But I realized that was what had been going on back in Valdon.

"They're safe, then? The-they're with you," Sven murmured, more to himself than anyone else.

"Yes. I have them. Please rest." I didn't know what else I *could* say.

For a moment, his eyes mirrored the emotions felt through the two relics around my neck. "Good," he breathed. "Is…Sefen alright?"

I nodded, "Everyone is alright." *Now, please, lay back down.*

As if he'd read my mind, Sven did just that, slowly leaning back and closing his eyes. "Everyone is alright," he repeated as his breathing deepened and he drifted back into sleep again.

Feverless, normal sleep.

Sven:

I was sore and stiff but alive. It was much better than the numb tingling sensation I had been plagued with the last two days. Still, my head burned like it was on fire, and every noise sounded like a roaring eruption cracking the earth open. Even the nearly silent drops of water on the cavern floor were unbearable. And then there was Maeko's eyes boring into me. I didn't blame him. As distorted as my memories were, I remembered enough to know that I still couldn't forgive myself.

I winced as I adjusted my sitting position, pain shooting up my torso. It had been two days since I'd first woken and I felt I had done nothing *but* sleep. We had to get going—we had to get the watch to The Crafters if any of this was ever going to be worth something. I had a feeling that Skayla would now be looking for them, too, now that she knew that I was with the watch. Now that I knew they weren't dead, like she'd made me believe. The memory of her making me search for them in the early years of my enslavement to her was vague, but it was still there. They'd gotten away, somehow.

"You look terrible, Sven," said Sefen. He'd been recovering nicely and could now walk about, while I could apparently hardly sit upright.

"I'm alive. That's good, ah?" Was it? Maeko seemed to think otherwise. Honestly, I didn't blame him. It didn't matter what my name was, I had still killed his Queen. I had no right to run from the ghosts I'd made, even if I couldn't yet remember them. But Serafina...Serafina I remembered, and it hurt to do so. I had been surprised enough that Aekon had been graceful; no Rugonian save Aekon would ever forgive me. No one on Baeno would forgive me for the lives I'd taken. *I* couldn't even forgive me.

"So, what now?" Sefen asked. "Where can we go?"

An excellent question. I looked over at the lump of feathers by the pool, thinking about the two little burdens she carried. If only I wasn't too much of a coward to carry them myself. It just hurt too much. Like carrying my family's sepulcher.

"We need to find The Crafters."

"Wait. The Crafters? Aren't they dead?" Sefen asked.

I was still kicking myself for believing that so easily. "No," I replied, "Skayla has apparently been still looking for them. They're alive, somewhere. I need to talk to Tanner...but first, I need to try and walk. Do you think Jaythos will help?"

283

"I don't know that's such a good idea, Sven." Sefen's brow creased.

"We can't stay here forever. Our supplies will run out. I need to see if I can ride," I insisted. If I could get up, I could maybe convince them to start off today or tonight. Time was of the essence, and if we couldn't find The Crafters, then all really would be lost. "I have a plan," I added. Sort of. I just...hoped we'd find some form of clue when we got there.

"Fine. But be careful," Sefen grunted as he stiffly made his way over to where Jaythos was keeping watch.

Soon, they had both made their way back to me, and Jaythos was extending a hesitant hand. He didn't say a word, and I was thankful for the lack of argument, at least, even if I could see the doubt in his eyes.

I straightened more, trying to hold in the grimace as every bone and muscle in my body groaned. Clasping his hand firmly, I pulled myself up. It felt like my body was on fire, and I wanted nothing more than to just sit back down. My legs gave way under me, and Jaythos barely caught me in time.

"Sorry," I muttered, forcing my stubborn legs to work. My left leg refused, however, and I had to lean heavily on Jaythos, who barely seemed able to keep me up.

"You should sit back down, idiot," Jaythos said with his usual charm.

"No. No. I'm fine. Help me walk," I replied quickly, stubbornly refusing to admit defeat. "We need to leave today, and I need to be able to ride a—" I stopped and leaned over, a painful coughing fit interrupting my urgent advice.

"You sure, Sven?" It was Sefen now.

In reply, I took a couple unsteady steps, testing my left leg and forcing it into submission. That wasn't so bad.

"Oh, you're...walking." The voice of a lady came from nearby, and a tall, dark-haired woman stood before us. "Did you clear this with Baey, Sven?"

I turned to Jaythos, completely lost. "Who is this?" I barely finished the question before another awful cough. My vision started to fog up, and I started to think that they were right—I did need to sit down. Why was she calling me Sven? I thought I was Feyn...Feyn Cavo, here to try and find out who the spy was in Valdon.... Oh, why did the Maras always cause so many problems...oh, wait. That was me. I was Sven, wasn't I? Oh great.

"You don't remember?" Jaythos's eyes narrowed, and he looked from me to the lady.

No. I didn't. Was I supposed to? I felt cold, and my vision started to darken a little.

"These memory lapses are going to get old, fast," he mumbled.

Memory lapses?

"You and Sefen got caught, Estasia got you out, Baey has the watch you gave her. We're in the cave you sent us to...ring any bells?"

It was like a chain reaction, and as the memories rushed in, my vision went black again, then cleared almost completely. Jaythos was right; this was going to get old, fast. In fact, it was already getting old.

Then another voice added into the mix. "What are you doing?" Baey asked desperately as she glided over.

I took in a labored breath and clenched my jaw, annoyed at my own weakness. "I just...needed to stretch...my legs." It sounded even more pathetic with the coughs. "We need to get...going."

"Yes, but you don't need to kill yourself," Estasia butted in with a huff.

I blinked and tried to focus more. "Skayla will find...this place soon." How could I get through to them?

"But if you kill yourself in the process, there's not much use in it, Sven." Sefen's voice rang out clear and stern, sounding even stronger than even last night.

I was starting to get impatient, and all my nerves were frayed in a hundred different ways. There wasn't time. We had to find The Crafters before Skayla found us. All that was left were those who stood in this room—and if we failed? Baeno would be gone. *Really* gone. "I'm...fine." I said stubbornly, continuing to walk with Jaythos' help. "This was a test to see if I can ride, and I have to say—" I coughed—"It's not going too badly." Painfully but not badly.

Sefen sighed. "Fine. You've proved your point; you can walk and most likely ride with help. We'll start packing, and if you're well enough we can head out today. But you should sit down and rest for now."

"Alright," I conceded. "But I need to borrow Tanner." I remembered one of the reasons I had actually gone to Valdon and wished my stupid brain worked better. MindHolds were almost worse after you got out of them.

Sefen looked hesitant, but nodded. "Fine. But Tanner...." He turned behind him to the boy, "You let him move, and I'll kill you."

So many threats of death...I would have thought the ones from Skayla and Kovo had been enough. But as Jaythos and Baey sat me down against the nearest wall, I took Baey's arm. "And, one more thing." I again caught sight of the precious burdens she carried. "I need the watch."

Baey:

Sven extended his hand, and I took the pendant from around my neck, handing it carefully over to him. I felt strangely responsible for it and letting it out of my possession was a little unnerving.

"Thank you, darlin'," he whispered as the gold watch and chain necklace dropped gently into his palm. I felt a little pull as I let go and knew the ring already missed it. I wondered if Sven felt the longing, too—after all, the ring did belong to him. Did he want it back? I noted how he caressed the watch, and again I thought of my hypothesis. If this was indeed Moira's, it was all Sven had left of his oldest sister.

The others slowly dispersed; Sefen back in charge and directing everyone in what to do. I wasn't sure whether I was glad or a little upset at him not telling me to do anything. I had begun to feel so useful, but now that everyone was getting their bearings back, I was afraid I would slip back into the shadows.

"So why do you need it?" I asked, sitting a little more comfortably down and resolving to stay and make sure Sven didn't break the deal. I pretended it wasn't also my curiosity.

"I need Tanner to find…something," he said, staring a moment at the watch, almost in a trance. For a moment, I was worried as his breathing almost seemed to stop, but then he handed it to Tanner, and the tension dissipated.

"See that crack?" he asked Tanner.

Tanner nodded, and I already had a feeling I knew where this was going. By the look on Tanner's face, he did as well.

"Can you only search memories...from people or... from objects as well?" Sven pressed quietly, confirming my feeling. Unbearable curiosity swelled in my chest, and I waited, wings twitching in anticipation.

"Of course, I can search objects." Tanner puffed himself up a little at the question, trying to look offended—and failing. "Especially if the memory is specific and shown on the object. Like this crack."

Sven's jaw clenched for a moment before he spoke. "Right...I need you to find where that crack came from."

Tanner looked down at the watch, and for a moment, I thought I saw a little hesitance in his face.

"There are going to be a lot of memories in there, Tanner. But we need to know when the crack happened," Sven repeated, looking nervous, himself.

I held my breath and watched as Tanner caressed the scarred glass, eyes closing for a moment. His body went rigid, and I reminded myself not to worry. Seldom did he have to concentrate so hard. I bit my lip, wishing he would tell us what he saw already. I was about ready to burst with tension.

Then his eyes shot open, and he stared from Sven to me, and then back to Sven.

I did the same, watching as Sven's face went even more deathly white. "What did you see?" he asked, as calm as death, faraway eyes staring unblinking at the watch.

Tanner was shaking. "I saw...I saw...."

CHAPTER XVI: Wrapped in a Ring

Baey:

Tanner was acting as if he had just woken from a horrible nightmare, and I was by my friend's side in an instant, putting a hand on his shoulder in the hopes of both comforting him and keeping him in the here and now. "Tanner. Ugh, come on. It's alright." He had never been so shaken up by memories before, not like this.

"I…." Tanner was swaying where he sat, as if in a trance. He didn't finish his sentence.

"Are you alright? I told you…not to get…lost," Sven said between coughs, moving over and putting a hand on Tanner's pale face, tapping it gently with a trembling hand.

Tanner's body convulsed in one last shiver before composing himself. Well. Sort of composing himself. He looked shaken to the core but wasn't trembling anymore at least.

"Tanner?" Sven's hoarse voice broke the silence only barely.

Taking a shaky breath, my friend shook his head. "S-sorry," he stumbled. "I…there were so many memories…so many…awful…I got lost." He stared at Sven for a long while, and the two passed a knowing sort of look.

What had happened?

"What did you see?" Sven asked.

"There was a-a lady," he began with a slight tremor in his voice, "and, uh, she was standing in front of—"

"But you saw more than that," Sven interrupted. I turned to see his face twisted in worried puzzlement, pale and drawn. He was now kneeling precariously next to Tanner and me, and I watched him sway.

"Sit back down, Sven," I ordered gently.

He opened his mouth to argue, but it turned into a grimace. Still, as he sat up against the wall again, he repeated his statement, this time as a question: "What did you see before that?"

Tanner stood up and brushed himself off with his free hand. He turned to me and slowly handed back the watch. "It was hard to distinguish," he murmured. He was lying. I had known Tanner for several years, and when he lied, he had this nervous twitch in his left hand. However, whatever the reason for lying, I wouldn't ask him now, in front of Sven. Maybe I'd try and get him to tell me later, after he'd had some time to process.

"Alright," Sven quietly. "Sorry. Go on."

"There was a lady," he repeated. "She fit Skayla's description. There was another woman—blond hair falling almost down to her waist. Blue eyes." Tanner paused there, clearing his throat as he seemed to start to recover. "Skayla called her Moira," he finished quietly.

I watched as Sven got paler and paler, and I wasn't sure whether it was because of what Tanner had said or because he was overexerting himself.

"Are you alright, Sven? Let me look you over." I made as if to go towards him, looking down to see the reddened stain through his tattered shirt. Ugh. He was hurting himself.

"No, no," He waved a hand weakly. "Let Tanner finish first."

I nodded reluctantly for Tanner to continue; clearing his throat one more time, he went on, "They were arguing. I couldn't hear all they said. Then a man—tall, I think it was Kovo—appeared next to Skayla with a captive. Kovo killed the captive—" Tanner paused to swallow, "and, uh, well. Um...well. Moira screamed...and she clutched the watch around her neck and...I don't really know what happened.... Something flashed, and Skayla latched onto her.... And suddenly it was in Skayla's hand, and she threw it on the ground and stomped on it...and when everything cleared, Moira was gone." The more he'd relayed the memory, the more excitement and confusion his features had shown.

Sven looked completely drained and lost, not moving a muscle. I overcame my own shock and confusion and left Tanner to go to him, inspecting his still-healing wounds. Ugh. He needed to rest. But it seemed no one could convince him. I looked around and saw the others in the far edge of the cave, loading up the horses. Only Estasia seemed to be paying any *real* attention.

"I'm fine. But I need to talk to Sefen alone. Tanner, could you go see if he has a moment. It looks like they're...just about done...anyway." Sven's coughs sounded painful, and his skin was clammy again.

Tanner nodded and hopped up, casting a quick look back at me before taking off at full speed.

"You *aren't* alright. And if you don't rest for a while, you could be in more trouble than you already are, Sven," I said fretfully, biting my lip and flexing my wings in and out.

"I am resting," he tried to convince me, but it was clear even he knew how pathetic the lie was. "I have to talk to Sefen, darlin'. I'm sorry. But it is important."

Ugh. How did we balance important with staying alive? I didn't really have time to come up with an answer, sadly, as I heard Sefen's uneven footsteps coming this way, and I turned to see him limping towards us with Tanner in tow.

"Why don't you and Tanner go see if the others need anything," Sven not-so-subtly hinted that he wanted to talk *alone*. While I was only more nervous about what Sven could do if I wasn't watching, part of me wasn't too disappointed by being left out of the conversation, for once. Perhaps I could get a chance to see what was bothering Tanner so much. Still. Sven had better not do anything stupid.

"What's the matter, Sven?" Sefen asked as he stopped before us, giving the man a look that summed up all my worries and annoyances with Sven.

"Tanner and I will go see if Jaythos or Maeko need help," I said, nodding to Tanner to follow me.

As we headed away, I heard Sven say, "We need to leave as soon as possible. Please."

I wanted to listen more but didn't have the guts to. Besides, I had a friend I was worried about. "Are you alright, Tanner?" I asked. He didn't *look* particularly alright. His hand was twitching as if his very posture was lying, but I realized it was more from nervousness than anything else.

"It was just…a lot of information." He said with a deep breath.

"Alright." As much as I wanted to know, I wouldn't press. He was clearly very upset, and he was my friend, not a source of information. But I knew that later—if there was a later—I would try again, maybe when it wasn't so dire.

"Is everything alright?" Estasia asked us, head cocked to the side as she looked beyond us to where Sven and Sefen were talking.

Tanner immediately returned to his usual self. His quirky smile flashed, and he shrugged. "Far as I know."

Estasia's stare never wavered from the two in the corner, even as she finished doing the girth on one of the horses.

I didn't really want to be around her, so I turned and went over to Maeko, who was securing the other horses until we were ready to leave. "Where's Jaythos?" I asked.

"Went to look and see if all was safe," he replied, jerking his head in the direction of the exit.

My brow furrowed. "You mean he left?"

Maeko's lips drew back in a small smile. "My Varnese is bad? I thought that was what I said. Maybe means something else?" I was about to reply in earnest when I realized he'd been trying to make a joke. Oh. Oops. My bad.

I rolled my eyes, but as much as I was glad Maeko was being something *other* than angry, this wasn't good. "How long ago did he leave?" It couldn't have been terribly long ago. I'd seen him packing up only a little while before. What if he got caught? The rain had stopped, and though it was still overcast, it would give the Drogans a lot better view of their targets. The cliff was a little way from the forest, so that detection would be much more likely when leaving the cave. We'd need to wait for cover of darkness, not that the Drogans would have too much of a disadvantage even then. If only it would rain again.

I huffed and my wings twitched in agitation. "Did he say when he'd be back?" I felt like there was a sturdy lack of coordination right now, and all this chaos was beginning to make me a little concerned. We needed to work together…but everyone seemed to have devolved to a state of disregarding any sort of communication. We just needed Sefen and Sven to get completely better. Perhaps then it would be better. Now I saw where Sven was coming from.

"Soon," was the only answer given to me.

Why did Jaythos have to be so vague? What if he was caught and our hiding place betrayed? I couldn't think of that, though. No. There had to be hope, and we would have to get out. But where would we go?

"Maeko, will you come over here?" Sefen shouted in our direction, and Maeko handed me the reins to the two horses.

I watched anxiously as Maeko strode over to where the other two were, and I bit my lip again. Maybe I should talk to Sefen, tell him my concerns. But I had no right. Surely, he saw it, too, and would fix it. He'd just been hurt and unable to enforce order. I would be completely overstepping to tell him my concerns. But I still didn't like the thought of Maeko near Sven.

"What are you doing, Feathers?" Tanner made me jump a little, hovering for just a moment in the air before recollecting myself. Had he really needed to scare me while I was holding the horses? I was lucky they hadn't balked too much at my sudden movement.

"Just holding the horses," I replied, stating the obvious. "You? Other than, well, scaring me," I added, giving an icy glare to show him just how unappreciative I was.

He smiled innocently, shrugging. "Estasia didn't want my help. She said they were done anyway…I still don't like her," he added, glancing over in her direction.

I was indecisive. She acted like she didn't like us, but I had a feeling she was one of those people that naturally didn't get along with other people. That being said, even though Estasia had told us why she'd helped, I felt like things were being left out—and that was never a good sign.

Estasia:

I kept an eye on the boy, trying to find out what exactly had happened over there. He looked shaken up—as much as he attempted to bury the fact—and I couldn't help but be curious. He had powers, that was for sure, but according to the rumors about Valdon, most everyone who had lived there had some sort of Gift.

"We need to leave as soon as possible." Sefen announced calmly as he limped back up to the two children and me. Maeko was still by Sven, and seemed about to help him up, but did not look happy about it. I wasn't either, but his murder stare had disappeared. Now it was only disgust. Though Maeko had apparently made the decision to so *mercifully* let Sven live, I still doubted him. Had he no comprehension of the pain Sven had endured? It wasn't like he'd *chosen* to be put in a MindHold.

"Where are we going?" the girl asked.

Sefen sighed, looking uneasy. "Hopefully somewhere safe."

"But we can't run, Sefen!" the boy jumped in, sounding indignant. "There's nothing but us left. We have to find a way to undo this! What's the point if we don't?" I watched as he threw his arms up, jaw set in defiance as he faced off against his elder. Unlike Baey, he seemed to have quite the streak of rebellion.

Sefen's face immediately turned stern, and you could have heard an insect's breath, it was so quiet. "We are *not* running, Tanner. Do not argue against what you do not understand. Just because I have not told you does not mean there is not a plan," he said, clearly not at all pleased with the little punk.

I secured the horses and moved slowly out of sight, doubling back over to where Maeko was helping Sven up. I needed to show them they could trust me, and I needed to see whether I could trust them to be competent before I explained anything of my information. So far, they weren't showing themselves to be very successful. It was a sad day when the last hopes on this planet were acting like a bunch of egotistical children—but then, I suppose it was better than a slave and ex-thief.

"Would you like help?" I asked drolly, stopping beside Sven's painful attempts to hoist himself up with Maeko's reluctant help.

Maeko glared at me as always, but Sven nodded. "Another hand wouldn't hurt."

I came up on the opposite side from Maeko, and together we were able to get Sven up and unsteadily on his feet.

"*How far is the sanctuary from here?*" Maeko asked Sven coldly in Rugonian. I wondered if Sven remembered I could speak the language. Intending to find out, I pretended to be mystified, looking at them in confusion briefly before returning to my task of helping Sven walk slowly to the horses. He seemed to be having a little trouble remembering things, so perhaps I would be in luck.

"*The old ruins are—about three- or four-days hard ride. Then, I, um. don't know.*" Sven's voice was vacant as he spoke, focused on just getting to the horses, and avoiding Maeko's glares. It would appear either this was a trick, or he really was having forgetfulness from the fever. Somehow, I figured the latter was more probable. What would I gain from this information to be tricked by anyway? I wasn't a spy, and if anything, this would show I wasn't. Whether they knew it or not, I could actually help them a lot more than they knew.

"*You need to be careful; you are not well, GhostMaker.*" Maeko's voice dripped with as much worry as I figured the Rugonian could muster. Sven just looked at him with a blank sort of sad smile. I realized Maeko really only cared right now because he was their guide and still he called Sven by that horrid name. Indignation for Sven grew, but I kept it down.

"*I'm fine.*"

Sven's accent was pretty atrocious, and he seemed a bit rusty. Granted he hadn't done much talking in the last eight years, let alone in multiple languages, so it made sense

Sven coughed, trying to put more weight on his own feet with little success.

"Careful. Maybe use us a little more for support?" I asked.

Turning to me, Sven looked mystified. "I've got it. I feel—" he winced—"splendid."

I didn't reply, just raised an eyebrow and showed how unimpressed I was.

"*What do you expect to find at the ruins?*" Maeko asked Sven, as if I didn't even exist.

I didn't bother hiding my annoyance but nonetheless didn't interject as we continued to walk towards the horses.

"A clue. Hopefully, Tanner can find another one."

"What did the watch show?"

"Not much in relation to ruins." Sven's voice was quiet, and I had a feeling that whatever had…happened…had revealed other things for him that he didn't wish to share. *"But pr-proved Tanner can get memories from more…more than just people."* His coughing renewed, but he managed to keep it under control. I didn't like him talking so much, but at the same time, this was important information he would give with or without me, so if I stopped him, he'd just give it somewhere else where I couldn't hear.

"Again with your tricks, GhostMaker." Maeko's voice hardened, and I grit my teeth.

Before anything else could be said, we reached the horses, and I took in a deep breath as I realized the difficulty ahead. "This…is going to hurt," I mumbled to Sven.

"Lovely reassurance," his reply was sarcastic, and yet I could hear the thinness in his tone. He was still so weak. This was probably a bad idea, but as much as I hated it, Sven was right. We didn't have time to rest here. We needed to find a more secure location…if one existed.

Maeko turned to where Sefen and Tanner stood, "Where's Jaythos?"

Sefen didn't look very pleased. "Not back yet. He had better be soon, too."

"Did he not tell you…he was going?" Sven asked with a cough, clearly as irritated as I felt. Yeah, this group seemed really incompetent.

Sefen said nothing, just turned shortly around and inspected the saddle's girth—probably for the thousandth time.

"Sefen...we need to stay together." Sven sounded pretty desperate and just a little perturbed.

This didn't help Sefen's mood, and he clenched his fist. "I am aware, Mara."

"*Tell that to yourself next time, Mara. You did the same thing to the whole world.*" Maeko's voice was quiet but still audible. I clenched my free fist. I wanted to say something but found it in my best interest to keep my mouth shut. I needed to get their trust, not their fury.

"He's coming! I see him!" The girl came running clumsily from the cave entrance, constantly tripping on her wings.

There was a simultaneous sigh of relief from all four of us, and Sefen muttered, "Finally," before limping moodily off to the cave entrance, with the girl leading the way.

"Well..." Sven whispered awkwardly in his faraway voice. He put his hands on the saddle and started mounting up. I reached to help him, but he was actually pretty spry and had mounted up before Maeko or I could lift a finger. He smiled slyly, cleverly hiding his grimace. "Told you to have faith," he retorted.

"Oh, I have faith, just in your habit of getting yourself killed," was all I would say. Then there was the clatter of hooves from the cave entrance, and everyone turned sharply to find Sefen, Jaythos, and Baey each leading a horse. My chest squeezed almost all the breath out of me, and I ran my hand over my hair. "Where did you get those?" I asked, frantic.

"I ambushed a small patrol," Jaythos said, glaring at me.

Naturally. Of course. I ran over to them and snatched one of the reins from his hands, looking over the horse and then lifting its hind left hoof. "You idiot, these horses are marked. Don't you know that?" Of all the worst-case scenarios there could be, this was getting up there.

Jaythos didn't seem to want to admit his fault, and I didn't care. I moved to the other horses, checking each of them. All but one was marked. "Skayla has the horses marked on their hooves. It's an old Bethynese trick she learned. It's easy to track thieves and escapees that way," I explained in exasperation to Sefen, completely ignoring the indignant Jaythos. Zeal without knowledge was not a good thing, and this just showed that.

"I am *quite* aware they are marked," Jaythos broke in. "We can lead them in the opposite direction. We're leaving today, aren't we? No one will find out what happened until several hours at the least, a day or two at best. If we let the horses go, then they will lead them on a wild goose chase."

I stood there, red-faced. I may have underestimated him…slightly.

"If you all…don't mind…lowered voices would be appreciated." I turned to see Sven wearing a pained expression, as if he was fighting a headache. It was clear that the arguing had worn on him, and he was anxious to get moving.

"We should get going anyway. We'll need to go slowly at first—to cover the prints of our horses. We'll be taking the supplies off these horses first, however. Baey and Estasia will be on one horse. Jaythos, you ride with Sven." Once Sefen started speaking, any remaining trace of awkwardness dissipated. Everyone was once more moving and getting ready, Tanner and Baey relieving the horses of their burdens while Jaythos and I held them still.

Jaythos gave a quick nod of understanding, and Sefen continued, "Tanner will ride on the other, and I'll ride for a while on the last one. Maeko, can you cover our tracks?"

"I could help," Baey's voice broke in meekly, but her face showed she instantly regretted the words as they came out of her mouth. Timid little thing, wasn't she?

"No, Baey," Sefen replied sternly.

"It would be helpful, Sefen. She could cover them without showing any, herself," Sven cut in to defend the little bird, showing another sign of aggravation. I didn't really like the way Sefen was belittling Baey either. I watched it only feed into her self-doubt.

Sefen released a pent-up breath, "Fine. Cover our initial tracks and then get on with Estasia, understand?"

"Mhm," Baey said, trying to hide the sparkle in her eyes. I hid my own smile. I thought I might get to like her.

The very air itself was taut as we started off in the gloom of a clouded night, the sound of Drogans' screeches sounding too close for comfort. Baey was squeezing me uncomfortably tight, her wings probably causing complications in her staying on. Still, it would be nice to breathe.

Sven and Sefen were at the front, taking it at a slow trot for a while until we got under the cover of the trees. Then Maeko somehow managed to get on the back of Sefen's horse and we were off.

"Cover." Sven whispered the signal, and I turned the horse swiftly to a nearby thick trunked tree. I felt a dark shadow cover over me, and Baey's wings fell around us as they had already several times before, shielding us from the outside world. A high-pitched screech sounded directly above us, and I held my breath, thinking that any moment we would be discovered.

Ten agonizing minutes passed before Sefen whispered the all clear. It went on like this most of the night, and no matter how many times we did it, it didn't get any easier. But gradually, the further north we went, the fewer and fewer incidents we had. The screeches became more distant, and the bigger worry became any ground-based patrols. Patrols looking for us. Hopefully, the horses Jaythos had released would help put a little more distance between us and our hunters.

All was silent as the delicate color of morning marked the sky; a warning that the cover of night would no longer protect us. As I watched Sefen and Sven, I could tell that they were wearing thin. They had definitely made quick progress in healing, but still, we really needed to stop to avoid relapses. However, by the looks of it, we wouldn't be resting any time soon.

Hours passed, and the sun began to shine brightly down on the autumn-colored trees. Another couple of weeks and our only cover would be gone. Hopefully, this sanctuary we were going to would indeed be just that—safe.

302

Sven:

I had told Sefen where we were going before we'd left, just in case I forgot...again. It had not been a good couple of days. I hoped our destination would, in fact, be safe, but the place we had to go to first might not be. Skayla knew of it, and it was possible she would expect us to hide there, or look there for information—the latter of which was true.

Tanner's words played over and over in my mind, and I tried to picture the horrible scene, unable to make complete sense out of it. "*Suddenly it was in Skayla's hand, and she threw it on the ground and stomped on it...and when everything cleared, Moira was gone.*" I recollected the memory to the best of my ability, trying to understand what had happened. Moira must have meant to go back in time and stop them from killing the captive, and when Skayla had broken the watch.... Was it possible that Moira was still alive? Or would it have killed her? I had to know...but I had no way to find out. And who had the captive been?

I forced myself out of deep thought when I realized everything was blurry. Where was I again? I barely stayed on my horse as my mind was tossed every which way in confusion, and I felt whoever else was on my horse try and steady me. What was I doing here?

The person in front of me slowed his mount, and we halted for a moment. I turned in my saddle and eyed the others. Everyone began to dismount—my companion went first then tried to help me down, which I refused. The way I was feeling, dismounting might mean not being able to get back *on* the horse. Instead, I looked around me, hoping *someone's* face would be recognizable. Behind me were two more horses, and a lady stood by the horse closest to mine, along with a winged girl. A glint of gold from around the girl's neck caught in the sunlight, and the important things came back. Unfortunately, I was still a bit at a loss.

"We'll rest for a moment. Drink if you need it, but remember, we don't have many supplies," the man in the front said. What was his name again?

The winged girl slowly made her way up to me. Baey. That was right. Baey. Her name made way for—at least for the most part—the rest of my memories.

"Sven?" she said hesitantly.

I leaned down a bit. "Hm?"

She reached around her neck and pulled the chain over her head, dangling it in front of me. "I didn't really have a chance to give this back earlier," she said quietly.

There, within grasp, hung my ring. The small green jewel glinted in the autumn sun as my eyes traced each of the barely visible intricate designs on the silver ring. I broke out of the trance and inhaled one ragged breath.

No. You seem to be keeping it plenty safe," I said quietly. I wished I never had to see that awful thing again. It was a curse, a memory, and even now I felt its aching pull in my chest; an ache I couldn't be rid of even if I *did* wear it.

"But it's not mine, and I'm really not good at it," she replied desperately.

I blinked, staring blankly as I tried to digest what she had just said.

"Get ready to leave," Sefen called out as he mounted his horse, interrupting just as I was about to make a bewildered reply.

Baey gave a hesitant look back to where Estasia had just mounted up.

"What do you mean, you're not good at it?" I finally managed to say. She couldn't...use it...could she? How?

She bit her lip, and her wings wrapped around her just as they always did when she was nervous. "I...well...um."

"Sven, Baey, is everything alright?" Sefen turned in his saddle and blinked at us in concern.

Baey nodded. "Yes, sorry." And before I could say another word, she floated over to Estasia and the horse.

As we took off again, my head whirred with her words. Not good at it. How could she have used it? No one could use our relics but us—it was a tested and proven fact. So, what could Baey possibly mean?

CHAPTER XVII: Forgotten Gifts...And General Amnesia

Sven:

We stopped for a longer rest around noon, finding a sheltered spot among the high Crysen trees. As I wrestled off my horse with Jaythos's help, I got an instant reminder that I was still not myself...whoops.

Using Jaythos as a support, I found a sturdy place to sit down under the tree, watching the others intently as they did the same. We were all exhausted, and I was surprised any of us were awake. It was probably only the sound of our sanity ripping at the seams that was keeping anyone up.

Estasia walked stiffly over to me, sitting down on my right and asking, "How are you holding up?"

"Like a tree." I tried not to sound as dead as I felt and leaned my head back on said tree, forcing myself not to close my eyes. Sleeping was probably the worst idea that was coming into my head.

"I would say so. You look rough."

I turned, only vaguely impressed at her comment, and sighed. "Where's Baey?" I asked, sitting up straight and forcing myself to be alert. Baey's words were banging around in my empty head again, and I still couldn't understand them.

"Talking with Sefen. She'll be over in a moment though to check on you. You should try to get some sleep, though, Sven. Jaythos and Maeko are watching the skies and ground, and we haven't seen a Drogan in a good four hours at least," Estasia replied, seeming to be in the loop of everything. I wasn't sure if that was a good thing or bad thing; spies had the knack for not letting anything get past them. Granted, she'd shown more loyalty already than Namaya had.

I was running out of the energy required to look rested and stable. "I'm fine, just fine," I muttered. I couldn't afford to sleep. Even though I'd explained to Sefen where we were going, there were a lot of other things in this useless brain of mine that I was afraid I would forget if I fell asleep. Even now, I felt I had forgotten something very important and that bugged me more than anything in the world. All those years of Skayla using me, putting me in a MindHold, and suppressing my memories were really getting to me. I'd hoped it would get better the longer I was free of it all, but it was taking so much longer than I'd hoped. At least I remembered who I was. Well, most of the time, anyway.

"Sven?" I snapped out of it to see a lady staring at me, face twisted in worry. Did I know her? I groaned in pure exasperation, ready to bang my head against the trunk of the tree.

"What's the matter?" she pressed.

I huffed, looking around for something that would make me remember who she was. Anything. I watched Sefen and Baey talking, Tanner patting down the horses and wondered why in the world it was just this one lady I couldn't remember. *Come on, Sven!*

"You don't look well. What's wrong?" Her voice was now a little more prodding, concerned and no-nonsense. "Sven?" She raised her voice slightly when I still didn't answer.

My brow furrowed, and I gave up. I looked at her with a very pathetic expression and said breathlessly, "Who are you again?" It was probably the most stupid question I could have asked, and by the look on her face, it could even be worse. But I just couldn't do this right now—I was too tired to think straight and too tired to remember.

She turned and crossed her legs, looking at me with sincere worry. "What?"

I looked around at the others again, clenching my jaw and repeating their names in my head over and over again, so hopefully everything *else* wouldn't fly out of my head. Then I turned back to her and smiled. "Never mind," I said, pretending I'd just been joking. *Come on...what was her name!*

"Sven...you don't remember me...at all?" Her question rang around in my head as I tried to put the voice to a name, but I couldn't. I just couldn't. "Wow. You really don't. Um. Alright...it's just me, Estasia."

I narrowed my eyes and said nothing. The name didn't click immediately, and it was quite possible that someone could just say that to try and get my trust. I hated feeling vulnerable.

"You and Sefen were in the Kovian Fortress. I helped get you out...Namaya was there?" Her voice stuttered just a little as she said the name. Namaya. Who was that? "Doesn't ring a bell?"

The sound of approaching footsteps distracted the very fruitless discussion, and we both turned to find Baey approaching. "Is something the matter?" she asked, looking me up and down like a fretful child.

Estasia started to open her mouth, but I promptly interjected, "No, darlin', nothin'. Just resting." I didn't need to add any more worry, though it was becoming clear everyone seemed to know. I just had to get this fixed…somehow.

"Why don't I look over you, just the same?" Baey only half-suggested, already kneeling down and preparing to inspect me.

Shaking my head, I moved slightly away. "No, no, I'm fine, darlin'. You need to go rest so you can keep a keen eye out. I'll tell you if anything's wrong. Don't worry." I patted her hand reassuringly and smiled. This didn't seem to convince her, but I gave her a face that made it clear that this was no option. I knew she would only push back so much, and I would let her know if anything was terribly wrong. I wanted terribly to talk about what she had said earlier, but not in front of Estasia. Still, I couldn't wait too long.

She finally gave a hesitant nod, backing away slowly and biting her lip to show that she did silently protest. But I just gave my best disarming smile and didn't waver.

As soon as she finally was gone, Estasia turned back to me. "You should be looked at. And do you *still* not remember?"

My brow furrowed, and I looked confused, "Wait. What?" I hadn't forgotten. What did she mean?

"Wait. Sven…What's my name?" she asked slowly.

Confused, I answered, "Estasia…" Then it hit me. Oh great, what had I forgotten? Estasia seemed no fool, and by the looks of it, she already had it half figured out. And had I just…forgotten I'd forgotten…? Great, this was getting too hard for even *me* to understand.

"Do you not remember any of the conversation we just had?"

I winced. We'd had a conversation? "You mean the one with Baey?" I tried, seeing by her face that I was very wrong.

"It's the MindHold, isn't it," she more stated than asked.

I tried to keep my confused expression, but it didn't work. Now I was just half-panicked. No one needed to know how bad this was, especially not Estasia. As much as she had helped so far, I still didn't know how far I could trust her.

"How long has it been like this?"

I started to get up, using the trunk of the tree for a firm support and the half sleeping horse on my left as the other.

"What do you think you're doing?" she asked sharply, jumping up and grabbing hold of my arm.

I grimaced as she accidentally hit a sore spot, muttering, "You're not helping."

Her grip lightened but didn't release, "Well, neither are you. Now, sit. Down. Now. This is getting old, Sven."

I sighed but obeyed.

"Now I know you don't trust me that much, but don't you think I would have turned you all over to Skayla by now? The girl has the watch, which is what Skayla wants, isn't it?"

Yeah. I didn't like this. At all. "You are treading on very precarious ground. Be careful." I didn't rein in how close to losing all favor she was, and I saw just the slightest glimmer of doubt in her eyes.

"You can't do this alone, idiot. And unlike *some of us*—" she glanced quickly at Maeko—"I would prefer to see you stay alive."

"Fine," was all I said. I needed to watch her—catch her reaction.

The tension in her body almost instantly released, and she let out a sigh, straightening and brushing herself off before breathing a barely audible, "Thank you," and walking off.

I watched her go, eyes narrowed as I tried to decide whether trusting her really was a good idea. Perhaps if I pretended to go along with her, she would herself go along with me, and tell me exactly why she was helping. Only time would tell.

Baey:

I really wasn't sure if I should have let Sven push me away like that, but I just found it so hard to argue. He did look a little better…. A little less like he could pass out or die or anything like that. But at the same time, he was clearly so spent. This long ride had taken a lot out of him, and he hadn't really had much time to heal at all. In fact, he'd had barely *any*. What were we ever going to do? I only wished I knew where we were going, and if going there would do anything at all except hide us. We needed to *do* something.

"Er…Feathers?" Tanner's voice came crashing into my musings, shattering the bird-brained thoughts that I was mulling over.

"Hm? Sorry." I yanked my eyes off of Estasia and Sven. I wasn't sure what I thought of her, but she kept steadfastly by Sven's side. So far, she seemed genuinely concerned for him, but Namaya had also been a supposed friend…and her actions alone spoke for our mistrust. Was it worth taking a second chance?

"Feathers. Hello? You still in there? Baey?"

Ugh. "Oh. Sorry, Tanner. I just can't seem to focus…I'm tired." I forced myself to break out of my self-imposed trance. I was just so exhausted, and everything seemed like something to watch and be mindful of: the skies, the noises of the forest, Estasia, Sefen, Sven. I was overwhelmed.

Tanner sighed. "Yeah. You look it. Get some sleep." He gestured to a nearby tree and made a face. "Not exactly a bed, but hey, it works. Besides, you're part bird or something, right?" That roguish grin of his appeared then, but I was too tired to laugh.

Nonetheless, I didn't want to sleep. Well, I did, just not yet. Not until I figured everything out a little more. I hazarded another look over to Sven and Estasia, just in time to see the lady brush herself off, huffing and giving one more worried look to Sven before heading toward Maeko. Suddenly, I felt someone's eyes on me, and I realized it was Sven. My own eyes narrowed in confusion as I stared back. Ever so slightly, he made a nod for me to come over.

"I'll be back," I told Tanner distractedly.

I trod over to Sven, wings twitching anxiously as I noted Tanner's quietness at my leaving. He seemed shaken up still about whatever he'd seen in the watch, and I'd been too caught up in my own thoughts to notice. Ugh.

"Sit down, darlin'." Sven motioned to an empty spot beside him, and I sat down.

My wings promptly folded around me, and I cocked my head. "You alright?" I eyed the bandages on his arms and tried to see if he was favoring his side any more than earlier, but all seemed as well as it could be in this position. Even the bruise on his eye was slowly fading, leaving only that sickly yellow-green color in its wake.

"Yes, fine. But I need to ask you something," he said with a wave of his hand. His vacant gaze was trained on me, but he seemed to be looking through me and to something beyond, as if I wasn't in front of him at all.

"What?" I asked hesitantly. He looked worried, and I wondered if it had something to do with me offering the ring earlier. Should I not have?

He cleared his throat and adjusted his position with a wince. "What did you mean you're not good at using the ring?" he asked at last.

I wasn't sure what to make of this. Was it not normal to not be good at it? "I...well, I tried to use it...but I really just meant I'm not very good...that's all." I looked down at my fidgeting fingers, feeling awkward and embarrassed. Was I letting him down? I'd always looked up to him, and I couldn't bear the thought of failing him after all he'd sacrificed for me. When he was finally here, *alive*, for me to look up to.

After a while of no response, however, I finally hazarded a quick look up, and found that he was staring at me with wide-eyed wonder, and no small dose of disbelief. I looked back down at my hands and then at him.

"Wh-what's the matter? What did I say?" I stumbled over my words, feeling oddly vulnerable.

"Show me," was all he replied with.

"Show you...what? The ring?"

"No, no. Show me how you use the ring," he clarified, with a gesture towards me.

The pressure was immense, and I really didn't want to. "Um...alright," I managed to murmur, slowly taking the ring and chain from around my neck and grasping it tight in my fist. I bit my lip a little too hard, feeling like the idea of falling short of Sven's expectations was enough to make my head explode. What if I couldn't do it? What if I failed in front of him...what if....

Stop it, Baey. You've been waiting for this. Maybe this is your chance to really prove yourself.

With a deep breath, I repeated that over and over in my head, hoping that if I said it enough, I would believe it. *You have to try. You're not just useless.*

I closed my eyes, picking out the first object I had ever imagined: Sven's sword. The beautiful silver, the slightly curved southern-styled blade. I saw new details too—the small message engraved at the base of the blade, and the intricate designs that ran down to the tip. When I opened my eyes, it was laying in my hand, shimmering a little as my focus wavered. I chanced a look up at Sven and found him staring dumbfoundedly at the blade in my hand. Any remnants of concentration vanished and, with it, the sword. My hands fumbled with the sleeves of my shirt, and my eyes darted hither and thither as my wings slowly began to fold further and further around me. I could practically feel them turning dark crimson.

"…What…what's wrong?" I finally made myself spit out the words, sounding as uncertain as I felt.

His free hand clenched and unclenched, and he kept shaking his head in disbelief. The way he just stared silently, eyes wide, was worse than a thousand words could have spoken.

The suspense was killing my nerves, and I couldn't stand it any longer. "What? What did I do, Sven?" I fumbled through the sentence, ready to just sit and cry. I couldn't tell whether he was astounded or disgusted. Had I done something amazing or terrible? I dared not hope for the best and, therefore, expected the worst…I had to know.

"You…you aren't supposed to be able to do that, darlin'…it's impossible," he said with a disbelieving shake of the head. "T-The ring only magnifies power. One isn't supposed to be able *to* use it unless they're the original owner," he added breathlessly.

I shrunk a little more within myself, not trusting my legs to get me up. Instead, I sat there helplessly, asking in a near squeak, "Is that a bad thing?"

"No, but I mean…I mean, how?" He stared at me, only making me more anxious. That was quite the reassuring answer I'd wanted. "How did you do it?"

I was so overwhelmed and not really sure what to do. "I-I just was thinking about the—the night I saw you, and I thought about something—really clearly—and I opened my eyes, and it was-was there. I'm sorry," I finished, about ready to cry but still having the sense to keep my voice down, so that Sefen or any of the others wouldn't come over to see what was going on.

"Shh, sorry, darlin', I didn't mean to scare you." Sven's expression turned worried. "It's just…well, it's not safe to explain here," he interrupted himself, giving a wary look around. "But don't worry. You've not done anything wrong. Quite the opposite." He gave a wink there, an attempt at lightheartedness that was dampened by the weight on his shoulders.

I nodded slowly. "Alright," was my squeaky reply. I wanted to believe him, but his reaction had been so…worried, and now I would live in uncertainty until he explained it.

"I'll leave you to rest, then." I wanted to stay and ask, but he looked so tired that I checked myself in my thirst to understand. It wasn't worth Sven suffering.

A few hours passed by, and I was satisfied to see Sven and Sefen at least close their eyes and *try* to get some sleep. Even I dozed off for an hour or so, still poring over what Sven and I had talked of but too exhausted not to sleep a little.

"We need to get going," Jaythos announced, looking at the late afternoon skies.

Sven, who had woken up about half an hour ago, got up and leaned on his horse heavily, not really looking too fit to travel. "Tell Sefen we need to divert our path a little. We can't lead them straight to it."

I mustered the power to command my legs once more and got slowly back on my feet. I wanted to ask where we were going but dared not. Anyone could be listening, and Sven seemed to be worried that ears were indeed everywhere.

"Baey. Why don't you fly near treetop level to scout?" Jaythos turned and half asked, half ordered. My wings pricked up as my attention was caught. Could I really? Pulse throbbing full of hope, I nodded vigorously. Then my faith dampened. "Did Sefen allow it?" Sefen was only now being awoken by Maeko. He obviously hadn't heard.

I was surprised when Sven broke in. "You should be fine, Baey." He seemed to answer my fears, scattering them.

I blinked at him, surprised. "But...should I? With what I have?"

"Everyone on the horses and stop gossiping like old ladies," Sefen's insult cut the air, and Sven barely had time for a nod before hoisting himself stiffly onto his horse.

I flew up, my fingers lightly brushing the tips of dying leaves as I hovered above my friends…my family. Looking down, I could just catch their figures as they rode through the thinning forest. The watch and the ring banged against my chest from inside my tunic, an ever-present reminder of the chance I was taking. Sefen had tried to stop me, but Sven had pointed out the lack of time, and that the sharp eyes of an Esmer should not be wasted. I hadn't heard the name of my kind since almost before I could remember, and it had given me a sudden and unpleasant start. It was a painful reminder that I was possibly the last, and I'd spent years trying to forget that. But, at the same time, it was nice having a name. Having something useful. 'Only an Esmer can help.' The thought was almost warm.

I looked up again, and ducked a little lower into the treetops, hovering for a moment so that I could get a good view of everything around me without being seen. The skies seemed clear in the area, but about thirty miles east, I could make out the dot of a Drogan. It was coming this way, but slowly, stopping to inspect and frequently disappearing onto the ground. Even from this distance, I could tell it was a massive animal, but I hadn't seen many, so perhaps it wasn't an unusual size. All the same, it was deeply unsettling.

After another sweep, I took off once more, forcing myself not to be careless. I could go for a good dive right now. The wind caressing my cheeks, the rush as I watched the earth flying up to meet me…. I shook my head and focused, slowing the speed I had started to build. I had already caught back up with the others and did not need to pass them. It had just been so long since I'd really been able—well, allowed—to fly. So long, in fact, that I'd almost been dulled to how much I'd yearned for it.

The wind blew harder, and I had to keep concentrating so that it wouldn't send me sprawling. It had been a while since I'd flown for this long, and in these conditions, it probably wasn't the best time to start up again. The watch untucked itself from my coat again, and I clung onto it for a moment before tucking it back in. My hand brushed up against the ring, and I thought again about Sven, his comments and obvious confusion. But now wasn't the time. I was burdened with watching the skies, and if I got lost in thought, I could lead us all to death. The terrible thought forced me to focus, and I did another quick pause to look around again. The Drogan was there again, but farther away than before and quickly growing farther. Other than that, I saw nothing—except suddenly to our left. The birds were stirring and above the roaring shouts of the wind I heard an ever-so-faint clamoring. Soldiers.

Taking off at full speed, I went slightly ahead of the others and landed where they could see me, yet still have time to stop the horses.

Sefen gathered up his reins and drew his horse up next to me, concern etched in his face. "What's the matter, Baey?"

"Soldiers to our left. Probably only ten minutes away. They seem to be heading to cut us off, and I don't know if your horses have much in them to outrun anything. I don't think the soldiers know we are near yet," I reported breathlessly, wings folded loosely around me as I tried to rest them. I was out of shape.

Sven drew his horse up as well, seeming to have caught the hushed conversation. "We need to back up and go left. If they don't know we're here, then we can move...right under them. How far back should we go...Baey?" he interjected himself into the debate with a labored question, surprising me half out of my mind. He was asking me? What if I was wrong?

"Uh...um...if we go about a half mile back, we should be able to duck under them. But we need to go slowly so they don't see us. When we start getting close, I'll have to land. But we don't have time," I replied as confidently as I could, which wasn't terribly.

Sven nodded quickly and turned to Sefen, who looked a little perturbed at being taken out of his place, but also knew when there was no time to argue. They turned around and followed me as I took off once more through the stained-glass fire of red, yellow, and orange leaves.

I watched the stirring birds carefully, and soon my eyes could even catch the movement, and before I knew it, I could hear them from afar. I put up a hand and halted abruptly, floating down to the earth and landing in the midst of my stopped friends. I said nothing, only putting a finger to my lips and starting ever so quietly off in a slightly altered direction. We'd almost gotten too close to them, but I had been so afraid of that Drogan— it had gained a bit on us since we'd had to backtrack.

Everyone dismounted and followed after me, not even the sound of breathing breaking the air around us. I myself wasn't even sure I *was* breathing. I had to admit, though, that Sven's presence was a calming one, and he stayed next to me as, together, we led the others.

Then I saw a movement in the trees and made the violent motion for everyone to duck. Unfortunately, the horses couldn't duck on command.... There was the rustling of trees, and, from my hiding spot behind a bush, I could just see a few of Skayla's soldiers, dressed in the mixture of metal and leather armor. I bit my lip, wishing my wings were large enough to shield everyone's presence. What if they saw the horses? We'd be done for. We were too tired to put up much of a fight, and I was afraid even our spirit wouldn't get us out of this one.

The soldiers moved closer, and I knew it was impossible that they wouldn't see the horses. My hand went to the sword at my belt, and I stroked the cold silver hilt with a regretful readiness. I was biting my lip so hard I thought I might put a hole in it, I was so anxious. I heard the muffled sounds of the others getting ready to make a last stand, and my heart threatened to pound its way right out of my chest.

But then I felt a hand fall over my own hand that gripped the sword, and I turned to find Sven shaking his head. He winked, inclining his head in the direction of the patrol. They...they were moving away...but...how had they not seen us? I felt the now all-too-familiar pulsing of adrenaline and realized the pounding I had thought was my heart was actually coming from...the ring. I looked back as the men moved on, some staring right at us for a moment as if we were not there but still I
couldn't believe it. I had heard the stories, and the legends, but never thought I would see him do this in real life—and he hadn't even been wearing the ring. Sven had used his Gift.

THE GHOSTMAKER

CHAPTER XVIII: To Ruins and Ambush

<u>Sven:</u>

I hadn't used my power to that extent in almost nine years. In fact, I had spent so much time forcing that part of my mind away so Skayla couldn't make me use illusions or take my old ones down, that I had almost forgotten what to do. True, I had used parlor tricks like hiding the watch from prying eyes, or changing my appearance ever so slightly, but making all of us disappear? This sort of thing was apparently no longer easy without my ring at hand. Now, with the ring next to me, I felt a vague sense of my old certainty creep back, and the patrol moved on without so much as a hesitant glance backwards. It was a shabby semblance of a once-greater power I had wielded, but shabby or not, it kept us alive.

After a while, everyone finally started getting back to their feet, throwing bewildered looks at each other before all settling on me. It would seem my reputation, no matter how old, preceded me. Baey especially was looking at me with wide eyes. I could see the question but didn't dare make a sound. No, I didn't need to wear the ring...only if I wanted my full abilities. Hiding people wasn't anything complicated. At least, it hadn't been. I was a little troubled at the difficulty I'd had in succeeding, even without the ring. I really was out of shape.

We walked a while in silence, still not daring to mount the horses. I thought again of Baey and the ring, but this time on a different aspect. Should I take it back? The answer was almost instantaneous. *No.* I couldn't...I couldn't deal with the painful aching it brought on. I was a coward and I couldn't face the yearning for a bond between siblings long broken. It hurt so much even to be around it, and I knew the reasoning that Skayla could use it to find us was only a pitiful excuse. Skayla would only feel me if I had it on when I was close by, but even from a far distance I would feel her—I would feel the absence of Moira. No. It hurt too much.

I could practically feel Baey's questions boring into me. However, when I turned to face her, she pointed to the sky. She seemed to be a little more focused than I was, at the moment, and I nodded. Before I even finished the gesture, she was off into the late afternoon sky, shadow falling on us like a small shelter from the destructive sun. Soon after, everyone mounted back up, and once more we spurred on our horses, giving them as much as they could handle—and as much as we could handle. The stress of the earlier encounter reminded me of how close to lost this cause was, and I only hoped we would find answers in the ruins.

Hopefully, if all went well, we would reach it by midnight. But I faltered as we were forced to slow down with the fall of darkness, showing not just how tired the horses were, but how incurably exhausted all of us were.

Jaythos had dismounted to do a quick scout ahead, and so I was alone when Estasia came up beside me on her horse.

"You seem well." Her comment rang sarcastic, and I decided not to dignify it with an answer. Instead, I put a finger to my lips, hoping that would silence any further argument. I didn't have time to not be alright.

She said nothing more, but her attitude was clear enough. An hour or two after nightfall we stopped, practically collapsing off of our horses as soon as we found a sheltered area.

Thunder sounded in the distance, and I sighed, heading under the large alcove that we had found under a mesh of Crysen tree roots and thick clay. It was actually quite large, able to easily fit our four horses and the rest of us.

"I'm assuming that was your piece of work, Watcher?" Jaythos addressed me directly as he referred to our run in with the patrol, using a name I had not heard in nine years—and didn't wish to hear again.

"Sven," was all I said in reply at first, confusing him for a moment before he realized what I meant. I did not have any right to that title. Honestly, I had earned my new one more than the first. "But yes, that was." I finally answered the rest of his question, hoping that would put the subject to rest.

Tanner came up and joined in the conversation, seeming very intrigued by the subject, to my displeasure. "Doesn't that take a lot of concentration? Most manipulations and Gifts take a lot of it, and I'd imagine yours would take an extra amount. But you don't seem…well, drained—all things considered." He half sat, half fell against the wall, sighing in lament of his exhaustion.

I was tired, too, actually. "Not much" was my half-truth. Concentration and attention were something I was rather short of these days, but that had not been a big trick, all things considered, and the weariness only showed how out of shape I was. I had been known for illusions, but had once been capable of…more. I only hoped that we got to a place where I could perhaps practice some more and maybe be of some use against my sister. But not now. Not yet.

Baey came back from tying up the horses near the entrance, wings shaking the new falling rain from her feathers. "I suppose we should be thankful for the rain."

Even with the completely unrelated comment, Baey seemed to know what we had been talking about but ignored it anyway. It was possible she was too tired to think, but it appeared she did desperately want to ask as many questions as the rest of them, so what was stopping her? The thought had barely finished crossing my mind when I had the answer in her eyes. She was a frightened little thing, wasn't she? How odd. I remembered all those years ago, when I'd known her and her family— and even when I'd rescued her that night. She'd been so calm, so courageous. So, what had happened to change that?

"Everyone, get a few hours' rest. I'll keep watch." Sefen stood up and brushed the dirt off from his trousers, handing out a hard biscuit to everyone as he continued, "We don't want to stay too long, so rest while you can."

"Sefen. You are not keeping watch. Maeko should. That leg of yours looks bad, as does the rest of you. Let someone who hasn't spent a week in a dungeon do their part," I ordered dryly, preparing for an argument. He'd been stewing over it for the last day, doubting my every word. I didn't like giving any orders, especially with my reputation among them, but Sefen was not thinking clearly at all since the fortress. Namaya's loss had been hard on him, no matter how he hid it, and as much as my memory was erratic, my judgement was quite intact. Mostly.

He opened his mouth to do exactly as predicted, but Maeko interjected, "Skinny right. Rest. Plenty of time to argue when dead." He said it all very matter-of-factly, and I was surprised that he had taken my side. Really, though, he was taking whoever's side was making Sefen rest.

The debate was settled with that, and Maeko stayed up to watch, allowing the rest of us to get some much-needed sleep. I felt a hypocrite for hardly drifting off, but I couldn't talk myself out of keeping a watch myself and promptly regretted it when we started moving again. I was running myself too ragged, but no matter how many times I told myself, I still fought the urge to sleep. I would be able to make myself rest when we found the sanctuary after the ruins. Hopefully.

The rain was intermittent and light, but still enough to make us all uncomfortable as we rode on for the next day and a half. I wasn't sure if it was enough to keep our pursuers much at bay, but we didn't really have control of the weather.

About an hour before dawn, the clouds broke, and the twin moons and pale stars peeked hesitantly through, bringing me back almost eleven years as the familiar landmarks greeted us. The howling rock, the old tree. I was surprised at myself as the bittersweet memories resurfaced. "We're almost there," I called up to Sefen.

We all spurred our horses out of the walk they had been resting in, and we were off once more, my heart sinking lower and lower and my gut knotting tighter as all the familiar sights assaulted me. I wasn't sure I was ready for this.

Then, almost without warning, we were in a clearing, standing in front of a place I had once known better than anything else in Baeno. A place that now lay before me in utter ruin.

A splintered and torn well was fallen practically at our feet, almost completely disguised by the tall grass and weeds that grew around it. Further on, there were the remnants of a cobblestone walkway, now grown over with ivy and more weeds. It twisted and curved, once-domestic flowers and plants spreading out of control along it. The walkway led to the path which joined eventually with the main roadway, though with the overgrown trees, you would never have guessed that many grand carriages passed through here little over a decade ago.

"What is this place?" Estasia whispered breathlessly as she came up beside me. She looked in complete awe, not at the well, not at the pathway, but at the ruins it all led to.

The building had once been The Crafters' finest work, metal, brick, and glass had come together to create a beautiful patchwork mosaic, complete with full-length windows, as well as a skylight for stargazing. In the front had been silver, gold, and other metals twisting together like spliced rope to form strong pillars that held together a bronze balcony. But now, this was all in ruins: Twisted frames were all that remained of what had once been a room completely walled with glass panes to let in the sun, with a smashed, barely recognizable harp hanging out of the gaping hole. The pillars once holding the balcony, too, were mangled and broken, listing over like a weary traveler.

I dismounted and led my horse up to the ruins. I felt as if I was in a dream, everything meshing with the here and now, and the before. I could still hear all of their voices in my head, beckoning, reminding me they were not forgotten. A biting ache gnawed within me, and only with a great effort did I push it away, replacing it with unquenchable anger. This was what Skayla's actions had brought. The ruins here summed up the complete ruin she had spread.

Tying my horse to an intact iron railing that had once been used to hold carriages, I made my way up the stairs, pushing back the ivy that stood between me and the now doorless entrance. Only vaguely did I feel the others' presence behind me as I entered into the darkness inside. Only vaguely did I hear their quiet gasps and reactions as they saw the bent and crushed interior.

I closed my eyes for a moment when I saw the inside, wishing to keep the old mental picture, and not have this awful reality reimprinted in my brain. But I made myself look—made myself take it in once again. All over the floor lay scattered and disfigured books, thrown from their metal bookshelves, with the various gears and wires that once served as pulley systems and book recovery devices now bent and tossed about the floor. A spiraling staircase came down to the middle of the room, frame bent slightly out of shape in evidence that a Drogan had been here long ago. But more had changed since I'd last set eyes on the ruins; plants now grew through the cracks in the floor and even along the walls, and ivy entwined itself around the rails and pulleys. It would eventually be so overgrown that none would even see the hints of beauty that had once been.

"What happened here?" Baey's whisper carried eerily through the building, echoing through the faraway corridors.

I didn't know what had happened; I had only ever seen the carnage, only ever guessed—and guessed wrong. But I needed to try to see where they had gone. Not until Skayla had gotten me had I known they were still alive. I'd always assumed she'd killed them—foolishly assumed she had caught and murdered the creators of the precious relics, the masters of so many beautiful things. But as much as she had taken from my mind, I had managed to get a little from hers, and her constant searching of this memory had made me realize that she had questions about this place as well. Someone had escaped.

"Sven?"

"I don't know," I answered Baey at last, her voice snapping me out of my deadly thoughts. "But Tanner might be able to tell us," I added, swinging around to the boy and giving a rueful smile. "Do you suppose you could find out? And see if they left any clue as to where they went?"

Tanner had been kneeling down upon the ground, and I had a feeling he'd already been looking. Without a word, he stood up and walked slowly towards one of the small corridors as if sleepwalking.

Baey and I were closest to him and were the first to follow, the others close behind—with the exception of Maeko and Jaythos, who were keeping watch outside.

We came into The Crafters' old study to find the room completely upturned. The desk where drawings and plans had always been was tipped on its side, moldering shreds of paper littering the floor. Still as if in a trance, Tanner slowly knelt on the floor, on the spot where the desk had once been. Without hesitation, he took hold of a loose panel from the wooden floor, reaching inside the apparently hollow underneath and pulling what had to be a hidden lever—by the sound of the click that echoed. The wall in front creaked, slowly opening from one side as long-unused gears worked in one of The Crafter's inventions. Baey gasped, and I looked up and breathed in sharply myself. There, blazing with a brilliant blue-green light, was a map.

"Do you see that?" she murmured, as if in a dream.

"What? A dead end wall?" Sefen's question dripped with confusion.

Estasia said nothing, but she didn't need to say anything for me to know she also didn't see it. The Crafters had some Gifts and tricks of their own.

Baey shook her head violently and pointed at the etched map in the air. "No. That! Can't you see it?"

"They can't," I intruded, before Sefen or Estasia could respond. She still seemed confused, but I didn't have time to explain it to her. Instead, I knelt down, picking up a larger bit of blank paper and a broken piece of charcoal. Slowly, I transferred the illusion onto paper, making sure to get even the smallest detail. After that, I handed it to Baey.

"Is that accurate?" I asked simply, wanting to make sure that I had missed nothing.

She nodded dumbly and handed it back, saying, "It's an illusion, isn't it?"

I smiled and winked at her. "Possibly. The Crafters could do a little bit of this sort of thing themselves. They made it so only I could see, it would appear." And her. Tanner pulled back down on the lever and hid the secret panel once more.

"But how did Baey—" Estasia's question never completely left her mouth, as suddenly the whole house shook. Sefen and I almost fell over, and Baey leaped into the air in surprise.

I turned around as I heard someone running down the hall, and soon Jaythos appeared in the doorway. "They found us."

CHAPTER XIX: Old Tricks

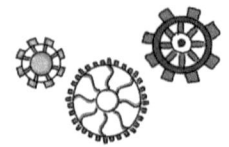

Baey:

He didn't have to say another word—we all knew what he meant.

"How? How'd they find us so quickly?" I'd watched the skies tirelessly, and the nearest Drogan had been hours away.

Sven steadied himself on the nearby wall as another quake shook the house. "I don't know. Where's Maeko?"

"He's in the main room. We blocked the entrance with one of the metal bookcases and a sofa. There's a Drogan on the roof," Jaythos replied quickly, starting back down the hall with us in tow. I fingered Sven's blade and would have offered it back to him had he not had another sword—and had I had something else to use as a weapon.

Tanner brushed up against me, and I bit my lip as I gave him a quick look of fright. We were going to have to fight. But how could we win against a Drogan? He flashed a quick smile, then ran past me and up to Sven and Sefen. I heard him whisper, "I know how to get out of here."

We came into the main hall to find Maeko standing over a few dead Bethynese soldiers with clear satisfaction.

"Is that all?" Sven said incredulously as we regrouped. "Where are the others?"

"On the roof," Maeko said with a grunt.

"Baey, go to the second floor. By that window—" Sefen stopped to point up to a long window where the second-story balcony ran all along the walls. "Don't do anything unless Sven or I tell you."

332

I wasn't sure if I was relieved or horrified, and had no time to figure it out, because just then, there was a crashing sound from somewhere inside the building, and we all looked up to see a group of ten or so soldiers rushing in through the upstairs hallway, followed by a large, silver-feathered Drogan.

"Scatter!" Sven shouted.

I shot up to the second level as instructed, watching as the soldiers flooded in, some running down the stairs, and a few at me. Ugh. Would Namaya's training pay off? I'd hardly ever been able to do more than watch others practice...

I landed on the balcony and drew my sword, nearly frozen in terror. I'd never killed a soul in my life, and it looked like I might just break that streak today.

The whole house shook as the Drogan burst into the room, looking smaller than I had thought it would be. It was large but not nearly as big as the one I'd seen in the sky.

But I had to focus. I snapped back to my surroundings just in time to duck the swipe of one of the men, using my wings to trip him as he tried to regain his balance from the missed swing. Another one ran towards me and swung his sword at me. Barely, I got mine up in time to block. I felt my arms shaking under the weight and knew I'd be easily overpowered with my lack of sword skills. So, while our blades were entangled, I beat my wings hard, knocking him over the railing and to the floor below. I tried not to think of the sickening crunch.

Fortunately, I didn't have time to think, as more soldiers than I could handle came barreling for me. I took to the air, barely making it far away in time to avoid their grabs at me. Below on the first floor was a merciless chaos. Sven and Maeko were trying to fend off the Drogan. Jaythos and Estasia ran between its feet, trying with little success to pierce its thick feather armor. Sefen and Tanner tried to fight off the soldiers. But it didn't look good. All of us were underfed and exhausted, and I knew we wouldn't have a chance. I had to help, somehow.

Without thinking, I dove in from above, surprising the Drogan by slashing my sword across its muzzle. The thing lurched back, taking half of the second-story balcony—and some of the soldiers—with it, and putting a claw to where I'd injured it. I quickly dodged to the side, trying to stay out of its sightline. But its blind snatches in the air hit their mark, and I felt its front claws hit me solidly on the back. My wing turned in an odd angle, and I gave a yelp of pain as I plummeted to the ground, giving my own sickening crunch as I hit the metal floor. Ouch….

Everything sort of went black for a moment, and when my senses returned, I still heard the chaos of the skirmish and the screeches of the enraged Drogan.

"You alive, darlin'?"

I blinked, finding Sven Mara leaning over me with a pained expression. I realized then that he must have dragged me into a corner, because I wasn't where I thought I had fallen.

"What…happened…" I muttered with a wince. My back didn't feel so swell.

"You gave that beast a mark he won't forget." There was a mixture of worry and pride in the quick explanation, and it was cut off as he ordered, "Stay here—" He turned abruptly and threw a knife, hitting someone who had apparently been coming up from behind. Then he turned back to me, eyes burning with a dangerous glimmer I had never seen before. "Quick.

I need my ring." He turned around again and put his sword out just in time to block a swipe from an assailant. My senses were quickly becoming more and more revived, and I realized we were very much surrounded by soldiers.

Without hesitation, I grabbed the ring, pulling the chain off my neck so that I could free it from the necklace. Before I could, however, Sven all but wrenched it from my hand and spun around.

"Stop!"

I had to cover my ears; his voice was so incredibly loud I thought my eardrums might burst. Everyone around did the same, and even the Drogan halted, staring unwaveringly at Sven. I noticed already that the thing's muzzle had seemed to heal.

"Dare you attack such a place? Are you animals?" he shouted again, though not nearly as loud as before. The soldiers seemed to regain their senses, and a few of them started edging towards Sven, swords at the ready, while the Drogan crouched down to about half its size and let out a low, growling sort of purr.

"Sven, watch out!" I couldn't help but cry out, trying to struggle to my feet. But my legs wouldn't hold me.

Sven just shook his head, making a tut-tutting sound and chuckling. "I told you to stop. You can't say I didn't warn you."

And that's when the ceiling fell. I couldn't help it, I screamed, putting up my arms as I prepared to be buried alive. My eyes squeezed shut and I prepared for the rocks to crush me to a pulp…but nothing happened. I peeked open one eye and couldn't believe what I saw.

The ceiling was back, as if nothing had ever fallen, but it was…raining? Pouring rain. Rain you couldn't see through, but I didn't feel a drop of it as it thudded down around me. Then I realized what was going on—Sven.

I found that I could easily peer through the sheet of rain to the shadows of the others. Sven weaved in between the confused soldiers, wielding two swords now as he fought. Could he make the illusions more convincing for the soldiers? They seemed to be swaying and confused, as if the floor was moving.

The rain froze suddenly, disappearing. The soldiers' legs wobbled and shook as if the earth had begun to shake.

I tried again to stand, but my legs were still like jelly from the fall, and all I could do was sit and watch. Maeko, Jaythos, and Sefen were practically on top of the wobbling Drogan, keeping it from getting at Sven as he dealt with the soldiers. Everything was chaos: One moment the soldiers would be fighting to stand, the next, Sven would literally disappear into thin air, reappearing somewhere else. Then the men would act as if they were blind or shout to each other as if they couldn't hear. It was unnerving, but I realized that was the point. The soldiers' numbers had significantly dwindled, and it appeared that they were now falling back.

Sven was not even fighting them any longer, just herding them to the open door. Then the Drogan managed to get free from Maeko and Jaythos for a moment and lunged at Sven. But in rearing up, a piece of metal lodged itself in its back and it came crashing down with a howling screech. Without even turning around, Sven stepped to the side to avoid being crushed, ready to bring his sword down on its head for a final blow on the beast. But then, suddenly, he just…froze.

My legs finally worked, and while the Drogan remained motionless, one of the few soldiers who hadn't fled yet came up behind Sven. I shouted his name, but my voice sounded soft and faraway, unable to help. I forced myself up instinctively and took out the knife in my belt. I wasn't terribly far from them, and with all my might threw the knife just like Jaythos had taught me. The soldier turned and saw the knife coming at him, but it fell short, clattering to the ground a little before him. But it was enough.

In that time, Sven had snapped out of it, and turned to plunge his second sword into the man. The man doubled over, but then looked at Sven, shocked. Sven winked at him and smiled, whispering, "Gotcha," and pulled the sword out, leaving the man completely…unharmed. The sword was just an illusion.

Now completely terrified, the four men remaining fled the room, leaving their precious Drogan behind in their haste. I dragged myself over to where Sven and the others were assembling by the beast. Sefen ran over and helped support me. "Baey, what did you do?" He fretted over me; it seemed that, as always, I was the one needing looking after.

Honestly, I felt rather sick, but I made a very unintelligent noise and then managed a soft, "I'm fine." My eyes were trained on the beast, lying slumped not more than a few yards in front of us.

The thing had seemed to get even smaller, if that was possible. Its breathing was hard and ragged and its eyes were half closed. The shard of metal stuck out from its back. I shuddered, trying not to imagine how painful that was.

"Baey. You should sit down; you don't look good." Sven gave me a quick look up and down, pausing the debate he had just started with Jaythos and Maeko.

I just nodded, and Sefen helped me over to a spot. Tanner was soon by my side, huffing and puffing like an old lady. "What were you thinking, Feathers..."

I wasn't really paying attention. I was watching as Sven seemed to be arguing with Jaythos about the beast, who was watching all of us with dimming eyes.

"I shall finish it," Maeko muttered to himself. I watched as he took a sword from the ground and started over to the neck of the beast. Its one good eye watched him lazily, and it let out a pitiful moan. I knew the thing would kill many more if we didn't kill it first, but now, standing here, I couldn't watch. As Maeko drew his sword up to give the final blow, I squeezed my eyes shut and prepared to hear the sickening thud of the sword point sinking into the beast's skull, but instead I heard Sven's desperate shout.

"Maeko, stop!"

My eyes shot open again, and I saw Sven had somehow run unsteadily over and gotten in the way of the blade. "What are you thinking? It doesn't deserve to die!" he shouted, swaying.

Everyone—including me—just stared at him.

"What in Baeno are you talking about, Sven? It would have killed us had we not gotten it first!" Sefen shouted over to him, getting up from beside me.

The creature let out another groan and tried vainly to scoot away from Maeko, the shock from its wound apparently wearing off a little.

"What's the matter..." I murmured softly, trying to get up. Sven had to have a reason for acting this way. Right?

"Oh, no you don't, Feathers. Stay put or I'll...I'll...I don't know, kill you or something." Tanner pushed me down, trying to cheer me up *and* make me sit at the same time.

"Very original," I mumbled.

"Stay down, Baey, and let me look at that wing." Suddenly, Estasia was by us, kneeling down with supplies she must have gotten from our saddlebags.

Tanner helped me move so she could see it, but I wasn't really paying attention. I was intent on the very heated argument going on over the Drogan. The one that I could see Tanner trying very hard to ignore.

"I think it might be in a MindHold." Sven's words made me curious, and I sat up a little straighter.

"What? How? Can animals even be affected? Its eyes—ow!" I shot right in the air as a searing bolt of pain flew up my wing and into my back.

"There. All fixed." Estasia seemed quite pleased with herself, a rascally smile touching the ends of her lips. "It was just dislocated. But I wouldn't use it if I were you. Your legs seem fine enough—you had the sense to not land on them."

The pain had definitely hit me like a brick, and I felt both dazed, and now very much awake. I landed, my wing sore, but at least better than it had been. I hit the floor standing; my legs weren't much better, but more from being scraped up than anything serious. "Its eyes look normal enough..." I said. At least, they did for a Drogan, anyway. But then I wondered; how did I know? What did Drogan eyes even normally look like?

Tanner had followed me closely, an arm constantly out and ready as if he was afraid I would fall, but he, too, was caught up in the heated debate to answer me. However, no one seemed to hear me; my voice was still a little hoarse, and everyone was too busy bickering. That was probably why one should not go so many days without rest or proper sleep...I turned to Tanner. "Check," I mouthed, and he didn't need any further encouragement.

I watched unsteadily as he knelt by the Drogan, putting a hand on its silver feathers and stroking them for a moment. Tanner's eyes got that conflicted look he always got when using his Gift, and then suddenly he shot up with seeming alarm.

"All of you, stop!" he yelled, not hesitating to get between the others. "Sven's right."

Estasia:

I had never actually been in a real fight like that before, so I was surprised at how easy it had been. I'd worried so much about the thoughts that could run through my head, the unconscious freezing I had heard took place in your first fight.... But in reality, it was much like dodging about in a busy marketplace. A very violent...perilous...sword-swinging marketplace.

Everyone was arguing—again—and I knew better than to get involved. Partly because we were all tired, and I could get awful if I got involved—but really, I didn't get involved because I didn't have much of an opinion on what they were talking about. Sven was the only one I knew who had gotten out of a MindHold, and I didn't even know much about his sister's abilities, so who was I to confirm or say otherwise? If I tried to take a side, I'd only make enemies of half of them, and while they would probably all forgive each other with proper rest, I had a feeling that would not be likely in my case.

That being said, the remnants of our attackers could easily find reinforcements and come back to finish the job. We really needed to get moving.

"All of you, stop!" the boy yelled suddenly, hopping up from the Drogan's side. I had been watching him out of the corner of my eye, and more and more I was getting a feeling he had some sort of ability to read minds, or something odd like that. I definitely felt relieved that I hadn't let him shake my hand. "Sven's right."

He and Sven turned back to the beast, and I heard Sven whispering something to Tanner. Then both Sven and Tanner touched the Drogan, and though I couldn't tell what was going on, I couldn't help but see the way the beast shuddered.

Tanner turned back to us. "It's...it's free now. But it's going to die if we don't get that stupid shard out of its back."

"I can help," Baey piped up, sounding completely exhausted.

"Why don't I," I stepped in, wishing I hadn't. If I got this animal killed, I would probably be permanently in Sven's bad graces, and I didn't want that. But my gut gave the first reaction, and if I could *help* the thing, I could also gain trust. "But we really shouldn't stay here long. This place will be crawling with soldiers by nightfall."

Sven nodded. "Agreed. Thank you. Do you need another set of hands?"

My eyes narrowed in thought, and I knew instantly he was offering up his services. But he wasn't strong enough, and his hands were shaking from adrenaline and the strain the fight had caused. Honestly, it was a miracle Sven hadn't died from overexertion, and Sefen didn't look very much better....

"If the big fellow here could give a hand, that would be great." I knew Maeko's name but decided not to use it. If he didn't give Sven the courtesy of his own name, I didn't feel like being any more cordial.

The man grunted, giving the Drogan a more suspicious look than he did me—which I supposed could be a good sign, even if I was not exactly helping myself to be in his good graces.

I turned to the conversation at hand. "But I need something to stop the bleeding..." But how in the world was I supposed to get enough of anything to do that? Looking at the wound, I knew already that would be impossible. Oh dear. It was going to die.

"Drogans can't bleed to death. You'll be fine," Sven replied matter-of-factly. Then he turned to Baey. "But some form of attention should still be given."

That was an interesting fact...but I supposed he would know that, having fought alongside them for eight years. Without another word, I started towards the Drogan. It was hardly awake but still it edged farther away from me—which wasn't more than an inch, with its condition and all.

"Death wish, I see," I muttered to it. "If you don't want to die, stay still." It seemed to understand me, and I put my hand on it, smoothing some of its ruffled feathers. I had never touched a Drogan before, and the texture of its feathers was different than I'd expected. It was as if each little filament of feather was infused with metal, giving it a natural sort of armor, yet still being soft to the touch.

"I'm just going to climb up, so don't go anywhere," I whispered to it, watching out of the corner of my eye as Sven moved to its head and Maeko came up behind me. With one deep breath, I grabbed hold of some of its feathers, hoping that it wouldn't jerk or try and fight.

It either completely understood me, or was too weak to do any more moving, and with a great deal of effort I made it up onto its bony shoulders. Maeko was behind me, a little more graceful than I, and together we sat on either side of the shard of what seemed to be all that was left of the staircase.

The thing was about twice my hands' width, and rather sharp at the ends. So how were we going to do this? I tore off some of my sleeve and wrapped it around a duller part. This was going to hurt.

"Who needs two hands, anyway?" I said with a casual shrug. "Ready?" When my joke got little response from Maeko, I cut to the point. Ha. Point...I hated jokes so much.

"Yes," Maeko said, tearing off some of his own shirt and wrapping a second layer around the chunk of metal before putting his hands around it.

I took a deep breath, "Alright. One...two...three." We both jerked up, and the thing came suddenly free, flinging me into the air. I slid off the beast's back and to the floor, blinking up in bewilderment as I lay staring at the ceiling, hands feeling...well, not feeling.

"Well...that was successful.... Are my hands still attached?" I mused to myself.

"I'm not sure, how many did you own before?" Sven asked, leaning over me and extending a hand. I grabbed it gladly, and he hauled me up, making me realize that while I still had at least one hand, it was not very pleased with me. I felt the small trickle of blood, and after inspection, found small slices on both my palms. Nothing big but definitely painful.

Sven took off his vest quickly, and handed it to me to wrap my hands. I took it and turned my attention to Maeko, who had just slid down the Drogan's back.

"You look worse than a prisoner in the Kovian Fortress," I commented dryly, looking him up and down. He was covered in a sort of blue goo—the Drogan's blood, I presumed. He just grunted and turned, going to its head where Sven had gone. I followed, looking up at the Drogan's back in ever lingering doubt. Baey had been helped up and was now attending to the wound, but I still couldn't fathom that the beast couldn't bleed to death. It just wasn't natural, and I supposed I just couldn't wrap my head around the fact that I didn't have to worry about the thing bleeding out on me. Wouldn't that be a nice thing not to worry about? I'm sure Sven and Sefen would have appreciated it.

"Is it still alive, Baey?" Maeko asked.

Baey looked uncertain, giving a halfhearted shrug as she continued to try and mend what she could. My attention then turned to Sven, kneeling by the Drogan and stroking its snout. It worried me at how caught up he was, as if this thing was his personal responsibility. But he seemed to be forgetting it had just tried to kill all of us—MindHold or not.

"Is it going to die?" I asked simply, looking around a little nervously. "Because I have a feeling that in a couple hours, we are going to have bigger problems than this wounded thing." Skayla would not stop until

344

she had that watch around Baey's neck; I didn't need anyone to tell me that. But I wasn't sure when I'd started thinking it was alright to speak so freely among those I barely knew. It seemed injured Drogans who couldn't bleed to death really brought people together—or I was too tired to care anymore.

"She's right," Sefen said, looking skeptically at the whole scene. "This beast isn't worth it."

Suddenly, the passion boiled in Sven's eyes, and he jerked his head around to face Sefen. "Neither am I, but you've kept me around this long," he growled unexpectedly, turning back without another word. Every inch of his body showed how tense he was, as if preparing to spring—or run. I wanted to say something, to try and help the obvious hurt he had suddenly portrayed, but it wasn't really my...well...thing. Honestly, none of this had been. I'd been a thief—and a good one—better off on my own and only tolerating people's emotions if I could use them for myself. Until he'd reminded me it didn't always have to be like that. Were the risks worth it though?

But I had to do something to pay him back, so I took a step forward and put a hesitant hand on his shoulder. He flinched away and I watched as his fists clenched and unclenched in ire. "Sven. I'm sorry...but we do have to go." I wished I had something actually soothing to say, but we did have to get going.

Baey slid off the beast and came back over, looking back at it with a mixture of doubt and sorrow.

Suddenly, the animal stirred, picking up its head a little and staring deadpan at Sven. Baey gasped, mumbling, "Tanner...do you think it worked? Are you *sure* it's free?"

Did I want to know?

The beast purred a strange sound then seemed to realize we didn't understand it and stopped, blinking in confusion at us. I myself blinked as its form shrunk even more, until it was the size of a large draft horse. I hadn't known Drogans could do that. I'd always assumed the wide variety in size had always just been the species' variable sizes, not the fact that they could shrink.

"You are one of the Maras." The beast's voice sounded like a mixture of scraping metal and deep rumbling as it tried to get to its feet. I heard swords being drawn, and saw Sefen and Jaythos standing at the ready, Sefen pulling Baey back behind him.

"One of them, yes," Sven replied, straightening with a wince. "And who are you?"

"Syvil," he—the Drogan—replied, stumbling a little as it started already to tire. "...I don't...I don't hear her voice in my head...how did you...?"

Sven's smile was cunning. "Old tricks."

THE GHOSTMAKER

CHAPTER XX: A Step in the Right Direction, Right?

<u>Sven:</u>

I'd talked Tanner through helping me free the Drogan, using my own powers as well as the anchor I'd once used against Skayla's tricks in order to escape. I had tried this for the first time when I'd helped Sefen keep out of her MindHold, but it worked even better with my ring, to be sure. Tanner had been able to share my memories of how to get out with the Drogan, and, together, we'd gotten it free of Skayla's grasp.

Now, it staggered before us, free, yet still dangerous. I wasn't quite sure whether I'd helped or made things worse for us, but my mind was racing faster than reason could keep up. Was this an oddity, or were all of the Drogans controlled? If so, how long had her plans really been going on? Since the creatures had come to this world years ago, I had thought that it had started then…but could it have started even earlier than that? I didn't want to believe that.

The creature stumbled forward, seeming dizzy with both pain and disorientation.

"Do you know where the patrols are and how to avoid them?" Jaythos asked the beast.

The thing blinked, legs buckling again.

"I can get us a good start," Tanner murmured beside me, apparently not knowing I was aware of the tunnels below the house. The Crafters had always had a fondness for tunnels.

"Patrols?" the Drogan asked in its version of a whisper.

"We don't have time for this," Jaythos muttered.

No, we didn't. "Tanner, get the tunnels open. Do you know how?" I asked in a low murmur. But I wasn't going to leave this Drogan.

"Yes." He nodded vigorously, then ran off and disappeared outside.

Now, what to do with this Drogan? It was pretty badly hurt, and even though it seemed to be healing quickly, it couldn't walk on its own—and none of us had the strength to carry it. "You have two choices." I decided to talk and think later. "Stay here and wait for Skayla, or come with us. But don't expect us to wait for you."

These choices did not seem to please Jaythos or the other two, but I gave them a quick stare and turned back to the Drogan for its response.

Instead of replying, it started shrinking again—but much, much smaller. Not only that, but its shape was, well, changing. In fact, it wasn't so much shrinking as its legs were bending and shifting, changing from the long, thick legs of a beast into the thin, lanky arms and legs of a...well...a *Human*.

"I will come," he replied, hoisting himself up on his two legs and standing unsteadily before us. The same silver and green of his feathers caressed his mussed hair, but he wore black trousers, a black frock coat, and a grey-and-black leather waistcoat with a silver shirt under it.

"Well, alright...then..." I couldn't help but show my utter mystification. I had definitely *not* known they could do that. The others said not a word, probably even more taken aback than I was. Then Syvil's feet gave out, and I was the first to rush forward and catch the tall beast—well, man. Then I painfully remembered I wasn't exactly in the position to be helping someone *else* hold themselves up, as my side gave a less than subtle twinge of pain.

"Thank you," he murmured, still carrying that odd purring tone that he had had as a Drogan.

I forced myself to bury my confusion, knowing we had to get going if we were going to get out of here before we really were done for. But first, I needed to figure out how to help Syvil stand. Fortunately, Jaythos—of all people—came and saved me, holding Syvil up from the other side. "You're too injured. I've got this."

I wanted to argue, but he was right; I could feel every inch of me protesting under the Drogan's weight, and adrenaline was now being replaced with a stiff fatigue.

So, I let go and allowed Jaythos to help Syvil, and instead turned to the others. "Follow me."

We got outside, and there stood Tanner by the well, looking triumphant as the cleared-away spot now showed a set of old stairs leading down into the darkness.

"Sefen. We'll probably need light," I said.

The man nodded, snapping his fingers and producing a little light that hovered above his fingertips. "But we can't bring him, Sven," he argued suddenly.

"Later, Sefen," I said through gritted teeth, turning to Jaythos in an effort to hold my temper.

"Maeko, a little help would be appreciated," Jaythos cut in sharply as he attempted to keep the Drogan upright. Maeko said nothing but came up and helped nonetheless.

Once everyone was inside, I pointed to the lever that hung against one wall. "Heave on that, would you Tanner?" I asked with a jerk of the head in the direction of the lever.

Tanner obeyed, and a groan emanated from some inner mechanics, causing the large well cover to grind over the top. Skayla might be able to find the secret tunnel under any normal circumstances, but with my illusion now over it, I doubted she would. She might know the trick to it, but hopefully this added obscurity was enough to keep it from even her sharp observations.

And so, with that thought in mind, we started off in the thick gloom, the dark broken only by Sefen's pale lights—there were three or four now. We were an unlikely bunch: the last of Valdon, a slave, the last Esmer, The GhostMaker, and a Drogan. I wondered how it had ever come to this.

It felt as if hours had passed since we'd seen daylight, and everyone seemed weary beyond description. The only ones getting better were, surprisingly, Syvil and me. Now that I was wearing my long-abandoned ring, the sensation of flowing strength had started to creep back in as it recognized its old master, and I hesitated to give it back to Baey. The overwhelming turmoil it brought was outweighed by the ability to be of more use, and I knew I would have to get over myself. But the pain...the emptiness in my chest as I longed for an impossible reunion of the other two relics was borderline unbearable.

I shook my head, even as I knew the feeling would never go away.

The Drogan, on the other hand, I envied for its quick healing. I also still couldn't quite wrap my head around the fact that he was now in a Human form, but nothing would surprise me at this point. However, it did worry me. This could explain how all the countries fell so quickly, and how Skayla could make Drogans seem to appear out of thin air. So how had I missed this?

"I…can't…go on…" Baey groaned, leaning against the wall. I didn't blame her. She'd been through more than anyone her age should have to go through, and that fall had still done her in. "I'm sorry…I'm sorry," she repeated over and over, acting as if she was choking back tears.

"No, no, darlin', it's fine. Why don't we rest a little?" It was risky, but hopefully we were far enough down the tunnel that, on the slim chance we had been followed, we could still get a little rest. It would be better done here than on the surface anyway.

No one needed further encouragement, and almost everyone sank down to the ground to rest. Only Syvil, Maeko, and I remained standing, Maeko replacing Jaythos in the watch of the Drogan.

"You had better hope you remember things well," I said sternly, crossing my arms as I looked Syvil up and down. I'd recovered my senses more than when we had been up on the surface. We needed to make sure Syvil was indeed out of the MindHold and would indeed help us. I'd let my own emotions cloud my judgement, yes, but hopefully for the better.

Syvil cocked his head and looked at us with a strange expression. "What...do I need to remember?"

"Do all Drogans have the ability to change into Human form?" I asked.

Syvil nodded. "Yes. I think. I..." He trailed off and started looking into 'the great beyond.' *And* the memory blanks were setting in. They still didn't seem as bad as mine though. Yet. Hopefully, Drogans took it differently.

"How long have you been in a MindHold?" I pressed, trying to juggle doubt and confusion at the same time. Drogans didn't have a good record, but if they'd all been in MindHolds, then they were just as much victims as we were. Perhaps they really had meant it when they'd spoken of peace after they'd appeared.

"I...don't remember. Ovok. It is his fault. That's what I remember. I remember it is his fault. He tricked us..." he mumbled, looking in deep concentration as his eyes focused on absolutely nothing, a look I knew well.

Ovok. The one who I had always suspected had started all of this. Had he allowed all of his kind to be subjected to Skayla's MindHold? Or was he actually in one himself? Syvil seemed to be blaming him now, but thinking of it, he and Skayla had talked often.... Had she put him in one first so she could manipulate his people? That would be something Skayla would think of...so why hadn't I?

The orbs of fire Sefen had created flickered above us, creating shadows on the walls of the tunnel and illuminating those around. I went over and sat by Sefen; jaw set as everything worked over in my mind. "We need to figure some of this out before we go any further," I said.

Baey was on the other side of Sefen, and immediately perked up, leaning forward so she could see past Sefen to me. I saw the all-too-familiar questions rioting in her eyes, begging to be spilled out. But she stubbornly held fast, only watching and listening. Tanner was not as patient.

"What is going on? Are The Crafters really real? I thought they were just a story the others made up. And that thing you drew? What did you and Baey see? Is it a map?"

"You're too young to probably remember them, so to you, yes, The Crafters are simply a story," Sefen replied to his first question, sounding weary and annoyed at the interruption.

I reached into my pocket and pulled out the worn scrap piece of paper I'd scribbled on, holding it in front of us in the dim light of Sefen's fire. "Yes, it's a map," I replied very unhelpfully, as I myself tried to figure out exactly what it was a map *to*.

"May I see?" Estasia had been listening quietly from her spot against the opposing wall, and her composed form didn't move an inch as she broke into the conversation.

I watched her carefully, trying to weigh my odds. She had proven herself again and again, but after Namaya—who had been one of Baeno's last *protectors*—had betrayed her friends, I wasn't sure I was ready to trust her. Yet here I was, giving a Drogan a chance? I hesitated only a moment and then finally passed the map over to her.

She scooted forward a little to catch one of Sefen's small lights, turning and adjusting the paper in the light. Then she flipped it around, holding it up to the light and smiling with quiet satisfaction. After placing it down again, she looked at all of us and finally voiced her discovery. "It's backwards."

"What?" Tanner stared at the map incredulously.

I smiled ever so slightly and nodded; it was just the sort of thing The Crafters would do. Make a map that was inverted. "Do you know where it is?"

"Yes," Estasia replied flatly.

I made myself remain collected as I pressed her. "Where?"

She shook her head. "Patelayna. More specifically, Alkemar. This leads us to The Crafters, I presume? It's to fix the watch?"

Great. Patelayna was one of the countries most firmly in Skayla's grasp. On top of that, it was across the sea—past Rugo, even. And in its capitol, no less. How in Baeno would we manage this? I observed Estasia carefully. Had she proven herself enough? She'd cared for Sefen and me in the Kovian Fortress; she'd helped us escape, fought with us, and helped Baey with her wing. Was it time I put faith in her?

Maybe it was time to have a little trust.

"Yes. It leads to The Crafters," I said after a while of silence. And maybe it was time I shared all I knew...before I forgot it again. "We—I thought," I had to correct myself, for some reason thinking back to when Moira had still been here. Idiot. "The Crafters had been killed by Skayla. Some of you may at least have heard of The Crafters—" I turned to Tanner and Baey—"But for those of you who don't know, their name was fairly self-explanatory. They are the ones who made the watch, the ring, and Skayla's armlet, from the Living Stone, making them into foci to magnify our powers." The Crafters had also been the ones to be told the promise of the Esmer rising up to fix what Skayla had destroyed—of Baey.

It had been through the Living Stone that The Creator had spoken, and through them I'd told Emarian. But still Emarian and Valdon had done little else than keep Baey hidden from the world. Hidden, when she should have been preparing to heal it.

"So, without your ring, you're just normal?" Estasia asked.

"No. The ring just enhances my Gifting." Not wanting to dwell on that part of the subject, I moved on. "But after Skayla attacked The Crafters, we never found them, and soon after that, Moira disappeared. The map we found hadn't been there when we arrived at the ruins the first time. That I am not sure of...unless one of them returned to leave it later..." I pretended all of this was completely casual to say—pretended it didn't bother me at all. There was no time for such nonsense. That's what I kept telling myself, anyway. "But anyway. Skayla wanted power—the Living Stone, itself, and when The Crafters wouldn't give her what she wanted, she settled for trying to kill them and going after the other two relics they'd made," I summed up, making sure not to delve into some very important details. We were desperate but not that desperate.

"Moira's watch and your ring," Baey whispered.

I nodded. "Yes. You were some of the bait to get me out in the open. Only it backfired on Skayla, and she only got me, not the ring."

Baey looked confused. "But...why would I have been such good bait? I mean, Skayla doesn't know about the...um...you know," she faltered as she looked at Estasia, and only implied The Creator's Promise. "And if she had known, she would have just killed me, wouldn't she?"

Again, I nodded. "Yes, but you were an Esmer, possibly the last. The Esmers had always been a wise race in Baeno and had been friends of my family." After all these years, I still hated how this had all happened.

356

The disaster all this had caused—all because of us. "And Skayla knew that, really, I would come with or without bait. She knew I'd be stupid enough to try and stop her." And to try and get her to tell me what happened to Moira and The Crafters. "But from what I've gathered, she knows now," I said. "Whether Namaya told her or she found out some other way, I'm not sure. For all I know, she could have gotten it from my own stupid head," I finished bitterly.

"Ah," was all she said.

"So, why do we need to find The Crafters exactly?" Estasia broke into the awkward silence with the practical question. "Wouldn't it just be better to keep them, well, lost? If Skayla doesn't know where they are, and only we know, then maybe we should leave it and keep them safe."

"And you said that no one else could use the relics, so how would Skayla benefit from getting yours or Moira's? And why do we want the watch fixed?" Baey added.

I decided to answer one question at a time, trying to keep my mind on track. "Skayla seems to feed off the other relics. She can't use them, but they make her stronger. So, I think that is how Syvil and I could get out of our MindHold. I stole it from her while I was still in one but in a more lucid moment. So, getting it from her and far enough away dimmed her power."

"So why do we want to fix the watch?" Tanner repeated Baey's question. Right. I'd already forgotten that question. Stupid brain.

I took a deep breath, not sure I was ready to give voice to the thought. I'd told Sefen but no one else. "Because…" I started quietly, "I think Moira may not be dead."

Baey:

The quiet that followed Sven's answer was deafening, and I myself had to let it sink in. "Wait...what?"

Tanner was the only one that seemed to understand, nodding as something seemed to click. "You're talking about what I saw, aren't you?"

I recalled him retelling it, and I found it beginning to click, myself.

"Yes. You said that Skayla took the watch and broke it. It sounds like—from how you described it—Moira was in the process of going back in time, and Skayla grabbed the watch before she completely disappeared. I don't know if there is any way to get her back, but maybe if we fix the watch...."

"Even if we did, no one can use it but her, and you said she's gone. What if she simply disappeared from time? She could still be dead, Sven," Jaythos pointed out bluntly.

Doubt seemed to creep into Sven's features, battling with the usual resolution he carried. "I think there is someone else who might be able to use it." He stared right at me, and a knot formed in my stomach. Ugh. What if he was wrong? I would feel responsible. What if I failed?

"Are you sure?" Sefen asked. It only made me feel more of a letdown. All my life had been building to these moments. I'd waited and wished for this chance, only to have my worst fear come true. I couldn't do it, and it was written clearly on everyone's faces. I wasn't a hero, the events of today showed that. I had been hurt and pulled out of the way like a child, watching as the real heroes saved the day. What in Baeno was I thinking?

I bit my lip as fear's grip tightened, and I felt almost paralyzed with it. The last hope of Baeno, indeed. I was just going to be the one to seal its doom at this rate.

"As clear as day," Sven's voice suddenly shattered into the spiraling thoughts, and I was back in the real world. I adjusted my position so I could see him, and he gave me a wink. "The Creator spoke through the Living Stone and said Baey would help us get back Baeno, so I don't see where the doubt lies."

There was a very uncomfortable silence after he said that, and I wasn't sure if I was grateful to him for standing up for me or filled with disappointment at how the others hadn't.

"But enough talking. We should get going again. I don't like the thought of standing still down here." With that, he heaved himself back to his feet, steadying a moment, using the wall before walking in awkward stiffness over to where Maeko was very keenly keeping an eye on the Drogan, Syvil. That was another thing. Drogans could turn into Human forms, so did that mean even *more* odds against us? But Sven and Tanner had said he was in a MindHold, and if that was so, could it be possible that he was not the only one? Could it be possible to get the Drogans—or at least some—on our side?

Everyone else got to their feet, while I found that I myself was putting the movement off. The reckless maneuvers from earlier were making themselves known, and I was feeling sore and almost frozen, unable to get the motivation or guts to move.

"Need help, Feathers?" Tanner extended his hand down, flashing a smile.

I grasped his hand in response, and he got me to my feet, keeping me up when I almost fell back on the ground. Ugh. "Thanks," I muttered. I felt embarrassed for needing help—once more, I was the one who needed to be carried, the one who needed to be protected, the one who couldn't hold her own.

As we started walking, I fell to the back and watched the others with growing fear. Did they think I was just a burden? Really, even the Drogan was healed and feeling better than I was, and he'd had a *metal spike* sticking in his back. I was useless, unable to handle the pressure of battle and war and death, just like I'd feared. I wasn't good enough.

"You don't look so swell," Tanner interrupted, having fallen back to walk next to me. "What's the matter, Feathers? You look like you just got finished digging your grave or something."

I turned and gave him a quizzical expression. "Um…."

"What? I just found it fitting as we were, you know, underground and all, running to certain death…thought maybe you were getting ahead of the game." And there it was, that impish grin that always appeared when he was being a little rascal and trying to cheer me up.

"How lovely," I replied dryly, rolling my eyes as I tried to ignore the reminder that we were, after all, underground. I hated being down here.

"But really, what's bothering you?" His grin disappeared and he looked genuinely concerned—I didn't like that. It just proved my point. No one was concerned about Sefen or Sven, and they had spent a week in a dungeon! No one was worried about the scratch on Tanner's arm, no one was worried about the bruise on Maeko's head. They all knew they could take care of themselves, just as much they knew I couldn't. All these years, and my worst fear had come true: I was too weak to do anything at all.

"Baey?"

"Sorry. I'm fine. Just thinking," I muttered.

Tanner sighed in exasperation. "Well, stop thinking and start talking. We're in a long dark tunnel that seems to go forever, and it smells, and I'm bored. Anything's better than silence."

Could he stop bringing up the whole tunnel thing? I sighed. "You've heard it all before. I'm just being silly." I somehow managed to lie and tell the truth in one sentence. I didn't even know that was possible. He'd heard all these tirades before and had always told me I was being ridiculous. But I wasn't being silly, I was being realistic.

I was distracted as I saw Sven slow his pace, coming back towards us. I thought maybe he was going to talk to Estasia, but he waited until he was back with us. Ugh.

"Tanner, why don't you go up and help Jaythos keep an eye on Syvil, ah? Maybe see if you can get anything off him?"

Tanner nodded and gave one regretful look at me, jogging up to the front of our line. As soon as he was gone, Sven was fiddling with the ring on his finger. "Darlin', what's the matter? Don't even try to say nothing."

My breathing grew gradually more and more ragged as I labored to stay calm. "I'm just still processing what happened, is all."

"Baey." He whispered my name in his usual, breathlessly hoarse voice, and it somehow made me feel less alone. Less isolated.

"I'm…I just…I can't do it, Sven," I somehow said, my wings clinging to me, but giving no comfort this time. "I'm just too scared. And useless and I can't do it." I tried to stop from blubbering, but it was hard.

361

He didn't say a word for a long time, and I began to think maybe he wasn't going to. What if I really was right, and even he couldn't say otherwise? But then he spoke, very soft, just like I remembered from a long time ago. "You were not useless today. You saved my life."

"I got in the way, is what I did," I murmured, hoping that maybe he wouldn't hear me.

"I beg to differ. A little idiotic of a move, perhaps, but I think we'll work on that so you're more prepared next time."

I blinked. "*What?*" What did he mean?

"I was under the impression you would be a little more prepared for this kind of scenario...." He trailed off, looking pointedly forward at the others. "You are not weak. You are a quick learner and will do just fine."

"But what if I don't?" I asked, confused.

Shaking his head, Sven let out a small chuckle. I realized it was the first time I'd heard him do anything close to a laugh. It was a pleasant sound that permeated the gloom of this tunnel.

"There's something my Mum had once said. If you think you're afraid, you'll be afraid. If you think you can't do something, then you can't. Besides, darlin', you can be brave and still be afraid."

It was funny how easy it was to forget that people like Sven had grown up a possibly normal life, with parents and all that. In fact, I never knew Sven had had any parents. I guess I'd assumed he had been in a similar situation to me. But it made me wonder...where were they now? Were they dead like the rest of his family? Well, besides Skayla, anyway....

Sven sighed, and I noted the way he was still rubbing the ring on his finger. It was then I realized it seemed the watch was pulsing, aching deep in my chest, almost to the rhythm of his rubbing.

"Are you alright?" I risked turning the question on him.

Sven didn't even seem to hear me, gaze far off as he continued to fiddle with the ring.

"Sven?"

This brought a flinch and a quick inhale, and he turned to me. His gaze seemed even more haunted than usual. "Hm?"

"It's the ring, isn't it? You feel the pull?" I guessed. But a pull to what? I'd thought at last I'd figured it out when we'd found out he was actually Sven Mara. I'd thought it was just the ring calling for him. But I felt it still— from the watch around my neck as well.

"The bond of siblings is a funny thing. It always calls," he whispered.

Oh. "Do you...feel Skayla?" I'd somehow never thought of it before, but if he felt the watch...why not Skayla, too?

He looked away; gaze now trained forward. "Sometimes."

"Can she feel you, too?" I had never felt Skayla, at least.

Another silence. "Probably. She shouldn't find us though, unless we're too close to her. And even then, I would feel her, too."

I wondered then what he really thought of his sister. I supposed...I supposed it was like Namaya, maybe. But worse. Namaya had turned back in the end...Skayla had made Sven's life a living nightmare.

"Do you miss her?" What was I thinking?

I saw the sorrow he tried to hide. "Sometimes," he said again.

The aching. The aching came from him now. I was sure of it. It was as if the relics could feel his pain and were sharing it.

"Are you okay?" I knew it was a stupid question, but I could think of nothing else to offer.

The smile was more of a grimace, but he didn't reply for a while. "Don't worry about me, darlin'."

But I did. I wanted to help and more than anything I wanted to help *him*. For years, the memory of him had been like that of an older brother or father, and now that he was here, he still felt like family to me. I wondered if that came from the watch I wore, or if it was just the fact that not many of the others seemed to care much for Sven beyond his obvious usefulness. Just as I was kept hidden for being useless, he was always pushed into things because he was *of* use. It was clear Maeko hated him, at least, and besides Estasia, no one really interacted with him beyond asking what to do next.

I didn't know what possessed me, but I asked, "Is there any way I can help?"

He smiled again, genuine and small, and his eyes at last returned to meet mine. He ruffled my hair. "Just being here, darlin'. Your presence is plenty. You have enough fight in you to carry us all on your shoulders."

I smiled back, hoping maybe Sven would find it as encouraging as I found his. Did he really mean that? I'd always felt so weak—so out of place—that the idea of being strong seemed like a joke. But he looked so sincere as he said it that I actually found myself believing him. And I did so want to believe that at least talking to him helped. It had always helped me, and I thought back on how he'd always seemed to be there— to push me forward. Even as Feyn, he'd been the only one to believe in me. And so, as we continued on in silence, I stayed by him, wishing I had more than my presence to comfort him, but hoping it was indeed enough.

CHAPTER XXI: Well, Isn't This Exciting

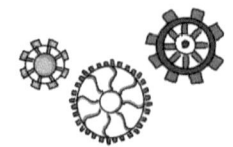

Estasia:

We'd rested again for a few hours in the tunnel, and after some shuteye, I felt a bit more refreshed, as did everyone else by the looks of it.

"Left. Soon we'll be out," Sven called out.

Maeko huffed. "Nice of you to join us, GhostMaker."

"I'm going to start calling you Kovo if you don't stop that," I muttered, not realizing I'd actually said that out loud.

Maeko just stared at me.

"To the left then, ah?" Sven acted as if he hadn't heard any of the exchange, taking the lead. Sefen went with him, starting a conversation, which I decided would be worth overhearing. I didn't like being left in the dark, and with as many risks as we were running, I wanted to know a little more than they saw fit to tell me, and I wasn't going to get anywhere by just asking.

"How far is this other hideout, Sven? We're running out of strength and eventually Skayla's going to catch us. She has more resources," Sefen started in a low voice.

I made myself back up, not sure if I would really be able to make it convincingly look like I wasn't listening in—but after all, we were in a very small, narrow tunnel, heading in the dark with no other place to go, so how much did they expect not to be heard? The same thing could be said about Sven's earlier conversation with Baey.

Sven huffed as he did a mental calculation, murmuring various measurements and modes of transportation. "Well...we've lost the horses...and it would be about a day and a half on horseback...but who knows, maybe we can convince Syvil." He jerked his head back in our direction as he mentioned the Drogan.

That made me feel a little better. Maybe that would give us all at least one night's good sleep. But could we trust the Drogan? At any moment, it could decide not to play nice anymore, and we'd all be deader than a rat in the kitchen. I did not want to be a rat.

Sefen voiced my concerns perfectly. "We shouldn't just trust a Drogan because he appeared to be in a MindHold, Sven. We aren't that desperate."

"We *are* that desperate, Sefen. But still, I'm not saying we should. It was just a thought. We need to see how well everyone's holding up before we start."

They started talking logistics—things I already knew, having looked at many maps of the area before planning the escape that now seemed so long ago.

It was interesting how Sven was rather attached already to the Drogan, even though we didn't know if it would help us or turn us over. Yes, it had been under Skayla's MindHold, but that didn't change its loyalties to its kind. What if it rejoined Skayla to stay with the other beasts? But Sven was determined, and I knew why. He saw at least a little of himself in it. What if this beast, like Sven, had been forced to do all the destruction?

I slipped back farther as my thoughts slowly started to wander. What had it been like for Sven to have his own sister do something as terrible as Skayla had? The closest thing to a family I'd had before the war was in Alkemar, where I'd been in a couple of gangs with some other kids and.... And those had not ended well. I supposed I understood betrayal at least. But then there had been the slaves at the fortress, and while some had been even worse than those I'd known in the gang, there were also people like Tanya, Aekon, and Ateli, who made me wonder if that was what it was like having a family. But Sven seemed somehow more deeply attached than even that. Did he still have that all-too-common delirium that he could somehow bring Skayla back? He didn't seem like that type, but it was his sister, after all. It was a bit much for my head to wrap itself around right now, to be honest.

"We're out!" Sven's sudden announcement jolted me from the rapidly deteriorating line of logical thought, and I gave my head a good, quick shake to stay focused. Man, I was tired.

We emerged from the tunnel to find it was not much lighter outside. It was as if we had been stone dead for days, only to come back and find the world as cold and dark as the grave.

I was glad that Maeko was at least taking the precaution of guarding the Drogan. It satisfied all parties and kept my countless conspiracies at bay.

The bitter wind rustled the tree tops and the smell of frost was in the air. Patelayna was a much more hospitable place, in my opinion, and the taste of freedom brought with it the desire to return home.

I stayed near the back—though Jaythos trailed now in the very rear—and I intently took an inventory of what I knew thus far.

Tanner was a cunning child, one who had seemingly dived into Sven's mind before. He was a young warrior in a world of old battles, but

I could see in his eyes that he knew much, and for one that age to know so much could be dangerous and unpredictable.

I found Sefen rather lost. He seemed quick to coddle Baey, fatherly but in a smothering sense. I wondered who he had lost. He took charge, and yet I didn't find him particularly good at it. And then Namaya's death—even traitorous as she was—still weighed heavy on his shoulders.

Then there was Jaythos. He seemed...closed off. Distant. I remembered the way he acted in the cave, when I had overheard his conversation with Sefen. It sounded as if Namaya had not been the first to betray him. He'd mention being a Bethynese deserter, and my stomach gnarled quickly into a knot at the reminder. I was not a fan of the Bethynese. At least his straightforward, seemingly emotionless approach to things made sense. But...how? There was no such *thing* as a Bethynese deserter. That just didn't *happen*.

My thoughts had to break away and focus on my footing, as the ground became rockier. Fairly soon, we began descending some steep, rocky hill. In the dark. That wasn't very easy. Syvil muttered something about wings and useless legs, but other than that, none complained. However, as the going got rougher, we had to rely on the strength of saplings to help us stay upright. More than once, I heard the sudden ruffling of Baey's wings as she stopped herself from a perilous fall. The girl seemed quite the klutz when on her feet. She really was like a little bird. Problem was, she didn't seem too much better in the air.... Did she even know how to use those things properly?

We continued down the hill and into a little hollow, where a small, cold stream ran. Above, there was just enough of a break in the trees to see the rare dot of stars peeking through the clouded night.

Hopefully, we had avoided Skayla and Kovo's wrath and gotten a good head start. But if Syvil was a trick, better find out sooner rather than later. True, Tanner had gotten memories...but how accurate were memories, really? *I* knew they were often not as trustworthy as it was said.

Jaythos seemed to be having a similar train of thought. He had once more taken his crossbow from his back and was walking more guardedly beside Syvil. I didn't like the way Jaythos looked at me either, but really, I had several things I needed to answer for myself.

"We have an explanation to hear, I believe," Jaythos addressed Syvil. "Now that you appear recovered." Indeed, Syvil seemed to already be almost completely healed. How was that possible?

"We can't just stop and tell everyone's life story though. We're still being pursued by Drogans and Skayla and Kovo's soldiers," Tanner said impatiently.

"If we wait until we are not running, then we wait for death," Maeko said gravely.

I actually rather agreed with the big fellow. With Kaedna being overrun and Emarian dead, we had nowhere to hide. Nowhere to rest forever. So, what was the point? I remembered my plan, and hope was restored. But at this rate, I wouldn't have the needed time to explain it to anyone until we got to Patelayna. *If* we got to Patelayna....

"I agree. Syvil—if that is your name. Explain yourself," Sefen said, staring hard at the Drogan.

I turned my attention to Sven, who was walking quietly by Baey. Neither said a word.

The Drogan's brow furrowed, perplexed as he spoke. "I...I told you. Ovok tricked us. He helped Skayla put her MindHold on us. I remember...I remember being called to see Ovok privately...and then...then Skayla..." He trailed off.

"So, there could be—" Sven began to break in, but something stopped him. I tensed as I, too, heard it. He put a finger to his lips. I touched the dagger in my belt.

The sound of a crossbow bolt severed the silence as Jaythos let loose a shot into the woods. I heard the thud of it hitting something, followed by a gurgled moan.

Oh, great. That was fast.

There was barely time to react—let alone think—before arrows came flying in response, and as quickly as possible, I dove to the ground, hearing the others do the same. My stomach lurched slightly as I heard Maeko grunt in pain, but there was no time for emotion or mistake.

The arrows assailed us from all sides, deeming my log poor shelter. It was a surprise I had not become a porcupine yet. I realized arrows were not being aimed directly at me but just shot willy-nilly. Perhaps Sven was using Illusions to hide us. That's when I also realized Syvil was no longer beside me.

I couldn't stop to look for him, but dread welled up in my gut as I crawled on my belly towards a large boulder. Its shape and position by the rocky hillside provided a slightly more effective shelter. Jaythos and Tanner had made it there, and Jaythos was now firing off the occasional bolt into the trees. More than a few times, I heard a satisfying yell.

Barely, I made it over to the boulder, diving behind it in a last-ditch effort only to get a stray arrow in my left leg as reward.

Agony coursed through my leg. Estasia, you *idiot.*

The arrows then began to subside. "Where are the others?" I asked Jaythos through a gasp as I leaned against the cold stone.

"Baey took to the air. Sven is behind the tree working his…illusions. Not sure what he's doing to make the archers stop, but it has to be him. They seem distracted now. Sefen got Maeko behind another boulder…but that no good Dro—"

Jaythos was cut off by a screeching roar as a Drogan came diving down right towards Sven—who I had craned my neck to see while Jaythos had been talking.

The Drogan was *not* Syvil, and it seemed fixated on Sven, its bronze feathers glinting in a chance ray of moonlight.

"Sven, watch out!" I couldn't help yelling. It was purely stupid and impulsive, but hey, I had an arrow in my leg. I was allowed to be a little stupid and impulsive.

The Drogan didn't even flinch at my voice, head swaying side-to-side, almost as if trying to discern where Sven was, exactly. I realized I was having trouble seeing Sven as well…as if my vision of him was blurred.

And then another Drogan dove swiftly down from the break in the trees and launched itself upon the other. *This* one was Syvil. I recognized the silver and green feathers.

We all watched in shock and awe as the two wrestled. I had never seen such a horrible, fascinating sight before, and the riveting fight was enough to tear my attention from the searing pain in my leg.

The two were blurs of bronze and silver, turning, twisting, clawing savagely at each other in what at first seemed a very uncontrolled, animal-like battle. But then, I realized that as they twisted and clawed, though fierce and merciless, there was an odd sense of...technique. It was like watching a pair of swordsmen dance, but in the air...with claws and teeth....

Suddenly, the bronze Drogan broke free of their deathlock and fled to the sky, chased quickly by Syvil. The forest was utterly silent. Even our hidden enemies in the surrounding forest did not resume their attack, and I felt that they were just as spellbound as the rest of us.

Then, we saw a dark shape falling back to the ground, but this time uncontrolled and limp. The soldiers in the forest cheered at the assumption of it being Syvil. Jaythos stopped one short with a bolt.

The beast made a sickening thud as it hit the earth. It was the bronze Drogan and never again did it stir.

Syvil flew to the ground and stood over it, and with that, the spell was broken. Only now, we were hearing not the sound of bold soldiers preparing to renew their assault on us, but cowards preparing to retreat. I could have laughed with relief, but it was short-lived.

"Sefen, look out!" Sven shouted suddenly, diving for Sefen and bringing him to the ground just as an arrow flew by, missing them only by a hair. This time, I dared not breathe a sigh of relief.

Jaythos let loose another bolt, and after that, nothing else came after us. But then I realized...if any of those soldiers found their way back to Kovo or Skayla, we were done for. They would know exactly where we were.

"We need to stop them!" I shouted as I managed to hoist myself up, grimacing at my leg.

I did not really expect Syvil to spring into action, as he had been standing stock still over his lifeless adversary. But he did. Within seconds he was out of sight, and for a long time I could hear the screams of the soldiers as the monster found his prey.

Baey fluttered to the ground. She had blood on her shoulder, and her wings seemed to be missing a few feathers. I realized that she had not, in fact, taken to the air to avoid the fight, but must have spotted the Drogan and helped Syvil. Clever girl.

"Baey! Are you alright?" Sefen, who had just gotten up and dusted some dirt from his trousers, came running up to her and inspected every blood spot. I tried to limp over to Sven, who was sitting up and holding the side where his still healing wound was. He wasn't far from Maeko, and that made me hurry more, making me almost fall. Jaythos caught me quietly and helped me along. Perhaps an arrow to the leg meant something in the ways of trust…. I still needed to get this arrow out of my stupid leg; however, right now I was dreading the procedure, and I was more worried about the others. Maeko was propped against another boulder looking very pale. An arrow was protruding from his right shoulder.

"I'm fine. But you all aren't—Maeko!" Baey caught sight of her big friend and ran over to him quickly.

"Little Baey. I am fine." Maeko whispered.

Sven managed to get to his knees, still holding his side but looking at me. "Fool, why did you have to go and get an arrow stuck in you."

He made it sound like it was an easy thing *not* to get one stuck in you….

"Jaythos, bring Estasia over here and Baey and I can have a look at her leg as well." Sven said absently, who had already snapped the arrow shaft that protruded from Maeko's shoulder wound and was inspecting the entry point carefully.

"I am fine, Skinny," I heard Maeko say quietly.

"Clearly."

Jaythos helped me limp over, and I sat down painfully next to the large man, giving Jaythos a grateful nod.

"You should really watch where you jump," Jaythos said dryly. That was possibly the most civil thing he'd said to my face. I must be growing on him.

Baey came over to take care of my leg, removing the arrow shaft and then tending to it. I tried not to scream like a little girl.

"Hold still, Maeko," Sven said impatiently beside me, still trying to tend to the Rugonian giant.

"I am fine, Skinny. I must stretch."

Sven's sigh was extremely audible.

I replied for him. "Stretching is a dead man's leisure."

I heard Jaythos...chuckle. Alright, was I delirious? "I like that one," Jaythos said after composing himself.

"Baey, did you help take that thing down?" Tanner's voice came from over by the fallen Drogan, and I saw him inspecting it in awe.

There was the flap of wings, and I tensed, thinking maybe it wasn't dead after all...which made my leg hurt even more. But it was only Syvil.

The beast again turned to man, and I realized his whole body was shaking. He ran his hands through his hair, murmuring something under his breath as he stared horrified at the dead form of his Drogan opponent.

"We need to get out of here," Sefen said, "These woods are probably crawling with patrols."

"I...I can take you," Syvil stammered, breathing heavily as he still stared at the Drogan's body. It suddenly struck me; he knew them. "It's dark. Everyone will think I'm...will think I'm Fryn—" He broke off and I heard him mutter, "Stupid Dragon" before taking another deep breath. "Is that fine with you? I just killed one of my friends for you." There was a bitter twinge to his voice.

No one said a word against the idea, and in a flash, Syvil had turned back to his Drogan form, staring at the dead form of the other Drogan as it...disappeared...? I gasped, but had no time to register, the need for flight more urgent than the dead Drogan disappearing. Drogans were weird. But at least we had one on our side now.

THE GHOSTMAKER

CHAPTER XXII: To Remember, or Not to…What?

Sven:

I stood there, bow in my hand and arrow in the other, ready to nock. My orders were clear, and every moment, I screamed against them. But it was only in the back of my mind, the last remaining place where Skayla's grasp didn't reach. The rest was ready to carry out her every word—ready to do whatever it took. I couldn't do it! And yet, still, here I was. Carefully, I adjusted the red-lensed scope on my mask, magnifying the view of the palace terrace.

I saw Queen Serafina walk out onto the terrace, her bodyguard, Maeko, next to her.

Think, Sven! Think of your friendship with her! Fight this, you weakling!

But I could not, and against my will, I prepared to aim. I felt as if I was shaking with dread, and yet every muscle was certain of its task.

Every bit of my soul seemed to scream out, and yet my arms didn't so much as hesitate as I prepared to kill yet another of my friends.

I aimed, took a breath, gave a wretched inward scream, and then I let go.

"Sven, wake up. Sven!"

I bolted awake, sweat pouring down my forehead and back. Who was Sven? Who was calling my name, where was I?

"Oh good, you're awake," the voice said in a sigh of relief, and I scooted back from where I was now sitting, trying to fight the panic surging through my blood.

Shadows formed in the dark, and my eyes started to adjust. With all the concentration I could muster, I forced my breathing to remain normal—but what was normal?

"Where's Moira?" I asked suddenly, almost not understanding the words until after they came out of my mouth. Moira. I had to find her. She'd left two days ago, by the looks of her letter. "I need to go. There's no time. Something terrible has happened." I started releasing the frenzy within me from its cage, remembering everything that had happened. Those treacherous Drogans! We'd offered sanctuary and instead they'd taken advantage of Skayla.

"Sven, calm down, you're confused. It's me, Estasia." The shadow became more defined, and I saw a lady kneeling by me, a candle in hand. "You don't look well," she added, brow furrowed.

"I'm...fine..." Estasia...Estasia...did I have another sister I'd somehow forgotten about? That *would* be odd. You'd think I wouldn't forget something like that.

She gave a huff and shifted her position so that she was sitting on the floor with her legs crossed. "Oh Sven, come on, remember? Baey? Sefen? The big fellow, Maeko. You saved my life, I saved yours. Seems to be a reoccurring trend. Skayla and Lord Kovo had you locked up? We went to The Crafters' old home, and now we're in the little hut you had hidden. Remember?"

Unfortunately, yes. I stared at her blankly, every vein in my body running cold as it came flooding back upon me. I sighed.

"Sven? You in there?" she asked, now sounding exasperated, and almost worried.

I nodded and forced myself to be fine. "Last time I checked."

I watched as her features relaxed, and she was so relieved she almost dropped the candle. "You scared me."

Eyebrow raised; I gave an incredulous look. "How's that, ah?"

She shook her head. "Never mind. You sure you remember *everything*? Even Syvil? Do you forget everything in general, or is it only certain things?"

"I doubt I'll ever forget you being pushy after this," I replied sarcastically, rubbing my aching side. The whispers of the cold of winter were making my battered body even more stiff, and I had no doubt the others were feeling their aches and pains just as much. "How is your leg? Syvil didn't get you until the second trip, correct? It was getting chilly when Maeko and I arrived here." I remembered clearly the surprising frost, the stubborn Maeko as Jaythos and I had to convince him to get on the Drogan. It had not been a pleasant night.

"Sven." Estasia's voice sounded worried.

I gave her a questioning look. What now?

"That was two days ago."

"Oh," was all I could manage to say.

She just sighed; her breath barely visible in the cold night air. Even in the hut it was cold, though Syvil had made a small fire to try and counteract the weather's bite. I turned my attention over to the Drogan sleeping soundly in the corner. Though in his Human form, he still slept curled up more like an animal, farther away from the others, who slept undisturbed by my waking.

"What else do you remember?"

I sighed, rubbing my hands together and not taking my eyes off the Drogan. I remembered...I remembered the stricken look on his face. He'd saved our necks.

"Sven?" Estasia sighed and scratched her head. "It's already been a long couple of days. Maybe you'll remember by morning? I really should make another round and make sure nothing else is amiss," she said absently.

My brow furrowed as memories flitted in and out like confused bugs heading for the nearest light. And then I realized..."Wait. You're on watch?" I didn't recall anyone trusting her enough to let her do anything like that.

"Actually...you were. But you fell asleep...and so..." She gave a half amused, half worried look.

I...*what?*

"I only woke you because you were...well...it didn't seem like you were having a very pleasant dream. You still haven't fully recovered, Sven, and you probably pushed it too far." Estasia sounded almost bored as she said the last bit. She noticed my expression and rolled her eyes. "Sorry. I know you won't listen, so not sure why I'm bothering to say anything at all."

True. We sat a moment in silence, and in that time, I desperately tried to knock my memory back into shape. What had Syvil told us? What if it was important? What if I'd forgotten something else that was vital? Dread filled within me as the thought rolled over and over in my mind.

"Is it almost dawn?" I asked finally.

"Mhm," Estasia replied as she stood up unsteadily, stretching her wounded leg as she prepared to most likely make another round to check on everything.

I stood up as well, observing all of the still forms on the floor around me. This had been the first good sleep anyone had had in a couple weeks. "Did you get some sleep?" I asked her.

"I'm going to check outside." She completely ignored me, limping over to the entrance and setting a candle on the pathetic little nightstand. Silently, she opened the door, slipping through the crack. I was close behind her, and soon we both stood in the pale glow of starlight.

Then she turned to me, looking unexpectedly angry. "You're being foolish," she started blatantly.

I did not answer. Perhaps I was. But the other option was going back to sleep.

Shaking her head in frustration, she puffed out a breath that looked like smoke in the cold night air. "You're careless and endangering all around you. You can't just forget, Sven, and expect to remember." Her free hand clenched in a tight knot as she spoke. "And what if you wake up one day and can't remember…ever? What will happen when we are all stuck not knowing what's going on?"

I didn't stir as she ranted, arms crossed and a very blank expression plastered on my face. Oh. She was talking about my memory. Right.

"Well, when I find out how to fix it, you'll be the first to know…" I mumbled.

Estasia sighed. "Alright. I'm not good at this. Sorry I opened my stupid mouth."

For a long while I said nothing, only staring fixedly at her, trying to figure it out. Trying to figure *her* out. Then, almost without me meaning to say it, the words came out: "You don't have to apologize. It's fine."

"No. I apologized and I'm not taking it back. So. Too bad." It was hard to know how to take any of what she was saying when she sounded so flustered.

Another moment of silence passed and I tried again. "I just mean, seeing my background, I'm rather surprised you went through all the trouble to break me and Sefen out of the Kovian Fortress. If you only knew me as…" I winced, unable to say the name out loud. "Why?" It didn't make sense. I was a murderer.

Estasia's appearance almost did a complete turnaround, and she looked suddenly very emotional, voice quiet as she replied, "Because. You changed how I see things."

I gave an incredibly concerned stare as I processed what she said. "I don't know if that's really a good thing…"

"Well, then. No. Let me explain." She took in a breath and then began. "It was many years ago. I was accused of stealing something, so Skayla wanted to teach me a lesson. You don't remember, obviously, but you were there. You were ordered to teach it. When you came in, though, your eyes weren't like the others. I could only see the one not hidden beneath your mask, but it constantly flashed from the violet of Skayla to the pale eyes you have now, almost as if you were fighting—like you could actually think for yourself sometimes. You took off your jacket and threw it on the ground. Then you took your whip and told me to scream, and you hit your coat with it. You didn't hit me even once."

She paused a moment, endeavoring to keep a calm composure. When she spoke again, her voice was thick with emotion, and as quiet as a breeze. "When I saw that, it made me wonder why you were fighting so hard—harder than anyone else in a MindHold—and if someone who had already lost the impossible battle was still fighting, what right did *I* have not to? So, I made up my mind." I thought she was done, but then she went on, voice stronger and defiant. "I fought every day. Seeing you so often in passing, but never able to ask why you had helped. Having to stand by and watch as you were forced to do whatever Skayla told you to. In the meantime, I stopped being so self-centered and actually tried to change things. I found there were other people who thought like I did. Aekon said he'd known you from before the war but wouldn't say how. I guess that it was because he knew you were Sven Mara...but that doesn't matter now.

"One day, some prisoners came to the Kovian Fortress, and I was going to try and get them out. Me and my companions. But it went wrong, and I got caught by three guards. They were taking me to Skayla, and I was so..." She paused. "So very afraid of what would happen. All these years, I hadn't really cared what state I was in, as long as I knew she wasn't...wasn't running around in my head. But now, I could lose it all—or worse. Die or...live and be forced to give up my companions because of a MindHold. I was numb all over—I can still feel it...and I knew it was all over." She took another long pause, bitter wind curling around us and making the both of us shiver. However, I knew she wasn't just shivering from the cold...but the memory.

Finally, she went on. "Then I saw you. You were coming down the flight of stairs as the guards were hauling me up them. We were still in the lower levels of the dungeons, so not many others were around. I—I don't know why...but I begged...begged for you to help. I didn't actually think you would." She sighed, and a puff of white mist escaped her lips. I stared at her, mystified. This all sounded so familiar, yet like a faraway dream that the more I tried to place, the further it ran away.

"You stopped dead in your tracks, and without a word, attacked the guards. You asked what I was doing, and too frightened to lie for once in my life, I dared explain what. You...just told me to return upstairs and do my chores. I didn't want to leave those prisoners...but I was still too selfish. I obeyed. The next day, I heard about a prison escape, and how three soldiers had been killed, but I couldn't wrap my head around it. The GhostMaker, the one everyone despised, the one everyone would kill on sight, was the one sticking out his neck for people who hated him. And you...you did what no one else had the spirit to do. You fought Skayla's MindHold. You kept trying to get out, even though you knew you couldn't. I had to know why. I just did."

A long silence followed as I struggled to understand her. All I remembered were the times I'd failed to fight against Skayla, to try and stop her from doing so many terrible things. It made it almost feel like this one thing didn't matter at all. It made me remember how much I'd failed Moira—I should have fought off Skayla's MindHold long ago, I should have stopped from doing more than just these almost pathetic and meaningless acts of kindness. What even happened to those prisoners I'd freed? For all I knew, I could have killed them right after, and this time Skayla would have made sure I did it. So, what was the point, really?

Then Estasia cracked through my spiraling thoughts. "So, yeah. There's my sob story."

I stared out into the night, lost in thought, processing Estasia's words. I didn't even know if it made me feel better to know if I'd done at least one good thing amid the horrors that followed in the shadows. Still...still I could not recall clearly much of anything. Who was alive, who was dead...what had happened under Skayla. It was like a dream; the more I tried to remember, the harder it was. Or perhaps, more like a nightmare, for I was so afraid to know. I now remembered Skayla's words after we had been caught, claiming she had locked my memories. That there was so much I didn't remember. What would happen when I did?

"Sven!"

I blinked, suddenly realizing I'd essentially blacked out. I felt numb all over and was only vaguely aware that Estasia was shaking me. "Sven, snap out of it."

Estasia:

I really hoped these memory problems would get better with time. "You really need to find a way to stop this."

Sven did not say a word.

Yeah. I guess I was being repetitive. I decided to change the subject...not that he would likely remember it. But if we were going to Hytat, he and the others really had to know. "Anyway. There is something you should know. I know where that map is, as I told you. And I think I can help get you in. It's the city of Alkemar in Patelayna. As you know, Skayla has moved most of the people into major cities, so she can keep a more concentrated eye on them. Alkemar is one of them. It also happens to be the city I grew up in." I took a deep breath, about to reveal what he had really inspired me to do. "But I know the slaves there. After how you helped me, I started building an underground network. I have eyes and ears in most of the fortresses and factories Skayla has made, and at least one in every city. Aekon was one—he said you knew him?" I watched Sven's reaction carefully, trying to judge if he was angry that I hadn't told him or relieved that there was a chance, closer than he saw. Well, if we could manage to cross the Ocean of Vek' n'Vol.

He said nothing, only nodding when I mentioned Aekon. Taking that as a possibly good sign, I continued, "Aekon and I have created a close system of code that we shared with a few other slaves. They then were transferred and moved around, and over the course of the years, the network grew. We may be able to stay ahead of Skayla, if I can get in contact with one of them. That was one of the reasons I came with you. We want to start an organized uprising from inside, but I need to really start spreading the word, gather information without being confined to being a slave."

Sven broke his silence then, doubt now mixed with an inkling of hope. "But how do we get to Patelayna? I don't suppose you know someone that can get us a ship? Syvil can't fly that far. Not with all of us."

I frowned. "No. But I could definitely steal you one."

He returned my frown, confused. "What?"

Sighing, I tried to keep my smile down, slyly saying, "Before the war, I may have been a...questionable citizen. Sticky fingers run in the family...I think. I guess I don't actually know. But anyway, a boat would be a good challenge, but I think I can get one. With some help, of course."

"I see..." he mused. "So, where is your nearest source of information?"

I closed my eyes, and once more made a mental representation of one of the maps I had studied, "A day or two from here, by foot. It's in the coastline city of Hytat. He's a slave in the city ruler's house. But how can we get in without being recognized?" I asked, knowing the answer already. The question was simple formality.

His whole body tensed, hand rubbing the ring around his finger and turning back to the little hut. "I can disguise us," was all he said as he slipped back into the dark hut in an obvious play to avoid further conversation, leaving me outside, alone with my now extinguished candle.

I let out a tense breath, keeping my train of thought going. I didn't like to dwell. And so, I turned to the next matter at hand. I knew that as nice as it was being able to rest here at one of Sven's hideouts, we would have to leave. I found it fascinating that even when he didn't have his ring on, the illusions still remained. How did that work? Regardless, we would be leaving soon. For Hytat. And I had to steal a ship.... For all my bragging, how exactly was I going to pull that one off?

Morning dawned as I continued to stand watch, and I shivered as a snowflake landed on my nose. Great. That was the last thing we needed. With another shudder, I went back inside, having just been relieved by Jaythos. I pulled my rags closer around me. Sven was already up again, looking much better physically, at least, than last night. Syvil was stretching more like a cat than Human, his eyes peering intently at the rest of us as he seemed to try and remember his surroundings. Having

Sven forget things was hard enough, but a psycho Dragon bird forgetting? That could be bad. I set my cold candle down on the ground and walked over to the beast, shaking my head and making sure to be extra careful. It did really look confused.

"You don't remember anything, do you?" I said wryly. I was really over the whole memory problems thing.

The beast's posture showed agreement, and he shrunk back from me defensively. "Syvil. We saved you, remember? We got you out of Skayla's grip?"

He relaxed slightly, but his eyes darted around the room warily, brow furrowing in confusion. "Where are we?"

"Still at the hideout." I tried to gauge how bad his, well, *brain issues* were, compared to Sven's.

"Right," Syvil replied, folding his hands and seeming to collect himself.

I sat down. I didn't like it, but I needed to evaluate, and...well, he had been quiet since that night. If I was going to keep tabs on who we could trust, then I might as well try and get to know everyone. I decided to start with the vulnerability he had shown after the scuffle. It would both show how much he could retain, as well as what I was dealing with. "It's been such a...tense couple days that I don't think anyone said thank you for saving our necks."

Syvil's jaw tightened, and the rest of his body followed. "No problem." The words were said bitterly. "What do you want? Drogans aren't dumb. Are you just seeking a reaction out of me, or do you want something specific?"

I raised an eyebrow. "Just evaluating."

"Yes. Killing my friend was clearly not enough for you." He rolled his eyes and ran his hand through his hair. "Fryn is going to hate me for that."

My brow furrowed. "What do you mean?" He had called the dead Drogan that. Right before they'd disappeared.

"Drogans have two lives. With the loss of the first comes a loss of the ability to shift to a Dragon. I have taken away Fryn's wings, forever," Syvil replied tersely.

"Well...I guess at least they still have one life left?" That had definitely not been the thing to say, and Syvil's red face proved it.

"It is just as much dying for us as it is for a Human. We lose a part of ourselves. Left for the rest of our lives to walk the worlds as a Human only. Some go another four hundred years after having lost their forms."

Wait. What? "How long do you live...exactly...?"

"I am two hundred and seventy-seven. Many don't live past a thousand, but we only die from disease or being killed. We do not age like other races."

Well, then.

Syvil kept going, frustration dripping in his tone. "And usually that is from being hunted. You all and your preconceived notions of our savagery and manipulations is what drives us to it. Ovok and his daughters were the only things keeping our race alive before we fled here. And then Ovok turned around and, with your so-called protector, used us."

I raised my hands slightly. "Hey. Until you, we were under the impression you all were helping willingly. I mean, you show up and suddenly Skayla just up and decides to turn on everyone?"

"Most of us are in a MindHold." Syvil grimaced. "Fryn was in one. And because of the stupid Dragon, she's dead."

My brow furrowed. "I'm...sorry?"

There was a pause, Syvil looking around doubtfully. His eyes settled on me with the gaze of someone who had walked a thousand miles, even if he didn't look it. "The Dragon. The beast side of us. Drogans aren't Humans that shift to Dragons, nor Dragons that can be Human. We are fully both. Because of it, we can assess a person as acutely as an animal but connect as a Human. That balance of beast and Human is a difficult one to keep and many succumb to The Dragon. The beast. Next comes Drogan Madness. If we spend too much time in one form, it...it runs the risk of throwing things off balance." He swallowed hard. "I never would have killed Fryn."

"Oh. I'm sorry." I didn't bother to try and not sound awkward. It was rather hard to find sympathy for the beasts that had ravaged my world. But at the same time...I was not going to be like Maeko. "So had you been in your, er, Dragon form much, then?" Should I be concerned about him going all...feral on us?

Syvil was watching Sven and Jaythos as they packed up some of their belongings. "Skayla did not allow us to be anything but the Dragon. I don't know how much of us are too far gone. I am not a fighter, nor do I want to be. That helped me stay...sane." He sighed. "But when I am in my Dragon form, the beast tugs. I will have to be more careful."

Well, this was...interesting. I was just starting to think of what to press about next, when our conversation was cut short.

"Time to leave," Sven said, coming by and tapping me on the shoulder before walking back to the others.

I gave an awkward nod to Syvil and turned to find Sven start explaining the plan. I listened intently as I helped Maeko prepare to leave.

"We're going to Hytat to get a ship."

Oh good, Sven was capable of remembering *something* at least. That was a good sign...right? I folded up the last of our pathetic blankets, bringing it over to the few saddlebags we had left. I'd need to get us supplies as well.

"Are you insane, Sven?" Sefen asked in a not-so-low whisper.

"A little."

I rolled my eyes at Sven's reply. 'A little' was an understatement. I started casually rationing out food supplies, throwing a stale biscuit at the quiet Drogan in the corner, impressed when he caught it without even looking at me.

"*How* are we getting a ship?" he asked with a hint of skepticism.

"I'm going to get us one," I casually chimed in.

"How will you do that, exactly?" Syvil's tone was one of dry amusement.

We all looked at him, but I didn't bother a direct retort. I had poked the bear enough, so I could deal with the claws it produced.

And so, instead, I continued to address the others. "I've stolen harder things and, with Sven's help, we could easily get a ship." If they all could learn to be a little more vigilant. I'd have to work on that one, too.

"What's taking so long?" Jaythos's agitation made itself known as he poked his head through the doorway, looking around at all of us. "I thought we were leaving? Time is not something we can waste, and we can always argue about things when we're all dead."

Short, sweet, and to the point. His dry lack of humor was starting to grow on me.

"Being dead allows no arguing," Syvil replied as he stood up.

"Shut your feathery mouth," grumbled Jaythos. He didn't quite have the same flair for patience, however.

"Well, shall we make like Jaythos suggests and get out of here? Maeko and I've got everything packed, I think. Not that there's too much left." I paused, looking over at Syvil. We'd had him carry the packs earlier—he was the closest thing we had to a horse—but now I loathed the idea of him being in the form of a Dragon unless we absolutely had to. "Why don't we separate the supply packs between the rest of us?"

"Why? The Drogan did before," Maeko said, clearly displeased.

I didn't want to explain. Maeko had enough distrust to get us all caught as it was, and I didn't need to worry about him pushing Syvil over the edge with any extra name-calling like 'monster' or whatnot. GhostMaker was enough.

"Because I figured we'd give Syvil a break, is all," I answered without tearing my gaze away from the Drogan. A knowing look passed between us, and nothing more was said on the matter.

"Shall we, then?" Sven broke into the very unfruitful discussion with the newest member of this…interesting…group, standing with Jaythos by the door.

Jaythos chimed in, "Yes. We've wasted enough time already."

And then, finally, we left.

Baey:

393

Ahh, it was so nice to fly. We'd been traveling for two days now, but no matter how often I got to fly, the moment my feet touched the ground, I felt the longing to go up again. The exhilaration of having the ground whirring beneath you like a splattered piece of art was a different kind of beauty. I checked beneath me to make sure I hadn't left the others in the dust, and sure enough there they were, like little ants in a far away, small world. I took a deep breath of the rushing air and then hovered to get a good look around. We'd not run into any more problems with patrols, at least. That being said, they would still be on our trail after finding the casualties of that other patrol we'd left behind.

I sped on once more, getting ahead of my friends, then behind, impatient that we no longer had horses. It felt as if we were going at a snail's pace, but at least we were alive. My hand went to the watch hanging from my neck, just as it always did at least a thousand times an hour. Sven's words came back to me. Was I really strong? No one had ever told me that before. I'd always thought that when the time came, I wouldn't have what it took. Maybe it was time to stop thinking like that. And what if I couldn't bring Moira back? Sven was just so alone—so lost—and no one seemed to really care. If I could bring just one person back who would help—one person who would maybe help bring *him* back….

He was right. I had to try.

I dove closer to the trees and waited for them, listening intently to make sure no one else was nearby. I heard the sound of a squirrel scrambling up a tree, a rabbit gnawing on a dying leaf, and a Kear leaping away into the forest, but nothing else. The others closed in, and I took to the clouds again.

My mind turned to Syvil and the Drogans, and I tried once more to wrap my head around what Sven had told me yesterday. He and Sefen had said they weren't from our world. At Valdon, I'd heard bits and pieces about the Drogans, but for the most part, no one had explained them to me. Tanner himself hadn't been able to help, being my age. I'd always thought they were some species Skayla had found or created, not one that had come to our world from another one. And about that. There were other worlds? What were they like?

I stopped when I realized I was pulling too far ahead of the others, forcing myself not to become too lost in thought. There was a spot in the very far distance, but it was going in the opposite direction that we were. Good. I tried to force myself not to relax, but it was hard. The further away from Skayla we got, the more relieved and renewed I felt.

When I stopped, I saw it. There, in the distance, the ground just seemed to disappear, melding into the sky. The faint scent of salt wafted in the air, and I could barely hear the screeching of a seagull. Excitement flushed my cheeks, and I felt as if I could do a flip—or try anyway. I had never seen such a sea or ocean, but I knew that was the only thing this could be.

I looked down just in time to see Sven motion for me, and I reluctantly descended back into the forest.

"How does everything look?" he asked.

I couldn't hide my relief and could almost laugh from it. "We're quickly losing them. I don't think they know where we're going."

"Good. Though I think we're moving slower than expected."

"Can you see the ocean yet?" Tanner asked, curious as ever.

A broad grin plastered on my face, and I nodded. "Yes. Though it's still far off." I already missed the sight of it.

"Can you see Hytat?" Sefen asked.

"I only just spotted the ocean. I'll have to look again."

Tanner shifted his weight impatiently. "Well, get up there already!" he ordered with a smile.

Syvil gave a sigh, and I knew he longed for the sky possibly even more than I did. But he was way too obvious, and he'd give away our position. Skayla had to know that we'd taken him with us.

"Be careful, Little Baey," Maeko said quietly.

I smiled and nodded, taking to the skies again. I turned my attention to the Ocean of Vek' n'Vol, and there, just before it, I saw the little city of Hytat, and a line cutting through the trees, the lines of metal leading all the way to the city. Sven had said it was the abandoned train tracks. I wondered what a train looked like.

Light started to fade, and once more, we were traveling in dusk. Sven had pointed me to an old bunch of ruins, and we reached them by nightfall. As we collapsed inside the fallen mansion, Estasia passed food out, and the sound of contented chewing emanated around the deserted place.

I felt a strange sense of sadness as I looked around at the fallen roof and the broken pillars that littered the floor. It was a haunting place, and

I shivered a little as the odd sensation grew. It was coming from the watch around my neck, I knew, but I didn't like it. What had this place been?

Tanner came to join me on the broken bit of marble I was perched on, and we ate our rations together in silence. But not for long. Tanner wolfed down his in seconds and immediately started a conversation. I wasn't sure if that was good or annoying at the moment.

"Do you know what this place is?" he asked.

I shook my head, mouth full.

"Hey, Baey, you ready?" Sven's interruption was so sudden that I actually jumped to attention, hovering an inch in the air as I swallowed my food.

"Uh, I-uh…." Slowly, I fluttered down to the ground, still confused as I stared at Sven, who was standing right in front of us.

Sven only handed me his sword—which I had long since returned to him—handle first. "I told you, we are going to make sure that next time, you keep both wings." His smile would have been imperceptible on anyone else, but on his face, it seemed like the most obvious thing in the world.

And it was catchy.

"Oh, um…" I looked to Sefen, who was now pointedly staring at us.

"It doesn't bite, promise. We'll be careful." Sven held it out further in encouragement.

Slowly, I wrapped my fingers around the hilt. The few times Namaya *had* let me spar, it had been with sticks or something much lighter. Never an actual, real-life blade.

"Sven, you can't be serious. She's going to get herself hurt." Sefen's interjection bittered the small bit of excitement I'd let myself have. Already, I was starting to give back the sword.

But Sven turned around. "She needs to learn. Otherwise, she's going to get herself killed. She should have learned a long time ago. If she'd known how, then she wouldn't have almost died back at the house."

"If she'd stayed out of the way instead of diving head first into a Drogan's mouth, then maybe she would have been safe." Sefen's reply left my throat feeling thick.

"That was *my* mouth, thank you," Syvil interjected. "I don't know why you're all bickering, anyway. I'd side with Sven. Clearly, the girl's been stifled—I mean, look at her flying. Sloppy. Doesn't have any sense of form."

I wanted to cry already.

But then Sven turned back to me. "We'll just ignore them, ah?" He winked. "Now, balance is essential; you can feel with the weight of the sword." Without warning, he pushed me, and I would have fallen face first into the ground had he not caught me.

"Sven!" Sefen shouted.

"See? Balance. We need to find your center." Sven steadied me and smiled gently, washing away my embarrassment. "Though with the wings, you are going to have a different center than most people...."

I tried to keep focus, even as Sefen got up to engage. "Okay," I said, taking from Sven's example and ignoring everyone else. I spread my feet a bit, flaring my wings and trying better to feel secure even with the heavy blade. "Is this better?"

Sven shoved me again, and I stood my ground—even if I wobbled. "Better," he encouraged, "but not there yet."

"Sven, I think we need to have a talk," Sefen was standing between us now. I pointed the blade down, afraid of tripping and hurting him.

"Sefen," Sven's voice was low. "This is not the time. She needs to learn. Trust me."

I heard Maeko scoff from where he was sitting, and my grip on my sword tightened.

"Sven, you don't know her like we do—"

"No harm will come to her, I promise," Sven said softly. "Now please, you're not helping. She can take care of herself."

There was a tense moment of silence, and without a word, Sefen backed up, slowly going back to his seat.

Sven returned to me. "Now, you are going to try and strike me. Never lose your balance for a moment, or you won't be able to launch a proper attack. Your primary concern is balance, understand?"

I nodded, adding, "But...what if I hit you?"

Another flicker of a smile. "Trust me. See?" Even as he said it, he waved his hand through the blade I was holding. Wait...wait, how was that possible? The sword wasn't an illusion, was it?

"Wait—" My brow furrowed in confusion.

"Just tricks, darlin'. You can't hurt me. Trust me."

Still confused, I nodded again, taking the stance.

"Oh, and Syvil? Anything that may improve the use of her wings will be helpful," Sven added quickly, before turning back to me. "Now, keep in mind, the closer your feet are together, the weaker your center. But too far apart, and you get a similar result."

"The same goes for wings, if you were wondering," Syvil chimed in. Got it...I hoped...maybe?

"Ready?"

I wanted to answer 'no,' but instead took the stance, a mixture of fear and excitement coursing through me and causing my hands to sweat. "Ready."

Sven folded his hands behind his back. "Alright. Have at it."

I took a swing, and Sven ducked without so much as moving his feet. Alright. So...we were doing this.... A thrill went through me and I tried again, planting my feet firmer, flexing my wings, and gripping the sword hilt as I went again.

"Now, don't toss it around like a rag, darlin'. The farther you extend the blade, the farther away from your center you'll be," Sven coached as he ducked and weaved around me, not even so much as breaking a sweat. I, on the other hand, was already panting, working through the frustration as I realized that, honestly, even without whatever trick he was using on the blade, I wouldn't be able to hit him.

But I was determined to get this.

"The air can be just as much an anchor, too. So, if you want to feel less like a fish out of water, feel the currents around you to push and keep yourself up." Syvil's interjections were more idly said, but I saw out of the corner of my eye how he was leaning forward now.

This continued for some time, Sven ever calm as he called out what I was doing correctly and incorrectly, and Syvil adding to his advice. I never knew there were right and wrong ways to hold my wings, or to swing a blade, or to stand...the list went on, but despite the exhaustion and frustration, I started to get it. Little by little.

At last, Sven announced, "Alright. That's enough for now."

I gladly relaxed, breathing heavily as I handed Sven back his blade. "Thank you!" I felt strangely elated.

Sven again gave that ever-so-slight smile and took back the sword, sheathing it in its place as he ruffled my hair again like he'd done in the tunnel. "You did well."

"Well, I have a good teacher." I tugged at my vest, my eyes flitting to Syvil. "Both of you."

The Drogan said nothing but did look a little amused, so...that was *something*, right?

"Well. I, personally, now want to try my luck against Sven." It was Jaythos, already getting up. "I need to give the arm a little workout anyway."

Sven seemed to mask panic quickly before replying, "I am not so sure that is wise."

Jaythos shrugged. "You don't even need your weapon. I just want to see if that fancy footwork is good enough to outmaneuver me."

This seemed to make Sven relax *slightly*, and he again folded his hands behind his back. "If you insist."

I quickly sat down by Syvil, intrigued to see what would happen. I'd often watched everyone at Valdon practice and spar, and Jaythos, while not as gifted at swordsmanship as he was his marksmanship, was no slouch.

Jaythos took a stance—which I now evaluated with a much more understanding eye, to my delight—and the 'match' began. It was almost unearthly the way Sven so calmly moved around Jaythos's deadly blade. Ducking, stepping to the side, and even getting around and behind

Jaythos. It was a little frightening to think what he could do if he *did* have a blade. I mean, I'd seen him in battle...but he'd been so hurt and stiff.

After a good ten minutes, Jaythos leaned over, panting and laughing as he gasped out, "I surrender. That was embarrassing."

"Alright, now I have to try," Sefen chuckled as he went up for his dose of whipping. And yes, it was definitely a whipping. Sefen didn't even get *close*, ending with the same gasps as Jaythos had ended with.

"That is...honestly, a little frightening." Sefen shook his head, chuckling as he sheathed his blade.

"He wasn't The GhostMaker for no reason." Maeko's comment caused a hush to go around, and Sven again stiffened.

"Maeko, would you please stop bringing it up? I think he's aware." I wasn't sure who was more surprised at the fact the retort had come out of my mouth: the others or me. I could feel my wings blushing scarlet, even as my cheeks burned with the same fervor. "I just don't see how it's helping anything."

"I agree with Baey." Jaythos was...agreeing with me? "We're stuck with each other. We should be glad that we have someone who can save our necks, along with Syvil and Estasia. We'd all be dead without them. I feel like insulting them constantly isn't really going to help anything."

Another reign of quiet.

"Perhaps," Maeko replied at last, giving Sven a long and uncomfortable stare. "My apologies. Jaythos is correct. The insults do nothing."

I saw the distance in Sven's eyes now; the hesitant smiles and humor he'd had were long gone, buried where I could no longer find them. "Well. I think I shall go do some surveillance around the ruins to make sure we are clear for the night," was all he said as he slowly turned around and left the area.

As soon as he was out of sight, I turned on Maeko. "Don't you get it?" I was uncharacteristically bold in showing my anger. "He *knows* what he's done. You don't have to keep telling him. What if Queen Serafina had been him? What if their places were switched? Would you still be as slow to understand? He didn't have a *choice*, Maeko, and he already treats it as if he did without you shoving it down his throat."

Awkward stares ensued, and Jaythos didn't really help when he said, "*Thank* you. It's about time you said half the things that were on your mind."

Estasia rolled her eyes. "Yeah. For once I agree with you. Now, let's all get some sleep before someone blows a gasket and we are at each other's throats."

I couldn't sleep. Instead, I wandered off into the ruins to think. I wished Maeko would stop being so antagonizing towards Sven. Yes, Sven had assassinated the Queen...but, could you really say it was him? Really, it was Skayla. Why couldn't Maeko see the way Sven reacted to it? Why couldn't he see that Sven was just as unforgiving towards himself?

"What are you doing out alone, Baey?" Estasia's voice came from right next to me, and I forced myself not to jump. She'd been on guard duty. Of course, she'd noticed me get up and leave.

"Just thinking," I said quietly.

"Hm," was all she said as she invited herself to sit next to me, swinging her legs lazily back and forth. "Bit distracted, are we?" she asked.

I bit my lip, nodding hesitantly. I still didn't really know Estasia well.

"You know. Before I was a slave, I was a thief." Estasia's lack of subtlety took me off guard. She didn't seem the type to open up, but I didn't say anything about it. If this was a phenomenon, I would take it.

"Sounds...exciting?" was all I could think to reply with.

"Mhm. I was a good one, too, if I do say so myself. You learn to be observant in that line of business. Like the way people react to things or the reason behind them."

I was quiet, resorting to twiddling my feathers.

"But more practically, I could maybe help you with swordplay in that sort of way. Paying attention is key in a fight. I mean, if you paid better attention, you would have a better chance at getting past Sven's guard anyway." She smiled mischievously.

"I do pay attention," I said defensively, hopping off the chunk of marble I'd perched upon. Estasia hopped off with me, putting an arm behind my back and beginning to steer me towards where the others were sleeping—though that was still a bit away.

"You do, don't get me wrong, but you have so much potential. And in the precarious position we are in, none of us can afford to not pay attention—whoops!" She tripped on a small pebble, using me to keep her from falling. "Sorry about that."

"You were saying about paying attention?" I said dryly.

She looked amused but said nothing, only patting my back and continuing on. "You see, when people constantly have something, they forget it's there. For instance, do you constantly feel your clothes on you? No. Do you always feel the feathers of your wings scraping against you?"

I shook my head.

"Exactly. But little things like that sometimes need to be kept in mind." She stopped and turned me to face her directly. "And you've gotten so used to the feel of your necklace and the watch, that you now ignore how they feel. How long have you been missing them?"

At first, I was confused, but when I felt around my neck, I was horrified to find she was right. They…they were gone!

"Don't worry, Baey," Estasia said hurriedly, before I had time enough to fully process. She held out her hand palm up, and there, snuggled nice and comfy in it, was the chain holding the broken watch.

I all but ripped the things from her hand, feeling defensive and angry at first. "Don't do that again," I snapped.

"But Baey, you said you paid attention. I was only making a point." Her voice was still calm as ever.

I opened my mouth to argue, but words failed. She was right. I didn't pay nearly as much attention as I thought I did, and now that I thought about it, I had a feeling that a good half of us didn't. "Can you teach me?" I asked.

The slowly growing smile on Estasia's face widened even more, and she nodded. "Of course. But not tonight. Tonight, you need to rest."

My spirits dampened, and I desperately asked, "But when?" When in the world would we ever get time again? We were running for our lives after all!

"Don't worry, Birdy," she chided. "We'll have plenty of time on the ship."

Assuming she *got* the ship, but after how she'd wrangled the watch from under my nose, I thought she really might be able to do anything.

"Now, get some sleep."

THE GHOSTMAKER

CHAPTER XXIII: Hytat

Estasia:

After I convinced Baey to sleep, I started the climb to where Sven was perched, seeing as he was also not actually asleep. The form of him on the ground with the others was clearly an illusion.

The wind howled among the rocks, and the air whispered snow as I made my way up. I had a feeling about what these ruins were, and between how close they were to Hytat, and how Sven was acting, I was confident my hunch was correct.

"You may not want to go for the watch, again," Sven said as I finally made my way to the top of the rubble.

So, he'd been watching. Well, he could at least help me get the others to be a little more observant then. "I was teaching her a lesson, that was all."

He said nothing at first, only continuing to stare off into the view of the ruins that we now had, so high up.

"It's not for you to touch," he replied at last, voice barely audible.

"Why, am I not *worthy* or something?" The words came out harsher than I'd intended, and I winced.

The silence that followed was chilling, and I rubbed my hands together to ease both the awkwardness and the tingling sensation that was running through them.

"That's not what I meant," he said quietly, fiddling with the ring around his finger.

I supposed if I had something left of my family, I'd want it to stay out of other people's hands, too. But then, he'd given it to Baey. I decided not to pursue that train of conversation any further.

"What do you want then?" Sven's tone turned a little irritable.

I came closer and sat down, allowing a little distance between us. "I was coming up to check on you," I replied. Now I almost wished I hadn't; but I had to try and do better. This group was dysfunctional at best, and all the arguing was not good for any of us. "How much of this is from that Rugonian jerk, and how much of it is this place?" I asked, referring to his behavior.

A puff of foggy breath escaped violently from Sven's lips. "You're very subtle."

"Yeah," was all I could think to say. I'd already blown sympathy out the window so might as well keep going now. "So, which is it?"

He didn't reply, again. As usual.

"I'm just trying to help, Sven. I know I'm not good at it. No one else really seems to be trying that hard, though, so I guess Baey and I are all you've got for now, sorry. I just...Maeko is wrong. They're all going to wake up one day and realize half the world is in a MindHold, doing things they would never do otherwise. If they can't forgive you, I don't know what they expect to happen when they 'free' the world."

Sven sighed and *actually* replied this time. "But I was supposed to be better. The Watchers were supposed to be different."

"No one's perfect. You couldn't have known Skayla would turn like she did. I thought *no one* saw it coming." I was in way over my head with these people, and yet the more I talked to them, the more I was slowly drawn into wanting to help them. First Syvil, now Sven. Everyone here had a story, whether they admitted it or not. Everyone was hurt in some way. Even The GhostMaker. Especially Sven.

"She was my sister. We were close. I should have been able to stop this." He motioned to the starlit ruins we were staring at.

"This was your home, wasn't it?" I asked.

The question seemed to prick Sven, but he nodded. "Yes. It's where we grew up after we were chosen."

I wasn't up to date on my history, what with living on the street and all. "How long did you live here?"

Sven put his hands in the pockets of his tattered jacket as if to force himself to stop rubbing and fiddling with his ring. "I was eight, I think." It took a while before he came up with the answer. "I don't remember much. Obviously. Still." The last statement was impatient.

"Wow," was all I could think to say. "Did you have parents?"

There was an awkward pause, and then he changed subjects with a clear and deliberate abruptness. "We should go over the plan for Hytat. We'll reach the city around noon tomorrow. What's the plan from there?"

I took a moment to relish the fact that he actually trusted me, remembering that only days ago he wouldn't have asked me the time of day. I had a feeling that ripping a scrap of metal from the back of a Drogan had something to do with it.

"Well, Jayler's mansion is by the ocean, but I won't want to go directly there. That would just be suicide. But I'll definitely need you." More specifically, his abilities.

So here we were, about two hours before noon as predicted. Maeko, Sefen, and Baey were to my left, Sven, Syvil and Jaythos to my right, and nothing but the looming, seemingly endless city of Hytat between us and the ocean of Vek' n'Vol. The city walls were surprisingly intact, as opposed to how I had left Alkemar. Where Alkemar had been decimated, Hytat must have been willing to surrender, for the marks of The Crafters were all over the intricate weaving of gears and metal towering above us.

Before us were the gates, the metals reflecting the autumn sun so that a beautiful patchwork of colors reflected on the ground and on the dozen or so people waiting for the gates to open. In the center of the gate was a large gear lock with a glass orb in the center that I knew was meant to refract the light to a mirror in a room in the gatehouse, allowing for a clear view of the outside. But, most importantly, I turned my gaze to the side of the gate, where a giant hourglass hung fastened to the wall, the sand almost all to the bottom. The gates would open soon.

"So, you remember how we're getting in, right?" I asked once again. They didn't even dignify me with an answer; I'd asked so many times. I just wasn't used to doing things like this with others.

Sven clicked his fingers together—purely for dramatic effect, I was sure—and then said, "We are invisible. But not for too long. Things could get complicated if we do. Once we're in, I'll just change our appearances." Stupid Skayla and her passports. They weren't something that could just be replicated—and Sven had said it was safest not to risk him trying to reproduce one, with the way his memory was—so invisible it would be until we were in the city.

We all nodded in understanding, and together emerged from the undergrowth where we'd been hiding. I couldn't help but feel nervous; I didn't like relying on someone else's abilities to get myself into somewhere—and definitely not Gifting. But Sven deserved my trust.

"Just remember," he added quickly, "they can't see or hear you, so people won't *avoid* you."

A guard passed along the wall above us, and I clenched my jaw in concentration. There was a casual shout from him to the other, and a moment later, the gear lock clicked like the turning of an hour hand on a clock, soon followed by the groaning of the opening gates.

Wagons started to pour forth from the gate, carrying supplies that would be brought from Patelayna and Rugo to the cities of Kaedovarna.

As the two-way traffic continued—with papers checked and double checked at the entrance—we slipped through, trying to be extra careful not to bump anyone. I took a deep breath as we made it inside.

"Watch it!" Sven shouted, grabbing me and yanking me to the side just in time to avoid a guard that was coming towards me. He walked right where I had been, and then over to another soldier, jabbering away as if he hadn't seen or heard us. Because, well, he hadn't.

I let out a breath and swallowed. "Sorry," I muttered.

"I thought you said you were good at this." Maeko's amusement wasn't helping.

I yanked myself from Sven's saving grip as soon as the guard was clear and glared at the Rugonian. "I am. I'm just not used to being invisible."

"It is harder than it looks," Sven reassured quickly, ushering for us to follow as we made our way to a quiet corner. "Once we're in the hub of the city, I'll just change our appearances, but here is still too conspicuous. Estasia, lead us somewhere that's possible?"

I nodded. That, I could do. Without another word, I started off in the direction of the populated areas, dodging a few soldiers here and there. I had never had to pay so much attention to where I was going. Well, I had, but I had always been able to rely on people not staring if I brushed past them. Now, I couldn't disappear in the streets like I was used to. It was a little frustrating.

The section between the first wall and the second were where the poor lived. The houses were older and often in disrepair, their ornate trim and stately colors worn and fading to nothing, making the metal parts of the houses stick out like a sore thumb. Skayla and her promise of prosperity. Yeah, right. I scoffed as all around were familiar sights: dirty little children sitting on heaps of rubble, the ones playing in the street, waiting for someone naive enough to pickpocket. One little boy with a worn flat cap ran out in front of us, and I barely remembered in time that he could not see us. Sven put a hand in front of me as an angry, better dressed man in a top hat and monocle ran after the boy, top hat under his arm so that he would not lose that, too, as he pursued the boy.

"Come back, you little rascal!" he shouted vehemently.

Sven dropped his arm. "Come. We need to move on."

He seemed to sense me keenly watching the boy, who was struggling to disappear in the crowd. I rebuked myself for breaking concentration, and then walked on, better noting my surroundings.

We arrived at the second wall, the one that separated the soldiers' barracks, stalls, and so forth from the rest of the city. This door was locked, but I pulled the two pins from my hair and quickly picked the lock. Child's play. Sven stopped my hand before I opened the door, pushing me aside and putting an ear to it. After a moment of listening, he opened the door, and I tried to hold in my annoyance.

A second later, and all of us were standing against the wall with the lively bustle of Hytat before us. The houses in this part of the city were in the best condition; the street had turned from dirt to cleanly kept red brick, and you could hear the clatter of carriages as they clunked about the street. There were also sidewalks here, and the pedestrian crowd grew even more prevalent. Ladies walked by in their layered, lace-trimmed dresses and perfect leather gloves, twirling lace umbrellas that did nothing more than keep out the sun. Men in waistcoats, frocks, and top hats often accompanied the ladies, and if alone they usually strode through the streets with some unknowable goal. There were others, too, those that didn't fit in—ladies with the loose hanging breeches or split skirts of Rugo especially visible. But I noted how few there seemed to be of foreign visitors—Skayla didn't like people traveling.

Buildings towered above us, some with giant glass balconies, others made of metal. Pipes and glass chutes ran between houses, some for heat and water, others for the message relay system. I could hear the click of gears as the delivery elevator pulley systems brought food or other packages up to apartments that were above the first story. It was hard to remember that this was a conquered city, the way everyone went about their business so normally. You could almost forget what you had just seen between the outer walls. The only hint were the dozens of people with the deep violet eyes that were not their own, walking almost too rhythmically as they moved through the streets.

The noise of the city tickled my ears like the sound of an old friend's voice, and the vile odor of horse dung, rot, and garbage intertwined with the savory smells of baking, the thick whiff of salt, the steam of tea shops, and other strange aromas that I had not experienced in a long while. The smells of food especially found my nose, but years of suppressing those urges came in handy, and I had little trouble stuffing the longing down. Besides, I had money to buy supplies. Money I hadn't told Sven about.

"Alright." Sven said simply, implying as planned that we could now be seen. "Lead on."

I turned to him to nod and had to force myself not to blink. Sven didn't look like…Sven. I had known he was going to do that, but still, it was hard to picture how convincing he could make it look. With his now-average height, added to by a tailcoat and top hat, he fit in perfectly. I was too afraid to look down at myself, not wanting to know what sort of finery he had posed me in. All I knew was that everyone else definitely looked…well, like they'd fit in with the rest of the crowd, at least. Even Baey's wings were hidden with an illusion of a voluminous fur coat.

Picturing the map in my head, I led us through the busy, winding streets, feeling very at home as I ducked and dodged among the people. To my surprise, Sven kept up very easily, but we both had to slow slightly when Sefen and Maeko lagged behind. Rugonians were not meant for speed or weaving through crowds. They were meant to part them.

The traffic increased as we grew closer and closer to the center of the city, and I immediately aimed for the marketplace. I kept calm, looking down and not at the surrounding people, just like I had for so many years. It also kept me from staring at the eyes of some of the passersby.

The sea breeze blew refreshingly through my hair as we arrived at the marketplace. The shouts of people selling their wares made the already noisy city overpowering, and instantly, we were bombarded with peddlers shoving birds, watches, and other things right in our faces. I sighed reluctantly as I stopped in a quieter area, digging in my fragmented pockets and touching the pouch I had long kept a secret. With one last pause, I took it in hand and all but shoved it at Maeko. "You all get supplies, and especially some new clothes for everyone. There should be plenty in here for anything we need. Then wait by the shipyard for us and get in position. We should be along in an hour or two."

Maeko stared at the bag of money, and Sven raised an amused eyebrow but said nothing.

"Come on. We have errands to run," I said to Sven, and soon we left Maeko and the rest behind us to do their shopping. I needed Sven in case we ran into any difficulties that required his power. They'd all fit in fine now for what they were meant to do.

Sven:

I followed closely behind Estasia, feeling as if I'd gone back in time as we wove through the streets. Once upon a time, Skayla, Moira, and I had done the same thing when running errands for Mum or Da. Now, we were still running an errand...just not for food but information. Dangerous information. I was rather surprised I'd remembered that.

The streets got less and less crowded as we neared the outskirts of the city, heading towards the cliff where the nobles' and Jayler's mansions were located.

"Alright. You really should stay out here."

I cocked a skeptical eyebrow. "Mm. No. I already told you that—so where do we get in?" I had once more shrouded us from the eyes of others, and we were now standing at the base of the mansion. With the strict schedule of the Bethynese soldiers who guarded it, it would, for now, be easier to remain invisible in order to at least get *into* the mansion. Entering under false pretenses and identities ran the risk of being found too soon—and we didn't want Skayla finding out about where we were going.

Estasia huffed. "I'm assuming we're invisible again?"

I nodded. "But as the sun starts going down, there are going to be variables that are harder to control. For instance, our shadows. Best to get this done."

"Follow me." She grabbed my arm to emphasize her annoyance, and I allowed myself to be pulled along.

"Well then," I said, very unimpressed.

She said nothing more, half dragging me to the west side of the mansion where a servants' passage lay. There was some traffic, but not much, and after waiting a moment for the right opportunity, we slipped inside behind a group of servants. We had barely enough time to slip to the side before they closed the door behind them, but we managed to make it without incident. Fortunately, the hall was large enough for us to press against the wall and avoid the servants brushing against us, and soon Estasia and I were alone in the hall.

"Alright. Back to disguises then," she said, repeating the plan.

I followed her down the hall, using my Gift so we didn't make a sound—that was easy enough.

We passed a noble or two, but they were too caught up in chatter to notice us. With heads bowed and the disguise I'd given us, we looked like slaves, so at least we would fool any of Jayler's visitors.

"Guards," I whispered, and Estasia and I ducked our heads low, waiting for the soldiers to pass before going on—as was common courtesy when one was a slave.

We made our way down several corridors until we got to the lower levels where the slaves were kept. Estasia took the lead here, weaving through like she'd grown up in the place and quickly finding her way to the barracks. A few of the slaves we passed by looked at us oddly but said nothing.

Suddenly, Estasia's face creased in triumph, and she trotted up to a middle-aged man just exiting the kitchens. "Gethnor, *Kedor ben tathey keva?*" She used so many different dialects that I could only catch one or two words in the sentence. Clever, very clever.

"*Gyt tov,*" the slave replied, after a momentary pause of confusion.

"Drop my illusion," Estasia whispered to me.

I glanced around uneasily and decided to do so, just so Gethnor could see her true features.

As Estasia briefly exchanged words, I caught some of the words: Skayla and Ovok.

"Thank you," Estasia finished, nodding and turning to me. "We have to get out of here. Gethnor said there are rumors that Skayla sent Ovok here to watch over the city. I guess they're searching for the Living Stone and there was something about them being disappointed it wasn't in Kaedna? Something about trying to get it so they can open up some doorway?" she relayed in a low voice.

Yes. We did need to get out of here. This was bad. "Lead the way," I said, shoving down questions of doubt. Now was not the time.

We started making our way out, once more dodging as much of the traffic as possible.

Entering the gardens and knowing this way would leave us exposed, I once more made us vanish from anyone's sight. Our plan was to locate the main gate and make our way out through there.

I saw a small door at the end of the garden, and we both made for it.

"Heh, Bethro, you see that shadow?" I heard a guard call to his companion from the wall. Great. I was slipping up. I put a hand out and stopped Estasia in her tracks, hoping I wasn't too late in making the stupid thing disappear. I chanced a look up and saw both the men peering down upon us.

"I mean...the sun does that." The soldier shook his head, as if musing on the things he had to put up with.

I dared not even breathe in relief, lest I was unable to contain the noise. We stayed put for another couple minutes, and when I was sure the guards were no longer paying close attention, we were able to cross over to the door.

The rest of the escape was pleasantly uneventful, as most of the guards seemed pulled into the inner parts of the mansion. By the looks of it, there were some visitors or even some sort of gala event. If Skayla wanted to gloat over Kaedna's fall, I wouldn't be surprised.

We scampered through the busy streets once more, this time heading for the shipyard. Estasia had explained the plan, but I was still a little on edge. Again, I was sorely out of practice, and this bothersome ring was being distracting enough. It pulsed, tugging at me as if calling me somewhere. That ache again, Skayla, Moira...it all mingled together.

A shadow passed over our heads, and I forced myself to stay calm as the black feathery form of Ovok flew above us. I could recognize that Drogan anywhere. Estasia shot a look back at me, but I motioned for her to keep going. We knew Ovok was here, and I just tried to ignore the bigger fact that the ring was bugging me about. Ovok was Skayla's closest confidant—even more than Lord Kovo—and if he was here.... Panic swelled as I wondered if that was why the pulsing of the ring was so strong. I only hoped Skayla wouldn't get too near us.

I directed my attention back to the ground. Estasia had slowed down, and I myself smelled the salty air as we grew ever closer to the docks. My eyes darted this way and that, and now, with Ovok hovering over the skies, I was even more on edge.

I spotted Maeko and Jaythos leaning in the shadows of one of the many crowded buildings. Estasia and I stopped, acknowledging them for just a brief moment before turning to the vessels docked along the pier.

The docks were, of course, for the flying ships that The Crafters had invented only six years before the war. The docks themselves were raised at least twenty feet in the air, steep ramps leading up to them, and ships hung suspended by the sturdy canvas and *tiskli* ovals that kept the wooden and metal vessels in the air, their back propellers stationary as they waited to be loaded or unloaded.

We needed something that would already be about to leave port—and something sturdy and not afraid of wind. My eyes settled on a small yet sturdy ship, and I clued Estasia into it with a jerk of my head.

I looked up at the sky and marked where the sun was. The others would be just about in position. I only hoped I could keep the aching of my ring under control, so that if Skayla was nearby, she wouldn't catch us.

Estasia:

So, now the fun part—getting everyone off that ship, without causing too much of a ruckus. Maeko and Jaythos had volunteered, but I still wasn't so sure it would work. That being said, by the angle of the sun, we were almost out of time, so it would have to do.

The captain came stumbling off the ship about ten minutes later, and Jaythos and Maeko, just as planned, lumbered up to the man. The captain was definitely exhausted, running his hand through his hair and easily distracted by noises.

"What do you want?" he asked, squinting his eyes at Maeko and steadying himself against the railing. Perhaps this wouldn't be as much trouble as I thought.

Jaythos seemed very bored as he replied, "We need to commandeer your ship."

"Are you ready?" Sven whispered from my left, and I turned to nod. He had changed disguises yet again, now in the regalia of a high-ranking officer in the Bethynese army.

"Yes," I replied.

He started walking towards Maeko, Jaythos, and the now very red-faced captain, looking as cool and collected as if he was just going out to lunch.

"What seems to be the problem here, Gadfer?" He directed the question at Jaythos, looking scornfully down at the air captain with a look that convinced even me. In fact, I had to keep myself from shuddering at the memories of how this once had *not* been an act. I could too easily remember him as The GhostMaker, and Maeko's uncomfortable posture showed that Sven's past was on his mind as well. I only hoped this would not cause him to go back to hating Sven.

"He's refusing the order from Skayla, sir," Jaythos said in perfect soldierly fashion.

The captain's eyes widened. "Wait, now that's not—"

Sven cut him off with a snap of his fingers, and a few other soldiers appeared from the crowd. Just as planned, I came up to him along with them. "Sir?" I asked, mimicking the military manner of the Bethynese, in my opinion not sounding nearly as good as Sven was.

"What? Wait, you can't just *take* my ship!"

Sven was a little bold and smacked the man right across his red face, grabbing the captain's fist before it could fly at him. "I would seriously reconsider that, Captain. Hitting a high-ranking officer is not exactly going to put you on Lady Skayla's good side." He smirked in cold satisfaction as the captain shifted uncomfortably. I had orchestrated the plan but was a little in awe at how well he was really executing it.

"We need to take your ship in order to make for Rugo—there are traitors on the loose and we must leave immediately. Are you *really* going to try and deny me? It gets so messy when Ovok has to get involved…and then Lady Skayla will need to be…and what a shame that would be." He made a pitiful little face and frowned at the man, who was now phasing between being angry and terrified for his life. "But maybe it would teach you a lesson."

"Yes, sir. I'll be right off." I turned on my heels like a perfect little soldier, not even getting a step in before the captain let out a petrified "Wait!"

I turned back on my heels and gave Sven a questioning expression. "Sir?"

"You're testing my patience," Sven mocked the captain. "Why do you try and tell *my* soldiers what they can and can't do?"

The man fidgeted nervously with his calloused hands, looking from them to the haughty Sven Mara, who was very comfortably acting the cold soldier. "I…er…" The man stumbled.

"Well, spit it out, man!" Sven shouted, annoyance dripping from his tone.

"I'm sorry. But…my ship…I just…" He stuttered.

With a cocked eyebrow, Sven let out a small snicker. "Oh yes, very convincing. It's too late, my little friend. I shall return." He snapped his fingers and turned around. Maeko, Jaythos, myself, and our little pretend friends followed. I marveled how now we could see his illusions, where, when we'd been attacked before and he had obviously used them, we could not clearly see anything. I wondered if it had something to do with him having complete possession of his ring. Or was it just his choice who saw his illusions? I stored the thought away as I focused on my task.

I carefully avoided eye contact with the few gaping spectators. Real soldiers would be here soon, now that we'd drawn attention, and we needed to get out of here before that happened. I had seen someone run off already and precious moments were slipping away. Sven had better not take this too far....

"Wait, please, I beg you, mercy!" The captain stumbled after us and grabbed Sven's arm. I watched as he swung around, utter disgust written all over his face. I wondered smugly if that part was an act or not. I personally felt no pity for this captain. I made careful note of the tattoo on his wrist and knew he'd been one of the ones to smuggle supplies to Skayla.

But this was exactly where we wanted the man. So, after a long pause, Sven nodded. "Fine. You have five minutes to get all of your crew off the ship."

The man bobbed his head up and down profusely then scurried back onto his ship.

Sven and I did not waver in our facade one bit, knowing there were eyes everywhere. "Tydran. Go alert Ovok that the captain gave us resistance. We will see how he feels about talking back after this." He addressed this to Maeko, and in a moment, Maeko had disappeared into the surrounding hubbub.

Within seconds of Maeko's disappearance, the captain gloomily marched his fifteen crew members off the ship, giving Sven and me an evil glare, his attitude having recovered from the shock of reality. I expected the man to leave someone hidden in there, but if he valued his life, he wouldn't. Stupid, prideful sea captains.

Sven left a few of his fake soldiers behind and brought me and Jaythos up to the vessel. We gave it a brief inspection and affirmed that this was a good ship.

Now for my bit. Sven had said his memories were still vague and didn't really remember much of how to sail. So, apparently, other than Maeko, there was no one who could really manage a vessel. Once we were out of port, I would have to somehow get the group to a point where they could competently handle the ship. It would be interesting, to say the least.

"I will go check on the others, and see if Tydran has returned," Sven announced, still in his assumed callous character. I nodded and watched as he disappeared down the gangplank. Now alone with Jaythos, we scoured the ship more thoroughly, checking its condition. It wasn't the best, but the ship was indeed a sturdy one, and the balloon part looked like it would hold well. It seemed to have run into storms on the way to port, as one of the propellers had just recently been repaired. It would do.

I turned sharply around at the sound of footsteps coming swiftly aboard and did so just in time to see Sven swiftly run up. "We need to go, *now*."

Oh, great. I didn't want to even know. "We can't just leave. I need help casting off!" I said hurriedly back.

"We have help." Maeko's voice carried up as he and the others came up as well, Baey, Syvil, and Sefen carrying the supplies that had been bought. "But we need go. Ovok coming. Not good."

Wonderful.

THE GHOSTMAKER

CHAPTER XXIV: The Great Vanishing Act

Sven:

As soon as everyone was on board, I whipped back around and bounded down to solid ground, taking my old sword in hand. I didn't want it, but Baey didn't need the burden of carrying a weapon with its murderous history. Besides, much as I hated to admit it, I fought best with my own blade.

The port was mostly deserted now, and anyone that still lingered in that doomed place was in the process of quickly exiting the vicinity. They knew what was about to happen.

"Mara!" The voice scraped and screamed without origin, echoing everywhere and nowhere. Ovok. I looked back, noting with satisfaction that the ship had disappeared. Though once such an act would have been simple, now the concentration it took to hide the vessel was overwhelming.

The large, black Drogan cast a long shadow over me as he spiraled down to land, almost appearing out of thin air. My heart stopped as I saw who was once more on his back.

The Drogan landed with a thump, and off his back slid none other than my wayward sister. I glared not at her, but at the animal who had started this all. I could no longer be sure, though, that he really had much to do with it. What if Skayla had simply put him in a MindHold as well? I was not close enough to see his eyes.

"Oh, Sven, how the mighty fall." Skayla puffed out her lower lip as she turned to face me, features a perfect picture of mocking self-pity and insanity. "You've really lowered your standards, little brother. I thought so much more of you." She laughed then, fiddling carelessly with one of her stray blond hairs.

"I could say the same for you," I replied, on the verge of completely losing my composure. I had not faced her with my ring in almost a lifetime, and the whirling storm of emotions it brought with it was almost unbearable—even more so than it had been before. Standing so close to her, it was as if the relic was screaming.

"You sound off. Aw, you feel it, don't you? You know, I may not be able to get you back, Sven, but I warned you; you don't know how merciful I've been. Holding back your memories, but you really don't deserve that, do you?" she cooed. "Your mind seems so much better now. I wonder how it would handle that memory jog, now, hm?"

I needed to hold my ground. I had to distract her. I had no idea if she was bluffing or not, and frankly, I didn't want to find out—but the others needed time, and Ovok had turned his attention to where the invisible ship was.

Come on....

A Drogan's screech echoed as the feathery silver form of Syvil flew through the air and flung himself upon Ovok, who was at least twice as big as our Drogan ally. That gave us only a little time.

"You've even started taking my pets? My *friends?* Sven, how could you?" Skayla sounded genuinely hurt as she spoke, making me nearly sick.

"You were the one that lost your friends, Skayla," I said through gritted teeth, fighting the wrenching feeling of betrayal and longing that welled within me. Stupid ring.

Skayla cackled, rolling her wild violet eyes and stretching as if she had just woken up. "Oh, come on, enough games, Sven. I've always been better at this than you. That's why I've already won. You're just being a sore loser."

"No. You're just being a brat," I countered, taking in a deep breath as I tried to focus. The variables in keeping the ship hidden took a good bit of my concentration, but I still had a little firepower left. I clicked my fingers and another sword appeared in the hand.

"Oh, good, I do love a challenge," Skayla giggled.

I couldn't take it. "What happened to you," I more stated than asked, tone deadpan as I prepared to fight my sister. The emotions from the ring were becoming overpowering, and all I could see was how much I wanted Skayla back—how much I wanted to just have it all as it once was. The yearning to go back, the wishing it never happened. I couldn't face the reality of it all...I had to....

Focus, idiot. How much of it was the ring, and how much of it was Skayla getting in my head again?

I did an unnecessary twirl with my swords and winked at Skayla, inwardly feeling sick. "So, shall we play the game of tricks?" Just like old times....

I heard the drum of the ship's propellers as the others started it up. I knew I had to stall and still hopefully get both Syvil and myself out of here and onto the ship before it got too far up. But how to stop Ovok from catching us?

Skayla made another mad giggle, acting the gleeful child. "Oh yes, I do love this game. Who first? Why don't you go, you're so out of practice. See? I play fair." She laughed again. "Sometimes."

I put a heavy foot down on the ground, envisioning the earth cracking beneath them, and my body weightlessly falling, falling into the ground. Skayla laughed, feeling the sensation. But I was rusty, and it was not easy to convince her. I looked up and realized it would be much easier to get Ovok. Syvil could use all the help he could get.

I threw the fake sword at Skayla as she 'fell,' but she just dodged it, smiling broadly. "Oh, come on," she retorted, closing her eyes and stomping down on the hidden ground with her own foot. The illusion dissipated, and we were no longer falling into nothing.

I snapped my fingers and Syvil slowly grew, just like a Drogan normally would, but passed what I'd figured out was his maximum size. He was now as big as Ovok as the pair tumbled through the air tearing at each other, and it threw the opposing Drogan off.

"That's a petty move, little brother."

I raised an eyebrow. "Oh?" I snapped my fingers again and then the streets were crowded, so thickly you couldn't see past the person in front of you. But I could and through them to Skayla. I had to move fast before she saw through the illusion and mingled with the crowd, my concentration pulled to the limit as I envisioned hundreds of people in the streets, pushing and shoving. I moved in behind Skayla, making the crowd of people panic just to add a little confusion.

As I moved closer towards Skayla, I saw her visible frustration. "Coward. That's not a funny trick," she said in irritated disappointment.

I got right behind her and brought my sword down towards her back. She spun around and whipped out her own blade just in time to catch mine, and, for a moment, it felt as if we were both frozen, staring heatedly into each other like the worst of enemies, when all I could think of was what fast friends we had once been.

The crowd of people disappeared, and we still stood there, blades interlocked as the Drogans screeched and fought above us. Then a slow smile crept upon Skayla's face, and ever so quietly she whispered, "My turn."

She flicked her wrist and ducked out of the way as our blades flung free of their places, and I barely caught myself from falling forward.

My blood ran cold.

"I did warn you I'd give you everything back." Her words rang from around the square, and she made that tutting sound, like she was a mother. "But you know, it's your own fault. You're being selfish. Look at you! You *killed* Serafina. And Emarian. And the Ostinars. Honestly, I've lost count. You could have told them to surrender. You could have tried to reason with them. But no. You had to fight. You had to be selfish and try and win the war that I already had. Do you remember them, Sven? Hm? No?"

I took a deep breath and created another blade in my other hand, and we once more entered the dance of battle, her smooth voice constantly harassing me. *Don't listen. Don't listen.* But it was so hard. Her words seemed to coax the shadows of my mind, the memories I couldn't take hold of. The nightmares just out of reach.

"You can try to ignore the truth, but you can't run forever. You've been costing lives for almost a decade now. Instead of fighting me, you should have just admitted you were wrong. This world could be so perfect, but you just stick to your stupid imperfections." She sighed in exaggerated annoyance as she blocked my blow. "Everyone was right. You were the weak one, the one who got in the way."

I swung my fake blade, and out of habit she ducked, causing her center of balance to go just slightly off. The old trick still worked, and I got another swing in with my real blade, inches away from her face. Had I miscalculated or pulled away?

"You feel it though, don't you?" Her tone changed as she said the words and a sinking feeling settled in my gut. She'd found it. Great. "The pain of being separated. Isn't it awful? That the pride of you and Moira should tear us apart forever? And yet you feel the longing to go back still. You can't kill me." She laughed. "You want to, but you're *still* too weak."

Everything around us went pitch black, and in my intense anger it was as if we were isolated from the outside world, the images around us blurred as if looking from the center of fog. "How dare you." I allowed a small glow of light to shine through the illusion, illuminating Skayla and I as we faced each other.

Skayla's giggle was bloodcurdling. "How dare I? You're so funny. Sven, you have no idea what I've done for you. All the things you wished to forget; I gave to you. The pain you felt from being separated from Moira, from being separated from me. The memories of the things you've done. *All* of them. I have been more than kind to you, despite your betrayal. No more."

As she spoke, the very things she had said came flooding back full force, freezing me right where I stood. Despair flooded with the memories and I drowned in it. I needed to stay focused! But all I could think of was the anger, the betrayal I felt. The betrayal *I* had committed. I could understand even more why even Maeko could not trust me; I could feel the pain I had caused so many. I could feel the searing emotions that pulsed with every heartbeat.

"Your Gift was supposed to help heal people! Look what you've done! Look at the chaos you've created, Skayla!" I yelled at her, making my voice as loud as a thousand rumblings of thunder. I knew it would not intimidate her, but I wanted to drown out the pleas for mercy, the screams of those I—The GhostMaker—had killed.

She only rolled her eyes, circling me like a fierce animal. "Oh, come on, Sven. You have just as much blood on your hands. Don't preach to me. I was going to finish our purpose! I *have* finished it—and without you or Moira's help." She was standing right in front of me now, childish smile adding to the madness in her eyes. She caressed her arm, where her armlet rested somewhere underneath her sleeve. "I will have what is mine back. You don't deserve it."

I held my sword only a hair away from her neck, but she did nothing, only chuckling. "Silly. You don't have the guts. I know you don't." With a graceful ease, she used her finger to brush the blade away, looking down condescendingly at me. "You've failed Father and Mother, you've failed Moira, you've failed me, and now you'll fail the pathetic group of misfits you've claimed responsibility for. Perhaps those rumors were true. I hope you were jealous of Moira and I—at least *we* had the guts to win or go down with the ship."

Memories continued to flood my mind until I couldn't think. Faces of friends no longer here—friends I had killed. Serafina, Darbeshay, Kyndle, Emarian. I couldn't stand it. I dropped to my knees, everything falling apart as her words sunk in. "Stop!" I yelled, but my voice seemed lost in the darkness. The memories she had given back were too much. I couldn't stop it anymore. I couldn't forget.

"Leave him alone!" Just as Skayla's blade was about to come down upon me, a figure jumped in between us, putting up their own blade in the nick of time.

Baey:

I stood there, hardly believing what I had just gotten myself into. But I'd been the only one to see past Sven's illusion and to where they were—somehow—and I couldn't sit back and watch anymore. I wasn't about to let Sven die for me a second time.

"Leave him alone," I repeated again, teeth gritted as I stood face to face with Skayla Mara. The Drogans were chasing each other through the skies in the city, and their screeches rent the air as I just stood there with my sword raised. It was all I could do to keep from panicking. Ugh. What had I gotten myself into now?

"Aw, sweet child. I remember you." Skayla chuckled, her eyes settling on the watch around my neck. Again. Ugh. I hadn't thought this through, had I? "And how thoughtful, bringing me back what I'd lost." Her smile was chilling, but I wouldn't let it get to me. Sven had all taught us the trick, just in case she ever tried to get us in a MindHold, and I knew that's exactly what she was trying. I could feel it.

"Sorry. I promised a friend I'd keep it safe." I felt her icy words try and grip at my mind, but as Sven got shakily to his feet, the feeling vanished.

"You touch her, and I will kill you." His voice sounded empty, and his eyes looked more hollow than usual. But it was the vehemence in his voice that was most frightening.

"Oh, don't deviate from the point, Sven. You've failed. I don't care if they keep their pathetic little wills, that only means I'll have to kill them, too."

The darkness around us faded, and once more we were in the abandoned street. The ship was no longer hidden, and it was beginning to exit the port, Estasia watching desperately and calling out to us. Syvil was pinned down by Ovok, and in short, I thought that maybe this really was going to end badly.

But then Sven really lost his temper. And I mean, really.

It was as if the whole earth was shaking, and there was a flash of light, then dark, then light and dark again. The buildings seemed to crumble into the air, and the sun darkened. Skayla was thrown back against the ground, and, amid the chaos I dared turn to Sven, his fists clenched so hard they were white. Oh dear.

"On the ship, now." He ordered me through the chaos. I dared not argue and took off, flying up to the airship and joining the others on deck.

"We need to go, Sven!" Estasia yelled down to Sven, still holding the rope ladder. I watched in horror as Ovok left a badly injured Syvil and started creeping over to Sven, constantly being thrown off course by the utter confusion that Sven was causing.

Syvil flew like a drunken bird up to the ship and shrunk to the size of a small pony, all but collapsing on deck. The ship started to get out of reach, and I yelled desperately to Sven.

"I'm going to get him." I wrenched my arm from Estasia's grip and took to the air, muttering to myself for ever obeying the insane man.

Trying to see through the endless illusions, I made my way to him, grabbing him by the arm and tugging. "We're leaving, *now!*" I didn't have time to regret the forcefulness.

He didn't even reply, in fact, he didn't even budge. It was like he was frozen. "Sven! Snap out of it!" I yelled, slapping him right in the face. Skayla and Ovok were getting closer as they made their way through the chaos.

"Sven!" I was desperate. Not having any time, I grabbed him from under his arms and took to the air, trying not to drop as he squirmed. As we landed on the departing ship, Ovok roared and started to take to the air, but suddenly, just as his wings unfurled and he prepared to leap into the air, a loud explosion wrenched from nowhere, and a blast of light blinded us all.

When it subsided, it was pouring—a pure unnatural deluge. It was real rain, though, for it was so heavy that I could hardly stay standing. Sven slouched to the ground, back against the side of the ship as he sat staring into blank space.

Estasia let out an almost mad laugh of relief. Strong, yet manageable, wind blew into the extra sails that had been put out to either side of the airship to help it get speed, sending us through the thick mass of rain. I peered desperately back to where I remembered the shore was, but I couldn't even see past the side of the ship as we climbed further up into the air and further away from Hytat. The others let out whoops and continued trying to manage the ship. I, meanwhile, ran over and knelt by Syvil, who was bleeding from several gashes on the deck of the ship.

"Let's see if we can put a safe distance between us and that madwoman!" Estasia hollered above the avalanche of water and sound of crashing waves growing steadily smaller beneath the ship.

CHAPTER XXV: The Crafters

Baey:

So, yes, no one had cared to clear up that we were going to steal an *airship*. I hadn't even known there was such a thing. And I. Was. So. Excited. We'd been sailing for two days now, and we were flying over the open ocean. I had been allowed to stretch my wings as I soared at sea level, hand touching the crystal water and leaving a stream behind me. The shadow of the airship cast a pleasant shade as I continued to fly about, leaving the ocean and its foam in order to practice the maneuvers and exercises Syvil had explained to me before we'd reached Hytat.

Syvil.

The Drogan had been badly beaten up after his fight with Ovok, but more surprisingly, he hadn't woken since. Estasia and I were both pretty confident he'd be fine, but for some reason, he had not healed as quickly as he had at The Crafter's ruins. In fact...he wasn't healing at an accelerated rate at all. And then there was Sven. He'd been awake but...not awake. Just staring into nothing, as if in a trance. What had Skayla done to him?

"Baey! Syvil is awake!" Estasia called down, her voice carrying surprisingly well for how far up they were. She was probably using the call horn we'd found on the ship.

I didn't hesitate, and with a few powerful strokes I was again aboard the ship, catching my breath and instantly following Estasia down below deck, where Syvil had been moved. As we went, we passed Sven, still sitting on deck. I bit my lip as we passed him. I'd talked to him but still nothing had gotten him to come back to us.

It had been two days.

There was a commotion coming from the room Syvil was in, and both Estasia hurried in to find Tanner struggling to keep a panicked Syvil from getting up and hurting himself.

"Syvil, it's alright, you're fine!" Tanner's voice rang desperate, and I quickly went to help hold Syvil down.

Slowly, the Drogan settled, though still shrunk as far as possible into the corner of the bed that was set as an alcove in the wall. He had at least been conscious enough after boarding the ship to change into his Human form and so, managing him was easier than it would have been if he was in his Dragon form.

"What happened?" he asked breathlessly, wincing as he inspected his bandaged arm. He seemed...terrified.

"You were injured," I replied softly.

"Tanner, why don't you go make sure they are all set up on top. Watch Sven?" Estasia ordered, and Tanner agreed without argument, muttering something about crazy Drogans.

"How are you feeling?" she asked Syvil, pulling up a stool and sitting down next to the bed.

"I...I didn't die, then?" Syvil took in a hoarse breath.

"Not exactly an answer but no. You're still alive," Estasia replied.

My brow furrowed, and I thought back to how that other Drogan had disappeared after dying. Syvil hadn't explained it much, but I wondered if that had something to do with recovering from a MindHold.

"Where are we?"

I was the one who answered this time. "Still in the airship, two days out from Hytat. Sven must have put a cover over the ship before he passed out though. We are safe." For now.

Syvil shuddered, again trying to make himself smaller. I was unnerved by the fact that such a fearsome fighter would seem so, well...terrified.

"But you'll be fine," I said. "Estasia and I have been taking good care of you. You're mending, and now that you're awake, there's nothing to fear."

He didn't reply.

"Speaking of," Estasia reentered the conversation, "Why didn't you just heal like you did the last time? These wounds weren't exactly 'impaling' status—" she made air quotes as she said the word—"and yet you've been unconscious for two days. As we said. Do we need to be concerned?"

A shudder ran through Syvil. "Ckaknimaen. Ovok has Ckaknimaen," he murmured almost feverishly.

"Cat knee what?" Estasia's tone mirrored my own confusion.

"The Drogan blade of death. One of the nine blades made by the Drogan Lords of old. They hold great power, and in Malnimor's case, wickedness. But they can wound a Drogan in a way other weapons cannot."

My brow furrowed. "But...you were fighting him as a Dragon..." I was pretty sure I would have noticed Ovok wielding a giant Dragon sword....

"They adapt with the owner. When he is in Dragon form, they are the claws he wears."

I thought back, remembering now the faint glint of gold and silver I'd seen on his clawed feet. I'd just thought it was just his claws, nothing more.

"Are you alright?" He seemed...*really* shaken. Like, really. Most wounded warriors I'd seen didn't have such open fear.

Syvil was just shivering, now, staggered breaths sounding far from calm. "He can't find us again. He *can't*."

I wished to help and yet felt completely lost. But I wasn't going to just sit there and watch the poor Drogan tremble. I had to try, and so I took on the most certain tone I could and said, "And he won't. You're safe now."

"I'm sorry. I'm not a fighter. I'm not brave," he breathed. "I liked art and books and storytelling. Marion was the fighter. If only you'd found her instead of me, you would be better off. I can't fight your battles. I can't do—"

"—Listen." Estasia's interruption was stern, and she stood up. "You faced off against Ovok and survived. I'd say you're pretty brave to me. You owe us for getting you out of a MindHold, and you're going to help us. You're going to get the other Drogans out of this stupid MindHold, and you can go back to your books and art and nonsense after we're done. But, so help me, everyone is pulling their weight, and you are too big of a beast to doubt your strength. You're weak, and you're hurt, and you're scared. That's fine. I don't blame you." She sighed, her expression turning a little more sympathetic. "I know we've asked a lot. You killed your friend. You're fighting your own...but I promise, we'll try and get them back if you hang in there. If the Drogans are just as much victims as Sven is, then I will do anything I can to help free them."

I looked at her, blinking. Then I looked back at Syvil, really thinking about his position for the first time. *Observing* for the first time. Estasia was right. He was with us, alone. All of his family and friends were fighting with Skayla, and I thought of how horrible it must be for him if he had to face them—well, he already had. For us. I guess the thought had never even occurred to me that he might not even be a warrior at all. I assumed that perhaps because all Drogans had claws and teeth and wings that they all had the desire to fight. But what if they didn't? What if they were more like Syvil? What if like Sven they were being forced to do horrible things?

"Now, rest. No harm will come to you, I promise. Do you trust me?" Estasia spoke again when Syvil didn't reply.

The Drogan was returning my stare, now, and I found myself relating to the terror in his eyes. I could relate.... He looked so scared. So alone. A bittersweet expression settled over his features, as he turned back to Estasia and answered her. "Yes."

"Oh, good. This would have been an awkward end otherwise." Estasia's laugh broke the tension.

I just watched, feeling out of place and yet...not. As we left the room to let him rest, I looked up at Estasia, wanting to say something but not really sure *what* to say.

"I'm not hugging anyone, if that's what you're wondering," she scoffed, but I realized she was feeling rather awkward and out of place. I guess I hadn't ever noticed anyone but me feeling that way. It was nice to see someone who appeared so usually calm and collected actually show emotions I could relate to.

I smiled innocently. "You're right. Observing really does make a difference."

Estasia's brow furrowed and she looked confused, tilting her head as we stopped at the foot of the ladder-like stairs that led to the top deck.

I turned mischievous as I dangled the small coin-purse I had snatched off her only moments before. "It's very handy."

She laughed, swiping it back and returning it to her very ragged skirt pocket. "Don't let it get to your head, Birdy."

Estasia:

Well, that had been eventful. The little girl was growing on me—even if I was turning her into a little thief.... I turned my attention back to where Sven sat as we returned to the top deck. He still hadn't so much as blinked. Physically he seemed fine, but I was afraid of what Skayla had done to his mind.

Baey saw me looking and asked, "Do you think *he's* going to be alright?" Her wings settled closer around herself as she spoke.

Before I could come up with some form of reply, both our attentions were turned as Sven gasped and stumbled to his feet, just like that. Well, what do you know?

"Get it off, get it off!" he shouted, clawing at his ring until it was off his finger. Without warning, he flung it into the air, and I watched in horror as it flew out of sight over the edge of the ship, towards the murky ocean water far below. Baey made some sort of squeak and lunged over the side after it, disappearing from view.

"Sven! What do you think you're doing! What's the matter?" I shouted at him, a mixture of panic and worry tumbling around in my already cluttered and exhausted mental state.

Maeko reached Sven before me, shaking him as Sven continued to mutter almost feverishly.

"What is wrong, Skinny?" Maeko asked roughly.

"I can't. I can't," he just murmured, shaking his head vigorously and acting as if he still didn't register where he was or that he was with anyone. I knelt by Maeko and shouldered him aside, hinting for the big man to ease up. The Rugonian actually appeared apologetic and moved out of the way so that I could take his place. Skayla had done *something* to him, and I did not underestimate the torment she could cause. I'd seen it before in the Kovian Fortress. It was more startling on Sven, though, who I had never seen like this. Syvil, I was not entirely surprised at. But Sven?

I snatched a quick glance back as Baey landed back on deck, and she nodded, slipping the retrieved ring on the chain along with the broken timepiece. I sighed with relief and turned back to the other mess we were now dealing with.

"Sven. We're okay. You're alright. Come on, it's Estasia. We're on the airship, far away from Skayla." I ignored the growing crowd as I tried to calm Sven, Tanner having also come up alongside us, Sefen and Jaythos left to manage the ship by themselves.

Sven tried to back away from us, and I had a feeling he really didn't know where he was…and quite possibly *who* he was. Naturally. "Come on, Sven, try and remember." I said desperately. "You're Sven Mara. You escaped Skayla's MindHold and—"

"—I know," he cut in breathlessly.

"Can I help?" Tanner asked.

"Go help Jaythos and Sefen with ship." Maeko ordered. "We need to stay straight."

"I remember everything." The way Sven said that made it sound like the worst thing in the world...and I suddenly realized what he meant. *"Everything."* The way he repeated the word was gut-wrenching. I noticed now the way the flecks in his eyes shone, the paleness diminished.

Oh.

"Sven. You're not that. Stay here. Don't get sucked into those memories."

He didn't say anything, but he wasn't making any eye contact. Not with any of us. All he did was get up, Maeko stepping in to stop him from falling over.

Maeko gave a great big huff. "Balance indeed," he muttered.

Sven brushed the Rugonian's aid aside as if any contact physically hurt him. Every movement was unsteady, and his hands were still shaking as he rubbed his hands nervously against the side of his breeches. "H-how long have I been out?" he asked softly.

"Two days," Baey said quietly from behind us.

"Ah." Sven flinched. "So, we're only a few days out from Patelayna, then? We can't dock in the main port, remember. Skayla could be waiting for us. A day away from the city, and I can try a quick hide of the ship. There's a little cove south of the city. That would be a good place to land her." His voice was a whisper as he attempted to appear calm. He still wouldn't look anyone in the eyes, only into the great nothing of the sky we flew through, brow creasing as he seemed to be reliving a nightmare.

I wanted to say something, but nothing came to mind. "Right."

I wished I had something better to say. Something more. Yet all I did was continue through the plan, hoping it would give his mind something else to think about. I wanted to kill Skayla for this. "Sounds like a good idea. Once we get to the city, I should have no problem getting us in. It has plenty of underground outlets." The city was fairly advanced in its drainage, and, in my earlier days, the tunnels beneath the city had almost been like a home. A very stinky, messy, cold home. I also thought of the information my contact in Hytat had given; we might have friends in Alkemar.

Sven nodded, pursing his lips as his eyes became even more distant. It was like I was staring at a phantom, and I wondered if he wasn't The GhostMaker's biggest victim.

The wind picked up, and it was back to work, Sven helping silently as we all pretended nothing had happened. I took Sefen's place at the helm, not really relishing anyone but Maeko or me steering the vessel, and watched him from there. Sven just worked quietly, a war going on in his eyes that I could only watch.

"What do you think happened?" Maeko had come up beside me, and his deep voice was an unpleasant intrusion.

"She gave him back his memories," I replied tersely, angry at Skayla. Angry at Maeko. "Now he remembers everything he did. So, hurrah for you, he's even more miserable. I hope you're happy."

Maeko did not say a word, but I saw what almost looked like regret settling on his brow. Maybe now he realized just what Skayla had put Sven through.

Baey:

"Alright, remember the plan? Follow me and keep quiet. Once we land, it's going to be about a day's trek to Alkemar. It'll be easier to enter the city under the cover of darkness anyway. But everyone needs to keep quiet. Syvil said he saw some patrols outside the city, and the last thing we need is to give a blatant message to Skayla that we're here," Estasia said as we finished securing the ship in the secluded little bay. It was almost daybreak, and the tips of the thin trees were just catching the faint light of day.

We'd reached the cove last night, about a week after fleeing Hytat. Sven had said that Skayla probably expected us to go to Rugo or Etho and not Patelayna—let alone Alkemar. After all, Patelayna was crawling with Bethynese soldiers, and as the first country to fall into Skayla's hand, it was now the most settled in her grasp. That was probably also why The Crafters—whoever they really were—had hidden here as well. Who would have thought they would hide in the center of Skayla's empire? It wasn't much different from how no one ever guessed The GhostMaker might just be a defeated Sven.

Sven.

I looked at him again. If possible, he seemed even worse than he ever had, having hardly spoken a word but to confirm the plan. All he'd done otherwise was stare at nothing, avoiding eye contact and any conversation. The color in his eyes seemed brighter now, holding more color and less pale, and yet the look in them was that of suffering. Why? Why did he deserve this? Why couldn't Skayla have just left him alone? As horrible as not having his memories was, now I would have given anything for him to have the blissful ignorance that had apparently been taken away. Now all that remained seemed a shell, a shadow. The rare smile he'd occasionally flash became extinct; any emotion other than emptiness vanishing with it. All I could do was stick close to him and hope I was *some* comfort, no matter how insufficient. Even if it only helped a little, I would be thankful.

We reached the shore on the small rowboat, hiding it in a bush that was brave enough to grow along the cold sand of the shore. As we hid it, I looked behind and saw the ship disappear as Sven worked his magic, once more wielding the ring. He'd only taken it when absolutely necessary, and it seemed to only make him worse.

He walked over to me and shoved the ring hurriedly back into my hand, a small shudder running through his body. I was still confused about how he didn't need the ring to keep the illusion, even after he'd explained it to me, but now wasn't the time to ask questions. He seemed to have enough on his mind.

Estasia led us off into the trees, this forest having a much different feel to the one back in Kaedovarna. These trees were comparatively short and skinny, leaves papery and giving off an almost minty smell. Hm. At least it didn't smell musty here.

We traveled through the trees in silence, once or twice stopping to avoid an upcoming patrol that Syvil or I heard. The sky continued to brighten, and soon a patchwork of sundrops filtered through the paper-like leaves and onto us, giving even more warmth to the already warm day. The weather was different here as well, and I found myself now thankful that Maeko had bought cooler clothes, though at the time I had not really appreciated it.

The day wore on, and we only stopped shortly for a quiet break, where my parched throat and empty stomach were at least partially satisfied. I really did much prefer the climate of Kaedovarna. And then we were off again, the silence driving us all out of our minds—or at least me. Noon turned to dusk, and dusk gave way to cloudy night, masking the two moons and forcing Sefen to give us a little light. But we had to be careful—the city couldn't be far away now.

"Douse the light," Estasia said calmly, and, almost on cue, we were left in darkness. But not for long. A second later, we cleared the forest and, in front of us, lay the huge city of Alkemar, a shining beacon of light in the surrounding darkness. I couldn't seem to find the end of it, and the large city easily put Hytat's size to shame. It was all I could do not to gawk.

"Not a sound. We need to get to the west wall," Estasia whispered, heading off quieter than her shadow towards the city, using bushes and the odd tree to cover her. We all followed suit, Sven taking up the rear. Another ten minutes later, we were sheltered beneath the west wall.

Estasia motioned towards a small grate along the wall, only a few yards away, and I barely stopped myself from groaning in time. Why did it always have to be so small?

We started our way down towards the pathetic little opening, when suddenly, Estasia held a hand up, and we plastered ourselves against the wall. Two guards, holding lanterns, came moseying past on the wall above us, chatting casually. I felt a sensation deep within, and suddenly realized Sven was hiding our presence.

After the guards passed, we moved on, reaching the grate. Estasia gave one tug on it, but it didn't budge. Every muscle in my body tensed, and I didn't like the way she rolled her eyes. Ugh.

She felt beyond the grate then and took out a small shovel from inside, digging at the packed dirt around the bottom half while we kept watch. Every heartbeat seemed hours apart, and I could hardly even remember to breathe. What if we got this close, only to be discovered now? I made myself dispel the thought, gritting my teeth in determination.

Another couple guards walked by on the wall, and everyone froze. This time the guards stopped, peering over the wall and narrowing their eyes. Oh no….

They said something I couldn't understand, shrugged, and then kept going. Estasia sighed in relief and, in another minute or two, had the bottom of the bars free. Ever so quietly, she pulled on the grate just as she had before, but this time the bars conceded, opening upwards with just enough room for a very brave soul to squeeze in. Not me….

Estasia motioned for Tanner to go first, and, a second later, he disappeared into the darkness that lay beyond. Next Jaythos disappeared—crossbow and all—and then Sefen. Maeko looked skeptically down at the hole, and for a moment, I thought maybe he shared my opinion, but then he too disappeared. Even Syvil went down without a fuss. Then to my dismay, Estasia motioned that it was my turn, and I gave a great big gulp. Nuh uh, not down there, not me. I shook my head and took a step back.

"Come on, darlin'. I'll be right behind you," Sven whispered from behind me. Even with the new sorrow in his tone, his voice was ever comforting.

That being said…. "I can't," I said back.

I felt him push me ever so gently and forced myself to take a small step forward. Then the sound of footsteps was heard, but this time, not from the walls. From nearby. Then voices.

"Now, darlin'." Sven's voice was more urgent, and Estasia was now motioning wildly for me to go down. A patrol was coming.

"I-I can't," I stammered. This felt like a repeat of when I had been leaving Valdon, but this time worse. This hole was definitely smaller…and more rank-smelling.

Sven's hand went over my mouth without warning, and I barely held in a squeak as he practically dragged me over to the hole. "Sorry, darlin'," he whispered in my ear as he made me get down. I tried to fight at first, but then the sound of the patrol got louder, and I allowed myself to be shoved down into the awful smelling rat hole.

I bit my tongue so I wouldn't scream as I fell into the dark void, feeling hands grab me.

"Just me, Little Baey," Maeko said reassuringly, carrying me out of the way just as Sven and Estasia jumped down, somehow managing to close the grate just before falling.

My eyes began to adjust to the darkness, and, as Maeko set me down, I kind of wished they hadn't. The smell alone was awful, let alone the rats that I saw scurrying about. Then there was the garbage that lay strewn, and the murky water that sloshed into my shoes. Ugh.

There were voices from above, but they walked past the grate with hardly a pause, and everyone breathed a collective sigh of relief.

"Alright. Follow me. Once we clear the grate, Sefen, would you give some light?" Estasia asked as she once more took the lead.

We were soon lost in the darkness, and I was glad when Sefen produced a small orb of fire to provide a little illumination. The tunnels down here were like a maze, and I could only imagine how much time Estasia must have spent down here in order to be so familiar with them.

"Can I see that map again, Sven?" Estasia asked, pausing our trek for only a moment. Sven dug the paper out of his pocket and handed it to her, and a moment later, we were off again.

The tunnel started getting smaller, and Sefen and Maeko were forced to bend uncomfortably low. I quickly lost track of how long we'd been down here, and I started to feel frantic. I couldn't breathe. I needed to see the sun, or the moons, or at least feel a breeze. This was torture. I couldn't stand being underground, and every time a rat ran between my feet I felt as if I would die. But I bit my lip every time I thought of asking Estasia if we were almost there—now wasn't the time.

But I hoped it would be soon. I didn't think I could handle much more. Unfortunately, I had to, and so resorted to *anything* that might get my mind off my situation. Counting back from one thousand, breathing exercises, counting bricks.... It felt like another hour before we reached a patch of dim light coming from above. But at least the ceiling had gotten higher once more.

"Here," Estasia announced quietly, her voice nonetheless echoing through the dreary tunnels.

She knelt down and picked up a ladder from the ground, placing it against the wall and starting up. "Douse the light," she ordered Sefen, who promptly obeyed.

She climbed up the ladder and peeked out from the hole where the light was coming from. A moment later, she made a grunting noise and moved what appeared to be a metal seal from the ceiling, pushing it up and to the side so that it rested on the ground above. "Alright. One at a time, it'll only be clear for a few minutes, so we need to move quickly," she said, disappearing into the street above.

I felt a slight push from behind and realized it was Sven telling me to go next. I had no desire to argue and made my way as quickly as possible up the ladder, gasping for air as I felt the night breeze hit me and ruffle my cramped wings. More than anything, I wanted to just fly as high as I could, but I knew better.

The others followed, and we found ourselves in a well-lit cobblestone street. Round lanterns hung from tall curved poles, illuminating the endless winding streets, and us as well.

"Baey, I...need my ring." Sven's request sounded as if it pained him to even utter it aloud. I wished I didn't have to give it to him, but nonetheless, I put it in his hand. It would be easier for him to hide us with it on him. Soon, we were masked from any prying eyes.

"Alright. We're only a block or so away. Follow me." Estasia took off like a Kear down the streets, and I flew low to the ground, knowing I would definitely trip if I tried to keep up with her on the ground. Suddenly, she froze, looking up at a very large house and looking puzzled.

"I...don't understand.... It should be right here," she mumbled, looking at everyone with an expression of utter confusion.

My brow furrowed. "What do you mean?" The house was right—oooh. She couldn't see it, could she?

Sven beat me to it, his dull eyes sparking with the most life I'd seen in them for days. "That's how they stayed hidden," he whispered. "They've hidden it." He walked up to the house, suddenly looking...quite pale and nervous, his hands working in and out of clenched fists as they always did when he was stressed.

I heard a collective gasp from the others and realized the house was probably now visible to the rest of them, and then there was eerie silence as Sven knocked on the door.

All of us stood with bated breath, and I kept anxiously turning around and watching the streets behind us. A guard came by, and I had to remind myself he couldn't see us. But what about the house? By the look on his very unaffected face, I figured he didn't see it.

We all jumped as the door creaked open; I, myself, startled to death. My heart leaped to my throat in a mixture of anxiety and excitement as I realized how close we were to possibly getting one piece of this impossible puzzle.

A woman appeared in the doorway, silver grey hair falling in a mess around her broad shoulders. She had a knife in her hand, and I held my breath. Please recognize Sven….

It was as if she'd heard my thoughts, and just at that moment her gaze fell on the pale form of Sven Mara. Her breath caught, and for a long while, her brilliant golden eyes stared at him as if he was some sort of ghost. Then, ever so quietly, she whispered, "Sven…? Is that…really you? How…?"

Sven grimaced, a nervous wreck as he replied, "Hello, Mum."

THE END

...For Now

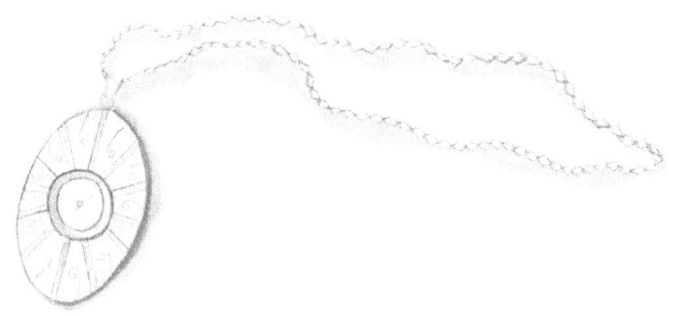

Next book in A Daughter's Ransom series:

THE EXILED: A GAME OF WITS

Astra is alive…

But barely. After escaping Tyron, she finds her way to help and slowly regains her senses. What she wakes up to is a mess; everyone wants something from her, and the king of Nythril is no exception. When he threatens to send her back to Tyron, will she cave and play bounty hunter for his idle pleasure? And what of the mysterious game that arrives, claiming she must play or face the consequences?

About the A Daughter's Ransom series:

The TetraWorlds live in ignorance of each other's existence...

One fallen behind in a Medieval time of fantastic and dangerous creatures, another fallen asleep in the comfort of their Victorian age, and the last torn apart by its own Modern innovation. When a dark threat rises up against them--one so quiet that none know to stop it, a Guard from each world must be called to protect their planet's source. But what will happen when these worlds entwine?

About the author:

NIAMH SCHMID:

Born in Clifton Park New York, Niamh is (unfortunately) a human being. She would much rather be off in some pretend world battling an ogre or taming a rabid pegasus, but instead is currently engaging in completing a bachelor's in Piano Performance. In her spare time she cares for her two mini ponies (or monsters), Freddie and Taffie, as well as her Dorkie (dachshund/yorkie mix) Tobie. She also loves to compose, collect stamps, and dabble in being a very mediocre artist.

www.ingramcontent.com/pod-product-compliance
Lightning Source LLC
Chambersburg PA
CBHW070830260626
47170CB00007B/2328